A QUARTER TURN OF THE SCREW

CHARLOTTE A. HUTT

 New Generation Publishing

With many thanks to my son Andrew for his help and encouragement.

This is a work of fiction. I would like to emphasise that it does not reflect or resemble police stations in Bury St. Edmunds. Any mistakes in police conduct or procedures are my own. All events described are fictitious. I have altered street names in Bury St. Edmunds as well as the outlay of the town and surrounding towns and villages so as not to cause any offence to inhabitants who might recognise locations. All characters are a fictitious, with the exception of a golden retriever, Ralph, who is still sorely missed.

And now the fancy passes by
And nothing will remain
And miles around they'll say then, I
Am quite myself again.

(From: A Shropshire Lad
By A. E. Houseman

CHAPTER 1

ON THURSDAY EVENING, Fred Foster felt a migraine coming on. That was all he needed, he thought, when he had to preserve his medicine as they would not issue him with a repeat prescription. Was it likely for him to end it all now he had paid his debt to society? Wasn't it time for society to pay its debt to him?

As he had only four tablets left, he swallowed some aspirins with limited effectiveness. Retching into the sink, he heard the steady thump-thump rhythm from next door,what they called music these days. He had a good mind to complain and swear at them, but decided against it, given that Vlad had told him that swearing indicated a limited mind. He also wanted to keep a low profile.

After a surprisingly good night he woke with a start. Seven forty-five! Even now, when he no longer had to attend a roll-call, he washed and dressed in a hurry and, as always, he was ready at eight o'clock. He cooked himself some breakfast, porridge, bacon and eggs and toast.

He washed the dishes and pans and then he got ready.

He rolled up a jumper under his shirt to simulate an old man's hump, put a sleeveless jumper over it and donned a beige, belted raincoat. It helped him get into the part of an elderly man. He straightened the brown wig and put a beret over it. He tested it. It seemed secure. He put on his glasses and chuckled at the thought of their name. Glasses. The lenses were made of actual clear glass. Trainers next. It should be shoes, but as he hadn't worn shoes for twenty years, he could not get used to them.

His liaison officer, probation officer or case

manager, whatever, knew he had altered his appearance from the hairless mug shot the country had been familiar with. Altered appearances were frowned upon but anybody could get their mitts on a wig and glasses, it was all too easy. However, he had kept his name. He saw no reason not to; there had to be thousands of Fred Fosters in the country.

The world outside had changed in twenty years, but so had the world inside, they had television controls but no computers at the open prison where he had been transferred to prior his release on parole.

Had his crime been out of character? Was it an unaccountable aberration of a clever man, a librarian, an OU graduate, a married man with a young daughter?

That was all they knew, but sincerity was the name of the game. He had expressed his sincere contrition.'THE SECRET OF SUCCESS IS SINCERITY. IF YOU CAN FAKE THAT YOU'VE GOT IT MADE.'

He couldn't recall who had said it, but whoever it was, they got it right. He had admitted to sincerely regretting his past life, his mistake. Too true! He didn't add that his mistake was to let himself get caught. Next time, he would be more careful.

When he was released, his wife came to pick him up with a car. It was taxed and insured for a year, she said, handing him an envelope with the papers. He put the envelope to one side and counted the cash, ten-thousand pounds drawn over the weeks before his release. She said Amelia had a degree. For a moment, just for a moment, he wondered how it was possible for a six-year-old to have a degree but daughter Amelia was twenty years older as well.

His wife never said Amelia wanted to see him, he knew that Amelia wouldn't, but his wife also said that she herself had made a good life for herself, (what, with *that* face on her? It had to be a miracle!) and he had promised never to get in touch with her. He found that funny. She had known that he wasn't like other people, he had no conscience, and yet she made him promise.

Inside, he had plenty of time to work it all out, and so far, it had worked out.

His ex had met him in the Grafton Centre in Cambridge, an enclosed shopping centre with trees growing inside. They drove to the car park in a glass-encased lift. She had a funny look on her face, amused, but he wasn't afraid of heights or of the outside world. Not now, although when he had been outside for the first few times he had thrown up. Twenty years inside did that, but that was when he had first left open prison.

The car was a pale blue Corola.

After she had left and he got in his car, he realised what the amused look on her face was, he hadn't driven for twenty years. Not only was the way down like a helter-skelter, he had trouble locating the switch to open the car window to insert the parking ticket when he reached the barriers.

By the time he finally succeeded he'd knocked his head, the beret had come astray and the other drivers behind him were getting impatient. He had to get out and beg someone to give him change for twenty pounds for the parking fee. He actually needed more than that, as the car had been parked there overnight. Besides, the charges had been paid upstairs.

'Why don't you try and put *the ticket* into the machine, fuck's sake,' the man next in line said impatiently.

His heart thumping, he finally drove out, straight into the traffic, approaching a three-lane roundabout with traffic lights. He got into the wrong lane and had to drive round Cambridge three times.

Finally, he came to a crossroads; it was either the A 14, a dual carriage way, or drive round villages and Newmarket. He chose the B-roads while he got used to the car.

He drew into a petrol station when a red light came on in the car and the petrol gauge hovered on empty. Where were the attendants? he wondered, and then he noticed that several drivers also used the pumps themselves.

Self service petrol stations, and wearing seatbelts, whatever next?

He got out, but how the hell was he supposed to open the petrol cap? There had to be a switch inside the car. He finally found a small lever and released it. The boot flew open.

The next lever did the trick. He filled up with ten pounds worth of petrol. 'How much is a gallon?' he asked the attendant behind the counter.

'Gallon? It's 99 pence a litre,' said the attendant.

'You must be joking,' he said, 'a litre is two pints.' He had watched news bulletins, of course, but the price of petrol had not figured largely in his life. The attendant asked him where he had been for the last twenty years. Somewhere you wouldn't last twenty minutes, he thought, but why it had given Her Majesty Pleasure he would never know.

Back at his flat, he looked at himself in the mirror. He had got used to his look and so had everybody else. People see what they expect to see. He was pretty sure he was under surveillance, most likely by some stupid copper. Whenever he turned round sharply, the bloke in an anorak and a baseball cap behind him bent over and tied his shoelaces.

Inside, he had developed a spot, an almost

electric warning sign, on the back of his neck. He always knew when somebody was behind him, and much good had it done him inside. That was until he had learned to look after himself with a sharpened tea spoon, and then he was segregated under Rule 43.

When he first came out the spot was working overtime. It reacted to people taking dogs for a walk awful, shitty things, he knew what he would do to them- shoppers behind him in the queue, footsteps behind him when he went upstairs to his flat. The flat time forgot; its decor just as it might have been when he went inside. A swirly black-and-yellow worn carpet in the one bedroom and a sitting room, and a bathroom with a shower, but no bath; at least the water wasn't brown.

He belted his beige raincoat, picked up his shopping bag and set off on his morning routine. He pictured the oblong glass school building trying to contain the children's pulsating energy. Locked away for twenty years, he had built up a head of steam and resentment, which was ready to explode. A fierce, tingling shot of adrenaline shot from the warning spot of his neck straight to his groin.

I'll give them energy! he thought.

Stage one of his preparation was complete. For a few weeks he had observed the chosen child in the playground. She was getting used to him. Pity the playground was ring-fenced and the gates locked. But he had been able to talk to her, the playground attendant, a fat woman with yellow hair, was always busy sorting out boys. He had told the girl, Emily she had told him, that talking with her was his secret, it was only fair she should keep *him* secret.

She had nodded.

She was a bit too knowing for his liking, she could spell trouble. He had his eye on a shy little girl who was now watching him. He beckoned to her, but she shook her head.

Emily it would have to be. Soon he would be beyond stage one. He would find out where Emily lived. She had already told him she wasn't met by her mother when she came out of school but by a young woman named Natalie, and that she had a much older brother, Gregory, now that might come in useful.

Presumably brother Gregory was a tidy sort. He would dress tidy, it would be helpful when the teacher saw him wearing black trousers,a grey sports jacket and grey hat when he waved to Emily as she came out of school. He could also suss out the parking.

Stage two. If she was late being picked up she would trust him, she would tell her teacher she knew him and she would go with him. After all, he was no longer a stranger.

When he reached the playground, the kids were already out of the building, letting off steam; However, the spot on his neck told him that he was being followed.

He turned round sharply and the cop following him fell to his knees, fastening his shoelaces. He faced the playground again.

The shy kid, thumb in mouth, stared at him, so he made a beckoning gesture with his hand, but it was Emily who came towards him. A car horn blared from a speeding car, nearly running over some silly sod of a bloke who had run across the road, shouting something about a lunch-box.

Fred Foster ambled off, turning around once, but he wasn't being followed.

Back home he 'phoned his probation officer, case manager, whatever. The silly cow denied that he was under surveillance. She asked where exactly he had spotted the so-called follower.

Only open playgrounds and the heath - not enclosed schools- were placed in an exclusion zone. To to be on the safe side, he said it had been outside the launderette in Harbinger Court. 'If you have no objections, of course.'

'I don't like your tone,' she said.

He didn't care. He knew he wasn't on the sex offenders register, his crime had been committed before the act came into force and his release had been kept secret.

'We will meet on Monday as arranged, and we'll review your current situation.'

He put down the 'phone and then he 'phoned friend Vlad. It was Friday, when he did the weekly shop. He began to make a list.

CHAPTER 2

AT THE TIME FRED FOSTER was retching his aspirins into the sink, George Hudson came home from work.

'Where's Rosie?' he shouted. He took off his shoes, hung up his car keys and put his overcoat on the peg in the hall.

'She's got a new best friend,' said his wife Christine. She was putting something in the oven, as he discovered when he walked into the kitchen.

'What's she like?' asked George, who took an interest in his only daughter and was -in his wife's opinion- overprotective.

'Emily? She's five going on fifty. She thinks she knows everything, but she's a gorgeous little thing.'

On his way upstairs to change out of his suit, George stopped in front of his daughter's bedroom. He listened at the door.

'I've got a television in my bedroom.' Rosie sounded proud of it, and so she should be, she had to fight hard for it.

'I've got a DVD player in mine. I couldn't live without a DVD player.' Another voice, presumably Emily's, interjected. 'On the telly, you got to watch what's on.'

'Yes,' said Rosie, 'that's true.'

'And I've got a pony.' A pause. 'You've got an old house.'

'It's Victorian,' said Rosie. 'We've got a cellar. It's a snooker room.'

'I couldn't live in an old house, 'said Emily. 'Have you got any ice cream in your fridge?'

George disappeared into his bedroom, as the girls clattered downstairs. He met them on the stairs, after he had changed.

'This is my friend, Emily Watson,' Rosie said, opening a choc-ice.

'We have Cadbury Flakes at home,' said Emily. 'Seashells or pine-cones are interesting,' she added.

'Or hedgehogs,' said Rosie.

Did children speak in code? he wondered, going downstairs into the sitting room, where he opened the paper to start on the crossword.

'Rosie was just saying how odd it was that you can never find a hedgehog when you need one,' Christine said, laughing. 'Apparently it's a project, *Interesting Things In Nature*. They need it for tomorrow. Rosie!' she shouted up the stairs, 'Does Emily want to stay for tea?'

Emily asked what was on the menu.

When Christine said that it was shepherd's pie, Emily said she couldn't live with it, sorry, Mrs Hudson, but her mother had made a vegetable bake.

While they had their tea, Emily sat on the chair, hands on her lap, legs neatly crossed at the ankles. Her dark hair was snaking down her back and she was looking at them through the fringe with her amazing blue eyes.

While Christine drove Emily home, Rosie finally chanced on an *interesting lettuce in* the garden. It was tall and spindly, not to mention soaking wet, rather than crispy, round and short. She pulled it out and put it on the worktop in the kitchen. 'Daddy was cross,' she told her mother when she came back.

'He doesn't like it when you bring dirt in the house,' said her mother.

Rosie stamped her foot. 'Nothing to do with dirt!'He shouted, "Where have you been? Next time tell me when you leave the house." I only went into the garden.'

Rosie's bottom lip didn't stop trembling until she was asleep, and finally Christine was able to tackle George. Overbearing, she called him.

'Overbearing? We back onto a main road and you left the side gate open when you took Emily home,' he said.

He had left Rosie in the living room while he put the dishes in the dishwasher. When he couldn't find her, he had raced through the house, shouting her name, his heart pounding. 'It was pitch dark.'

'Don't you think you are getting a bit over-protective?' she said. 'Shouting, "Where's Rosie?" the minute you come in? There isn't a paedophile around every corner, you know.'

That's all you know, George thought. Should he tell her about Foster? Perhaps not. It was enough that one of them knew and worried about it, but Christine was like a dog with a bone, she wouldn't let go. 'You're not even happy when she spends Wednesday nights with my mum. It could affect her confidence, you know.'

'Rubbish! I'm just looking after her,' he said.' What is Emily's family like?

'You mean is Emily good enough for Rosie?' asked Christine.

What he meant was, did Emily's family look out for the children? but he let it go.

'As a matter of fact, they are loaded and live in that double-fronted Georgian house on the way to Wheystead,' she stated. 'The one we always admire when we drive past it, the grey one with the pillared porch and the conservatory winding around the sides.'

He was protective of Rosie; he knew that. 'There are lot of nutters about,' he said,.

There always were, Christine thought, and it had never bothered him before. Why now? she wondered to herself.

Unlike George, she didn't know that Fred Foster had been released from prison and was now housed in Bury St. Edmunds.

Next day, the lettuce was limp and very uninteresting. On the way to school, the traffic moved very slowly, the windscreen wipers very fast, and Rosie's father said a very rude word.

'My friend Emily Watson said she couldn't live with a grey lunch-box,' said Rosie. He could very easily live without Emily Watson, he thought. He watched Rosie skip off to meet her friends and drove off to a meeting with the architect overseeing the new development on the market site. He took Mira, his secretary, along with him, to keep notes.

'What's that?' she asked, pointing to the back seat.

'It's Rosie's very interesting lettuce,' he said. 'Oh, God, she forgot her lunch-box. I'll make my excuses at the meeting and take it to her later.'

It was playtime when George drove up to the school. The rain had stopped and the children were out in the playground, letting off steam. The noise was incredible, George thought, slowing down and stopping, mentally separating groups of children into single girls, looking for his daughter.

There she was. Her fair hair swinging, Rosie was hopping on one leg, her head bent forward. She was with a group of girls, she was probably trying to get in a word edgeways, and then his heart stopped.

The paedo was there in his beige raincoat and black beret. George's mate, Ritchie, wasn't far off, slunk into his anorak, wearing a baseball cap. He bent down, pretending to tie his shoelaces. A little girl was watching him from across the playground. The paedo beckoned to her, his arm straight, his hand opening and closing, pointing towards him.

She shook her head.

A girl detached herself from Rosie's group and was walking slowly towards the paedo.

The paedo looked around and moved closer to the rails fencing the playground. As Emily Watson walked up to him, George grabbed the lunch-box, got out of the car and sprinted across the road, narrowly avoiding being run over by a grey Saab, horn blaring.

'Emily!' he shouted over the noise, 'I've got Rosie's lunch-box. Catch!'

The paedo pulled down his beret and ambled off.

Ritchie waited for George.

'You all right? I thought you'd had it,' he said. 'He's at it already,' he added. 'I told you, he's got his eye on that shy kid, but she doesn't want to know. It looks like that dark-haired girl is getting used to him.'

George rocked back on his heels. Emily was being groomed. 'And she's just daft enough to go with him. She's nothing more than a baby, but she thinks she knows it all. The police won't be able to do anything; they can only act when a crime has actually been committed.'

'When he's done anything like...,' Ritchie trailed off, as if scared to finish the thought.

George inhaled sharply and Ritchie looked at him.

'Right, we'll put our plan in action this evening.' said George, exhaling. 'We'll rough him up and frighten the life out of him. We'll show him the error of his ways. I'll 'phone Alf and let him know. We'll meet in the road on top of the lane, half four.'

CHAPTER 3

PAUL WILLOUGHBY STOPPED in front of his garage just as it started to rain. Summer was not even a distant memory on this wet November evening, although he would be hard pushed to recall it. He went back to the front door to get his car keys, and then he remembered he wore an old raincoat because he was walking to the shops.

He belted his raincoat, pulled down his hat and started off, reaching the supermarket. Cigarettes were bad for you, but the walk would do him good and make up for it, he thought. And the rest! One day, very soon, they would become dangerous and he would have to give them up, but not today.

He consulted his list and bought cigarettes, a bottle of sherry, (his daughter liked a sherry trifle), and a frozen lasagne for his supper. Normally, the woman who came in most days, (Miss Thingy, he called her because she was Polish and had an unpronounceable name) cooked for him, but not on this Saturday when he expected his daughter.

He put his purchases into a plastic carrier bag. WARNING, it said on the cigarette packet. The woman next in the queue finished her conversation where she had told her daughter she was on the phone in the Supermarket, closed her mobile and, with a tut-tut, shook her head at him, more in sorrow than in anger.

'I beg your pardon?' he said as he was about to leave.

'Plastic bags kill animals, don't you know? Or is it that you just don't care?' she said.

'And talking on mobile 'phones about the bleeding obvious gives you brain cancer,' said the man next to her in the queue

She turned round.

'You've been listening to my conversation?'

'Everybody has, we've got no bleeding choice, so get a move on.'

Whatever had become of this country? A man couldn't go to a shop without being disapproved off, Paul thought, pulling down his hat, setting off. The rain had sprung a surprise, it now came at him sideways.

His mobile phone rang. It was his daughter, Natasha, he finally discovered after putting his bag down onto a small wall beneath the dim light of a lamp post, wondering as he always did, why the buttons on it were so small. Still, being able to use a mobile phone cheered him up. Frank's pills are doing the trick, probably, he thought.

'I'm bringing Hester tomorrow, Lewis can't have her for the weekend,' said Natasha.

'I've got some of those yoghurts she likes in the fridge, he said, 'and I just got the sherry for your trifle. And cigarettes. There's a warning on them. Apparently smoking will spoil my chances of getting pregnant.'

She laughed. She had a lovely laugh, very melodic.

'I thought you'd given up.'

'I have, this is just in case I need them.'

'I'll let you go. It's your chess night, isn't it?'

Is it? he wondered.

He closed the phone, put it in the little bag and then onto the small wall next to him and looked around him in the semi darkness. For a moment, he didn't know where he was, who he was and what he was supposed to do. The Aricept was in his pocket, he had taken one today but he chanced another one, even though they made his legs more than a bit shaky. He got the small bottle of water he was never without and swallowed the tablet, crossed the road and started to

20

walk on the lane.

'I can see Foster coming now,' said George to Alf and Ritchie, on top of the wall on the garden leading to the lane, 'turn round and lower yourself hanging from your hands. Now.'

The three men landed heavily in front of Foster.

Muggers, Paul thought, momentarily frightened, surrounded as he was. It wasn't the first time he had been mugged. The first time was in Barcelona, the second time was in ..., wherever it was. They would let him pass when they had relieved him of his possessions.

'You can have what cash I've got on me. I'm afraid I don't have any credit cards. I don't use them,' he said.

''We want you out. We don't like *your sort* here,' said Alf, shoving his face into his.

What was *his sort*? He did not understand it, but he thought it was better to apologise.

'I'm sorry,' he said.

'What's he sorry for?' the man to his left said sharply. 'Are you sorry for hanging around the school playground?'

The playground? Was that where he had been mugged the second time?

'I used to wait at the school gates,' he said, 'but not lately.'

'School gates? Look what he's got in his bag, fags, a frozen lasagne and a bottle of sherry. Are you a secret sherry drinker?'

He couldn't stand the stuff.

'No, my daughter likes a sherry trifle, my granddaughter is coming as well.'

He paused. 'Or is she?'

And then it came to him.

'Alf!' George screamed, 'Don't!' as Alf lifted the sherry bottle and hit Paul on the back of the head.

'Amsterdam,' Paul Willoughby said. He fell slowly to his knees as if he was praying, and then he toppled sideways.

Ritchie bent over him feeling for his pulse, he lifted his head and the hat came off.

'Oh, my God, he's dead.' he said, straightening up, letting go of the head. 'He can't be, I mean he was talking and everything a moment ago.'

He looked at the dead man again. 'Oh my God,' he said, clutching his face, 'Oh, Jesus, what have we done? This isn't the paedo. The paedo wears trainers, and this bloke's shoes are black, the paedo has hair, lots of it, and this one is bald.'

Then he fell to his knees and started to hit his head on the pavement.

'Are you sure, Ritchie?' said George, bending over what was now a corpse, looking at the black, polished shoes. His father always said you could tell a lot about people by looking at their shoes.

Why was he thinking about his father?

Just a split-second before Alf hit the man he had known this man wasn't Foster. Foster was a loner, he didn't have visiting daughters or granddaughters. Moreover, this man had sounded educated. It had come to him just too late, just before the man said, 'Amsterdam.' If you thought about it, which George didn't want to, these were damned odd last words.

'Stop it, Ritchie,' he said, grabbing him by the scruff of his neck. 'Pull yourself together.'

'But it's *Doctor Willoughby*,' cried Ritchie. 'He is a nice man. I've done a spot of decorating for him. His granddaughter is the same age as my Bobby. He used to meet her from school.'

George looked around. 'Where's Alf?'

Alf was heaving his guts out against the wall.

'I didn't hit him hard, hardly at all when you screamed at me,' he said. 'Honest, I didn't.'

Lights sprang on in the houses behind him. Five o'clock. People were returning from work. They couldn't go back the way they had come, even assuming that they were able to climb *up* the high wall, and somebody was bound to take the short cut through the lane soon.

'Move him over the lane into the allotments. One, two, three now.'

They rolled the body into the allotments which were lower than the lane. George removed and searched the raincoat.

No mobile.

Then he took the signet ring and the watch off the dead man. He found the wallet and looked in the little side pocket where he found the driving license issued to Paul Anthony Willoughby.

The small photo purported to depict Paul Anthony Willoughby, but it could equally have been a monkey with glasses. The dead man. He wished to God he had looked at the license a few moments ago.

'What are you doing?' asked Alf.

George was going through the wallet. 'He had nearly two-hundred pounds on him, but like he said, no credit cards.' He closed the wallet. 'When they discover the body, it will have to look like a mugging gone wrong,' he said.

The three vigilantes had decided something would have to be done when Fred Foster was released from prison, having done twenty of his twenty-five years for abducting, raping and killing a six-year-old girl. He was out on parole and was moved into The Flats, as the halfway house on the Harbinger road was called.

His release was supposed to be a secret, but the liaison officer of the open prison, where he was transferred to prior to his release' employed a typist who happened to be Alf's sister.

All three men had school-age children. It wasn't right that they lived in fear for their children. Something would have to be done. Somebody would have to do it.

They all had to work in the day, so they divided shifts. Ritchie did an hour in the morning, George an hour at midday (not a peep out of the paedo), and Alf did the evening surveillance. Every Friday between half-past four and five o'clock, without fail, Fred Foster would enter Somerfield, he reported. When he came out with his few groceries he invariably took the shortcut past the allotments, and he always wore a belted raincoat and a beret.

'A beret, not a hat,' said Ritchie. 'Look.' They all looked at the man who now entered the lane. He was wearing a belted raincoat, had a beret and was carrying a plastic bag. They instinctively moved closer together. What now? Foster, moving silently on trainers, walked with his head down because of the rain. He didn't raise his head until he saw their feet in front of him. Three pairs of feet.

He looked up.

'What the..'

'We want you out, and we want you out tonight. We know every move you make in every hour and on every day.' said Alf, stabbing him in the chest with every word. 'If you're hanging around the playground tomorrow morning we'll get you when you least expect it.'

'I don't know where to go, I haven't got any money,' said the paedo.

The dead man's raincoat slipped off George's

arm when he threw some of the notes on the floor. As the paedo bent down to pick them up, George kicked him and he fell down. George grabbed the bottle and smashed it on the ground to show that he was serious.

The paedo steadied himself after the kick, but, falling hard on his palms onto the glass, he cut one of his hands. He wiped the blood off on Willoughby's raincoat on the ground. As he tried to straightened himself up, he lost his glasses in the process. He picked them up, turned round and scrambled to get away, stumbling once at the end of the lane, and vanished into the gloom.

'I think we better do the same,' said Ritchie.

'Are you mad? The paedo looked in the direction of the body, we'll have to move it to be on the safe side,' said George, who watched CSI: *Crime scene Investigation*. 'This is a crime scene. A crime scene is where your DNA is found.'

The others had heard about it. Everybody left something of themselves behind. Alf certainly had, but that could be any drunk throwing up against the wall if it was found, if the rain hadn't washed it off.

'You didn't have to hit him with the bottle,' said George.

'I don't think I hit him hard, maybe he has a thin skull,' said Alf hopefully. 'I didn't mean to hit him, but when I heard him say something about hanging around the school gates, my blood boiled.'

Same here, thought George. He knew little Emily Watson, the little girl the paedo was grooming.

'We should go to the police, we can explain it all. We didn't mean to do it. They will understand,' said Ritchie straightening up and wringing his hands

'Of course, we killed a man going home from the supermarket, it's an easy mistake to make,' said George. 'All of us will do time and won't see our children grow up. Our businesses will go bust, and our families will be destitute.'

He paused, thinking, leaning back on his heels.

'Foster has gone, that was our aim. So think of this other man as a martyr to the cause.'

Ritchie couldn't quite picture it.

'So,' said George, clapping his hands, 'this is an allotment.'

'So what?' said Alf.

Three men moving a body would look suspicious, George explained, but men with a wheelbarrow on an allotment would not. Allotments had wheelbarrows to move stuff with and most likely brooms in the sheds. Sheds were usually locked, but sometimes people forgot to lock up, especially if it started to rain. Alternatively, they could smash a window to get in.

Ritchie understood about the wheelbarrow but not the broom, but he was sure that George would tell him, so he kept quiet.

Alf said people would wonder what they were doing in the allotments at this time of the year, and in this bloody weather.

'What people?' said George. If anybody walked past while they searched the sheds, they should bend down and pretend to do a spot of gardening.

'Fetch your car, Ritchie, and take the coat with you. Burn it.' said George.

'What? Now?'

'Later, birdbrain,' said Alf.

'Let's not fall out,' said George, who had found a wheelbarrow and a broom in an unlocked shed and started to sweep the blue shards from the sherry bottle off the path.

Why me? Ritchie wondered, taking the dead man's coat, as he ran off to get his car. What would they do without George, he thought, when it occurred to him that the whole bloody mess had been George's idea in the first place.

CHAPTER 4

WHILE RITCHIE FOLDED the raincoat nicely before he put it in the boot of his car, (Dr. Willoughby had been that sort of careful man) George put the cigarettes into his pocket. He swept up the broken glass and the dead man's glasses and put them into the carrier bag with the lasagne. He had just put them into the wheelbarrow next to the dead man's body when he noticed something. What a stench! The dead man had lost control of the bowels.

He had replaced the broom in the shed, where he had also found a black bin liner and a torch, when somebody came click-click-clicking down the lane.

'Alf!' he hissed. They bent over, pretending to be busy, tending to some soggy weeds.

What awful weather, Maggie thought on her way to do the evening shift at Somerfield, wishing she wore more sensible shoes as she walked past the allotments. Somebody was actually working on it. In this weather!

She couldn't understand people growing vegetables full of dirt, organic as they called it, when they could easily buy clean vegetables from the supermarket. There was no telling about people, so she thought no more about it, crossed the road and stopped to fasten her headscarf more securely.

A mobile phone in a small bag was on the little wall. She put it in her bag. She would hand it in at work, somebody was sure to miss it.

There was quite a lot of traffic on the road, people were returning home from work, when Ritchie drew up with the car next to the allotments. They had put the body in Ritchie's car boot when a police car, sirens blaring, flashed past. They hastily tipped the wheelbarrow into the boot, shut it, got in the car and drove out of Bury St. Edmunds onto the Brandon Road, turning off towards Thelford, stopping just before the sign, 'WELCOME TO NORFOLK, NELSON'S COUNTY.'

George knew his bearings. 'Take the lane to the right, all the way up to the trees,' he said.

'Nobody goes for a bleeding walk in this weather, it'll look suspicious,' said Alf.

'Fly tippers do, and you can drive beyond those short bushes,' said George. He used to take his dog for a walk there. The last time the gorse bushes had been as yellow as the streak down his back. He didn't like what they were about to do.

Their eyes soon grew accustomed to the dark. Scot pines were sparse at the wood's edge and sprouted straggly branches high up, like spiky, useless umbrellas.

Alf and George, who was shining the torch with his left hand, grasped the body beneath their right arms, while Ritchie struggled with the man's legs. They carried the body into the woods where trees were more closely massed. Nobody swore, it didn't seem right. When they chanced on an abandoned mattress, George stopped. Now to the unpleasant part, but it couldn't be helped. Nothing could be overlooked.

George's father had an old saying (amongst many): *For want of a nail the shoe was lost. For want of a shoe the horse was lost, for want a horse the battle was lost.* Leave nothing to chance was the same, but shorter sentiment.

In the end, he wasn't up to it, it was Alf who partially undressed the body, the top part and the shoes. When keys fell out of the man's jacket, George picked them up. Probably house keys, he would look at them later, he thought, as Alf took out the dentures. Ritchie nearly fainted, so George put them into the carrier bag with the lasagne, while Alf put the dead man's hat back on his head, closed the staring eyes and the gaping mouth.

Rain was dripping through the canopy of the trees, so they put the top half of his body in the bin liner and then placed the body under the mattress. They didn't want him to get wet.

'We should have taken a spade and buried him,' said Alf.

'And get home filthy dirty? What would the missus think?' said George, who thought that Alf had a fair point, but he wasn't letting go of the upper hand.

'I'll be over later,' said George, when Ritchie drew up in the car park where Alf and George's cars were parked.

'Later?' said Ritchie, looking at his watch. He thought it had to be about midnight but it was only half six.

'Later. I'll bring something that will calm you down,' said George whose wife had suffered with her nerves.

Alf needed watching. It was he who had inflicted the fatal blow, so George had given him some of the man's clothes to dispose of to keep his mind going. However, Ritchie was a priority, he hadn't stopped shaking since Alf had removed the dentures. It would hit him hard; he had known the man personally.

'Remember, both of you, not a word to your wives, not if you value your freedom,' said George.

He thought that he smelt of sherry, so he drove off, stopping at Somerfield where he bought a bottle of Harvey's Bristol Cream. He was going to stuff the money he'd taken off the dead man into a collecting box for the blind; only it wasn't there.

He disposed of the lasagne in a bin and threw

the dentures and the keys down a drain. He then drove home, parking the car in the garage. As he still had the ring and the watch in his pocket, he placed them in a small, white, plastic bag, which he hid in the boot of his car where it would not be disturbed. Christine drove her own car.

He sank back into the driving seat feeling limp, like that doll of his mother. All the sawdust had run out when he had vandalised it after she had left him. He lit a cigarette with the car lighter and inhaled deeply. He hadn't smoked in years, but after a hefty bout of bronchial coughing, it felt as if he had gone to heaven. He wondered why he had ever given up.

Christine caught him going into the hall. She sniffed. 'Have you been smoking?' she said, raising her voice. That was good. When she was on the happy pills, she acted like a zombie.

'Where's Rosie?' he asked.

'She's drawing.'

He went upstairs, changed his trousers and went into the bathroom. He peered into the mirror. He had hidden a dead man who shouldn't be dead, and who deserved a dignified burial. He was envious of men without dreadful secrets coming home after a days' work, soaring high without a burden, whereas he felt earthbound.

Yet amazingly he still looked the same- a familiar squarish face, blue eyes, a slight frown, light-brown hair springing from a clear forehead. He opened the bathroom cabinet. Aspirins, the Pill, a small, full bottle of Valiums, dated third of March. Good. She hadn't used any for months.

He went into the living room, sat on the settee and opened the paper on the crossword section. Clue; *One word - two syllables. Charades*, he thought. They're not kidding either, he thought; *When is a dead paedo not a dead paedo?;*

'I got a star today, Daddy,' said Rosie, drawing at the little table. 'A silver star. Emily Watson got a gold star.'

'I bet she couldn't live with a silver star,' said her mother.

Rosie was amazed. 'How did you know that?'

'You're both very clever girls,' said George. To his annoyance, he felt a tear in his eyes. He wiped it away, being sentimental wouldn't do.

Christine looked up and smiled at him. She had smooth skin, smooth blonde hair and a crooked grin. It made her looks memorable.

She said something to Rosie. He looked at both blond heads shining in the pool of the lamplight. He was the man of the house. He provided for and protected his family, unlike his father before him. Perhaps he ought to go and see the old man. He hadn't seen him in years. So what was it that made him think of his father?

'What's for dinner?' he asked.

Christine said she'd put a lasagne in the oven. He didn't fancy it, the very the thought of it made him feel sick.

CHAPTER 5

UNLIKE GEORGE, Alf was a bit of a slob when it came to his hygiene, although he cleaned his shoes before he went into the house. His wife was vacuuming the lounge. When he tapped her on the shoulder, she jumped about two feet into the air, clutching her heart.

'Oh, it's you. Silly sod.'

'Who were you expecting, Simon Cowell?

She switched the hoover off. 'Look at you, you're soaked,' she said.

'It's raining,' he said. 'I got wet walking to the car park,' he added in case she wondered, but she didn't. She asked him instead what he was doing in a car park. Usually he parked in front of the car-repair shop he ran and had no reason to get wet coming home from work.

He wished he hadn't mentioned it, so he tapped his nose.

'Who has a birthday coming up?' he said.

Somebody's was bound to; in fact, he saw that it was Margaret's when he glanced at the calendar on the kitchen wall. He told her not to look in the car boot; it was a surprise. He went into the kitchen and put the kettle on, swaying slightly. He sometimes did that.

'You really should get your blood pressure checked,' said Margaret, who had followed him.

'Nothing wrong with my blood pressure,' he muttered. 'Nothing that a good fry-up won't cure.' He paused, hopefully. 'Or egg and chips.'

Margaret pointed out that she also worked full time and had no time to cook. She offered to put a frozen lasagne in the microwave. Alf said that he didn't fancy it and that he would fetch fish and chips instead; he might as well, he was wet through already.

'Where are the girls?' he asked before he went

out. Apparently, they were busy doing their homework. He went upstairs and opened the door to their pink bedroom.

'Knocking first would be polite,' said eight-year-old Victoria, his eldest daughter, lying on the floor, watching *'The Weakest Link* on *Freeview'*.

Eight years old, and already she was too good for him.

'I'm off to the chippie,' he said. 'What would you two you like?'

'Same as her,' said five-year-old Kylie, pointing to her sister with the TV control, inadvertently switching it off.

'Give it here,' shouted Victoria. 'Why do I have to share a room with an idiot? Haddock, and no bones, mind, 'she added, 'and shut the door when you leave.'

'That's what comes from treating daughters like princesses, you become their servant,' he said to Margaret on his way out.

'Who has turned up his nose at a lasagne?' she asked.

When he apologised before he left, she wondered if he was all right, normally he was a stranger to apologies.

'There must be an infestation of lasagnes,' said George, rocking back on his heels when Ritchie joined him and Alf at the chippie with tales of lasagnes.

'Can't stand the things,' said Ritchie, 'all that pasta with runny stuff inside.'

'Mince and cheese sauce,' said George. Although Ritchie was less of tremble, he was still shaking a bit. 'What did you tell the missus?'

Ritchie had told her he had been scraping Aertex of a ceiling all day. It made you shaky; it was nothing but the truth. 'Have you ever tried it?' he added when George congratulated him on his powers of invention.

'They're always arguing,' Alf said, pointing to the Korean couple who ran the chippie, now waiting to serve them.

'It only *sounds* as if they do,' said George, 'They're Koreans and they speak, what language do they speak?'

'*We* spikk Korean when not spikk English,' the Korean said, waving his fish slice at him, 'You here all night?'

They left the chippie and parted, going home, clutching their warm parcels, united in brotherhood. If one fell, they would all fall, that much they knew. They arranged to meet up at The Volunteer for a swift unit or two, as George put it, to discuss how to get rid of the old man's clothes.

'I'll drive, I pick you up about half-eight,' he said.

Ritchie said he got him, car-born footprints.

'CARBON footprints, idiot,' said Alf

'Same thing,' said Ritchie.

It was all so normal. Normality and company would see them through, thought George, but he knew it would be another story in the long hours of the night when it was one lone man versus his conscience.

CHAPTER 6

NOT FAR AWAY, Fred Foster put his plan into action. True, if it was premature, it was his own fault. His everyday routine had betrayed him, but routine was the lifeblood of being institutionalised.

He had a long time to think about it, but first things first. He had a nasty cut on the inside of his left hand, which was also his own fault. Acting in impulse never worked, he shouldn't have said he didn't have any money. If he hadn't said it, he wouldn't have his hand pushed into the broken glass.

He stemmed the blood with a handkerchief and then checked his First Aid kit where he found everything from the last migraine tablets to aspirins to bandages and Elastoplasts, but no iodine.

He would go to hell and back rather than facing that snot-driven doctor again, so he poured some Vodka onto the wound to disinfect it. The pain made him feel dizzy for a minute, but luckily the cut was on his left hand and he was able to pull the cut together and apply a butterfly-plaster.

He removed the rolled-up jumper simulating an old man's hump from his back, changed into a pale-blue shirt, grey trousers, a pale-blue v-neck jumper, a short, blue weatherproof jacket, but he left his trainers on. He replaced the brown wig with a short, slightly curly one between light brown and blond, and put on a different pair of glasses.

He had lost a lens out of his old pair when he fell over in the lane, not that it mattered, the ones he now put on were rimless, with small lenses. He looked positively intelligent, completely different from the hunched elderly man he had been, apart from the two deep grooves running from nose to chin. He would grow a slight beard, he thought.

He packed up everything in his case, then he picked up the phone.

'Homeward Bound?' said a woman's voice.

'Ah, Mrs Warner, it's Howard Cole here.'

'Lovely to hear from you,' she said.

'I'm just coming off the A14,' he said. 'I'll be with you shortly, if that's convenient.'

'A bit earlier than expected,' she said.

Silly cow. He had paid a fortnight's rent without being there in case things went wrong.

'Of course it's all right, your room is unoccupied.' she added. 'I Look forward to seeing you.'

He took one last look around the flat.

He hadn't intended to go so soon, but the men who attacked him had to be punished. The memory ignited his fury, he had been running away with his tail between his legs. They would have to pay, especially the one with the bad breath poking him in the stomach. One of the other ones had been watching him by the playground, so it hadn't been the police.

The B&B on the Farn Road was conveniently central to Bury St. Edmunds. He knew that he would find his attackers in one of the pubs and when he did, they would be sorry. He picked up his case. One final look around. Pity he had to leave the food he had just bought, but otherwise all cupboards and drawers were empty.

He was about to shut the door when he spotted the YELLOW PAGES, open at Hotels and *Bed And Breakfasts, Homeward Bound* underlined. He opened his case and put it in, wondering what else he had been careless about.

Next. He would do a pub-crawl, starting tonight. He would also enjoy watching the hue and cry when it was discovered he had gone underground. But only if he didn't make any more mistakes, he thought, looking in the mirror.

The bloke in the mirror lifted his wig and scratched his head. Something else to watch for until his hair grew a bit longer, he thought, leaving the flat.

He never left the car at The Flats. He walked to the Ridley estate, a large council but orderly estate where he parked his car every night, always in a different place.

He would have to change the car soon, he thought. It was bound to be registered to his wife.

Scouring the countryside a couple of weeks ago for abandoned buildings convenient for his intentions, he had hit on Clacton, a seaside town in Essex, dismal and grey in the winter and as forlorn as a seagull's lone cry.

His mood lightened when he had chanced on a caravan park, shortly to be closed for the season. An empty caravan was ideal for his purposes. It would be locked, of course, but it was amazing what you could do with a hairpin and bits of wire.

Not far away, he spotted a car showroom. It was a bit shabby, fitting in nicely with his plans. He made a note of the address and the phone number.

He wanted a five-year-old Corolla, as lucky a car as this one was. Not having a log-book, he phoned the car show-room, but when he said, 'no questions asked,' the receiver was replaced.

He now had a mobile phone. Although at first he had wondered about all the mobile phones sprouting like malignant growths from people's ears, he was no longer surprised by them. What was more, he really needed one, as the only phone booth he had found and been able to use had been at the railway station.

Now he got into his car and drove the short distance to the B&B, where he reversed into a tight space.

He congratulated himself, went inside to Reception and pinged the bell.

'Mr Cole, welcome to Homeward Bound, said Mrs Warner, coming down the stairs. She was a tall, thin, woman, probably in her fifties. Her lips were tightly pressed together when she wasn't speaking. 'You came on the A14?' she enquired, going behind the desk, opening the register.

'Through Newmarket,' he said. She sounded as if it was impossible.

'That's why you avoided the traffic jam, my hubby is still stuck on it,' she said, looking for a pen. 'There's been an accident just after you turn of the A14 towards Bury St. Edmunds.'

He put his hand inside his jacket, as if searching for a chequebook he did not possess. 'A cheque for next month? Or would you prefer cash?'

'Cash will be fine,' she said, opening her hand, taking the notes and closing the book. It was all the same to her, he had signed it when he booked in a fortnight ago on reserving the room.

She closed the book, handed him the keys for his room and for the front door, explaining that the house was shut from twelve to seven am. Then she smiled and came from behind the desk.

'I'll show you up to your bedroom,' she said, 'you have one of the large ones on the top floor. It has a television and tea and coffee-making facilities.'

He bloody hoped so, the money she charged, forty pounds a night. 'I have seen it, thank you, Mrs Warner.'

'And all our rooms are en-suite.'

En-suite. The bog was practically in the bedroom. What a bright idea, it would make him feel right at home. He followed her up the stairs when she turned round.

'By the way, this is a no-smoking establishment,' she said.

Who-ever had heard of a B&B where you couldn't smoke? Bugger that for a tale of soldiers. 'In that case I will have to look elsewhere.'

She looked at the notes and waved her hand. 'We'll make an exception in your case,' she said, 'you are on the top floor, and here we are.'

Nice and private. He would familiarise himself with computers, it wouldn't take him long, he had a logical mind. 'And computers?'

'Computer access?'

She opened the door to his room. 'Of course. You can Google away on your laptop at your heart's content.'

As his hostess wound her way downstairs, he sank on the bed, wondering for a moment if Mrs Warner was being filthy. Googling on his lap top! But it suddenly came to him that it might be computer speak.

'Oh, one more thing.' He got up.

'Mrs Warner?'

'Yes?'

She turned around on the half-landing.

'I wonder if you could let me have the name of a barber,' he said. 'I'm not familiar with Bury St. Edmunds. Tomorrow will do.'

I should think it will, thought his hostess, while Fred Foster had planted the seed. A man going to a barber would not be wearing a wig. As ever, people saw what they expect to see.

He would change the car tomorrow, he thought. How long was it taxed and insured for? How valid was his licence?

He opened the envelope with the papers his ex

had given him. His car was neither taxed nor insured. The lying cow! But he found his old driving licence, dated 1985, several building society accounts and a bank account, all of which had been closed.

It came to over three-hundred-thousand pounds before she had closed the accounts, and she had left him with the measly ten-thousand he had left behind when he was banged up.

He wondered where the money came from, not from selling her body with that face on her, she probably inherited the cash when her dad croaked it.

According to the log book, she lived in Haslingfield in Cambridgeshire, over the Suffolk border. He would pay her a visit tomorrow. He would wipe that smug grin off her face all right, he thought, but a smile was slowly spreading over his own face. Nobody knew he drove a car, and if they did, they wouldn't find a record of him in Swansea once he'd changed his means of transport.

She had done him a favour after all, he thought as he wound his way downstairs on his way to a pub.

CHAPTER 7

CHRISTINE LOOKED UP from her fish supper.

'I don't know how you do it,' she said. 'I really, really fancied a cold, dry sherry and I found a bottle in the fridge. Thanks, Mira.'

It had to be the smell of the broken bottle on his trousers, thought George.

'You're being silly, Daddy's name isn't Mira,' said Rosie. 'Mira's name is Mira.'

'That's all you know,' said George, 'my name was Mira once.'

Mira, his secretary then and now, was a marvellous typist, but when computers galloped over the horizon, she had to learn new words. Cut and Paste, File, Edit, Format, and of course, Switch On.

She refused to go on the computer course, but as it included a good lunch George went instead and spent the whole day sporting the nametag Mira on his jacket. Nobody had laughed more than the girl who taught the course, her name was Christine. She wore a tight beige suit, very high heels and had shiny blonde hair.

It wasn't only Mira who had to learn new words at the office. George's new vocabulary included accountability, benchmarking, and finally redundancy. He had joined the firm after getting his engineering degree at twenty-two, which meant he got twelve years salary when he was laid off.

He bought, not rented, (never rent, money down the drain, his father said when he was young and they were still speaking) a run-down workshop on an industrial site. He married Christine who inherited the Victorian house they lived in from her grandmother.

They had run hand-in-hand to the car taking them to the airport, happy ever after, they thought.

In the next five years, Christine suffered two miscarriages at five months pregnant. It was heartbreaking for him to see her going through labour and giving birth to dead boys; it was equally heartbreaking to lose his boys. It was a difficult time for them both.

If only you could synchronise suffering. Instead, they seesawed between feeling up and down at different times, but they came through it together. When they finally had their perfect little girl, Christine didn't want her to be an only child. However, she miscarried once more, again it was a boy, and that was the end of that. She was prescribed Valiums, and now that she was free of them, she lived her own life again.

'I know,' cried Rosie, who had brooded on the problem of Daddy being mistaken for Mira. 'We could ask Mira to our Bonfire Night Party.'

'I thought we were going to the Abbey Gardens,' said George. He hated the general idea of standing about in the cold, craning his neck, clearing up afterwards, people coming in his house with dirty shoes and, most of all, he hated eating burnt potatoes. 'On the other hand...'

'We could ask a few people,' said Christine.

'We could ask Alf and Ritchie,' said George. 'I'm seeing them tonight as a matter of fact. At the pub.'

Christine lifted an eyebrow.

'We're thinking of starting a five-a-side football team.'

At the pub? With three people? Christine wondered, but she let it go.

It was Quiz Night, Fred Foster noted when he entered the pub. He was soaked and found himself a small table

43

near the blazing fire. He picked up a menu. He sometimes wondered what had happened to the country in the twenty years he had spent inside. However, good pub food was definitely an improvement, he thought, as he looked about him with concealed interest.

Bits of paper and pencils were handed round by the landlord to a group of elderly people sitting to the left of the room by the fire.

'Do you want to do the quiz?' the barmaid asked Ritchie, who was standing at the bar.

'Naw, thanks,' he said. 'I don't know nothing.'

That's a double negative,' she said, handing him his pint.

'It cancels itself out,' she explained when he looked at his pint, puzzled.

He found George and Alf in a corner, finishing their first drink, so he went back to the bar.

'Alcohol-free beer is a lot more expensive than real beer,' he said when he came back with their drinks. He didn't know why, but he felt sure George would tell him.

'They brew it first and then take the alcohol out of it,' said George.

'They ought to take the gnat's piss out of it, if you ask me,' said Alf, who was drinking the real stuff. 'Ritchie mate, we are invited to the Bonfire Night Party at George's.'

Ritchie was doubtful. 'We stand outside our house and watch the fireworks from the Abbey gardens. They go off in the air,' he added.

'They generally do,' said George, but Alf said he got him. 'We'll burn the clothes,' he said.

Ritchie wondered what sort of clothes they were burning, but he got it by the time it was Alf's round; Dr Willoughby's raincoat.

Bonfire Night was on Wednesday, George said.

He would build a big fire at the bottom of the garden.

'Start in the morning,' said Alf. 'I'll bring some wood round.' His greengage tree had lost a main branch in the recent gales.

The landlord coughed and looked in their direction, so they joined in the quiz. It was ok, the questions were mostly about football or the telly. They didn't do that well, considering, when it came to the last question: Which Shakespearean character wore yellow stockings?

'Who knows?' said Ritchie.

'Who cares?' said Alf.

'*Malvolio,*' George wrote, folded his paper and handed it to the landlord.

'How did you know?' asked Ritchie.

George said he had played Olivia in the sixth form when boys played all the characters as in Shakespeare's time.

The jackpot rolled over to next week, they came second and they won a set of cheap glasses. They couldn't stop laughing, what with George being the lovely Olivia, as well as at the pub owning more than enough cheap glasses to donate as prizes.

It was time for high fives as they were about to part. All three agreed to come back again next week, when a man padded past them silently.

He was a tidy-looking man, with curling hair, wearing rimless glasses.

They watched him leave the pub.

'There's something familiar about him,' said Alf.

'Like what?' said George.

'His trainers,' said Alf. 'The paedo wore trainers.'

'So what?' said Ritchey. 'So do I, sometimes.'

It set them off again, middle-aged men, going

on thirteen, thought Alf.

A hysterical reaction, George thought. He had somehow ended up their unelected leader. He was perhaps more afraid of the consequences of their actions, but even as he laughed, he knew their laughter was a brief escape from the burden they all carried.

Three fucking idiots, thought Fred Foster lurking by the bushes. He wasn't sure if the short, red-headed bloke was the one he was looking for. He had mechanic's hands, engrained with grease and dirt. He didn't remember that. All he recalled was the man's bad breath. He didn't have his car and couldn't pursue them, but next time, he would get closer to him.

While Ritchie was gone, Iris, his wife, ironed the children's clothes she had sorted out for Oxfam. She put them in a bin liner and went to the garage with it.

When she opened Ritchie's car boot, she found a wheelbarrow and a man's beige raincoat, an old man's coat. It was probably her dad's, he had told her he was having a sort-out.

She placed the raincoat on top of the children's clothes, tied the bin liner and put it on top of the wheelbarrow. God only knew what it was doing there, it was probably something to do with Ritchie's work.

She was going to ask him about it when he came in, but when he said George had invited them to his Bonfire Night Party, she forgot all about it.

'What? Posh George?' she said, amazed. She might have forgotten the wheelbarrow, but she remembered the clothes for Oxfam.

'They'll be closed when I finish work,' he said, but she said it would be all right to leave them outside the shop overnight. When he promised to take them, she wondered how many more times she would have to remind him.

'Oh, don't forget,' she said, 'Alf and Maggie are having the kids tomorrow, we're going to the flicks.'

CHAPTER 8

'BURY ST. EDMUNDS POLICE,' said PC Connor, answering the telephone on Saturday morning.

'Is that the police?' a querulous voice inquired.

'It is.'

'I want to report a fly-tipper.'

'You'll want to speak to the council.'

'No, I don't. I have spoken to them on untold occasions. In fact, I have sent them my telephone bill.'

'And?'

'Nothing. They are my servants, you see, just as you are, because I pay my taxes.'

'I am not your servant, I am the Queen's servant as an Officer of the Crown.'

'I'm not a Royalist, so save your breath to cool the tea you lot seem so fond of drinking. Despoiling the environment, these people are,' continued the whiny voice.

'Right. Can I have your name and address, please?'

'Albert Rusty. Winfred Close, Stow,' said Mr Rusty. 'I saw three men removing rubbish from the boot of their car on Friday evening. Make a note, this is a new complaint.'

'Where?

'By the woods, on the way to Thelford.'

'Can I just stop you there; you will have to get in touch with Norfolk Constabulary.'

'I said o*n the wa*y, you see, it's just before you get to the sign.'

PC Connor, who was on temporary desk duty, lost the will to live, let alone ask what sign.

One of the those callers, he thought, replacing the receiver, when the phone rang again with another one of those calls.

'I want to report a felony,' said another angry voice

'Right. What felony are you reporting? Let's start at the beginning.'

'I always do. I want to report a break-in and a burglary.

'Right.'

'When did this take place?'

'How should I know? I've just returned from my holidays. You see, the wife and always go to Madeira. We fly Thursday to Thursday, so on the Friday, late evening, I went to the allotment to see how my sprouts were doing.'

'And?'

'Doing well, thank you, just needs a frost on them. When I got there, my shed was open, wide open, and my wheelbarrow, my torch and my very last bin liner were missing. Plus, my broom had been used. I always put it away upside down.'

'Where is your allotment?'

'Where the road branches of towards either Culham or the supermarket. On the left-hand side. Oh, one more thing, it might not have been a break-in, I seem to have forgotten to lock the shed, you know how it is when it's cold and raining.'

'Right.'

He paused, counted to ten, and tried to retrieve *the friendly face of the police,* as recommended in the latest communication now in front of him.

'May I have your name, address and your telephone number, please.'

He made a note of it, promised to pass it on, and put the phone down.

'A Claude Ford is missing a torch and a wheelbarrow from his allotment, can you believe it?' he said to his mate from *Traffic* who had a heavy date he wanted a report on.   'A torch and a wheelbarrow? Would you believe it?'

His mate could believe it.

'As a matter of fact, we spotted something being loaded into a car boot when we passed the allotments on Friday night on our way to investigate an accident in Culham.'

Constable Connor made a note of it.

CHAPTER 9

'WHO INVENTED MUESLI?' Rosie asked on Saturday morning. The Hudsons were having a late, leisurely breakfast.

'A very clever man from Switzerland,' said George, who had to have a tooth crowned after biting on something unidentifiable, but very hard, he had found in his muesli. 'One day he said to his wife, 'Vifie, vhy not put cat litter in a box and call it muesli, Liebling?'

'You're being very silly,' said Rosie.

'I was,' said George, reaching for the toast, 'it vas food for ze budgerigars.'

He looked forward to a relaxing morning, gathering his strength for the afternoon ahead; he intended to visit his father.

'Mummy said you would take me swimming *and* to ballet,' said Rosie.

'What? Why? Why can't your mother do it?'

If George hated anything it was socialising in swimming trunks. Swimming, in fact going anywhere with Rosie, invariably led to socialising. He also disliked sharing a shower or a cubicle with Rosie. Although he was her father, it could lead to funny looks from the attendants.

'I thought it would be nice to have some people round for dinner tonight,' said Christine.

'I thought you wanted to finish that painting of fruit you're on.'

'It's a Still Life,' said Christine.

Christine was a good if self-taught amateur painter.

'I thought it might be time to show our sociable face,' she added.

George didn't know they had one, but he was

willing to support her.

'I've invited Mum and Eddie, as well as Mira and her sister for dinner.'

He liked her mum; he found her lively and good company, and so did most men, it seemed. She was on her fourth marriage. He wasn't sure about her latest, Eddie, a large man with a matching round face, nor about Mira. Mira had a huge crush on him, which she translated into a great passion.

'Mummy's doing a Beef Wellington,' said Rosie, who seemed to be better informed then her father, who had spent a terrible night chasing sleep. When he finally did, he dreamt about his father being buried. The coffin was light and floated away. George shouted, 'there's no body,' and everybody laughed.

Jarring laughter was ringing in his ears when he woke up, and never had he been so glad to see a new morning.

When Christine got up and started to clear the table, he followed her into the kitchen. 'Can't she miss ballet for once? I was going to see my father this afternoon,' he said.

She had to steady herself on the sink.

'YOUR FATHER? You haven't remembered you had a father for years. What has brought this on after all this time?'

'A boy can see his father if he wants to.'

'Some boy,' she said. Still. Normally asleep the minute his head hit the pillow, George had tossed and turned in bed like clothes in a tumble drier. 'Have you finally forgiven him for having an affair? I mean, you were only a child.'

He hadn't put two and two together until he was an adult. His father used to disappear on a Sunday, probably once a month, as far as he could remember.

Although he clearly remembered the sound of crashing from the kitchen where his mother was slinging saucepans about.

'Where's Dad?' he used to ask. She just shook her head, her lips a tight line. One Christmas, he had looked under the tree and some parcels, previously hidden behind the settee, had disappeared.

'Who had my presents?' he asked his mother.

She was mad as hell and burned the turkey.

One day he came back from school and his mother was gone.

'I thought mothers liked their families, but she didn't like us,' he said to his father, who told him he wouldn't understand it.

'Why not?'

'Because you are too young,' said his father.

George would make damn sure Rosie had her childhood happiness intact.

Mixed swimming, or whatever it was called, was from ten until twelve. Rosie's ballet was from three to four. Christine also wanted him to get some lemons and eggs for a lemon meringue. All in all, it would have to be a late afternoon, or an evening, visit.

He finally dialled the number.

'Dad?'

'Yes?'

'George here,' he said.

Silence.

'I thought I might come and see you tonight.'

'Hang on, just checking my appointments,' said his father, 'I believe I am going out later in the evening.' George could see him between half-five to seven, he added. Apparently, there was nothing worth watching on telly at that time.

Charming, George thought, putting the receiver

down.

Rosie, wearing pink armbands to match her swimsuit, looked pityingly at the children splashing about in the starter pool. '*I was* in the big pool,' she said to a woman who was watching a dumpy little girl shivering in the water, 'this is my daddy.'

The woman was slim and delicate, with an exquisite face. Her dark hair was parted in the middle, drawn back and gathered into a low chignon.

Eat your heart out, Julia Roberts, he thought.

'I'm Natasha,' she said, 'and,' she added, pointing to the girl in the water, 'this is Hester.'

'Can Hester come to dinner tonight?' asked Rosie.

Natasha must have seen the horrified expression on George's face. She laughed. 'I'm afraid we are going to my dad's for tea. He's making a sherry trifle for me. For some reason he thinks it's my favourite.'

'And you can't stand it,' George said. 'Fathers!'

What a woman, he thought, walking away to the showers.

'Do you ever play with Hester?' he asked Rosie on the way out. Rosie pulled a face and shook her head. 'Please! She can't dance; she can't even do a pliè.'

However, it wasn't the pliè that had George worried, it was the sherry trifle.

Hester might not have been able to do a pliè, but neither did she want to.

'You might have to miss ballet toady, your granddad likes to see us about four,' Natasha Marshall, Dr Willoughby's daughter, said, getting into the house and putting their swimming things into the machine.

When Hester pulled a face, her mother almost agreed with her. Her father had become difficult a few months ago. He was moody, calling Hester *the child*. 'Don't let the child hoover up its food, Natasha,' he'd said when Hester was too low-seated on his deep dining chairs.

Not only was he moody, he'd become slovenly in his habits, so she had organised a home help, a lovely Polish woman, who had done him the world of good.

He normally came to her once a week for a meal except, this week, he had invited her for a change, but she knew that she should really see him more often.

'I don't like ballet,' said Hester who was more concerned with missing dancing than meeting up with her grandfather. 'It's silly.'

'But it's nice to see the other girls.'

'They don't play with me. I want to talk to Emily at school, but she talks to the man in the black beret. I don't like him.'

'Which Emily? Emily Watson?' asked her mother. She wasn't sorry about that; Emily Watson was a precocious little madam. Still, Hester seemed to have a problem making friends with her peers, although most adults adored her.

'I would like to have a friend,' said Hester.

'You will,' said her mother, giving her a hug. 'I was exactly like you at your age.'

It wasn't true, of course. She had been one of those polished, popular little girl's parents were so proud of, but Hester had always been a bit slower than the rest in the competitive mother-child world; slower walking, slower talking, but she had a lovely smile reflecting her true nature. *She wouldn't change her for the world*, Natasha thought, but she would certainly change the constant worry nagging at her about her daughter.

The phone rang. She answered it, pulled a face and told Hester to go and play.

'Is it Lewis?' Hester asked.

Her mother put the hand over the phone.

'Yes, it is, but you really ought to call him Daddy.'

Lewis had changed his mind again. First of all, he wanted to have Hester for the weekend, then he didn't, and now he did again.

'She isn't a parcel you can post whenever you feel like it,' she screamed into the phone, even though she knew that it wouldn't make the slightest bit of difference.

'*Marry me*,' he had written on a greetings card after they met. It sounded like a command. '*Says who?*' she wrote back. God! What fun! Back and forth, they batted as in a game of tennis until it was game, set and match to Natasha and Lewis. Still, she had paid for the fun.

They sat on the settee, eating their lunch, and afterwards both had a little nap. When they woke up, Hester declared that she wanted to wear her new blue jumper for the visit.

'Blue suits me, it brings out the blue in my eyes, Lewis says.' said Hester, admiring herself in the mirror, and so, relaxed and happy, they set off on their journey.

The milk was on the doorstep when she drove up to the bungalow, her father hadn't taken it in, nor was he there to greet them when they got out of the car.

'Maybe he has gone to the shop, but he would still pick up the milk first.' she said, fumbling for her own key, letting herself into the house.

She picked up what looked like the day's post.

The Guardian, and junk mail. *'Don't miss this opportunity! Win a weekend for two,* it said on the envelope,and also a gardening magazine. She put the mail next to *The Mercury,* the free newspaper, on the hall table.

'Yoo-hoo! Dad!'

No answer.

The house felt deserted.

She went into the kitchen and saw his car keys hanging by the door. He was walking to the shops, she thought, perhaps he had forgotten something. He was getting absent-minded, he used yellow Post-it notes as reminders. All the while-despite trying to reason with herself-she knew that she was wrong; his absence was serious.

The sink gleamed, not a thing was out of place in the kitchen, the tray with the blue-sprigged best china cups and saucers was ready for her visit as it always was when the help had been in.

The Afghan blanket her mother had crocheted was folded on the armchair by the fireplace, and her father's reading glasses were on top next to a small notebook. He wore his long-distance glasses when he went out.

She looked at the notebook, but his famously neat hand (for a doctor) was deteriorating into in squiggles. Probably chess-speak, Natasha , who hadn't inherited her father's brains but her mother's looks thought, as she went into the main bedroom. The room was neat and tidy; the bed was made, with the nap of a white sheet folded neatly over the top of blankets. Her father didn't believe in downies.

A Post-it note was on the dressing table, it read ; Put dirty laundry in the basket in the bathroom.

How odd.

'Where is he?' she said to Hester. 'I talked to

him last night; I know he *was* expecting us.'

The sherry trifle, she remembered. He was getting the sherry for it; he had bought it, as a matter of fact. He had said so yesterday. It should be here, but she found no trace of it anywhere.

The free newspaper was normally delivered about three, half-past three on Friday afternoon. When she had phoned him, it was coming to six o'clock, perhaps a bit earlier. He was missing since then, she was sure of it. His bed had not been *made*; it had not *been slept in* since yesterday.

'I better 'phone Aleska,' she said to Hester. Aleska Wawrinska was in her father's small phone book under *Thingy (Miss)*. She was her father's Polish home help and Hester's babysitter, the cheerful sort of help Natasha looked on as a life line.

'I came in morning, as always I do,' said Aleska, answering the phone. 'But your father, he is not there, and the bed he is not sleeping in, but everythink I left as should be. Perhaps he is going away, I think.' She sighed. 'Such a man! So many hard things in his life, eh?'

There was something compassionate in her voice. Was there something Natasha had missed?

'Oh?'

'His wife he lost, and then Lewis, your man. He like him much. And people riding him, how you say? Taking him for ride. Nice woman down the road, she take him shopping.'

'Yes, he told me. Magda, isn't it?'

'Magda, yes. She take him shopping and make him pay for everythink.'

'For *her* shopping as well?'

'I stop him, and she goes on holiday, very nice? And your brother. Papa ask him to come, visit, but he say no.'

58

'I am sorry,' Aleska whispered. 'My Man, he wanting to speak. Saturday is time for him.' She put the phone down.

Aleska often had bruises on her arms or on her face; apparently she was always walking into doors. Neither Natasha nor her father were fooled, but the girl loved her Man. So she said, and she always pronounced it with a capital letter.

So many thoughts were racing in Natasha's head, and so many worries. She felt abandoned, trying to ignore the creepy stillness of the house. She wanted to phone the hospital, but she didn't want to worry Hester.

Besides, who could she phone on Saturday night? except there was *somebody* at a loose end, she remembered, Lewis. She picked up the phone reluctantly.

'Your daddy is coming over to get you, Hester,' she said, putting down the receiver after a while.

'And then you can find my granddad,' Hester said, sounding not particularly bothered.

'Hopefully,' she said, watching for the car out of the window.

'There's Daddy,' shouted Hester, and ran to the front door.

He carried her into the living room.

'So, Natasha? How are you?'

'My father is missing,' she said, 'That's how I am.'

'Oh God, how awful, I'm sorry it has come to this.'

'To what? What do you know?'

'We don't want to worry Hester,' he said, sitting next to her, looking as polished from his blond head to his neat little beard to his gleaming brown shoes as he ever did.

'I think you had better take her back to the house to sleep,' said Natasha. 'She hasn't got her night things. I'll be over as soon as I can. '

'Mummy has got some more jigsaws for us,' said Hester. They completed jigsaws donated to Oxfam to make sure no pieces were missing. 'We can do the one with kittens,' she added excitedly.

'My absolute favourite, I can't wait,' said Lewis, holding her hand.

'Make sure she's strapped in,' Natasha said over Hester's head before they left the house.

Lewis started the car. Then he got out.

'The house key,' he said, holding out his hand for it. 'And before you ask, I put Hester on the car roof.' He drove off, with Hester sucking her thumb in the back seat.

The bungalow was full of her father's belongings; his chess set, his books, his CDs, but he was gone. Phonebook. Where was it? She didn't know where her father kept anything, and she didn't know any of his neighbours. She had never lived in the bungalow; her parents had moved into when her mother was diagnosed with bone cancer and could no longer use stairs.

Finally she found the phonebook and started making enquiries. Nobody with that name had come in, the nurse at A&E at the other end of the telephone said. Apparently, she was consulting the register.

'Is everybody registered there?' Natasha asked, as she had no idea how A&E actually operated. 'Is an elderly man there waiting to be seen?'

The nurse took her number, said they were very busy, and she would ring if a Paul Willoughby is admitted.

'How about ambulance admissions?

Accidents?'

The nurse was losing her patience.

'They would be in the book,' she said, ringing off. Just as she had, the phone rang.

'It's Phil here,' said an elderly voice. 'Are you Paul's daughter?' when she answered it.

'He's not at home, I think he's been missing since yesterday evening,' she said, 'and even my ex is worried. Oh, I forgot, it's your chess night.'

They played via the telephone.

'We don't play now, I'm afraid,' said Phil, 'Paul said he wasn't up to it any more. Maybe you should be worried. He could be wandering about, not knowing where he was. Maybe he fell in a ditch.'

Idiot, she thought, but maybe he had a point?

'What makes you think so?'

'His condition?'

'What condition?'

Her father had told him he had Alzheimer's disease, Phil said.

She couldn't believe it. Is this what Lewis meant when he said '*it had come to this*'? If so, how had he known?

'If I were you, I should try and find him,' he said, (idiot!) when a car drew up on the gravel. It was Frank Somersby, her father's former -and younger- partner at the surgery.

She and Lewis were not formally separated, they lived apart, and since then Frank had appointed himself her guardian. It annoyed her when Frank insisted on calling Lewis her ex. *She might call Lewis her ex,* but in her heart he wasn't.

'Is Hester with your ex?' Frank asked, and Natasha gritted her teeth, alas, in vain.

Meanwhile, George was in the Brownie hut where ten

little girls in pink leotards were urged to be little pixies, all bar Emily, who was in a strop. 'I shan't,' she said. 'I couldn't live with being a pixie.'

'Which one is Emily's mother?' he asked Rosie, pointing to a group of women.

'I don't know, Emily's always with her omp pair,' said Rosie.

'Au-pair'.

'That's what I said,' said Rosie. 'That's her,' she pointed to a girl barely out of her teens who was looking severely bored. 'Natalie. She's French, from France,' she added, 'but Hester's not here and I was going to be nice to her. How annoying is that?'

'She's probably at her granddad's,' said George. Hester's mother had said something about it this morning at the pool, something about a sherry trifle.

A nagging worry wormed its way deeper into his brain.

He tried to dismiss it, but it was wriggling away as he got ready to visit his father later that day.

By the time he was ready to leave, darkness was descending rapidly on a grey November evening.

Before he left, he wanted to Google *Rigor Mortis* on his computer, not a good idea as Christine wanted to check a recipe at the same time. So he went out and selected a spade from the garden tools hanging on the garage wall, graded according to the handle length. He found a torch, a bin liner and gardening gloves, got in the car, and drove off to see his father.

Charming, his father thought, just dropping in after all this time.

George wanted something, probably money.

Who was it who had wrestled him into his anorak and shoes and taken him to the pictures after his mother had done a runner? Who had made sure George had his dinner-money and clean clothes and a bed to sleep in? Who provided the roof over his head? And who had cleared off to college just as he grew hair on his face and in unlikely places and became reasonable company for his father?

George's father had always told it like it was.

After George's wife miscarried, he had told him it was just as well; he would have had idiots or cripples for boys.

Maybe it had been a mistake not to tell George about his sister. She was a Mongol, Down's syndrome they called it now, but it was the same thing. She had been handed over straight after her birth. Her mother couldn't bear to look at her, but he visited his daughter once every month. That smile when she recognised him! A smile big enough to light up the world. She had died when she was twelve, something to do with her heart.

He had been to the funeral where he remembered the smile. It seemed forgiving; after all, she hadn't asked to be born like that.

He thought on these things as George drove with his spade out of Bury St. Edmunds.

CHAPTER 10

GEORGE DROVE OUT OF BURY towards Thelford, where his father lived in sheltered housing just outside of the town. When he looked up the address again, he found he had driven past it and had to turn back. There it was, to the right. *Bethany,* the sign said. He turned into the development and parked in a place marked with VISITOR PARKING..

Bethany, wasn't that something biblical? Something Christian? he wondered, getting out, locking the car and getting his bearings. Yellow-brick bungalows and houses with trellised porches and little front gardens surrounded the centre lawn. It had a tree in the middle under which ducks were sheltering from the drizzle, heads buried under their feathers. The tidy development projected an air of order, of serenity.

Number seventeen was an upstairs flat. When he pressed the bell, the front door opened into a small hall with a staircase, with a stair lift at the bottom.

He walked upstairs and knocked.

'Are you ill?' he said, when his father answered the door.

'Not so you'd notice,' said his father. 'Come in. What makes you ask?'

'The stair lift,' said George.

'That's for decoration at the present moment,' said his father. 'What do you think of the place?'

The living/dining room, when table and chairs were pushed against the wall, was a good size. Double glass door led to a small balcony overlooking a stream. Decorated in magnolia throughout, the living room was lit by a central light. Flood lighting was for football pitches, thought George, but he said it was very nice, which it really was.

'Don't pull that red cord by the wall,' said his

father, 'that's for emergencies. If I have a stroke and collapse it will fetch the warden.'

'Let's hope you can reach it if happens,' said George.

He was really impressed; everything was so neat.

'I tidied up when I knew you were coming,' said his father, beetling off to the kitchen, putting on the kettle. 'You always were a prissy little sod, you take after your mother like that, but it turned out for the best. You married a girl with her own house.'

It wasn't quite like that, George thought.

'I should have told you about your sister,' said his father.

'WHAT SISTER?' asked George, groping for a chair behind him.

'Your sister was what you call a Down's syndrome child nowadays, I believe. It was kept quiet in those days, hushed up.'

George sank onto a chair.

'You see, your mother was very beautiful, a right Rita Hayworth head-turner.'

'Was she?'

'I always wondered what she was doing with me. And then she had Lorraine, only she couldn't face what she had given birth to. They told her of the baby's condition straight away. They can tell, something to do with no lines on the hands. Our daughter was taken away, and she never went to see her, not even once. As I said, it was different in those days, so we kept it from you.'

'Let me get this straight.'

His father didn't have an affair, he had visited his disabled daughter. He took her presents at Christmas, the presents that went missing. And he did it alone. How lonely his father must have been, and how brave.

'Your mother liked everything nice, she cleared off when you were seven and lost your baby charm. Anyway, Lorraine died when she was twelve. Your mother never saw that smile of hers, but I did.'

'I'm not airy-fairy, I tell it as it is, that's why I said what I did about your stillborn boys,' said his father.

'You like everything nice, how would you have coped with a Mongol child, Down's syndrome, whatever, or a child with another disability? Believe me, it would break your heart to see some of them in the *Home*, especially when they grow older, as babies will do. It's no life for anybody. One of them in the *Home* was a man, born well before his time, his mother told me. He was blind and deaf and incontinent, he had epileptic fits and he dribbled constantly. His chin was like a bit of red meat.'

He paused.

'Day in, day out it went on. Nobody could inflict a worse torture on a person. Your sister smiled once a month for twelve years. I wouldn't call that a life either.'

George stared at him, trying to take it all in.

'Not always,' he said. 'Sometimes you see one-year-old babies born at five or six months in the papers. Perfectly healthy.'

'And why do you think they make the papers? I'm an opinionated old so-and-so, maybe you're right, and, as for Downs, I believe you can have a test now,' his father said uncertainly.

'As a matter of fact, Christine didn't have the amniotic test.'

'I thought I ought to have told you, in case it can be inherited like, but then you had Rosie.'

'We wouldn't have had an abortion. We

expected a baby, not a condition.'

'So some things may have changed, but there are degrees with Downs, and your sister had a severe case.'

He looked anxiously at George.

'You did your best. You took me to the pictures when Mum left – I remember seeing Pinocchio. And you made sure that I had clean clothes every day and my dinner money,' said George.

He paused.

'I remember that day as clearly as if it was yesterday. I begged Mum not to go, I tried to take her shoes away. She put on some lipstick, picked up her case and told me to be a good boy when I left for school. When I came home, she was gone. I sat huddled in the dark. It was winter and I was cold.'

'That's right,' said his father.

'All the good things were gone, security, warmth, and then the door opened. You switched the light on. You knew how I felt without being told, you knew everything and I felt safe again. You smoked a packet of cigarettes in the cinema.'

'Number Six. Those were the days, smoking in a cinema.'

'You remember what the Blue Fairy in Pinocchio said? "Prove yourself brave, strong, truthful and unselfish, and someday you will be a real boy."'

George paused.

'She was the teller of truths. You said, "I suppose you believe that sentimental rubbish?"'

'No supposing about it,' said his father. 'When am I going to see my granddaughter?'

'Soon, I promise. But I must go now. We're having some people in for dinner.'

'I'm sorry for having been such a lousy son,' said

George some time later, after they have talked some more. 'You see, I thought -when I grew up- you had an affair when you disappeared once a month, and then you said what you said about our babies. What are you doing tonight?'

Apparently, his father had never cooked a dinner since he moved in, he had never had it so good.

'I always dine in a restaurant in Warsaw.'

'WARSAW?'

'There are more Poles in Thelford than in Poland,' said his dad. 'Are you in trouble, son?' he asked, seeing him to the door.

'I might well be, Dad,' said George.

'Well, you know where I am.'

His father shut the door, wishing his son had never been to see him; he would worry about him from now on. He had forgotten how that felt.

George drove off, images of his father in his head. His father dressing nicely, putting on his hat, leaving to visit the *Home* where his sister lived, his mother resenting it, clashing saucepans in the kitchen.

His father had proved himself brave, strong, truthful and unselfish, he thought, and he would never forget it.

If only everything wasn't kept so bloody secret, he thought, stopping by the forest where they had disposed of the body.

It was dark and deserted.

He drew in behind the gorse bushes and parked his car. He took out the spade, put on the gloves, and got the torch. An eerie shriek of all the dead souls in the world filled the air. *Probably an owl*, he thought when his heart finally stopped hammering in his chest. A fox barked near-by, strengthening his resolve; it was the thought of foraging animals that had brought him here.

A five-minute walk, he reckoned; but it seemed a lot longer before he spotted the stained blue mattress. He lifted it up, dragged it to the side and dug a man-sized hole, the sort that wouldn't leave a hump, which was easy in the soft forest soil.

The dead man was next to him, his legs sticking out of the black bin liner. He put the spade down, wondering about Rigor Mortis. He (he didn't like to name the dead man) had died on Friday night, yesterday, would it have worn off?

It hadn't. He didn't have to break any bones, (thank you, Lord) as the limbs had been straight when they put him under the mattress. When he laid the body in the shallow grave he had a feeling of floating above the trees. He was looking down on a man who shovelled dirt over a dead body, saying over and over that he was sorry, sorry.

When he returned to earth, it was done. He dragged the mattress over the grave and walked towards his car, carrying the bin liner and dragging his spade. He opened the boot, put in the bin liner that had held the body into a fresh one, put in the spade, and, totally drained, he sat in his car where he took off his gloves and lit a cigarette.

A car stopped opposite as George drove off, driving off shortly after. Another one parked soon afterwards behind the gorse bushes. A busy night for a god-forsaken spot, George thought, but his house looked reassuring and welcoming when he got home. Lights were switched on, smoke curled out of the chimneys. After George parked in the garage, he threw his gloves and the bin liner into the wheelie-bin.

He had better join the living. He had seen the two cars parked in front of the house, the sodding dinner party. *Why couldn't people eat in their own houses*, he thought, letting himself in.

When he opened the living room door, it was like a film set lights, camera, action. Secretary Mira looked at him as if he was made of chocolate; however, his wife Christine didn't, she disappeared into the kitchen. His mother-in-law came towards him, brandishing a bottle of champagne.

'Champagne,' she cried. 'If you visit the best, you bring the best.'

The best! He nearly cried.

'Much appreciated,' he said, giving her a hug, 'but I better go and change first.'

Washed and changed, he crept downstairs and took his mobile into the toilet.

'Alf,' he said when he got a signal. 'I thought you should know I made my peace with my dad.'

'What? What makes you think I bloody well care?

'You should also know I went back and buried the body.'

'When?'

'About thirty minutes ago.'

'I also went to bury the body, and when I looked under the mattress it was gone,' said Alf, 'I think you should know I'm having a nervous breakdown.'

'Where are you having it?'

'In front of your house,' said Alf. 'I'm in the car.'

CHAPTER 11

'I JUST THOUGHT I WOULD check up on your father,' Frank Somersby said to Natasha, standing awkwardly in the hall, 'I often do.'

'Come in, do. I'm sorry I flew at you when you called Lewis my ex. I'm just so worried. Did my father really have Alzheimer's, Frank?' Natasha asked. 'I can hardly believe it! He never told me. Is that why he had all these Post-it notes around the house?

'He didn't want to worry you,' said Frank. 'It was my idea to prepare him for a time when his memory would let him down, it would give him a few more months of independence.'

He paused.

'At first, I prescribed tranquilisers, which didn't help much, so I discounted them.'

So that was why her father was getting slovenly and uncaring and feeling so tired all the time.

'He is now on Aricept and that will do him good, providing he takes it of course. I assume that you already phoned the hospital. I had better take charge,' said Frank, getting up and going to the bathroom.

'He has taken his medicine with him,' he said when came back.

Frank was taking charge.

Sometimes she longed for a strong shoulder to lean on, to make her feel safe, to be there for her. The part of providing the shoulder belonged to Lewis, while Frank now admired her looks. Natasha was classy, she had been a beauty even in childhood, with her wide brown eyes, slim nose and her luminous skin.

'We had better inform the police,' he said, picking up the phonebook and then the telephone.

Natasha went into the kitchen and put on the percolator. It bore a little yellow sticker. '*Water in first*.' Her father had written himself little notes to remind him of the simplest tasks. Well, he wouldn't have to; from now on, she would look after him, she thought, when she saw a sticker on the fridge.

> *Natasha: Sherry trifle*
> *Hester: Fruit yoghurts.*

She took the sticker. Her father had written it. In the hours and days to come, she would look at it from time to time. It would remind her that her father had once been alive, caring, and writing notes. She was somehow already certain that she would never see him again.

DS Cunningham drove up shortly afterwards, much to Natasha's amazement. He was tall, good-looking, well-groomed and well-dressed. He was wearing a suit and a grey overcoat, with a red scarf hanging from the collar.

She always thought policemen travelled in pairs like Jehovah's Witnesses and they would turn up a fortnight after they were called.

He took notes, tapping his teeth with the biro, Natasha wished he wouldn't do it, while he waited for information on her father; name, age, hair and eye colour, and other preliminaries.

'Has he taken his toothbrush? In my experience, people staying away even overnight take their toothbrushes.'

The toothbrush and the rest of the toiletries were all in the bathroom. Next, he checked the doors and windows for signs of a break-in.

'There is no sign of an intruder,' he said. 'Is there anything missing?'

Natasha shrugged her shoulders; nothing was missing as far as she could tell.

'Unless your father had some sort of disability,' he said, sitting down, tapping his teeth, 'I'm afraid there is nothing we can do. He is an adult and he can come and go as he pleases.'

'My father is suffering from Alzheimer's disease, but I didn't know until today. He never told me, and frankly, it wasn't that obvious,' said Natasha,

'Frank,' she pointed to the man sitting at the table next to her, 'has just told me. Frank Somersby has been our friend for years, as well as his doctor.'

'That makes a difference. Dr Willoughby might have been disorientated. He might have wandered about, not knowing where he was,' Cunningham said, tap-tap, 'due to his, er, condition.'

'I didn't know he had it, as I said,' said Natasha. 'As a matter of fact, I talked to him on his mobile yesterday evening. He could use a mobile. (Why did they think her father was a small child?) He did some shopping and was on his way home. Normally he comes to us on Saturday evening but he doesn't stay for the night, he likes his own bed, but sometimes we go to him, like today.'

She thought of something else.

'He has a signet ring, silver, I believe, and an expensive watch, a Tag Heuer, the sort where the strap clicks on. It cost nearly ten thousand pounds. My mother bought it for him, but he didn't use credit cards, only cash.'

Her mother had liked to throw money about like confetti. Those were her father's words, but they were true. She remembered the time her mother had promised her tulips from Amsterdam. She flew to Amsterdam and came back with a bunch of wilting tulips.

Her ex, Lewis, had the same flair for the *Grand Gesture*.

'That's the first time a woman told me I reminded her of her mother,' Lewis said when she told him. Like her mother, he didn't care what other people thought.

When her father discovered yet another credit card statement going into the thousands, he cut up all credit cards, but that was nothing to do with anybody else.

'He normally drew enough cash to last him a month,' she said, getting up, going to the bureau where she found his chequebook. 'According to the stub, he drew out two-hundred pounds on the twenty-fifth.'

The DS whistled.

'Did anybody else know that? He wore an expensive watch; he had a lot of cash on him and a mobile, as you said.'

It looked like a mugging to him, although the man's condition would have to be kept in mind. 'Where was he when he spoke to you? I mean roughly?'

Natasha didn't know. Avenue Lane, where her father's bungalow was situated, was an equal distance from Tesco, Asda, and Somerfield, or he might have visited an off-licence for the sherry.

'He did his weekly shop in Tesco,' she said, 'with a widowed neighbour.' They had such a laugh, her father had told her, eating an English breakfast full of cholesterol.

'Poor Dad. His home help told me the woman made him pay for her own groceries as well as his own.'

'She fleeced him? Could she have robbed him?'

'I don't think so, I believe he just paid for her company, but all I know is that her name is Magda and that she is on holiday at the moment.'

'Escaping this awful weather on her takings, but it rules her out,' said the sergeant. He accepted her offer of a cup of coffee although it would keep him awake all night, but people always felt he was showing an interest when he did.

Good coffee, he thought, putting down the cup.

'I'll get Sergeant Tomlinson to organise Uniform to look out for Dr Willoughby. I'll also get in touch with my inspector; we'll probably put a Missing Person Appeal on tomorrow's About Anglia and Look East news bulletins, also on Ceefax and Teletext. Can you describe his appearance? And what he was wearing?'

Natasha went into the hall. Normally he wore the blouson-type grey jacket, now hanging on a hook, when he was driving.

'A cap? A hat?' asked the DC.

'A beige hat, and a scarf in a red tartan, it matched the lining of his old Burberry. 'He might wear a blue donkey jacket if it was cold.'

When she returned she shook her head.

'The jacket's here, but the red tartan scarf and the hat and the beige Burberry are missing. Once I had a crafty cigarette in the hall in our house, before they moved to this bungalow. When they caught me, I burned a hole in the sleeve, and my mother wouldn't let him wear it after that.'

Perhaps he did wear it, but it was a guess at best.

'We'll prepare a draft and have it ready to phone in to HQ if he doesn't turn up or we don't find him.' He handed her a card. 'Please ring me on this number if your father returns.'

**

'I shall have to go home very soon.' Natasha said to Frank, looking through her father's bureau after Cunningham left. Her father's monthly statements were in a small bundle, but using cash, he only checked the stubs against the bills he paid by cheque, and he paid for day-to-day expenses by cash.

'We should check supermarket car parks,' said Frank. 'Or perhaps he took the short cut from Somerfield past the allotments, what do you think?'

'I know it,' she said. 'The lane is unlit and would be deserted this time of night. Let's do it first.'

Shortly after, they parked near the shortcut. Frank got out and scrutinised the lane with the torch. They hadn't got far, when she found what looked like a lens Frank had trodden on.

'My father wore a type of glasses this kind of lens would come from,' said Natasha, stumbling after she'd picked it up.

'Please go back to the car,' said Frank, steadying her. 'I'll go a bit further.'

She watched the pinpoint light retreating, and then coming towards her. He shook his head. 'Nothing.'

'What now? I need to get back to Hester.'

Frank drove her to Wheystead, where she was renovating a sixteenth-century farmhouse. Lewis opened the door just in time to see a car driving off.

'Frank gave me a lift, before you ask,' she said. 'We found a lens from my father's glasses in a lane. Frank will stay at my dad's bungalow tonight in case the police get in touch, and before you ask, it was his idea. Did Hester go to sleep all right?'

'Who is Frank?' he asked. 'Is that a new admirer?'

'Must you get everything wrong?' she asked, 'It's Uncle Frank, but I haven't called him that in a long time.'

'Can I stay the night?' he asked hopefully.

'Of course you can,' she said, as he followed her upstairs, overcome by his good luck.

She opened the door to the little spare room.

'I haven't got around to this room yet,' she said.

A naked light bulb overhead illuminated a small bed with a mattress, pots of paints, and a decorated chamber pot. For a minute, he wondered if he had been taken hostage and would be chained to a radiator.

'I left my meeting early for you. I had a feeling you needed me.'

'Don't wake Hester,' said Natasha, putting a finger to her lips before she disappeared into her bedroom.

Oscar Wilde was right, no good deed goes unpunished, he thought, leaning against the doorway.

'There is something you should know about your father,' he said, but she was gone. He would tell her another time.

'Sorry to disturb you on a Saturday night, sir,' said DS Cunningham. He was on the phone to his inspector.

'Are you working overtime? You'll soon earn more than I do.'

'I was late at the station, finishing my report on the smash-and grab for the Super when the call came in,' the DS said. 'It looks like we have a missing person.'

'How long missing? Where? How old?' asked DI Wilson.

'He's been missing for about thirty hours, in Bury St. Edmunds; he's sixty-five.'

'A person is considered missing after forty-eight hours have elapsed.'

DS Cunningham was aware of it, but the inspector was in full flow.

'In fact, if he had been reported missing to the desk officer, he would have suggested to come back in a week, as the man is old enough and ugly enough to go where he pleases without having to fill in a sheet in triplicate.'

Cunningham waited until the inspector drew breath.

'Dr Willoughby, the victim, might have been disorientated, according to his doctor, a Frank Somersby. He had Alzheimer's, so he can be entered on the computer as having a disability.'

'God bless computers.'

'It's the programme that allows it, you see. He also had nearly two-hundred pounds on him, he had a mobile phone, a silver signet ring, and he wore a watch costing nearly ten-thousand pounds, so it might have been a mugging.'

'If I had a watch like that I would spend all day checking the time to get my money's worth. How old was he again?'

'Sixty-five,' he said. 'Plus, we have what looks like a lens from the missing man's glasses found in a lane by the man's daughter and a Dr Somersby.'

Bloody nuisance, those types of glasses, said DI Wilson, he had a pair like that himself. He always thought he had gone blind in one eye when a lens fell out.

'Prepare a draft and let the relevant TV stations have it if the man doesn't turn up. Get an accurate description and other personal details and e-mail it to me.'

'Right,' said DC Cunningham. 'I lean towards a criminal offence myself, Sir.'

DI Wilson wasn't leaning towards anything as far DC Cunningham was able to ascertain; his over-exuberant golden retriever had knocked the receiver out of his hands. Cunningham drew this conclusion from Wilson's repeated shouts of, 'Down, Ralph.'

Cunningham wasn't a detective for nothing.

CHAPTER 12

ON THE DAY OF GEORGE'S DINNER PARTY, Alf had started decorating the spare bedroom for his eldest daughter Virginia. The junk from the spare bedroom became a pile on the small landing, strategically placed for the unwary to fall over it.

'Ritchie and the kids will be here soon. Why don't you take the rubbish to the tip, dearest,' said his wife Margaret in the late afternoon. Or words to that effect after falling over the rubbish several times.

Driving off with a car full of assorted rubbish, he found that the tip was shut.

One thing leading to another, he remembered the wood with the mattress and what was under it.

He drove home, got a spade and drove back to the woods.

Deep at night, when law-abiding citizens were in their beds sleeping the sleep of the just, images of foraging animals and dead bodies began to haunt him.

Mustering his courage and a torch and shouldering his spade, he made his way to the spot where they left the body. He lifted the mattress.

The body was gone.

He counted to ten and lifted the mattress again.

A large bird overhead shrieked and flapped down from a tree, Alf dropped the mattress, spade and torch and took to his heels. Sitting in his car, breathing heavily, he realised that he would have to go back for them. Finding his way without torchlight to guide him meant bumping into trees, stumbling over tree roots, swearing and eventually falling over his spade.

Starting the car with a bump, a heavy box full of old magazines tipped over on the backseat and onto his head.

Alf buried his face in his hands and sincerely

wished he was dead. Finally, he drove to George's house. Sitting in front of his house, his mobile rang, which he answered with shaking hands on account of the ring-tone being the overture to William Tell, who ought to have been shot with his own arrow up his own arse.

He spoke to George and closed the mobile.

George opened the door and he got out of his car.

'Are you moving house?' asked George.

'What? Oh, that's just rubbish from our spare room.'

'Come in, we're having a bloody dinner party. You better have a drink, you look all in. We ought to let Ritchie know about what happened in the woods before he gets himself into a state,' said George, ushering Alf into the hall. 'Is he at home?'

'Ritchie's gone to the pictures,' said Alf. 'The boys are at ours.'

'What's he going to see?' asked George, as if it mattered.

'No Country For Old Men,' said Alf sadly.

The door opened before George could ask if he was taking the piss. It was Christine, wearing a red apron over jeans, a spoon in her hand, a frown on her forehead. Right behind her was her mother, dressed in a pink suit a size too small, still clutching the champagne, a fixed smile on her face.

'We better open this in the kitchen,' she said, 'this is going to fizz.'

'Evening,' said Alf.

'This is Alf,' said George. 'He thought we were going to play snooker tonight.'

'I got it wrong, I must have mixed up my dates,' said Alf.

'Not at all,' cried George's mother-in-law.

'You're most welcome to eat with us first, isn't he, Christine?'

Christine didn't say anything.

'We'll just set another place,' said George's mother-in-law. 'Everybody was always most welcome when Christine lived at home.'

This was news to Christine. Her mother had been hard-pushed to put a few fish-fingers under the grill to feed her family, let alone any surprise visitors.

'I don't want to intrude,' said Alf, taking his shoes off. 'I'm a mechanic. Excuse the state of my hands, Mrs..er.'

'We'll forget surnames,' said George's mother-in-law, laughing her mountain-stream laugh.

Christine winced.

'I have changed it so often I'm hard-pushed to remember it myself. I'm Dawn, dawn by name and dawn by nature,' she added.

Alf looked bemused.

'I'm a bit of a night bird,' she said, going into the living room, followed by Alf, yet another slave added to her army of admirers, although husband number four, a large man with a jowly face, stayed where he was.

Christine shrugged and went back into the kitchen. The kitchen was hot, the oven was on, and something smelt wonderful.

George had heard about warm welcomes, but this wasn't it. Something bubbled on the stove, and so did Christine.

'You're late,' she said. 'I have it all to contend with, especially a mother with a memory-malfunction. You knew we were having people for dinner.'

'Actually, I didn't until today. You never asked me,' said George standing in the doorway, leaning towards her as if he was approaching a dog of dubious temperament.

True, thought Christine, I *told* him, I didn't ask him. Nevertheless, it still didn't make it any better.

'Anything I can do?'

'You can set a place for Alf, and then you can entertain our guests.' She lifted a saucepan lid. 'Concentrate on the Twitter-Sisters. All they do is twitter on and on how wonderful you are.'

'Very true,' said George modestly, 'but *you* invited Mira and her sister'.

Also true, but it didn't make her feel any better either.

Rosie was in pyjamas and dressing gown, ready for bed. He put her to bed, clearing a space between her soft toys, and watched her drift off to sleep. Her face relaxed, her fingers opened. All strain was gone. Lucky girl, he thought.

Alf was also thinking that somebody was lucky. George, in fact. He had a lovely house, Victorian, with an attic and a cellar. Not a semi like the terraced houses down the road. There was also a beautiful long garden and ample parking space, protected by two side gates. The rooms were softly lit, fires were burning in grates, and polished floorboards were covered with scattered rugs.

George also had a blonde, sexy wife, a wife who not only could cook but actually did, and a mother-in-law who didn't get on his nerves.

Early Victorian houses were originally built for an emerging middle class before falling on hard times. Christine's grandfather bought the superior property before prices moved into the upper atmosphere again, but Christine's mother harboured no regrets about moving out.

'You see, Alf, I can only live in houses nobody has ever lived in before,' she said.

And now she did, in an identity-kit house on an identity-kit development, George thought. But if he was in trouble, and he knew he would be one day, he would do the unlikely; he would go to her for help and advice.

He hoped it wouldn't come to it, he thought, crossing his legs as his fingers were otherwise engaged, when he thought he had heard mention of his father.

'Oh, Dad? He's very well, actually we fell out over a misunderstanding I regret but which I won't go into,' he said, putting down his fork. 'He doesn't look that much different from a few years ago. Grey, of course, but upright.'

He explained his father had sold his house in Cambridge, a run-down semi, for half a million, and bought a flat in sheltered housing for one fourth of it. 'They clean his windows and cut the grass. Apparently, he gets up late, goes out for breakfast, goes to the library and eats out in the evening.'

'Where is it?' asked Secretary Mira who had been left out of the conversation.

'In Thelford. He calls it Warsaw on the account of the influx of Polish immigrants.'

Marvellous. A stroke of genius. The conversation turned to immigration, on which everybody had not only an opinion, but an informed one, which they turned it into a fact. He would tell Rosie about her grandfather tomorrow, George thought, the little worm in his unconscious mind wriggling away.

It was after midnight when their guests finally left. Christine got into bed, asleep the minute her head touched the pillow, as if she was casting off the day. It hadn't always been so, George thought, so he let it be.

He fell asleep quickly himself. It was two o'clock when the worm finally wriggled into his brain. The worm had teeth and bit him hard. He sat bolt upright, his heart a drum-beat in his ears.

The little girl, Hester. She and her mother, Natasha, were having tea with her father who was making a sherry trifle because he thought it was her favourite.

Paul Willoughby had bought some sherry for a trifle he was making for his daughter who was bringing his granddaughter.

However hard George looked at it, the pieces fitted perfectly.

Two o'clock.

After an hour of staring at the ceiling he couldn't see, he got up, went downstairs and made himself a cup of coffee, sinking on the settee in the living room, when he remembered the bottle of Valiums he had earmarked for Ritchie. He took it out of his coat pocket and looked at it, but he didn't open the bottle; Christine might need them later.

CHAPTER 13

AT SEVEN O'CLOCK ON SUNDAY MORNING, George had cleared the debris from the kitchen and dining room abandoned to their fate the night before. The boys (ha, ha) had played snooker whilst the girls (ha, ha) watched an old Cary Grant film on Film Four.

He cleared the dining room, soaked the saucepans, loaded the dishwasher and wiped the surfaces. He wanted to clear the grates but decided not to, as not to disturb Rosie and Christine, who were still fast asleep.

He crept upstairs into the bathroom, showered and changed into his sweat suit, clean and folded in his sports bag. He peeped into the bedroom. Rosie, asleep, was snuggled against her mother who was blinking up at him sleepily.

'I'm going for a jog. Do you want to come?'

'Do I look insane?' she whispered, not unreasonably. 'Couldn't you sleep? I expect you're worried about your dad.' She yawned. 'I didn't sleep much either, I'm really worried myself.'

'What about?'

'I can't remember how many people I've asked for Bonfire Night.'

I hope that you never have to worry about anything else, thought George fifteen minutes later. He was in New Park, his feet pounding, his arms going like pistons, pound, pound; working up a sweat, trying to forget anything to do with a sherry trifle.

If only.

His mobile rang. It was Alf.

'He had Alzheimer's,' Alf whispered. Whispering was difficult when you were excited.

'Who?'

'Haven't you watched the news?' whispered

Alf.

'Why are you whispering?'

'I don't want to wake Margaret. She is bloody annoyed with me. I said I was going to the tip at five o'clock and it was past midnight when I got home with all the rubbish still in the car.'

Alf cleared his throat.

'Dr Willoughby had Alzheimer's. It was on the local news.'

The local news. George felt as if he had been hit with a cricket bat. He had worried about knowing Dr Willoughby's daughter and granddaughter, but he had never actually pictured the moment when he would be reported missing.

Alf said he was in the kitchen. He was so relieved Dr Willoughby had Alzheimer's. 'It's not quite so bad, him dying,' he said. 'It's not pleasant living with it, so I've heard. We might have done him a favour."

'That's going a bit far, but you could be right,' said George.

'And another thing, that little girl up North? Nothing to do with Fred Foster.'

George knew the one Alf was talking about. She had vanished from a playing field and was found dead on waste ground two weeks later.

'They arrested somebody, I can't remember his name, but apparently he was on the Sex Offenders Register and served four months for downloading kiddy porn. He was judged harmless, apparently.'

Harmless, thought George? Because the paedo didn't display any tendencies towards harming children in prison where he encountered other prisoners and not small children? It focussed his mind. The state had released a paedo, the state had killed the little girl up North, and the state would have been responsible if

87

anything had happened to little Emily Watson. What would have happened if he had reported it? Zero. Zilch. The paedo hadn't actually done anything.

'Thanks Alf. If they hadn't released Foster, Dr Willoughby would still be alive, but we have to be careful. And be prepared! Before long, the authorities will realise they have a missing paedo on their hands. It'll go nationwide. Don't forget to bring the clothes for the bonfire.'

Ritchie phoned next. He had seen the news and said much the same thing about Dr Willoughby.

'See you on Bonfire Night. Don't forget to bring the raincoat.'

'Is it going to rain? I suppose it always does.'

'The one in the boot of your car, for the bonfire,' said George.

'That's going to be a problem,' Ritchey said unhappily. On Saturday, just before the shop closed, he had taken a bag of clothes his wife had sorted out to the Oxfam shop.

He had also returned the wheelbarrow and the torch to the allotments.

'Iris wants the car next week, so I cleared the boot. I'm having the van, I'm plastering next week.'

George counted to ten.

'We were going to the pictures later, Iris and I, so I bought a bottle of wine for Alf and his missus. A thank-you for looking after the kids.'

George breathed in and counted to twenty.

'Anyhow,' Ritchie continued, when he went to the car and opened the boot, it occurred to him the old man's raincoat was missing. It was in the bag of clothes for Oxfam, Iris said, when he asked her on his return.

'Does it matter?'

'Maybe not,' said George. 'It was pretty dirty as it had been on the ground. 'They don't sell dirty stuff.'

Ritchie said he wouldn't buy anything dirty, and as for Iris!

George breathed in, then he told him to be prepared for the hue and cry that would be raised when the paedo was discovered missing He waited, but Ritchie apparently understood straight away, so he closed his mobile.

Ritchie was the nicest bloke who had ever stood in a pair of shoes, but not the brightest. The three had been friends since their primary and comprehensive school days, a friendship that grew into an unbreakable lifetime bond. Ritchie was a much-sought-after plasterer, Alf was a genius with a car engine and George had gone to university, and all three were now successfully self-employed.

When he let himself back into the house, Christine was up and dressed, sitting on the settee next to Rosie, having a cup of tea.

'I came down to clear up,' she said, 'but the good fairies were ahead of me. Thanks.'

She still looked worried.

'Hester's granddad has gone missing,' said Rosie importantly.

'You won't believe it, I didn't believe it either,' said Christine, switching on the television, putting it onto regional Teletext. 'You read these headlines and think, how awful, but then you forget it because you don't know the people involved.'

Man missing in Suffolk.

Officers in Bury St. Edmunds are trying to trace an elderly man who has been missing since Friday night. Paul Willoughby, aged 65, of 49 Avenue Lane, is 5 foot 9.
Wearing a beige raincoat, and a red scarf and

hat, black shoes and trousers, he was last in
touch between five and six o'clock on Friday
night. A retired doctor, Paul Willoughby is
thought to be suffering from Alzheimer's, but he
could be the victim of a mugging.

George sat down as the public was urged to get in touch with Suffolk Police.

'It must be awful for Mrs Marshall and Hester to know he's missing,' said Christine.

'Do you know her?'

'Not well, just from waiting at the school gate,' she said, 'and Hester's not one of Rosie's friends.'

She got up for another cup of tea.

'Mrs Marshall used to be a model,' she said, back in the living room, 'not catwalk. Magazine shoots, catalogue fashion, that sort of thing. She went all over the world modelling. She has the sort of face that makes everybody else's look like a potato.'

'A Maris Piper,' said George, who liked his chips.

'Hester's mum is called Mrs Marshall. We saw her at swimming yesterday,' ventured Rosie. As if he needed reminding. 'What are we doing today, Daddy? Mummy said maybe we could go and see my new granddad.'

One granddad lost, one granddad found.

'Good idea, kiddo,' George said, remembering the ducks sheltering under the trees. 'We'll go to Thelford and take him some bread.'

'Oh, poor Granddad, hasn't he got any? Is Thelford like in the Third World?'

Before he got into a discussion about the Third World, George got up and told Christine there were two more guests, Alf and Ritchie for Bonfire Night. 'Oh, I forgot, that's two adults and four kids. That's six.'

She had known two and four made six, but she wasn't thrilled. And then Rosie had another idea she wasn't thrilled about either.

CHAPTER 14

NINE O'CLOCK ON SUNDAY MORNING, Lewis and Hester watched Natasha getting into Frank's car. She turned around, looking worried but as fabulous as ever, in an oversized blue cashmere jumper and slim-jeans.

'Stone me,' he said, 'isn't that my jumper your mummy is wearing? How very annoying is that?'

Natasha had always borrowed his clothes. He had promised to share his worldly goods, BUT NOT HIS CLOTHES!

'I'll have to wear the yellow, I suppose. I'll look after you today, moppet. Bath first.'

'Not a hair wash,' she said.

'All right, not a hair wash,' he said upstairs, running the water in the bath, making sure it wasn't too hot.

Downstairs, a paper plopped into the hall.

Civilisation has reached the wilderness, he thought, making a cup of coffee and settling down in the living room. He had an awful creek in the neck, although Natasha had relented and slung a duvet and a pillow into his room. He glanced through the paper and the supplement and then switched on the local Teletext.

Poor little Hester, her granddad's missing, he thought. What will we tell her?

My God! Hester!

In his Cambridge apartment, he left the bathroom door open so he could hear her splash about. Could five-year-olds drown in a bath? Of course they could, children and drunks could drown in a couple of inches of water. He raced upstairs. It was quiet in the bathroom.

Please God, no! he thought, opening the door.

Where was she?

With trembling knees, he approached the bath and forced himself to look. He peered into the bath, but she wasn't there.

He found her in her bedroom wrapped in a pink towel.

'Stone me, Lewis,' she said, 'I was getting cold.'

'Sorry. Daddy really loves you, moppet.'

'I know that, silly,' she said, when the phone rang.

'Lewis here,' he said. 'Natasha's ex.'

It was a friend of Natasha, Christine. Was there any news about Natasha's father?

'Not at the moment,' he said, 'they've gone off to..' he didn't really know what they were doing.

She was sorry to disturb him. Apparently Hester was a friend of her daughter, Rosie. Rosie wanted a word.

'Can I speak to Hester?'

Hester shook her head.

'I'm afraid she's incommunicado,' he said.

'In where?'

'Communicado'.

Rosie digested this.

'Will she be back for my fireworks party? I would like her to come.'

'Is it that time of the year again?' he said. 'Just a moment, I'll have to consult Hester.'

'Right,' he said. 'As far as I can make out, she's not keen on fireworks, but she'll come if I'm allowed.'

Christine, who had by now taken over, laughed. It sounded a bit forced. 'The more the merrier,' she said.

Lewis disappointed Hester so often, calling at the last

minute to break a scheduled date.

Natasha reminded him of it that evening when he asked if he could go with her and Hester to a Bonfire Night party.

'Only if you don't change your mind at the last minute and let her down.'

He might have let Hester down before, but not after today. He still recalled the awful silence outside the bathroom door. He went upstairs to check on Hester, who was fast asleep. Her little round face, the curve of her cheek, and her long, dark eyelashes curving out at the ends tugged at his heart.

'She prattles on a lot about a man in a beret and Emily Watson,' he said when he came down.

'Emily is a spoilt little madam,' said Natasha.

She looked tired, so he made her the hot chocolate she used to enjoy when she was whacked.

'Did you find out anything about your father?' he asked.

She shook her head.

'Did you check the bus shelters?'

'Yes, and the Monastery Gardens, and the hospital car park and a lot of other places Frank thought of.'

'Do you want to end this communication forthwith and shall I clear off?'

She nodded and he drove off. He knew of old that when something worried her she wanted to be alone.

She went upstairs and looked in on Hester when a car drew up on the gravelled drive. She crossed to the front window and peered out. It was Frank. He got out of the car. Leaning against the willow tree, he looked up at the house, a dark silhouette, half hidden by drooping branches. He was keeping a watchful eye on her. She was always thankful for his care, but she

94

wished Lewis would return.

Nine o'clock on Sunday morning. Karin Lewis from the Probation Service and case manager for Fred Foster turned over in bed. Should she do anything about Fred Foster? He had said that he was watched by the police.

Not so.

Was he being stalked by vigilantes? Outside a laundrette? His release wasn't general knowledge and he wasn't on the Register, so this was unlikely. Furthermore, he was somewhat paranoid about being followed, she concluded as she stretched out, reached for her cup of tea, and decided to leave it until the morning.

Nine o'clock, Sunday morning, Fred Foster, known as Howard Cole in the B&B, was enjoying a full English breakfast, the paper propped up in front of him. Two other tables in the dining room were occupied, one by an elderly couple, and one by a younger couple who looked indulgently at a small ginger-haired boy with glasses who stood in front of him, staring unblinkingly.

He made an impatient, shooing gesture, keeping his arm straight. 'Bugger off,' he said through clenched teeth.

The boy ran back to his parents, who were trying to decide if the black pudding on their plate should be there.

'That man,' said the boy accusingly, pointing a trembling finger at him.

Howard put down the paper and smiled at the horrible child's parents.

'Boys will be boys,' he said, adopting the confident manner and speaking with the English of a man of education. The Howard Cole he had easily fallen into seemed to do the trick. They smiled and told him they were touring English Cathedral cities.

Americans by the accents.

'Excellent choice,' he said.

Please, he thought. In this fucking downpour?

His hostess, wrestling with the coffee machine, was full of the terrible news. Local news. Apparently some old bugger had wandered off to God only knew where.

'He wore a red scarf and a hat,' said her better half, coming in with more toast.

Howard hoped he wore bit more than that.

'Awful,' he said, 'really tragic, these old boys.'

He pushed the chair back.

'Off, are you?' said Mrs Warner. 'We were wondering if you were connected with the new development on the old market site.'

He considered it, but decided against it. In case.

'I'm afraid not.'

'Shame', she said, 'we're expecting somebody connected to the site next week.'

'I'm going through a nasty divorce,' he whispered. 'I'd rather my wife didn't know where I am at present.'

She tapped her nose.

Too right, noisy bitch, he thought, going upstairs, getting a wad of notes. He got into his car and looked for his mobile. He phoned the garage in Clacton and asked if they had a five-year-old Corolla.

'Funny you should say that,' the bloke said, 'somebody was asking for one a little while ago. No questions asked, he said.'

'And have you got one?'

'As a matter of fact,' the bloke paused and coughed, 'I haven't. I thought you might be the police.'

Howard could have strangled him.

'We have got a very nice four-year-old red

Corolla.'

Red? It was probably better than to change to another light colour.

'Would you be willing to part-exchange for a five-year-old pale-blue Corolla missing a log book and service history?'

He would. Howard said that he would be along later.

Next onto item number two; sort cut his wife. He pondered on how to get to Haslingfield in Cambridgeshire, and decided to go through Cambridge. It was probably the long way, he thought, finally pulling up in the village. Church bells were ringing, cars were parked under a huge cedar tree close to the church, people on foot were hurrying to the morning service.

He waited.

Ah, a few women worshippers.

He got out, trying to look puzzled.

It worked.

'Can I help you?' asked one of the women. The others stopped.

'I'm looking for a Mrs Foster,' he said. 'She lives in Cambridge Road. I believe she has a daughter at University. I have a parcel for her, only I've forgotten the house number.'

They looked at each other, shaking their heads. No Mrs Foster was known to them.

'Could be Mrs Forester,' said one of them. 'She was a deputy head. She had a daughter who has just finished her MA in Norwich.'

'I believe that is her,' he said.

'She lived at number fifty-five '

'Lived?' he asked?

'She sold up and moved abroad a few weeks

ago, Spain, I believe, or Portugal, or the Canaries. I mean, she kept herself very much to herself, so I'm afraid we can't help you. If you come tomorrow, you could ask at the Post Office.'

'If we still got one,' one of the women said, and they went off laughing.

Silly bitch, he thought, but it was clear his wife had sold the house and had done a runner. Now *that* had never occurred to him. No wonder she had so much money in her account *and* that smirk on her face when she met him at the Grafton centre.

An idea suddenly flashed in his mind.

The bells stopped their clashing din, and suddenly it was silent in the churchyard by the cedar tree. He inspected the row of parked cars and, sure enough, one was left unlocked. He went back to his Corolla, removed the out-of-date tax disc, went back to the unlocked car and switched them. His new car from Clacton would be taxed until next March.

He drove to Clacton, his fury with his wife barely contained. As she wasn't there, he directed his vengeance towards the three men who had driven him underground, but the car first.

By the afternoon, Howard Cole was five-hundred pounds less well off and the proud owner of a red Corolla, no questions asked. He was relieved, but he also had a headache.

Nine o'clock on Sunday evening, he leafed through the YELLOW PAGES under Public houses in Bury St. Edmunds. *The Volunteer* was a short walk away; in fact, he could see it when he looked out of the dormer window, it was two streets away. Of course, it was the pub where he had seen his three suspects winning the pub quiz a few nights ago.

He looked at the cut on his hand. It didn't

seem infected, but to be on the safe side, he doused it with Vodka. It concentrated his mind nicely, but it didn't do much for his headache or his exhaustion; decision-making left him drained. For twenty years, he had been given three meals, told when to exercise and gone to sleep when the lights went out. Open Prison had helped, but even there he had arranged his day around the roll-calls.

He took a migraine tablet when he saw stars in front of his eyes and was beginning to feel sick. He could hear the television from the room next door. There was also laughter; that ginger kid was laughing, would you believe, when *he* was being tortured.

That kid would have to pay for this.

Nine o'clock, Sunday evening. Karen Lewis from the Probation Service had second thoughts. She'd better check on Fred Foster. *If* he had done a runner on Friday, he had some time to go underground, and she would be in deep trouble, she thought, driving along. She parked in front of *The Flats*, a half-way house *for* parolees.

The undercover officer watching him for the first week had reported nothing unusual. Fred Foster didn't drive a car, he didn't go out much, apart from shopping and keeping his appointments with her. Other than that, he had gone to the Post Office once, probably to cash his Social Security cheque, he had gone for a job interview at a nursery he had turned down on account of his hay fever. Mostly he was in the flat, watching television with the sound up loud after the evening's nine o'clock curfew.

The Flats, without a warden, housed newly released, but not generally dangerous prisoners. The powers-that-be had decided that Fred Foster, who was out on parole, should not be sent to a hostel with other parolees of similar inclinations. Instead, he was released to a town where he would be kept under surveillance although not taking in the constraints of the local police. As he was not on the sex offenders register, he would be less well known, and his crime had been committed twenty years ago.

'I'm looking for Fred Foster,' she said when she met a young man in the hall.

'Is he that old bloke?'

'Yes, relatively.'

'Na, haven't seen him lately'.

'Can you get me the video from the surveillance camera?' she said.

'It isn't working,' he said, before he disappeared. 'What's he done?'

She climbed the stairs and rang the bell to his flat. No sounds emerged from it. She fumbled for her key. When she opened the door, she found the place deserted, with cupboards and drawers empty, apart from groceries in the fridge and on the kitchen shelves.

She looked in the wastepaper bin where she found a bloodied handkerchief and a pair of broken glasses. There was no other alternative; she had to phone in.

CHAPTER 15

ON MONDAY MORNING, the first thing Natasha did after waking up and dressing was to ring Bury St. Edmunds Police. A PC Collins answered the phone and said that he would re-direct her call to DS Cunningham as soon as possible.

She got Hester ready and took her to school. Strangely enough, Hester said that she knew her grandfather would be back soon.

What makes you say that?'

'Well, my Daddy always comes back,' she said, which rather shook Natasha. The rows she had with Lewis about not disappointing Hester because she didn't want her to be insecure!

'When I see Granddad, I shall tell him you were worried,' Hester said. 'Do I have to go out at playtime?' she added.

At the school, Natasha had a word with the Head and explained the situation about her grandfather. She was sympathetic. She said that she would keep an eye on Hester. 'It will be a pleasure,' she added. 'Hester is such a little dear.'

There's nothing more cheering than your child being admired, it bucked up Natasha no end as she drove home. She worked part-time in a council office as a typist (something to fall back on, her mother had said, presumably when her face fell off), having Mondays off. The rest of the week, she was able to pick up Hester at four.

On the way home she stopped at Aleska's house, who was not only her father's Polish home help but also Hester's child minder, and she looked after Hester during the holidays. Aleska lived on the Riley estate. It was council–owned, but it was one of the nicer ones. Houses and blocks of flats were set on either side of a wide, tree-lined avenue.

Aleska lived in a first floor flat.

'Dear, oh, dear,' said a stout, middle-aged woman closing the door on the ground floor flat in the echoing concrete staircase. 'I nearly called the police last week. He gave her ever such a beating.' She shook her head. 'A nicer girl than Aleska you could not wish to meet, but she is devoted to that animal she lives with.'

'I had my suspicions,' said Natasha to the departing woman's back, 'but she won't admit to anything.'

'Is nothing,' said Aleska opening the door, sporting a fading array of yellow bruises. 'I clumsy, my Man says.'

'If you are tired of being clumsy,' said Natasha carefully, stepping into a narrow hallway and then into an open-plan lounge-diner decorated in pale green, 'you can always come and live with me.'

Aleska shrugged, 'I like here. My own place. My Man, he bring presents.'

He was a dustman, or refuse collection operator. She pointed to the mantle over an electric fire sporting an amazing array of odd glasses, mugs and candleholders. 'My own things he brings me,' she added. 'So. How yesterday?'

'Lewis looked after Hester,' said Natasha. 'Tell me Aleska, was there something going on between my father and Lewis? I mean, did they ever meet?'

'Lewis is good man, so,' was all she would say.

Next, Natasha drove to her father's bungalow, but there was no sign of him, and Frank had left for work. When she got home, she rang the police again. No luck. DS Cunningham was not there yet. Now, to the call she had dreaded. Phoning her brother in Australia, wondering what time it was over there, when

102

he answered the phone.

'I've got some bad news,' she said, a catch in her voice, 'Dad's gone missing.'

'How? What happened?'

'We don't know,' she yelled.

'There's no need to yell. Dad's not a child, so I don't understand it.'

'He's got Alzheimer's,' she said, 'and he went missing on Friday night.'

'That's bad, but you are there to look after him. I couldn't possibly come over.' He paused. 'I borrowed a lot of money off Dad,' he said, 'and I want to pay it back when I see him. I'll see how it goes.'

Next, the phone rang. It was the manager from Oxfam. Natasha sometimes spent a few hours sorting out and pricing *Labels*. He asked her if she could spare him a couple of hours this morning. They had some dresses for the party season.

'Party season?'

Apparently, Christmas was coming, he said sadly, as if Christmas was an unwelcome disease.

He didn't mention her father, which would suggest that he didn't know that he was missing, not everybody knew she was Dr Willoughby's daughter.

The car park in Bury St. Edmunds wasn't full. There's a surprise, she thought, making her way to the shop. Reg, the manager, was deep in talk with a woman. 'Re-organising the shop,' he said, 'thanks for coming in. Bric-a-brac Peggy is upstairs.' She fought her way through the small vestibule full of donations in black bin liners and went up the narrow stairs. Due to her irregular few hours, she didn't know many of the women who worked there.

'I'm Natasha, I'm doing *the Labels*,' she announced, taking off her coat and hanging it in the cupboard with her handbag.

'I'm Peggy,' said an elderly, well-kept, good-looking woman who was sorting out ornaments. 'I sort out the bric-a-brac. I hear you're a model.'

'Used to be, until life intervened,' said Natasha, running her eye over half-a-dozen assorted garments.

'We used to get really nice things,' said Peggy, pricing and putting ornaments into a basket prior to taking them into the shop and putting them on shelves, 'but people are getting wise to e-Bay.'

'Too right,' said another woman, opening a bag of clothes.

There was a vast gulf between what people thought of as donations and what they would actually buy.

'Look at this! Nice, clean good quality children's clothes, and a filthy man's raincoat.' She shook it out. 'Looks like there's blood on it as well. Who do they think is going to buy that?'

'What sort of a raincoat?' asked Natasha, her heart beating fast.

'Beige. It's actually a good make.'

'Is it a Burberry?' she asked, her heart now thumping. 'Has it got a small hole in the left sleeve?'

She went over and looked at it. 'Let me see.'

She clutched the raincoat and sank to her knees. 'Oh, my God! It's my Dad's. He went missing on Friday night.'

The two women looked at each other, and then at her.

She got up and rushed to cupboard for her bag, finding DS Cunningham's number. He didn't answer, so she phoned the police station.

'Natasha Marshall here,' she said. 'Tell DS Cunningham I have found my father's raincoat. You can also tell him that it has blood on it. Perhaps he will be good enough to answer the bloody phone now.'

CHAPTER 16

'WE HAVE GOT A PROBLEM, JOHN,' said Chief Superintendent Nicholson sitting behind his desk in Storwich, Headquarters of Suffolk Constabulary.

'Yes? Really, sir?' said DI Wilson.

John Wilson, fifty-two, had been transferred from London to Suffolk Constabulary in Bury St Edmunds after he had rejected promotion. It meant a drop in salary, but he had made a killing on the sale of his London house. The lower house prices in Stowmarket, the large village he now lived in, in a substantial house overlooking a village green, more than made up for it.

Stowmarket was conveniently situated between Storwich and Bury St. Edmunds, and was even more conveniently situated near Felixstowe with a beach onto which dogs were allowed.

He handled cases in Bury St. Edmunds and surrounding areas including the parts of it in Newmarket in Suffolk, and he had successfully brought before the court the killer of young man who was found murdered in a ditch in Farnham. His strength was that he knew how to assemble a good team and get the most out of each member.

He also successfully liaised with neighbouring police forces, as crime and jurisdiction more often than not crossed county borders. Criminals were such inconsiderate buggers.

A widowed man, he lived with a schoolteacher called Dorothy and a golden retriever called Ralph, and he had one daughter in New Zealand. God bless New Zealand, he often thought.

John Wilson was tall and thin, over six foot. The Super was a supremely handsome, dark-haired man, albeit short, and he was always sitting behind his desk. Sometimes Wilson wondered if Nicholson had lied about his height when he joined the police before height restrictions were abolished. If anyone could lie about his height standing before an interviewing board and get away with it, Nicholson would be the man for it.

'We have got a problem,' the Super said again. 'Fred Foster, who we released on parole six weeks ago, seems to be connected to a further child rape. The victim was six-year-old -old Denise Stocks.'

He looked at some papers in front of him.

'So Devon informs us. Budgets don't allow for Cold Case reviews, but the pathologist, a Dr Williams, is about to retire. They're DNA testing a hair-band found on Denise Stocks, but as you know, it takes a month or more for the results to come through. And, of course, it's not certain a clear..err.. DNA link can be established from old fibres and so on.'

'Quite,' said DI Wilson, to whom science was as much of a mystery as it was to the Super.

'What's the link between Devon and Fred Foster?'

'I'm glad you asked me. Apparently, Fred Foster worked there as a librarian at the time the child killing took place. it was a mobile library, as a matter of fact, so he got about.'

He paused.

'Dr Williams carried out the DNA test entirely of his own bat without informing Devon Police, that is, until he realised Foster had been released on parole. That is why this case is now taken over by a team.'

He looked up from his notes.

'That was four weeks after Foster was released.'

He consulted his notes again.

'Anyway, Foster was rigorously risk assessed

and, according to the psychoanalyst, he was judged as posing no further risk.'

He paused.

'Apparently, he wanted to turn the clock back. It was an aberration, completely out of character for a family man. He repented, in other words, and to deny him his freedom would deny him his humanity.'

'You said that without laughing,' said Wilson.

The Super ignored him.

'He has a Masters degree from the Open University. But as he already had a degree, it isn't as marvellous as it sounds, it apparently only involved one course. Obviously, he had no access to computers.'

'I wish I didn't, but it doesn't make me a Master.'

When the Super said that it all helped towards Foster release, Wilson tried to take it all in.

'As I understand from Karin, you have mislaid Fred Foster.'

The Super nodded.

'Unhappily, yes. Well, not me personally, but he seems to have vanished on Friday when he reported to her, well, complained, that he was under constant police surveillance.'

'And he wasn't.'

'He was in the early days, but you know how tight our budget is, and open playgrounds and the heath are in an exclusion zone he observed. But no surveillance, certainly not in the last few weeks, and not on the morning when he complained about it.'

Wilson thought about it.

'Vigilantes?'

'Could be.'

'He complained on Friday morning, and today is Monday. Karin is supposed to report anything out of the ordinary to me.'

The Super sighed. Apparently, he was off to a meeting were these matters were being put on the table.

'Heads will roll,' he promised. I have to take you off these eeer..,' he looked at the papers again, 'current cases. And also, with the Felixstowe people-traffickers, the violent cross-border Essex robberies, the rapes in Tavern Road in Storwich, you won't be able to draw on Storwich. Not for the present moment, anyway. However, I have been on the phone with Sergeant Tomlinson and you can also have a word with him.'

He looked meaningfully at Wilson.

'I suppose I had better,' said Wilson. He had never liked Tomlinson who talked in clichés and bore the permanently bewildered expression of someone who was supposed to laugh at a joke he was not getting. The feeling was mutual, they had probably clashed in previous life, Wilson thought.

'I'm not asking you to marry him,' said Nicholson.

'Matters in hand. It is of the utmost importance that we keep up a visible presence to the public. You have Connor plus Constable Smith, who is back from maternity leave. Both are taking their Sergeant's exams, so they will be keen, and you also have Cunningham.'

'Good man,' said Wilson, who liked his company and brains, and who liked to do some legwork himself to get a feel of things.

'So there we are,' said the Super, handing him Fred Foster's photo. 'Good, good. I've got a report here from the Karin, that will fill you in.' He paused and looked at Wilson over his interlocked fingers. He must have thought that it made him look impressive; it did in photos, anyway.

'But it looks like Foster has gone underground.

He's familiar with Bristol, so taxis and trains and buses will have to be checked, of course, and also boarding houses in Bury St. Edmunds, where he might have stayed on overnight.'

'Could he have changed his appearance?' asked Wilson.

'You might have noticed it when Foster reported to your station,' said Nicholson reproachfully, 'but you were away in foreign parts.'

'That's right, Hunstanton. It has a beach dogs can use. Besides, Karin came to the station, it was convenient for both of them. I never saw him, she merely sent in a report on him.'

Wilson had a feeling he was getting on the Super's nerves when the Super sighed.

'Talk to the probation officer. I'll send her to Bury St. Edmunds after the meeting,' he added. 'And of course, don't forget, there's the missing man. I've seen the appeal.'

'Right, Brownie points; find at least one mislaid man.'

'We'll draft a statement concerning Fred Foster for the media at the meeting.'

That seemed to be all. Wilson left Storwich and drove to Bury St. Edmunds Police Station.

He paused at Sergeant Tomlinson's desk .

'I have spoken with the Super about your two constables. How are they on computers?'

Tomlinson looked up.

'I hear what your are saying,' he said, 'we are singing from the same hymn sheet.'

Nobody was singing, and if there was a more stupid expression used by someone he was actually talking to he had yet to hear it, Wilson thought, making his way through the large, open-plan room with computers on every desk to his own, small but private, cubbyhole at the back.

**

When the 'phone rang at the station, it was a Claude Ford, who reported that his stolen wheelbarrow and torch had been returned.

The desk officer, Collins, made a note of it. A borrowed wheelbarrow and torch.

Next was an old man who had a bee in his bonnet about fly-tipping and asked him if his memory was going, he had talked to him last Friday, it might have been Saturday.

'That wasn't me,' said Collins, 'I was on leave.'

'So you say.'

He had caught them at it, he said, and he had made a note of the car number.

'When and what was the offence?'

'Fly-tipping. Last Saturday evening,' the querulous vice said. 'About seven in the evening. I was driving home. I live in Thelford, you see, and my married daughter lives in Bury St. Edmunds.'

'So?'

'I slowed down and stopped, and then I saw him.'

'The fly-tipper.'

The caller hesitated.

'Not the fly-tipper as such. The fly-tipper drove off, but I saw a man going towards his car, he had a small dog on a leash. He was sort of dragging it along, it was an awful evening.'

'And the dog didn't want to go walkies.'

'Yes, that sort of thing.'

'Taking dogs for a walk who don't want to go is not actually against the law,' said Collins, who by now wished he was still on leave or else filling shelves in Tesco.

'You are missing the point entirely. He might

have seen who the fly-tipper was,' said the caller. 'Do I have to spell it out for you?'

Collins declined the offer.

'I have your name and address on record,' he said

The phone rang again. Some woman, Natasha Marshall, was in a bit of a state, wanting to talk to DS Cunningham, who was not yet in. Apparently, she had found her father's coat, and there was blood on it. Now what was that about, he wondered, when DS Cunningham came in.

The phone rang again.

'Just a moment,' he said, 'DS Cunningham is here.'

Words mercifully failed Wilson when he studied Fred Foster's file in his office once more. Then he went onto the desk sergeant's notes. He had said something about nutters, fly-tipping, and missing and returned wheelbarrows and torches..

Wilson lifted an eyebrow when Cunningham came in.

'It's a Natasha Marshall, the daughter of the missing man,' he said. 'She found her father's coat apparently.'

Wilson lifted the phone.

'Inspector Wilson here,' he said. 'Where and when did you find the coat?'

'Just now, at Oxfam's,' said Natasha. 'It was with a bag of children's clothes. They probably came in on Saturday, according to Reg, the manager.'

'It's unlikely your father would donate children's clothes, so somebody will be along and interview the manager.'

Natasha put down the phone. The ladies and Reg looked at her. She shrugged her shoulders. She was good at not talking when she didn't want to, as Lewis would have been able to testify had he been there. She sat down and decided to wait.

CHAPTER 16

WILSON CLOSED HIS FILES.

'Right, let's leave this lot, ' he said to DC Cunningham. 'With regard to Natasha Marshall, we'll carpe the diem, as you wouldn't say.' He rubbed his hands. 'First, I'd like a word with WPC Smith about Fred Foster.'

Constable Smith was dark-haired, trim, fresh-faced and had black-fringed Liza Minnelli eyes. An unlikely-looking married woman and even unlikelier mother; at thirty-one she looked more like a teenager. He thought a few welcoming words wouldn't come amiss.

'You know you're getting older when policemen and women start looking younger,' he said.

'That applies to you in that case.'

'Kind of you to say so,' he said gallantly. 'I hear you had a little girl.'

'Yes,' she said, beaming, 'we're calling her Brie.'

As in cheese? he wondered.

'French, is it?'

'No, English, it's short for Bridget.'

Right.

'Glad to see you back,' he said.

He explained the situation and handed her photos of Fred Foster.

One was the old mug shot with the bald head and wide-spaced eyes, giving him a reptilian look. The other was with the dark wig and beret when he was released.

'Can you make copies and let me have one. Put them through letterboxes and flash them at taxi rinks, at the bus station, the train station and rental cars. Relevant times are from between Friday morning to

Sunday night.'

'Nutters and missing wheelbarrows, and bloodied raincoats left at Oxfam's,' said Wilson after she left, going to the canteen. 'It sounds like one of those plays Dorothy dragged me to.'

'Oh?' said Cunningham who liked going to the theatre.

'You might well ask. It was about three people in a dustbin, a bloke who couldn't sit down, and a bloke who couldn't stand up.'

'Samuel Becket, Endgame,' said the Constable like a contestant on a game show, although it was unlikely that Wilson would award him a prize. 'One has to put one's interpretation on it.'

'Really? And what did one make of it?'

'All three maimed people are dependent on each other, and as their actions are repeated over and over again, it would suggest the sameness of life.'

'They should have joined the police force,' said Wilson, who now was more interested in a bacon sarnie and a cup of very sweet stewed tea in the canteen. It was rumoured Wilson would eat anything with four legs as long as it wasn't a coffee table.

They parked in a small loading bay in front of Oxfam, went into the shop and located the manager. Then they fought their way through what looked like an obstacle course of packed black bin liners, toys and bags of books, following the manager into the crowded room above the shop.

A dazzling young woman clutching a beige raincoat got up.

'I'm Natasha Marshall,' she said. Long legs in tight blue jeans, a black polo-neck, a curtain of dark hair held loosely back by a comb; Wilson momentarily wondered if she was the same sex as the countless buggy-pushing young women, walking along the pavements exposing rolls of fat midriffs and builder's bums.

'DI Wilson,' said Cunningham introducing him.

'Perhaps we could talk somewhere else,' Wilson said, looking around him. There wouldn't have been room to swing a cat, what with a rail full of clothes, a container with black bags, a steamer and two interested ladies, plus a pissed-off manager.

'It's much smaller upstairs,' said the manager. 'The computer cubicle and the toilet take up room.'

Smaller? Impossible.

'Is this the raincoat with the burnt hole you described to me on Saturday, Mrs Marshall?' asked Cunningham

'Yes, I'm afraid it is.'

'You identified it by a small hole in the sleeve. It's not much to go on. Have you looked in the pockets?' asked Wilson.

'No, I haven't. A shopping list!' said Natasha going through all the pockets,' sherry, sponge fingers, custard, lamb chops, he was shopping for our dinner. It is Dad's. It's his handwriting.'

'I found the coat when I unpacked a bag of clothes,' said one of the women opposite. 'I'm Lena.'

'Any idea when it was left?'

The manager had a good idea.

'Last thing on Saturday evening,' he said. 'I took it upstairs after I locked the shop and cashed up.'

He explained that Monday's donations hadn't yet been taken upstairs, they had to clear the cage first, he pointed to the container with the bags. Saturday evening, just before five, a man and a woman had come in. He had been at the till and had indicated to leave their donations in the corner of the shop. He saw them leave, but he couldn't tell if the man and woman had come together, or separately.

'Were you on your own?'

Reg was aghast. Two people had to be there at all times during opening hours, Maggie had been upstairs, turning taps and lights off, so she wouldn't have seen them. He couldn't describe the people either, having his eye on the till mostly, but he would say they were in their thirties, early forties.

'Now, eh, Lena. I believe you unpacked the bag?'

'That's right,' she said. 'It contained boys' summer clothes.' She paused. 'Seven to eight years old.'

'Probably last season's clothes,' said Cunningham.

She pointed to a large yellow bag. 'We put them away for next year.'

'The coat does belong to the missing man' said Wilson.

He 'phoned the station.

'Connor, can you come to Oxfam and help Lena go through the clothes in the yellow bag.'

'For identification purposes,' said Lena, 'I don't suppose the bin liner would be any good for finger-prints.'

'Why would that be?'

'It's been handled by too many people,' Lena explained. 'It was well- used, nearly torn. You would have to fingerprint half of Bury St. Edmunds.'

Wilson was impressed.

'You should be in the force,' he told Lena.

'So we are looking for a family with young boys who might or might not have the raincoat,' said Wilson. Cunningham was dropping him at the station where the probation officer was due to fill him in on Fred Foster. 'It could have been the mother or the father dropping the bag in.'

'It's a start,' said Cunningham

'There might be a label sown in somewhere.'

'They don't do that any more,' said Cunningham who had a sister with small children, 'but Lena might be lucky.' He paused, but he couldn't help himself. 'She should be in the force, and may The Force be with her.'

'*I* was going to say that,' said Wilson.

'I can't help wondering why we are concentrating on the missing old man,' said Cunningham after a while. 'I thought Fred Foster was a priority. Brownie points, I suppose.'

Not so old, thought Wilson, sixty-five was nothing these days.

'I suppose Bury St. Edmunds is a provincial town,' said Cunningham.

'So?'

'Small-town living is more connected than, let's say, than London'

Not so. Small town or large, people lived in communities where they shopped, went to the cleaners, the cinema, to hairdressers, all in the same area, perhaps with more choice of shops and get-away options, Wilson said..

'As a matter of fact, I met Dorothy when I investigated a missing young woman and finding a dead body in Cricklewood. Dorothy and the missing girl, Tessie, were both living in a boarding house, but everything was closely connected locally,' Wilson said.

Neither he or Dorothy had been looking for a partner, for want of a better word. He had settled into a widowed state, Dorothy, whose mother had died after a long illness, was moving into rented accommodation, but if the time wasn't right, they were certainly right for each other. Dorothy and the girl had been friends, and the girl, Tessie, was now a mother of two, married to a multi-millionaire and lived in Canada.

But Cunningham was right, he was looking for links. Once he had found enough links, he could form a chain.

A paedophile goes missing. A man goes missing the same evening. The man's overcoat turns up in the charity shop his daughter spends a few hours at. A raincoat with blood on it is found.

'I'm looking for connections. Fred Foster's photo shows him wearing a raincoat, so two men wearing raincoats have vanished,' he said. 'What does it suggest to you?'

'It was raining.'

'Precisely. It started to rain in the afternoon.'

'On Friday?' said Cunningham. 'I believe you're right. That doesn't mean Fred Foster was still in the area on Friday evening.'

'And how many men do you know who wear long coats flapping around their legs? A coat like Foster was also wearing?'

'Not many. Not if they're driving.'

A missing paedophile, a person with a young family bringing in a bloody coat, two men wearing long coats, possibly not driving, thought Wilson, and a lens found in a lane. It wasn't much to go on.

'When you meet Mrs Marshall back at the bungalow, perhaps you could ask her for her father's glasses' prescription. He seems to be a type of person who would keep these things,' Wilson (who wasn't that sort) said back at the station, just as Karin Lewis from the Probation Service drew up, 'and also find out what doctor he was registered with.'

Karin Lewis looked worried, as well she might, when she handed Wilson her report and Fred Foster's file.

Karin Lewis was large and stolid in a Concentration-Camp-Hilda manner, which could possibly be intimating to some, but not to Fred Foster, Wilson thought. She told him very honestly she had neglected to check on Fred Foster after his phone call on Friday morning.

'I didn't think he would go anywhere,' she said.

'Why?'

'He had only his Social Security. The money he earned in prison was spent on tobacco and TV and he had turned down one job.'

She was unimaginative.

'It would get him out of Suffolk.' said Wilson. 'He might also have money we don't know about. For instance, was he in touch with his wife?'

Karin Lewis didn't know. She didn't know her address.

'It would be in the file.'

'Well, it isn't, I asked around, but she's disappeared.'

Wilson made a note of, but he didn't blame her..

'The undercover officer watching him for the first week reported nothing unusual,' she said. Wilson already knew that, it was all in the report.

'Just tell me,' said Wilson, making notes.

Apparently, Foster didn't drive a car, didn't go out much, did his shopping, went to the Post Office. or he was in the flat watching TV after the curfew, supposedly, the surveillance camera had been nobbled.

'I have only just found out. Oh, I forgot, the

first week he went to the doctor, and once he went to the railway station.'

'What? You didn't think it was important?'

'Not really,' she said smugly, 'he only used the phone box. Besides, he knows if breaks the terms of his parole he'll end up inside.'

'If you ask me, you're not up to the job,' he said. 'Which surgery was he registered with? Don't tell me, you don't know.' Wilson looked it up. Foster was registered with the Angel Mount Practice.

'By Sunday night he was gone. He left perishable goods in the fridge, and also a handkerchief with some blood on it,' she said. It was in a plastic bag, which she handed over.

'Did you talk to any of the other people at the house?'

'Only briefly.'

'Well, you can do it in depth now,' he said.

When she said it wasn't in her remit, he reminded her she was lucky to still have a remit.

'I expect a report on my desk by two o'clock this afternoon. Delegate your other duties, and let me have the key to Foster's flat, I want it secured and given a thorough going over.'

'No can do, I'm afraid. The cleaners are already in,' she said, handing him the key

'I asked the Agency to come in, and before you say anything, I may be Foster's case manager, but I'm in the Probation Service, not the Police Force.'

Wilson studied the desk officer's report again, scratched his head, made some notes himself. Why was a fly-tipper important? He had reached no conclusion, except he wasn't surprised the man's name was Rusty, he spent too much time in the rain, he said to Cunningham who had returned with the lens, possibly from the missing man's glasses, and also his doctor's name and surgery.

'A cup of coffee,' Wilson said, and then we're off.'

'Where to?'

'Haslingfield, according to the report,' said Wilson, 'to visit Fred Foster's ex-wife.'

'If.'

'Too true. If. If Fred Foster was in the neighbourhood and short of cash, he might have paid her a visit.'

CHAPTER 17

WILSON FULLY INFORMED Cunningham of the Fred Foster saga as they drove out of Suffolk.

'He behaved himself in prison. After a while, he was moved from the windowless steel cell to another with a window, and so on. He was re-arranged down below and suffered various other injuries, but he never complained -what he did on the quiet is another matter- he said he deserved it. See? He repented.'

He paused.

'Evil doesn't even begin to describe him,' he said. 'He got off on inflicting pain and terror on little more than babies. I won't tell you in detail,' he swallowed. 'Let's just say they you are lucky not having to look at the photos of the little girl's remains.'

'And they let him go,' said Cunningham.

'We must not forget his human rights,' said Wilson. 'Don't ask.'

They drove into Cambridgeshire onto Haslingfield where Fred Foster's wife had moved to. She had changed her name to Forester.

'As far as we know, they were in touch by phone before he came out, but we don't know if she had changed her name, or where she had moved to.'

Haslingfield was a nice village even in the rain. Wilson and Cunningham found the house in London Road, Mrs Forester's abode, but they were informed that it had changed hands five weeks previously.

The present occupier, a young woman with one baby on her hip and a small child hanging onto her skirt, had no idea where the previous occupier had gone. 'My husband handles that sort of thing,' she said, 'and no, nobody has been asking questions.'

Next to the Post Office.

'Morning,' the woman behind the counter greeted them with, 'Will it ever stop raining?'

'I have no idea,' said Wilson, 'but I'm thinking of building an Ark.'

The woman laughed. Two shoppers, women, busy comparing prices on tins of soup, looked up, when Wilson introduced himself and DS Cunningham.

'Has there been a stranger around asking questions?'

'When?'

'On Saturday or Sunday.'

'I don't know about a stranger,' she said, 'but I noticed a car parked on the side of the road when I dropped my mother off to church. Something about it worried me.'

'What was it?'

'I can't remember,' she said, 'but as for seeing strangers, you had better ask my mother,' she said, shouting, 'Mum!' explaining that her mother knew everything there was to know. 'But she will go all around the houses before she gets to it.

Wilson had a dog like it, Ralph, a golden retriever. He wouldn't settle until he had gone round and round preparing his bed for the night entirely to his satisfaction and ended up exactly where he had started.

'She goes to church and Mother's Union,' she explained. Her mother, a sprightly woman in her sixties, drew breath and opened her mouth. 'And don't tell the inspector your life story, he only wants to know if you've seen a stranger over the weekend,' the woman behind the counter said.

'All right,' said the elderly women. 'We were going to church Sunday morning, my daughter dropped me. It was raining. A stranger, a man, approached us, me and two friends, he said he was trying to contact Mrs Foster from Cambridge Road. He had a parcel for her, only he'd forgotten the house number. He said she had a daughter at University. Mrs Forester had a daughter who has just finished her MA in Norwich. And then we told him they've moved abroad, Spain or Portugal.'

Wilson looked at her.

'And then we went to church.'

Apparently the man was tall, had greyish hair, and he was smartly dressed in black trousers and a grey jacket. He wasn't wearing a hat.

The two other churchgoers Wilson and Cunningham located said much the same thing, except one said the man was of medium height, had curly, reddish hair and wore a wine-coloured anorak, and the other described him as a man on the short side, with a receding forehead, and he wore a brown anorak.

None of the women could say if he was driving, but they assumed so, even though they hadn't seen a car.

A blank was drawn, Cunningham concluded, walking back to the Post Office. 'From their description, we're really looking for three blokes.'

Just as they were about to get into the car, the elderly woman came out of the Post Office. 'I just remembered, and I don't know if it makes any difference, but the man was actually asking for a Mrs Foster.'

'So you assumed that he meant Mrs Forester.'

'That's right. One thing that struck me as unusual,' she added, 'he was smartly dressed, as I said, but he wore scruffy trainers.'

Wilson waited.

'He acted normally when he asked questions,' she said, 'but not like anyone normally would, if that makes sense.'

Long-time prisoners acted furtively, Wilson

thought. Looking over your shoulder or sideways to see who was behind you becomes ingrained. He kept quiet, he couldn't implant that thought.

'He was sort of looking sideways,' she said, 'from side to side, like very slowly, in-between talking.'

Wilson showed her Fred Foster's mug shots. She studied them intently, then she shook her head.

'There's something about the eyes, but I wouldn't swear to it. All I can say is he gave me the creeps. I couldn't wait to get away from him.'

CHAPTER 18

'THE MAN MIGHT HAVE acted furtively,' said Wilson, getting in the car.

'Or he might have been getting wet,' said Cunningham. 'He might, or he might not, be Foster, who might or might not have done a runner.'

'Gut feeling?' asked Wilson who believed in instinct and coincidence.

Cunningham, who preferred to rely on science, shrugged his shoulders.

'Let's see what we can find out about Mrs Foster, or Forester, from her employer.'

They were on their way to Sawston, a large village in Cambridgeshire, where Fred Foster's wife had been deputy head of a primary school.

The news of Foster's disappearance would have been made public. Wilson intended to look at it on the six o'clock news purely to satisfy himself that Nicholson had legs and didn't propel himself along on wheels, he thought, drawing up in front of the school. The building was all large windows, purposely designed for small children to get easily distracted.

The Head, (Olive Palmer it said on the door) was gaunt and tall and wore her greying hair in a tight bun. She wore a twin-set, tweed skirt and sensible shoes like Her Majesty favoured in her off-duty moments, and she too appeared not easily pleased. She was especially displeased with Wilson and Cunningham for releasing a dangerous paedophile into the community, so she said.

Wilson didn't apologise, *he* hadn't let him loose, he said. 'It was handled from Storwich.'

'Handled from Storwich? Mishandled, I would say. Let us face it, Foster could be anywhere,' she said, arranging paper, a stapler, pens and pencils on her desk.

'What exactly has it got do with me? Or Mrs Forester?'

She sighed.

Apparently, Mrs Forester had kept herself to herself, reading in the staff room and eating alone. She was never one to partake in social activities, staff barbecues and volleyball competitions, that sort of thing.

And did this Queen look-alike really play volley ball? Wilson thought, when the woman smiled and showed him her hands, fingers spread wide. Like bloody dinner plates, he thought.

'They all underestimate me where balls are concerned,' she said sweetly. Wilson crossed his legs.

'Matters in hand,' she added. 'Heidi Forster was an excellent teacher until a few months ago. Then she stared to lose it, as they say these days. She was distracted, didn't prepare timetables, got impatient with the children. All in all, I was glad when she handed in her notice. And she took a day off to get a passport when we had our Sport's Day. Most inconvenient.'

She never told anybody where she was going, it was either Portugal, mainland Spain or the Canaries.

'But if she was the wife of this Fred Foster, I can't say I blame her for putting an ocean between them.'

'Didn't Shakespeare have a word for it?' Wilson asked when the left the school.

'The Head? I should think so. "Methinks the lady does protest too much."'

'I thought of the other one, something or other "in the state of Denmark."'

'Something rotten.'

'I bet Foster's wife is still in the country,' said Wilson. 'Olive Palmer might be good at volleyball, but as a witness, she made a serious mistake.'

They stopped at a pub, drawn by the sign that simply said *FOOD*. It appealed to Wilson who had a hunch these new-fangled chefs hadn't yet invaded the premises.

He was right.

He demolished a plate of egg and chips, washed down by a pint, while Cunningham picked at a few limp lettuce leaves and grated carrot masquerading as salad.

Going outside for a smoke, he wondered how Wilson did it. He ate all the wrong things, never put on an ounce and was as fit as the blonde barmaid, in a different meaning of the word, of course. In contrast, Wilson wondered if Cunningham inhaled cigarette smoke right down to his kneecaps.

'Your smoking and my eating chips makes us morally inferior,' he said, 'any ideas why?'

'Search me,' said Cunningham glumly. 'I suppose it's visible and some people have nothing else to be superior about,' which cheered Wilson momentarily.

The woman from the Post Office rang after they got back to the station. She had just remembered what had been worrying her about the car. It was a pale blue Corolla. Mrs Forester had driven a pale blue Corolla.

'As she had left the village a few weeks ago, I thought it was strange, she didn't have any friends and she wasn't a church-goer,' she added.

So that explained the stranger's (Foster's?) side-ways looks at the car, if it was him, Wilson thought. He thanked her and replaced the receiver.

'While I'm ringing Olive Palmer, perhaps you could look into unpaid parking fines, Foster might have left a trace there,' he said to Cunningham.

'Inspector Wilson here,' he said when she

answered the phone.

She sighed. 'I didn't think I had you fooled. I'm not a very good liar. What do you want to know?'

Finally he replaced the receiver and picked up Karin's report on the other occupants at The Flats.

One, a Charles Wilson, had reported he had knocked on Fred Foster's door one night (possibly Wednesday or Thursday of last week) wanting him to turn down the TV. He got no reply, so he went twice more. The last time, after ten o'clock, Foster had answered the door. He said he had been asleep and had apologised, but his trainers and trouser-legs were soaked.

Charles Wilson decided the wise course would be to follow the man from Coventry's example and mind his own business. He had seen Foster the previous Friday in question, leaving the flat about four or five o'clock or thereabouts, when he carried a shopping bag.

'Fred Foster might have gone out, leaving on the TV to indicate he was in the flat,' Karin concluded, and it looked as if he was shopping (for groceries?) on Friday evenings, ex-prisoners being notoriously creatures of habit. The fridge on the night in question had been well stocked, so it looked as if Foster had been shopping, and had left unexpectedly.

Had something happened on his way to, or from the shop? Wilson made a note of it. He phoned Karin to thank her (surprising her) for her thorough report. He was about to replace the receiver, but he didn't. She seemed to hesitate.

'Right, let's have it,' he said.

'I only took the handkerchief with the blood out of the waste paper bin.'

'What did you leave behind?'

'A broken pair of glasses,' she said. 'And the cleaners, as you know, have already been to the flat.'

PC Connor got the job of going through the bins.

'Which bins? Brown is kitchen waste, blue is paper and stuff and black is everything else.'

'Life used to be a lot easier with just one metal bin,' Wilson said, noticing Connor giving a longing look at the desk on his way out.

He then phoned Boots, the Opticians.

Apparently Paul Willoughby was on their list. They would be able to check the lens against the prescription, the girl from *Boots* said. Wilson sent for Cunningham, who thought life became very difficult when two people went missing at the same time.

'It's downright inconsiderate,' Wilson said.

The Corolla couldn't be traced without knowing a number plate. However, he got WPC Smith to telephone Swansea to find out who owned the car seen and reported by Mr Rusty as a fly-tipper.

Apparently, there was a software enabling the user to check for themselves, she said.

'Good. In that case, use it.'

'We haven't got it yet,' she said sweetly before she tripped off.

Wilson drummed his fingers on the desk, looked at the bloody raincoat, handkerchief and the lens, all now bagged up. Next he moved to Fred Foster and Paul Willoughby's doctor at the Angel Mount Practice. He was not so lucky there, however, as the receptionist flatly refused to give him any information.

'Anybody could say they're inspectors,' she sniffed,

'Quite right,' said Wilson, using his authoritative voice, 'except I am an Inspector, and we are trying to find Fred Foster's whereabouts.'

'I've heard about that,' she sniffed. 'Talk about

stable doors and horses. Just a minute. He was with Dr Graham, and Paul Willoughby was with Dr Somersby.

'Thank you,' Wilson said 'I'll be along shortly.'

He didn't keep Dr Graham for long. He noted Foster's blood group and that Foster suffered from migraines. Dr Somersby looked like a TV doctor, well-dressed in a chalk-striped suit, very good-looking, black hair, maybe -but not obviously dyed- and he appeared to be in his late forties.

He got Willoughby's blood group and then he drove to the Flats, not too far away. He parked, went round the back where he found Connor deep in a black bin. He told him to carry on and drove off.

Two lone men in raincoats, shopping on Friday evening. Asda, Sainsbury, Tesco, Somerfield. Or Off Licence for the sherry?

He drove back to the station, added to his notes, and picked up Cunningham who took him to the lane where Natasha had found the lens. A high wall to the left of the lane enclosed houses and sloping gardens. These householders would have to be questioned, probably in the evening, said Cunningham.

More overtime, convenient for some.

To the right were the allotments. Wilson scratched his head. Hadn't the desk sergeant muttered something about nutters and fly-tippers and missing and returned wheelbarrows?

'Wheelbarrow. What springs to mind?'

'Carrying stuff. Difficult to carry stuff, possibly heavy, possibly in a black bin liner.'

'Whatever did we do before black bin liners? Right. So somebody borrowed a wheelbarrow to carry something heavy, and then returned it. We'll have to find out what that something is.'

'Or was,' said Cunningham gloomily.

Back at the station, Connor had returned with the broken glasses missing a left-temple lens, a stroke of luck Karin had remembered it.

'Perhaps you can ring the dispensing chemists,' said Wilson, 'and ascertain if Fred Foster has been in for a repeat prescription for migraines. While you are at it, also check the optician, and find the address of the alleged fly tipper.'

After the sergeant left, Wilson labelled the coat and the handkerchief when Cunningham returned from the optician. Apparently the lens did not come from Paul Willoughby's glasses.

'It was glass, clear glass, not a lens from prescription glasses,' he said. 'It's from a pair of glasses worn for effect.'

'Or disguise,' said Wilson, putting the bagged-up glasses with the other items. 'Forensics will have to deal with these, but if they don't belong to Fred Foster and got broken in that lane on Friday night I am Queen Esparanta of Rumania.'

He drummed his fingers on his desk. 'I think I will have to ask for the incidents van for the lane,' he said.

'Mobile Unit, you mean. That should please the Super, bearing budgets in mind,' said Cunningham. Wilson said he wasn't in the business to please the Super, when Smith reported she had the address of the man who might have spotted a fly tipper on Saturday evening.

Wilson said he would look into it if nothing else broke tomorrow.

Then he went to the white board and drew a vertical line.

On either side, he added a man wearing a long coat and carrying shopping bags. The board screamed something at him but as he was deaf to it, he went for a cup of coffee.

When he came back, he looked at the board and put Paul Willoughby's name on one side, Fred Foster's on the other. He entered what he knew about either man and looked where the lines converged, or rather, didn't. Two men, and then none. He was about to go home, by Royal Appointment, as he told Cunningham, who wasn't surprised.

'That film about the Queen is on again tonight, so my mother tells me.' (Cunningham was divorced and lived with his posh, single mother)

Apparently, the Queen bore a remarkable likeness to Helen Mirren, he added.

Wilson put on his coat and got his car keys, feeling sorry he hadn't thought of that one, when the phone rang.

It was the Super.

'Any developments?'

'We have found the missing man's raincoat, bloodstained, and what appears to be a lens from Foster's glasses.'

'You think the two are connected?'

'If you put the unlikely together you get surprising results. Well, sometimes. The missing man had plenty of cash on him and he also wore an expensive watch, a Tag Heuer. Apparently they cost thousands.'

'I suppose that could mean robbery.'

'We'll get onto it,' said Wilson. 'Tomorrow, I'm going to see Foster's wife.

'What? Nobody knows where she is,' said Nicholson. 'She vanished off the face of the earth, according to Cambridgeshire Police.'

'I'm meeting her tomorrow as I said, although I'm not able to tell you where. Her former head

133

mistress arranged it for me.'

'Well done.'

Wilson took the bull by the horn, 'I'd like a mobile unit on Friday, afternoon to evening.'

'I suppose so, we have to make some headway with the missing man,' said the Super. 'Have you looked at surveillance tapes from the supermarkets yet?'

'They don't use tapes any more. Apparently. it's all digital, they can transmit it. I thought we'd do it later.' said Wilson. 'I have Willoughby's blood group from his doctor as well as Foster's. I'll send the raincoat to forensics with the bloody handkerchief found in Fred Foster's flat.

'Foster's DNA is on the database, so we'll have a conclusive result fairly fast. They're still working on DNA fibres from the old Devon child-rape,' said the Super. 'We should hear in the next few days. We have a warrant out for Foster, as he's broken the conditions of his parole.'

'Wherever he may be,' said Wilson, rather unnecessarily.

CHAPTER 19

THE NEXT DAY, after Dorothy left for work, Wilson put up the ironing board in the kitchen. The dog jumped up, released a few sharp barks, and sank back into his basket. 'I have done this before, you know,' he said, selecting a blue shirt and ironed the bits of the shirt sticking out.

Last night they had watched a repeat of *The Queen*, the film. When Prince Charles appeared, they looked at each other, but when Tony Blair came onto the scene, they both started to giggle. Helen Mirren moved her head in a queenly sort of way, as if it was screwed too tight into her neck.

When they switched channels, there was a Celebrity Pig Farmer and a Celebrity Greengrocer on a quiz show. The upshot was that they had a good laugh, Helen Mirren got an Oscar and the ironing was still waiting in the basket.

Once he was dressed, Wilson polished his black shoes, the dog keeping a close eye on him, wagging his tail half-heartedly.

'All right, you can come,' he said, getting the lead and the car keys. 'as long you don't bark if a call comes through.'

He was meeting Mrs Foster in The Buckingham Lodge in Buckingham in Buckinghamshire. 'Easy to ask for directions if we get lost,' he said to Ralph, who, as always, had sunk into a deep slumber on the back seat the minute they had hit the road. He always wanted to come but did exactly the same as he did at home, he slumbered on.

Wilson liked classical music. It used to be Berlioz, Holst, Beethoven and Mozart, but now he had settled firmly on Mozart, the Master.

Although he usually listened to Mozart when

he drove, he preferred to drive in silence when he was involved with case. He gave his brain free rain, well, at least that part of it not concerned with keeping an eye on the road and other motorists, but he perked up when they approached Milton Keynes.

Walton Hall, home to the Open University, was prominently marked. Everybody had degrees, Dorothy, Cunningham, and of course Fred Foster, whereas he only had A levels. When he retired, he would join and get a degree. He had read in the local rag of an eighty-year-old woman who had completed her degree course. It made a change from a hip replacement.

There was more to getting a degree, of course. He would have to study something, but what?

The Buckingham Lodge was a smart hotel, as he discovered when he parked in the car park. The dog woke briefly when they stopped, loomed up behind him, decided it wasn't worthy of his interest, and went back to sleep.

The foyer sported a good display of the large indoor plants Dorothy was always trying to grow but always killed.

A board announced conferences.

A large room doubled as lounge/dining room with a bar at the end, where he spotted a slim, tall woman.

'A waiter will join us shortly,' she said, walking up to him. 'I'm Heidi Foster. I assume you are Inspector Wilson.'

They shook hands and sank into one of the small divans facing coffee tables, where a waiter came to take their order shortly after.

A shifty-looking man with a black goatee squinted at them from a portrait on the wall.

'I wouldn't want to come across him on a dark night,' said Wilson.

'The Duke of Buckingham? He came to the same sticky and as Charles I. He was beheaded. Reputedly they were lovers when he accompanied Charles to Spain to ask for the King's daughter's hand in marriage.'

'Oh?'

'Sent off with a flea in his ear, apparently. That was before he married Henrietta, who was French, and Catholic, not good, of course.'

'Of course,' said Wilson. Why? he thought He could study history, he thought briefly, but there was nothing for it.

'That must have hurt,' he said, looking at the two deep scars, running right down both her cheeks.

'It did,' she said. 'And Foster found me through the scars.'

She had been interviewing for caretakers for the school. Covering them up meant more than a bit of concealer. She hadn't bothered for a long time, she said. 'People got used to how you look. However, one man applying for the job as caretaker was immediately suspicious.'

'Oh? How?'

'Most people stare at my face, they can't help it, but he looked away. Since the Huntley horror, we are extra careful. Were you involved with that?' she said.

'It was cross-border,' he said.

'I won't prey, it must have been horrendous, but as I said, I might otherwise have looked with more compassion at a middle-aged immigrant trying to settle down. Vladimir Glubis was from one of the Baltic States and had degrees from Vilnius. However, there was something so very unpleasant about him, we wouldn't have dared put our backs on him.

'How unpleasant? Disfigured?'

'No, not disfigured, I suppose it was the

expression on his face, kind of knowing? sneering? combined with the soft voice.'

She paused.

'Next thing, Foster rings me at the school. He wants to me meet him in Cambridge when he got out with ten thousand pounds and a car, which I did. I hoped he would use the money and disappear. Olive Palmer drove me home. We invented the abroad story between us. She is a marvellous woman, but she isn't a very good liar.'

'She also made a serious mistake, she connected you straight away to Fred Foster without being told,' said Wilson. 'I'm telling you this in case somebody else inquires after you. Perhaps you can tell her to keep the interview short next time and refer to you as Mrs. Forester, if she has to.'

She nodded. 'It could be the press.'

'Right. I think Foster is going to be bad news, big bad news. So he has money and a car.'

'A pale-blue Corolla.'

'He might have changed it, but that answers one of my questions. The other question is, did you report this Vladimir Glubis and his connection to Foster?'

'And draw attention to myself as the wife of a perverted killer? '

He made a note to get Cambridgeshire Police to make a check up on Glubis, Sawston was in Cambridgeshire and toes had better not be trodden on.

'Next. How does Foster operate?'

She stirred her coffee.

'A psychological profile, you mean?'

He nodded. Criminal psychology, another subject for his consideration.

'There are no cold-blooded killers,' said Wilson, 'something or someone always sets them off.'

'Is he psychopath? Probably. He likes to terrorise children. He is also adaptable in that he can take on facets of other people's personalities.'

'We lived in a second- floor flat, so on her sixth birthday we took our daughter Amelia and her friends to a park,' she said. 'They played games, but Foster wanted them to do handstands and cartwheels. Most of the girls were like baby elephants, but Amelia was graceful, cart wheeling effortlessly.'

She paused. 'Red balloons, blue sky, green grass. A small triangle of white knickers.'

'He chased the girls until they squealed and cried and finally sobbed their hearts out. I dried their tears, cut the park frolics short and went to McDonald's for tea, and the girls went home.'

'"My friends don't like you, Daddy," I heard Amelia say.'

'Unbeknown to Foster, my father had arrived and was using the toilet, and I was in the kitchen when I heard Foster say that naughty girls had to be punished until they learned to please him. One of Amelia's presents was a kitten, a tiny bundle of beige fur. He got up, took the kitten into one hand and Amelia's hand in the other and went out onto the balcony. He opened his hand with the kitten. "Your present's gone, all gone," he said. "That's what happens to little girls who don't please me."'

'I went into the bedroom and threw a few things into a case. I really ought to have left on the spot, but that is the benefit of hindsight. Foster came in and asked me what I was doing. I said that I was going to leave him. He went into the bathroom and came back with a razor and cut both my my cheeks. My father, a widower and a policeman, -he retired with a heart condition- came up behind him and hit him over the head with his upturned walking stick.'

'There was blood spurting from my face, Foster was knocked out by the antique handle made of pewter, my father collapsed, and Amelia screamed.'

She paused.

'Foster likes to terrorise, as I said, and I was very pretty, but this was a punishment,' she said. 'I was visiting my father, who later died, some weeks later when Foster was arrested and I was out of hospital, but I never divorced him because the press would have found out where I and Amelia were. And whatever anybody thinks, I had no idea he had killed that little girl.'

A group of bright young things, well-suited and booted, came in. When Wilson got up, she waved to somebody.

''My daughter is attending the Eco Conference and I'm spending a few days with her,' she said. 'I count myself blessed that I have her and that she came through it all.'

She paused.

'But she still doesn't like birthdays?' offered Wilson.

'She both hates them and loves them in a peculiar fashion,' she said. 'You see, when Foster was in hospital with concussion, he was was kept in for a day and somebody else drove the library van at short notice. That was the start, when nasty child porno was found under his seat.'

That was how the finger started to point at Foster.

'"*Blood will have blood*." Amelia quotes Shakespeare because that birthday in all its horror set us free.'

Wheels had a habit of turning, Wilson thought, but another thought was uppermost in his mind. How did she reconcile having a daughter with Foster's genes?

'What makes you think. she is his daughter?'

CHAPTER 20

WILSON, ARMED WITH HIS pooper-scooper, let the dog out in a secluded spot What his old dad would have made of grown people clearing up after their dogs didn't bear thinking about.

As he drove back and into Bury St. Edmunds he noticed cars parked on roads near schools where knots of parents, mostly women, were waiting for the children to come out. They were probably discussing the news of a paedophile having been in their midst.

'And none of us knew,' said Christine, talking to Natasha. 'I always thought George was too protective of Rosie, but now I think he was right.'

Natasha agreed.

'Lewis, Hester's father, will be devastated. We are separated, not officially, but he lives in Cambridge, and he loves Hester in his odd way. He treats her like an adult, he brings her florist flowers, he takes her for good haircuts and out to proper restaurants.'

Christine wondered how shallow she was. A dangerous man had been on the loose, and yet she noticed Natasha's looks. She wore blue jeans, boots, a grey jacket with a stand-up collar and an Oliver Twist cap, when her mind returned to the children coming out of school.

Rosie jumped up and down, apparently what she had to say was , as always, of extreme importance.

'Can Hester come and play?' she asked.

Hester wanted an ice-cream, so Rosie went into the living room, where her mother was watching the news. She stopped when the photo of the man with the beret came on.

'Is he famous? The man with the beret?' she asked.

142

Before her mother could answer, she said he talked to Emily Watson through the railings at school.

'**He what?**'

'He goes like that to Hester,' Rosie said, making a motioning movement, 'she won't go, but Emily does because she always wants to come first.'

And yes, Rosie said, she knew about strangers, but he wasn't a stranger if they knew him, was he?

George Hudson let himself into the house. Before he had a chance to go into his routine of coat and key and 'Where's Rosie?' Christine rushed out of the living room.

'You have got to phone the police.'

'Why? What's happened? Is Rosie all right?'

'She's fine. Hester is here, she came to play. The telly was on and I was watching the news of Fred Foster' disappearance , I suppose you've heard?'

'I heard he has vanished, broken his parole, the police say he's left the area.'

'*That's not the point.* Rosie pointed to him and said that was the man who hung around the school. She says that he was interested in Hester but she is shy, so he talked a lot to Emily Watson.'

George had seen it himself, he thought as he phoned the police station.

'I have some information about Fred Foster,' he said, 'can you put me through to whoever is in charge?'

'That would be Inspector Wilson.'

'Yes?' said the inspector when George got through.

'I'm George Hudson. My daughter Rosie, she's five-and-a-half, recognised Fred Foster, the man on the News. She says she saw him hanging around her school.'

'Which is?'

'Reardon Infants and Primary. I warned her about strangers, and she says the man in the raincoat wasn't a stranger because he was often there at morning break.'

'Is it an open playground?'

'It's ring-fenced. The gates are locked at nine. Late-comers buzz and are let in by the girl in the office after being identified.'

'Was he interested in any of the girls?'

'Yes, he was. Not in my own daughter, as it happens, but one of her friends, Hester Marshall, who was too shy to talk to him, and also in a girl called Emily Watson, who apparently talked to him frequently.'

'Morning break, you said. Was this only in the morning?'

George said he would ask Rosie.

'Apparently it was only in the mornings.'

'Leave it with me. I'll have to get in touch with the Head and see how best to handle it, we don't want to frighten the girls. On the other hand, we will have to talk to Emily, Hester, and your daughter. I'll arrange a meeting on Monday morning. Have you got the Head's address and 'phone number?'

Back in Wheystead, Natasha felt at a loss. It was the first time Hester had gone on her own to play after school.

She lifted the phone to ask Christine how Hester was, but instead she dialled her father, a reflex action. Listening to his measured tone on the recorded message was like a blow to her stomach, a reminder of what had been but no longer was.

Then she phoned Lewis, but his answer-phone kicked in too. 'Leave a message, dears,' he said, 'if it's not too much trouble.'

No wonder everybody thought he was gay, especially with his love of pink, lemon and pale-blue cashmere jumpers; all, except for her father , who had recognised the chemistry between them.

Bewaring chemistry, she made a start on the spare room in case he wanted to stay the night. She was screwing in a light bulb, fixing a lampshade, making up the bed with fresh linen and carting pots of paints and boxes into the garage, so she didn't hear Lewis's car.

'I 'phoned you,' she said accusingly. 'I told you on the 'phone that we found Dad's coat.'

'I heard, awful, just awful, but I'm here now,' he said, bearing a bunch of flowers and a carrier bag, when she fell into his arms.

'I came as soon as I could,' he said, 'I'm here now. I bought some steaks, you need bucking up. Where's the moppet? I brought her some oranges and some orange roses for you.'

'She's playing with Rosie Hudson.'

'I suppose she will be all right. My blood boiled when I heard that pompous little twit, Chief Superintendent if you please, spouting forth Fred Foster had been rigorously risk assessed and was found to pose no danger. Apart from which, I nearly had a nervous breakdown'.

However, that was nothing compared to how he felt when George brought Hester back at seven and asked for a private talk, so Lewis took him in to the living room

'We need to handle this carefully, so it might be wise to calm down,' George said. 'Brace yourself, but Fred Foster has made advances towards Hester through the fence at the school playground, but she ignored him.'

'My Hester? How dare he?' said Lewis. 'If he has disappeared because vigilantes saw him off, I hope they made a good job of it and strung him up by the balls.'

If only we had, thought George, but we got the wrong man.

'And the same goes for the police. Fancy letting him loose.'

'I feel the same way.' said George, 'You have no idea how hard my wife and I fought for our family. We have lost three little boys at five months.'

Lewis fetched him a whiskey and soda.

'All we have are little markers with their names on in the graveyard, and Rosie. We have come out of it, but believe me, I will fight tooth and nail for my family, with no holds barred.'

A few short sentences. So much living had gone into it, and why was he telling this to a perfect stranger?

'And you never thought, blow this for a lark, enough is enough, and waltzed off into the sunset?'

'Never.'

Lewis said he had his absolute, perfect admiration. He hadn't been able to cope when Natasha had transformed herself from a girl who threw a pair of jeans and some tee-shirts into a suitcase and took off for a week-end in Venice, or wherever, into a stay-at home mother with one thing on her mind; her child.

'Hester became everything to her, everything. I suppose I couldn't understand it. I mean, Hester's important to me, and I don't know what I'd do without her. But I still have to function in the outside world, earning a living for instance. In contrast, she became Natasha's sole reason for living. She slept in our bed at night and was carried in a sling until she was twelve months old. To be honest, I felt like a sperm donor.'

He couldn't cope when it was just the normal baby stuff, he admitted it freely.

'And this house,' he added, curling his lip, 'didn't help much.'

A seventieth sixteen-century farmhouse set in a few acres, and beautifully furnished, George thought. Dark oak floors, needle-point samplers and botanical prints on the wall, a Victorian chair with a fringe, a beat-up striped settee, dog's head and irons and a coal scuttle in the hearth.

Lewis liked to see houses and roofs, hear traffic, walk to a pub on streets with street lights and not wake up to the bugger-all they called the countryside. 'It's worse in the summer with all that yellow stuff.'

'Rapeseed.'

'It's a ghastly colour, and it makes me sneeze.'

'To each his own, I suppose,' said George. 'My mother-in-law was brought up in our Victorian town house, and she hates it, the high ceilings, how hard it is to heat and how many people have lived there before her. She can only live in a new-built, she says.'

He paused.

'She was an amazing help in our trouble. I think if I was in trouble again, I would go to her.'

George spoke sincerely. Lewis couldn't help wondering what sort of trouble he could get himself into.

'Come to think of it, Hester was also talking about a man in a beret,' Lewis added, helping himself to a whiskey and soda without the soda.

'Would you believe, she was afraid of a man in a beret? She was always prattling on about him, as a matter of fact, she wouldn't let Natasha wear hers.'

He sank onto the settee and looked at George.

'Can you just explain to me why nobody ever

listens to children? Not properly?'

Maybe it was because they had other things on their minds, he added.

Three weeks ago, his father-in-law had asked him to dinner. A good dinner it was too, a perfect Château Bryant, cooked by his Polish helper. Over coffee he said he was contemplating suicide, and then he prattled on about a foreign holiday.'

'Amsterdam?' George said promptly.

'I should think not,' said Lewis, 'he was mugged in Amsterdam.'

'That would explain it,' said George, remembering the dark evening in the lane.

'Explain what?'

'That he didn't want to go there.'

'It most certainly would,' said Lewis, 'he said his mind was packing up, but maybe I talked him out of it.'

George felt a great relief sweeping over him. Killing a suicidal man, even by accident, did not seem quite so bad.

'I'll certainly keep it in mind if the worst comes to the worst,' he said. He nearly added 'when we get caught,' but he stopped himself in time

'What?'

Lewis stared at him.

'With my own father, he's getting on a bit,' George said lamely, making for the door. 'Time I was off.'

Lewis looked after the departing car. What was going on with George? But they all had their secrets, perhaps it was time he told Natasha.

'There is something you should know about your father,' he said to her. 'A few weeks ago we discussed suicide.'

'Whose suicide?'

'His.'

'*My father* and you discussed HIS SUICIDE?'

'I asked him who he wanted to punish, I mean it is an aggressive act. He said he hadn't looked on it like that, but he would not shuffle meekly towards dementia. He would rather terminate his life than have a negative impact on others.'

He paused.

'But I think I changed his mind for him.'

'What did you say to him?'

'I told him not to be so bloody stupid and that it was a privilege to know him. '

Paul Willoughby had followed Lewis to his car and had looked at him through the car window.

'Promise me you won't tell Natasha until later,' he said. 'And promise me to take me to Switzerland when the time comes.'

'Why did he want to go to Switzerland, I've wondered ever since? And how would I know when the time was right for a little holiday?'

'It's Dignitas,' said Natasha, 'it's the clinic in Zurich where they,' she shrugged her shoulders, 'you know, but Frank has -had?- put him on a new drug. I am glad Dad came to you for help, I don't know how I would have coped on my own.'

Now they faced a conundrum. Should they tell the police that Paul Willoughby was suicidal?

Maybe next week. They had had a meeting with the headmistress on Monday morning concerning Fred Foster, said Natasha.

They.

Back in the bosom of, thought Lewis, and for good this time.

CHAPTER 21

UNLIKE EVERYBODY ELSE, Fred Foster had a good evening. He had enjoyed his news coverage before he went shopping. He wished he had cleared out his fridge and saved some money, ten thousand didn't last forever

He had one leg out of his car on Somerfield's dark, drizzly forecourt, the part that wasn't fenced off due to re-surfacing, when a fat woman loading groceries from a trolley into her boot next to his car tripped and fell. He was going to ignore her, of course, except her handbag flew open, displaying a red purse amongst the usual rubbish women kept in their handbags.

Another woman shopper rushed over to help her up. All he had to do was get out, help himself to the purse, get back into the car and drive off. He drove back to the B&B and opened the purse. No cash, but a Visa card. The pin number was folded into a side pocket, he noted, when somebody knocked on his bedroom door.

It was the American couple and their horrible kid. It was their last evening in Bury St. Edmunds, they said, they were packed up and ready to leave early in the morning. They would like to invite him to dinner, as it had been such a pleasure to meet him.

'Ethan is playing at being grown-up, so we're leaving him in bed. Mrs Warner will listen out for him.'

Ethan was their kid. What sort of a name was that? He hoped it would be their last evening on earth, but he declined their offer politely.

'I'm dining with friends, alas.'

Had he really said 'alas'? he wondered, looking after them as they disappeared on the landing's half-turn, all bar the kid, who, in his pyjamas, went into the room next door. It was tempting fate, of course, but the kid had it coming. He removed his wig and took off his glasses, and then padded down onto the half-landing, listening to the vanishing murmur of voices in the hall. He tried the door handle of the next room. The room wasn't locked. He opened and closed it a few times before he went in.

Ethan was happy, terribly happy. He wondered if this was the happiest day in his life, apart from flying in an aeroplane next to the white clouds. It was also close to the last Christmas, when the fairy lights caught fire and a real fire engine came, so they had to go to Grandmother who let him eat everything he wanted.

The rain lashed the window.

He felt safe, cosy, sitting up in his warm bed propped up on his pillow in the small pool of light cast by the bedside lamp, the TV control in one hand, a whole bar of Cadbury's Fruit And Nut in the other. What should he watch, he wondered, when he looked up.

The doorknob rattled.

It turned slowly.

The wind, Ethan thought, heaving a sigh of relief when it stopped.

The doorknob turned slowly again and the door opened even more slowly.

The wind, the wind, go away, wind, he thought desperately even though he knew it wasn't the wind. It was a dark figure coming in silently. He had a white face and a white skull. It was Death. Nathan had pictured Death when his grandpa died in the night. Grandpa had 'been taken,' they said. Death had taken him, and now he was coming to take him, closer and closer. Ethan was taken in the night, that's what they would say.

'Do you know who I am?' whispered Death.

Ethan wanted to nod, but he was totally frozen.

'I am the bogeyman, I tear children limb from limb and eat them. I am very fond of little boys,' whispered Death.

Ethan wet the bed, but his pee was nice and warm; he was still alive. A scream was slowly building up in his insides.

'Do not scream, if you do, I will know,' whispered Death, putting a finger to his lips, walking backwards out of the room, silently closing the door.

Fred Foster retreated. Back in his room, he put on his wig and the anorak collar up high and looked at himself in the mirror. It would have to do.

He turned out the light in his room and waited. He didn't have long to wait. Ethan's scream, building up in his innards, finally reached his mouth, and he let go. Ahhhhhhhh! Ahhhhhhhhhh! Ahhhhhhhh! His blood curdling screams finally reached below stairs. Doors were flung open, and somebody knocked on his door.

'He's gone out, he's meeting friends,' a voice said.

'Soon,' he said to himself, waiting for the moment when he could slip out of the house.

The rain was beating on the roof. He tiptoed trough the hall and grabbed Warner's hat from the hall stand. It was tanking down as he walked into town and pressed the button for *Statement* on the cash machine outside the Post Office. Lo and behold, the fat woman had five-hundred pounds left to draw. His finger-prints would be on the purse, so he put it in his pocket and walked to the pub where he treated himself to a well-deserved meal.

Mrs Warner was behind the desk in the hall when he came back, the hat in his pocket.

'Here, Mr Cole,' she said, confidentially, 'have we had had some trouble while you were out.'

'Oh?'

'The boy from upstairs, the American,' she said, 'well, he won't go upstairs, he absolutely refuses.'

'Oh?'

'He says Death is waiting for him. Death is apparently the bogeyman, who will get him and tear him up and eat him. Talk about screaming!'

When the lounge door opened, he saw that it was the American couple. The boy's mother wanted to telephone her mom, the father wanted to nip upstairs to get the boy's toy monkey.

'Would you mind sitting with him for a moment?' They looked at him imploringly. 'Ethan is so very fond of you.'

'No trouble at all, I will be more than pleased to oblige,' he said, 'except a boy needs his mother at a time like this.'

When he opened the door, the boy was shaking like a leaf in a breeze. White as a sheet, his freckles standing out like organ stops, he stared at him wild-eyed.

'I told you no screaming, you promised,' Howard Cole whispered and put his finger to his lips.

'MOM! '

His mother rushed in, looked at him, and he shrugged his shoulders.

'That awful screaming has started again,' said Mrs Warner when he went out.

'It's Mr Cole.'

'Mr Cole, he's asking for you,' said his landlady.

'Neurotic?'

'I should say,' said Mrs Warner as he wound his way upstairs, secure in the knowledge nobody ever listened to children. Not properly.

He went to bed. In all the excitement, he had forgotten to keep an eye open for the three blokes who had assaulted him in the lane. The power of three had eluded him, although he was sure they would be in the pub next time. There was always a next time.

CHAPTER 22

ANOTHER BUSY DAY, Wilson thought, at the station at eight, where he assembled his team for a briefing, and put his findings on a whiteboard.

'About time I put you in the picture,' he started to his assembled team, 'but I didn't have much of one before, so:

> *Missing man.* (he wrote)
> *Paul Willoughby, sixty-five years old.*
> *Exhibit..*
> *His mug shot. Last spoke to his daughter, Natasha Marshall, on Friday, October 31st, between five and six pm.*
> *Clothes:*
> *Beige Burberry. Beige hat. Red Scarf.*
> *Retired Doctor.*
> *Suffers from Alzheimer's.*
> *Expensive watch, a Tag Heuer, reputedly worth ten thousand pounds.*

Gasps.

> *He has roughly two-hundred pounds on him. Robbery? Or accident?*
> *Hobbies. Chess, County Champion some years ago. Supports Norwich FC.*

'No wonder he's gone missing,' said Connor.
Laughter and groans.
'Right, let's get back to it.'

> *Friday October 31st·Reported fly-tipping..Vehicle unloading rubbish in woods about quarter to six pm.*
> *Place:*
> *Before you leave Bury St. Edmunds*

'Nuisance callers, or perhaps not, the information might or might not be relevant to the missing man, CONNECTION IS THE AREA. If we find him quickly, it'll look good for us,' said Wilson, turning from the whiteboard, 'and we do need something in our favour as we turn to Fred Foster.'

156

Wilson turned to his team.

'An unsolved child killing in Devon may be connected to Foster. He was twenty- eight at the time, working as a librarian who drove a library van to remote villages.

Everybody sat up.

'The point is, they started DNA testing a few weeks ago, four weeks into which Foster was released. And this unsolved murder bears Foster's hallmark. Now, I come to the part where you will all wish you had chosen another profession and wouldn't want to know the exact details or view the photos. I know I did when I read it.'

He paused.

'It's the pathologist's report on Claire Baldwin's cause of death. Her mother called her 'a blessing.' They found some of Claire's baby teeth in her stomach.'

Dead silence.

'Right,' he said, 'now we come to the part where we are glad we joined the force, let's find the bastard, if he's still with us.'

Back in his office, the desk sergeant reported that a woman insisted on speaking to him.

'She says she's been robbed,' he said. 'I made a note of it, but then she mentioned the man wore trainers. It just seems odd.'

'Wheel her in and ask Smith to bring us both some coffee. If you don't mind.'

Wilson knew from experience victims liked to start at the beginning, always supposing they could find it, and he might as well make the most of it.

'I was robbed when I fell over,' the woman, a Miss Hillman, said, sinking one of her haunches onto the chair, which creaked. The woman was enormous, wearing a tight black tee-shirt and black leggings in which her enormous curves flowed into one another like sets of spare tyres.

Never mind, thought Wilson, who prided himself on being tolerant.

'Yes? Tell me what happened.'

'What else? Honestly!' she snapped. Wilson went right off tolerance. DS Cunningham came in and was about to leave, but Wilson motioned him to stay.

'Who's he?' she said.

'DS Cunningham, but please carry on.'

'I did my shopping, like I always do...'

Wilson drifted off. He came to when she reached the previous evening, about to open her car boot for her groceries.

'I slipped and fell on my back,' she said. 'I had my car keys in my left hand.'

'In your left hand?'

'Where else? I'm left-handed and I put my handbag into my right hand. When I fell, I let go of it and it split open. A woman came to help me up and she also helped put the groceries in the car boot.'

'Which side?'

'The left, of course. I'm left-handed.'

'Who was on your other side?'

'I can't say. It was dark and it was raining and crowded, only half the car park was in use. All I saw was an open car door and a man's leg. He had dark trousers on and he wore trainers.'

She paused.

'My partner had a pair like it, very unusual, with a chevron pattern. Anyway, I drove home and thought no more about it, apart from my headache, of course,'

If she fell on her back her head was in a funny place.

'What did you mean when you said you were robbed? What was taken?'

'My purse, of course, what else?'

Wilson reminded himself that he was being paid to do this.

'I noticed it missing later that night, about midnight. I was watching a DVD, Indiana Jones. That Harrison Ford turns me on. I fancied some .... ice-cream.'

She paused.

'Smoking in your own home is not a crime, not yet,' said Wilson. Ice cream in the middle of a cold November night?

'All right then, cigarettes, and I told Burt to go the garage and get some. I told him my purse was in my handbag, only it wasn't. I had it when I paid for my groceries. It had my credit card and some cash in it.'

Wilson made a note.

'It couldn't have been the Good Samaritan.'

'What?'

'The woman who (he was about to say winched) who helped you up, because she was on your other side.'

'You finally got it. I have been in touch with the bank. It's a special number, see, and they cancelled my card. They checked my account and somebody has cleared me out, reached my limit. Five-hundred pounds.'

'What about the pin number?'

'In my purse, I can't be expected to remember fucking stupid numbers.' She sounded indignant. 'So, are you going to do anything about it, or are happy to sit in your nice warm office all day?' she said, rummaging in her bag, waving a photo under his nose.

'My partner took a photo with his digital camera and printed it out on the computer. It's of my backside.'

'Really?' He thought it was Europe's butter mountain. Did they still have one?

Smith appeared in the doorway with the coffee. Wilson waved her away.

'Yes, really. He noticed I had a big bruise on my backside. I walk about in the nude before I shower.'

'That's when he noticed it. But why take a photo?'

'Because I'm going to sue Somerfield's arse off.'

An unfortunate expression under the circumstances.

'That is up to you, of course, but I wouldn't bother, car parks are run by another company,' said Wilson. 'So, let's see what happened. You finally found a space in the crowded car park and were about to drive onto it.'

She nodded.

'And then you noticed an abandoned trolley blocking the bay, so you stopped the car, moved the trolley somewhere where you could get to it without hunting for a pound, had a word with someone you knew, and then you drove into the vacant space. When you got back, you slipped on some oil and fell down. This "woman"who helped you was the woman you had a word with."

She nodded again, looking amazed.

'The conclusion I reach is that your car's MOT is overdue and if you don't do something about your oil leak, I'll report you to traffic.'

'How did you know?' the woman gasped.

'I sit in my nice warm office and think about it,' said Wilson, 'so I don't need to go out.'

'You took a chance with that oil leak,' said

Cunningham.

'I had one on my front drive, 'said Wilson. 'I have wasted my time with that woman, but does she think I came over on the banana boat?'

'You could lose your job over a remark like that.'

'That's why I haven't made it. So, recap. All she noticed before she fell over was a man's trousered leg to her right about to get out of a car. The man wore trainers with a distinct chevron pattern.'

'A lot of men wear trainers,' said Cunningham.

'So they do, but the man in Haslingfield also wore trainers. So, let's suppose the man is well dressed. So well dressed, that his trainers look out of place. Let's suppose Fred Foster is still in the area, and let's suppose he is greedy. We know that he has money, and this woman's purse lands in front of him like manna from heaven.'

'He would have altered his appearance, perhaps he's discarded his glasses or wears another pair,' said Cunningham. 'Although, according to psychologists, adopting another persona isn't easy, it can lead to confusion.'

Wilson asked him to surprise him, but Cunningham took no notice.

'It can lead to confusion in what we term 'normal' people. Normal people like to belong. If we are talking about psychos, however, it is a different story.'

Wilson thought story-time had lasted quite long enough.

'We better get the surveillance tapes from the cash points. Connor can do it.'

'I'll arrange it with the Technical Division here,' said Cunningham.

'I didn't know we had one.'

'We don't, it's wishful thinking. What about guest houses?'

'We'll do it while Connor views last night's tapes. Can I have a word with Constable Smith?' asked Wilson.

'Now, if you were a woman,' he said when she came in.

'I am,' she said.

Wilson sighed.

'I mean if you were a woman like the one who has just left, wouldn't you do something about your weight?'

'Is that why you wouldn't give her the coffee?'

'She showed me her bottom,' said Wilson sadly, 'and there really was no call for it.'

Apart from which, he had wasted his time, or so he thought.

'Perhaps you better get onto the cash points first, find Connor, and see what turns up there. And Paula, seeing it's Monday morning, it might be time for your school interviews,' he said, but apparently she already knew it.

CHAPTER 23

NOW, DON'T FORGET, DADDY,' Rosie said before she got out of the car at the school, 'when you get into school, no running in the corridor, and a*lways* walk on the left.'

George said he would try to remember it.

'And remember, your left is on the other side when you turn round.'

George promised to think about it and possibly make sense of it.

The parents of the children involved with Foster were meeting at the school.

It took place in an empty classroom, so the children wouldn't feel they had been summoned for some kind of wrongdoing. That was the explanation offered by the head mistress, a twinkling women in a smart dark suit. She looked as if she knew a joke she was keeping to herself. This might have been due to her two prominent front teeth escaping over her top lip, or the small chairs accommodating roughly half an adult buttock.

The room was decorated with children's bright, optimistic drawings done mostly in crayon and pinned to the wall. The parents, George and Christine, Natasha and Lewis, and an older woman with a mass of grey hair, Emily's mother, didn't quite know where to sit until Lewis took charge and shifted some tables and arranged the chairs in a half-moon.

Emily's mother looked untidy, the sort of woman who probably wouldn't eat anything with eyes and considered her body a temple. She would have back-packed around the world in her younger days, a rucksack on her back, long skirts and sandals. She also looked tired, frazzled. Did she have a husband?

'Now,' twinkled the head mistress. Ann

163

Granger it said on a piece of paper pinned to her jacket. The parents knew her, of course, but not Constable Smith. 'What we have to remember is that children interpret events in a different fashion.'

'Stone me, who would have thought it,' whispered Lewis. Natasha poked him in the ribs.

'Yes?' twinkled Ann Granger.

'Different from us,' he said. 'To us,' he added, feeling he should be standing in a corner.

'Exactly. Children have a different criteria. Bear it in mind.'

Rosie came in first in her role of observer. She was told Constable Smith was a police officer.

'I knew that, she wears those clothes.'

She walked slowly up and down in front of them, hands on her back, feeling Very Important.

'She looks untidy,' whispered Christine. 'And I don't think the red uniform does anything for her. She looks washed out.'

'I lost my hair-clip,' Rosie announced. 'Sorry, Mum.'

'You look very nice. Now, Rosie, tell us what you saw in the playground on Friday morning,' said Ann Granger. Her direct approach took George by surprise. He had imagined the children would be asked about the playground over the last few weeks.

Rosie looked at the police woman, who, in George's opinion, could have been any age between fourteen and fifteen.

'I'm Paula,' said Constable Smith.

Rosie thought it was a funny name for her, more like a man's.

George coughed.

'I didn't see anything on Friday morning. I was playing with my friends. We played Matthew, Mark, Luke and John.'

'Ill show you,' she announced, stretched out her arms, stood on one leg, and pointed at WPC Smith.

Matthew, Mark, Luke and John
Hold my horse while I get on.
If he hollers,
Let him go ...

George coughed again.

'What I told Daddy,' Rosie broke off. 'The man in the beret wanted to talk to Hester. He went like that,' she made a beckoning gesture. 'Emily was going to talk to him, but then she said I'd forgotten my lunch-box and Daddy had brought it for me.'

She paused.

'He forgot to bring my interesting nature thing. In the winter, nature isn't very interesting, except when we get snow. Can I go now?'

'In a minute,' said Constable Smith. 'Now this is very important. You must never, ever go with this man,' she held up an enlarged photo of Foster. 'You must never get into a car with him, and if you see him, you must tell a grown up at once.'

Rosie nodded and left and Hester came in. Hester sucked her thumb. Lewis signalled for her to take it out. She gave him a little wave with her other hand. He nodded at her until he thought he should be a toy dog sitting in a car.

She finally got it.

'I didn't like him, the man by the playground,' she said. 'Him with the beret. My mummy has got a beret. I didn't want to play with him. I don't want to play with boys either, they're rough and fight. I don't really know how boys play with girls.' She paused. 'I expect I will find out when I'm older.'

'Stone me,' whispered Lewis.

'Why didn't you like the man in the playground?' asked Constable Smith.

'He looks like the man in the wardrobe.'

'Can you explain that to me?'

'When my mummy leaves the wardrobe door open it looks like a man is there. It's only her clothes and at night. But he's gone now, so that's all right.'

After Constable Smith's official warning, Hester gave her parents little wave and left. She was followed by Emily, who said the man by the playground had said it was a secret. She shrugged her shoulder. 'So, I can't tell. I'm not allowed, you see.'

'You can tell us now, Emily, we can all keep secrets,' said Constable Smith.

She threw her dark curls over her shoulders.

'I told him I didn't like this red school uniform. Gregory doesn't like it either.'

'Who is Gregory?'

'Gregory is my brother. He's twenty-four. The man said his name was Uncle Fred, and he said I could choose my own clothes if I wanted to. He wanted to know my name and who was meeting me from school. I told him about Natalie meeting me.' She shrugged her shoulders. 'Sometimes she is late. I told him that.'

Her mother gasped.

'I talked to him quite a lot,' she said proudly. 'He said he had a nice caravan by the seaside. There was another man behind him, but he always tied his shoelaces when the man talked to me. You fall over if you don't tie your shoelaces properly. I expect he wanted to speak to me as well, but I wouldn't have. He was there on Friday, and then Mr Hudson came with Rosie's lunch-box.'

She paused.

'Mr. Hudson shouted, "Emily, Rosie forgot her lunch-box" and threw it over the rails, so I took it to her, ' Emily continued. '

'Thank you, Emily,' thought George when everybody looked at him. His face momentarily froze, and Lewis thought, *Hello! George was there. George saw him, but he never mentioned it.*

'And the man behind him tying his shoelaces, did you recognise him?' asked Ann Granger.

'No,' Emily said, 'he wore an anorak with the hood down even when it wasn't raining.'

Thank God they didn't ask Rosie who was following Fred Foster, George thought. She might have said, 'It's Uncle Ritchie.'

He relaxed visibly, and Lewis, hearing his sigh, thought again, *Hello, what's going on?*

'I had no idea about Fred Foster,' George said after Emily, severely warned off Foster, had left. 'After I'd dropped off Rosie on Friday morning I picked up Mira, my secretary, for a meeting. She noticed Rosie had left her lunch-box in the car. I parked opposite the playground and looked for Rosie amongst the children so I didn't have to waste any time, I had to go back to the meeting. I threw the lunch-box to Emily, who was at the railings.'

The parents left the school and headed to their cars, WPC Smith stayed behind to question the playground attendant and then warn the children in a general assembly.

A few adults were loitering by the school entrance, and a flash-light went off.

'Good God,' said George, 'can this be the press already? How did they know? I'll tell them what they can do.'

He was about to tell them to bugger off, when Lewis took charge.

'What do you think is happening here?' he

asked them, stepping forward.

'We understand Fred Foster haunted this playground,' said a balding man with glasses. 'I mean you look like worried parents.'

'I'm very much afraid you have the wrong school,' said Lewis smoothly.

They looked at each other.

'Gregory said,' said one of them.

Emily's mother gasped.

'If only my husband was here,' she sighed.

'Where is he?'

Apparently he was on a fact-finding mission for 'Save The Children.'

Stone *me*, thought Lewis.

'Emily might be wilful, but she is never disobedient,' said her mother.

Fred Foster had earmarked a caravan for himself and Emily. If it had been for Hester, he wouldn't be able to speak. First things first, thought Lewis.

'We were here for an inter-school competition meeting which we, naturally, want our children to win, so we might look a bit worried, although this is an excellent school,' he announced.

The press, three tidy, well-dressed individuals departed, the heavens were about to open again, but before they did, George stopped and looked at Lewis.

'That was good,' he said admiringly. 'Or well good, as they say these days.'

'Think nothing of it,' said Lewis. 'I could lie for England, wouldn't you say, Natasha?'

'For the whole Western Hemisphere,' said Natasha, 'but for once I'm very grateful. I wonder why Gregory, who seems to be Emily's brother, tipped them off.'

That wasn't the only thing Lewis was

wondering about. *What's up with George*? he thought as they got into the car. The frozen face, the lengthy lunch-box explanation, the sigh of relief. He might find out more on Bonfire Night, if he was allowed to take Hester.

'Allowed to take her?' said Natasha who had got into the passenger seat through sheer force of habit, which annoyed her greatly, 'Have I ever stopped you from seeing Hester?'

They drove off to visit the police to inform them about Dr Willoughby's suicidal thoughts, although they had no idea if it would be helpful.

CHAPTER 24

'I THINK WE CAN SAFELY discount the Angel Mount Hotel and the Young Men's Christian Association Hostel, also B&B's with Saunas and whirlpools,' Wilson said after Constable Smith left for the school, closing the Yellow Pages, having let his fingers do the walking in a book rather than on a computer before checking possible hide-outs for Fred Foster. 'Do we include the ones in Rilsby and Great Barlow?'

'Fred Foster has a car, we know that,' said Cunningham.

'I must put it on the board. Do it now.' He got up. 'But as they're near, we'll include them.'

They dodged the rain and ran to the car.

'Things to do before I die,' said Wilson. 'I'd like to get the better of Constable Smith, just once.'

'Impossible,' said Cunningham.

'Oh?'

'She knows everything, or she thinks she does. But what she doesn't know she keeps quiet about; plus, she is a genius on a computer.'

'Best not to upset her then; she can deal with the surveillance tapes. I wish I was but...'

'you didn't come over on the banana boat.. and all that,' said Cunningham, parking on the forecourt of Sunny Hill B&B, which wasn't sunny or on a hill but hidden by an impressive array of shrubbery, a greenhouse adjoining the grey flint house. It was run by Mrs Hargreaves of Hengrave, better get it the right way round.

He pressed the doorbell.

'Oh, no, it's you again!' cried the woman who opened the door. She was a redhead, although it was a shade of red not usually seen in nature. She had lively eyes, but there was a downturn to the corners of her mouth. 'What do you want now?'

'Can we come in, Mrs Hargreaves?' said Wilson, 'unless you are about to water your son's cannabis plants in the greenhouse.'

'I thought they were tomato plants,' she said ushering them into a square hall.

'An easy mistake to make,' said Cunningham.

'Growing a few cannabis plants doesn't make my son into a drug baron,' she said. 'Have you come to tempt me with your good looks again?'

Wilson assumed she meant Cunningham, who smirked.

'What's Paul done now? He is a good boy to his mother.'

Aren't they all, Wilson thought, before he explained his mission.

'You're looking for a man going on for fifty,' she said, fetching the register. 'No can do. Actually, we never have single men in that age group. We have three young men working on the market development, they came in a fortnight ago. We also have an elderly couple wanting to sample Bury St. Edmund's lively culture.'

'If they can find it,' said Cunningham.

'Quite. Elderly couples stay here during this period. It's the seventy-five percent discount, see. They can drive themselves to distraction in a different environment.'

'It always helps,' said Wilson, who really didn't want to know. 'May I?' he asked, looking at the register, passing it to Cunningham. 'Johnnie Walker of Fort Williams.'

Footsteps overhead. A tall, thin youth with a mop of curly hair came lolloping down the stairs. 'Oh, no, it's the fuzz. You can just off-buzz.

He paused. ' Rhyming couplets. Interesting.'

'Oh, no, it's the fuzz.
You can just off-buzz.
Looks like I am a poet,
'And I never knew it.'

Having delivered his epic poem, he disappeared into the kitchen, judging by the smell of coffee wafting into the hall. He was last seen furtively depositing something in the kitchen waste-bin before going outside, pretending to put something into the dustbin. It was witnessed by Wilson and Cunningham who peered round the corner and retrieved a block of cannabis resin from the kitchen bin.

'After he's charged he'll be locked up until bail is set,' said Cunningham.

'I don't have money for bail,' cried his mother.

'Don't worry about that, Mum,' said Paul, tapping his nose, 'I have friends, and it won't come to that. Illegal entry and illegal search, see. Human Rights.'

Wilson nearly choked.

'I couldn't possibly operate in a prison environment. Eating meat, see. *'We are the living graveyard of animals.'* George Bernard Shaw, a fellow vegetarian.'

A laxative would take care of that, thought Wilson.

'You could leave me alone now.' He closed his eyes, presumably enjoying his high in peace, which was rudely interrupted by Wilson who asked him why he didn't think his mother had any human rights.

'Like what?'

'Like she shouldn't have to flog her guts out to keep you in idleness.'

'In a nation ruled by swine, all pigs are

upwardly mobile,' he said. 'Hunter S. Thompson.'

'The police have been called pigs before now, at least in prison you will have some time to make up your own, original quotes.'

Then he phoned the station. 'Hengrave, Sunny Hill B&B. Don't use the siren.'

He took Paul firmly by the arm. 'Paul Hargreaves, Under the Police and Criminal Evidence Act 1984, I'm arresting you for possession of illegal drugs. You do not have to say anything, but it may harm your defence if you do not mention when questioned something that you later rely on in court. Anything you do say may be given in evidence.'

'That's a lot to remember,' said Paul, closing his eyes.

'I would come clean about your friends, if I were you.'

'Ah, but you're not me,' said Paul, opening his eyes reluctantly. 'That's why we've got different names, see, but you're too good at your job.'

'Too good?' screamed his mother. 'You let a paedo loose and arrest my son for smoking a bit of cannabis.'

'I'm sorry, Mrs Hargreaves, but I suspect he's on something else. He's also dealing and he's now over eighteen,' said Wilson. He handed the block of cannabis resin along to the officer who arrived in a remarkably short time and cuffed Paul Hargreaves.

'Search him when you get to the station,' said Wilson, and then nodded upstairs. Cunningham and Connor rushed round the back with him where a figure was dangling from the sill of a first floor window and jumped, landing lightly on his feet.

'Sod it,' he said when he looked up. 'I ain't done nothing.'

'Quite,' said Wilson, 'that's why we're taking

you in. Turn round.'

'That's good stuff you planted on me,' he said sadly.

'Who shopped me?' he asked after he was cuffed.

'You shopped yourself. You should have used a different name when you booked in.'

'I did,' said Michael Ross of Felixstowe.

'You have used the 'Johnnie Walker of Fort Williams' routine once before. Remember?'

'I do now. How did you know I was here?'

'Pure luck,' said Wilson. 'We're looking for somebody else. And we heard footsteps. Now, let's see what you have under your jumper.'

Michael Ross wore a belt containing numerous small, sealed, bags of white powder, possibly coke, certainly not chalk.

Wilson time-travelled. He remembered a time when 'coke' was something people put on the fire, but that wasn't it.

'And 'a joint' was something women cooked on Sundays,' said Cunningham.

Wilson thought he might have mentioned it before as the police car left, sirens blaring, when Mrs Hargreaves came out, wielding a poker.

'Don't be silly,' he said quietly, going towards her. 'You don't want to be arrested for threatening a police officer, do you? He'll be back soon enough. You can pick yourself up again. You know you can.'

She lowered the poker and sat down on the nearest chair, sobbing broken-heartedly. 'I thought he was clean when I didn't smell it. How many more times? What we'll he get?'

'Ten years, but possibly he'll get away with wearing a bracelet.'

'Like a tagging thing? But he never goes

anywhere,' she wailed.

'It's out of my hands,' said Wilson. 'Can we look upstairs?'

She nodded. Cunningham went up and came down shortly.

'All the paraphernalia but nothing else,' he said

In the car, Wilson phoned the Super who had to be dragged out of a meeting, but agreed Paul Hargreaves and Michael Ross could be persuaded to give them a few names. He thought that the information could be helpful in springing the drug ring operating in Felixstowe, under investigation at the moment.

'It might be worthwhile if you can send the squad to the market development, the name does keep creeping up.'

'I will. Send them to Storwich, we'll deal with them there,' said the Super. 'Well done. I'll mention it at the meeting.'

'Sad really,' said Wilson, back in the car, 'husband clears off, wife tries her best to make ends meet, helps daughter through university who becomes too bloody good to speak to mother, and this happens. And he's a nice lad with a brain the size of Europe.'

Cunningham was surprised to hear it.'Not exactly the John Donne of East Anglia.'

'Certainly not,' said Wilson who didn't want to know. 'He's just too bloody idle to get his arse out of the house, employing it. And another thing, I didn't smell any pot either.'

'I used to dabble a bit. Pot, of course, at Uni, but I also tried heroin,' said Cunningham. 'I tried I once. Heroin is morphine based, you see, and once in the bloodstream, it reverts to morphine. Didn't do a thing for me.'

'But you only did it once?'

175

'Too true, I might have liked it better the second time.'

'Addicts obviously do. Stupidity seems to be a marketable commodity, according to the celebrities falling out of nightclubs with their bodies ageing before our very eyes. Better not mention your dabbling to anybody else in case you go far in your career,' said Wilson, now time-travelling into the future. 'I can see headlines. 'Chief Constable was drug user.'

'At least we have learned something,' said Cunningham, greatly cheered by his career prospects, 'single men in Fred Foster's age group rarely visit Bury St. Edmunds.'

Unless they were clergy. Two were visiting the Cathedral, staying in Rilsby, an aunt and her niece were visiting Cambridge but also stayed in Rilsby because it was cheaper, and the B&B at Great Barlow had no takers at all. Perhaps it was because the owners wouldn't reduce the tariff in the winter. 'Why should we?' the owners whined in unison. Wilson and Cunningham weren't really interested in their grievances, but at least they were served with some excellent coffee while they pretended to be absolutely fascinated.

Last on the list was '*Homeward Bound*' in Farn *Road*.

A Mr Warner was behind the desk.

'We have two men staying in that age group,' he said, looking at the register. 'One is a Michael Oliver, who came on Sunday, and we have a Mr Cole. Howard Cole. He booked in,' he leafed through the book, 'a fortnight last Friday.'

No good then, thought Wilson, when Mrs Warner came traipsing downstairs.

'We've also had an American couple and their little boy staying here, they've left very early this morning for Heathrow. They don't drink tea, Americans don't,' she said, 'but we've had some rare excitement last night.'

'Oh?'

'The parents put him to bed and the little boy screamed the place down. Something on the telly, I suppose. He was on the top floor, but we could hear him down here.'

'Who has the room next to him?'

'Howard Cole, as a matter of fact, he's from Cambridge, but he was out when it happened, he was having dinner with friends.'' She lowered her voice. 'He's going through a nasty divorce.'

Fred Foster paused on the half landing, hearing voices below him. He pulled the hood over his head. People booking in, no doubt.

Or perhaps not, he thought when he reached reception. It looked remarkably like Plain Clothes had arrived. A tall man, wearing a winter jacket and dark trousers. Where had he seen him before. A younger one looking like a model, was perfectly packaged, one of these bright sparks they employed these days.

'Ethan, that's the boy's name,' said Mrs Warner, 'was especially fond of Mr Cole. He wanted him when he came in last night, but Mr Cole said the boy needed his mother. He looked in on him in the lounge, and when he left, Ethan cried, "Mr. Cole!" It was pitiful to hear.' She looked up. 'Isn't that so? Mr. Cole?'

'Indeed,' he said, pausing briefly by the door, 'poor child.'

'I won't keep you, Mr Cole,' said Mrs Warner, 'but here's the address of the barber you wanted.'

'I'll have it later, he said, 'I need to keep an appointment.'

They watched him pad out.

'He's fussy about his haircuts,' explained Mrs Warner.

Fred Foster drove off. He felt a migraine coming on, the bloke was definitely a copper but it was the younger one he had seen at the Station. Now was the time for a sharp exit, but he couldn't bring himself to do it. Everything was working out nicely. It was a masterstroke, asking for a barber, it was bound to fool the plods.

'He wore trainers,' said Cunningham, 'but not everybody who wears trainers is Fred Foster.'

'Apart from which he booked in ages ago, he has friends he dines with, and he wants to know where he can get his hair cut, so he isn't wearing a wig.'

They were having a pint at *The Volunteer*. Food was only served until two, the barmaid said, but there was still time for an omelette.

'Omelette is French,' she said when she put them on the table. 'It means 'flat plate'.'

'Very aptly named, we had better get back to the station,' said Wilson to his DS after paying the bill. 'You can pretend to be our Technical Division and exercise your mastery of the computer with the CCTV tapes from the supermarkets.'

Back in his office, he looked at his notes and started to transcribe them onto the computer when Constable Smith came in. He turned round, leaving his fingers where they were. When he looked at the screen again, it was blank. 'Look what you've made me do!'

'May I? I've brought my report about the interviews at the school,' she said, coming over. 'I see what you've done.'

'Of course,' said Wilson.

'Just minute,' she said. He shifted in his seat, she pressed a few keys, and Hey Presto, the screen was restored.

'I would back it up, but I am too busy,' he said, 'perhaps you better do it.'

His talent laid more with delegating than with computers, so he 'phoned Nicholson.

'If I were you,' said the Super.

*B*ut you're not, that's why we have different names. I'm mentally quoting Paul Hargreaves, he thought, surprised.

'Right you are, Sir,' he said.

'If I were you, I would view the surveillance footage we received from the supermarkets.'

'We have made a start,' said Wilson, 'but there are four supermarkets within roughly the same distance, I also have Constable Smith's report, (he looked at it) where Fred Foster was seen near a school. Apparently, he was grooming a little girl. He said he would take her to the seaside. Three girls saw him, and they identified him from the news bulletins.'

'I'll get in touch with Forensic,' said the Super, 'and see if they have matched Foster's DNA with the old fabric in Devon.'

Wilson left his office, leaving the officers' reports on his desk. His mind on still on Fred Foster and nasty divorces.

'Have you ever heard of nice divorces?' he asked Dorothy, his partner, over a dinner of cottage pie.

'I wouldn't know,' said Dorothy, a tall and slim woman in her late forties, with dark hair and brown eyes and an up-turned mouth, 'given that I have never been divorced. Or married, for that matter.'

Neither did Wilson. He was a widower when he met Dorothy.

'Do you want to get married?'

Dorothy said it wasn't the most romantic proposal she'd had, but, no, she didn't.

'We don't want to spoil what we've got,' said Wilson, hugely relieved, when the dog made his daily appearance, walking slowly into the room with his head down.

'Out, Ralph!' commanded Wilson. 'Dogs are not allowed at the dinner table.'

Ralph lifted his head and looked at him, astonished to hear this.

He turned round, looked at the ground where he saw the perfect spot before him, the very spot he had looked for all day. He slowly circled it three times and sank down. Unfortunately, his nose pointed towards the kitchen. He shuffled round slowly until he faced them, looked at Wilson accusingly, sighed and stretched out with his head between his paws.

'He does it every time, that dog is compulsive obsessive or something,' Wilson said, poking his plate. 'What's in this pie?'

'Aubergines,' said Dorothy. 'A little boy brought it in for 'Interesting Things In Nature' day. He said, and I quote, "It's an oboejean, Miss." I asked him what was interesting about it, and he said, "It looks like a black man's willie, please Miss."'

'What did you say to him?' Wilson asked after the merriment died down.

'I called our 'Next',' she said. 'All the kids gasped and covered their eyes, but I can safely expect drawings containing phallic imagery.'

'I shall remain non-committal and not say he should be so lucky. Some fed-up parent put him up to it.'

Dorothy agreed, but the four seasons were inexplicably on the curriculum. 'The children's general consensus was '*that nature is good for you* ', so I took the aubergine home and made a cottage pie. Some people might call it a Moussaka.'

The Greek had a word for it, but that wasn't it, Wilson thought. He said it was very nice. He smuggled some of it to the dog in the kitchen, who looked at it, rolled his eyes and started barking at his dish. Traitor.

'A nasty divorce,' he said much later sitting up in bed, explaining the situation. 'Should I pursue it?'

'You might actually experience it,' said Dorothy giving him the fish eye, 'if you were married.'

He turned out the light, but he couldn't sleep.

It wasn't the divorce mentioned in connection with Howard Cole, something else in the back of his mind kept him from sleep. Dorothy slept beautifully, hardly breathing, until she turned over and began to snore lightly.

Below, the dog grumbled in his sleep. Wilson got out of bed, donned his dressing gown and padded downstairs. Until the case was finished, he would be lucky to grab two or three hours sleep, he thought, when the 'phone rang.

'Yes,' he said, taking it into the conservatory.

'It's me, Dad. Just wanted to know how you were.'

'Heather,' he said to his daughter, 'it's one o'clock in the morning.' New Zealand was twelve hours ahead, so he was talking to her in the future.

'Sorry,' she said.'

'We are well,' he said, 'anyway, how are you?'

'Oh, *anyway*, is it? I wonder how my dad is. I bother to lift the phone and it's "anyway." Are you and Dorothy married yet?'

'No,' he said. 'We had an in-depth discussion about it this evening, as a matter of fact, and we

181

decided against it.'

One good thing about Heather was that she made him feel so tired, he forgot all about his case while he wondered why she couldn't be happy. He found a blanket and fell asleep on the settee.

Something licking his hands woke him up. He opened his eyes and stared back at a pair of large brown eyes. Ralph was looking at him, resting his golden head on the settee, inches from his face.

The dog barked and wagged his tail, excited to see he was still alive. Well somebody was, as Dorothy had left for work, she left a note for him.

'I hope I didn't snore. Sorry I didn't listen to you, will do tonight. Ralph has been out and had his breakfast. Won't disturb you.
Love D.

God, it was nearly nine o'clock. And then it hit him.

Cunningham was at the station, the desk sergeant said when he telephoned.

'Fetch him.'

'Cunningham.'

'Take two uniformed officers and go to '*Homeward Bound*'. Arrest Howard Cole.'

'On what charge?'

'Anything you can think of. He's Fred Foster. I'll explain later, and use the siren to get past the morning traffic.'

He put the phone down. 'How could I have been so stupid?' he asked the dog, who neither knew nor cared; he just wagged his tail and looked meaningfully up from his dish to Wilson, hoping he could wangle another breakfast.

CHAPTER 25

FRED FOSTER WAS PUT OUT. He had a terrible night, his hand had throbbed and his brain was working overtime. At three o'clock, he was standing at the window, looking over the streets at *"The Volunteer*, ghostly in the yellow street light.

If it wasn't for the three men who attacked him in the lane on Friday, he would be safe in *The Flats*, getting Emily ready for a caravan trip to Clacton, and then on with his plan.

It was his own fault; he was acting on impulse.

He ought to have resisted the urge to terrify the American kid, and now he would have to pay for it, delicious as it had been. The police weren't stupid. 'When he left, little Ethan cried out for him. It was pitiful.' Mrs. Warner's words would penetrate their skull eventually.

It wasn't pitiful, it was accusing.

He couldn't wait for night to end. When morning finally broke into a grey, drizzly day, he heard next door's occupier stirring.

He looked at the card he had pocketed. Michael Oliver, 21 Gloucester Road, Stroud, Wiltshire.

Could he get used to yet another identity? he wondered as he packed his few belongings. His ten-thousand, in fifties, were untouched in a large padded envelope. He also had the money from the fat woman's Visa card. *Life wasn't all bad*, he thought, going downstairs for his breakfast where he was the dining room's sole occupier.

He had a feeling he was in for some heavy driving, so he got Mrs Warner to bandage his hand. Back upstairs, he wondered if he was panicking for nothing when he heard sirens blaring. He thought it might be a police car stuck briefly in the traffic.

He rushed downstairs with his bag.

'Why Mr Cole, are you leaving us already?' asked Mrs Warner, barring his way. 'Will you return?'

'Most likely,' he said.

The sirens were getting louder.

'Let me know when, so I can keep your room for you. In the meantime, can I have our keys back?' she asked.

The sirens were getting nearer.

'Bitch, piss off,' he said.

'And just who do you think you're talking to?' Mr Howard asked, standing right behind him.

He turned round and hit him in the face with the keys before he chucked them onto the floor, and while Mrs Warner bent down to pick them up, he kicked her, hard. 'Why don't you .....'

He didn't finish the sentence, but it was nothing to do with swearing indicating a limited mind. He rushed out of the house and to his car where he started the engine and drove out, passing a police car driving in.

He joined the traffic, turned left at the junction and parked in the car park of 'The Volunteer,' deserted bar a couple of staff cars, where he watched the B&B's driveway with interest.

The police weren't stupid, but he was clever, that was the difference. He was expected to clear off, so he would stay put. He would get rid of the wig and the glasses and book in somewhere where they would least expect him to.

His hand felt a lot better, Mrs. Warner had put some anti-septic cream on it and bandaged it well; and so she should, given that he hadn't used up his pre-paid days at the B&B yet. He waited until the police car came out of the B&B's driveway, started the car and drove off.

The landlady was traumatised and in the care of WPC Smith.

'Why exactly did he assault you?' Wilson asked her.

'I wanted my door keys back,' she said. 'We can't have strangers walking about with our keys.'

'And did you get them?'

'He threw them on floor,' she said. 'He kicked me, and I fell down when I picked them up.

Wilson had pressed her to bring charges for assault, but she was horrified.

'And have him threatening me when I'm out and about? What could *you* do about it?'

'So, why did you say he booked in a fortnight ago?' he asked Mr Warner, who was developing a nasty eye.

'It was in the book. Apparently, he signed in when he reserved the room. I work as a Supervisor for supermarkets, you see, and I'm not always here. As a matter of fact, I'm off today to Felixstowe. Well, tomorrow. I'll drop my wife off at her sister's in Great Yarmouth and close the B&B.'

He sighed.

'I'll get a team of cleaners in and put it on the market, it was running at a loss anyway. My wife will have to find something else to keep her occupied.' He sighed again. 'He seemed quite ordinary; nothing weird about him,' he added. 'The Americans liked him. I expect you'll want their address.'

'Still in mid-air, I expect, with a traumatised child,' said Cunningham. 'We'll get in contact later.'

Wilson nodded.

Foster might be many things but never ordinary, and he was also clever, he added.

'Looking early for a bolt hole and asking for a

barber were master strokes, it put me right off his scent,' he said. 'I've sent the glass he used to forensics for dusting, by the way, but I'm certain it's him. If you would be good enough to call at the station later with the address of the Americans. We might also have Foster on a CCTV tape for your identification, Mr. Warner, and you will also have to make a statement.'

'What made you think it was him?' asked Cunningham when they left the B&B.

'Mrs Foster told me Foster liked to terrify children. So when Mrs Warner said the little boy had been terrified and he had cried, "Mr Cole," I think what he actually said was, " It's Mr. Cole." I recalled Foster had the room next to the boy, the room where the screams came from. Foster must have paid him a visit, but it didn't come to me until this morning.'

'Foster probably went out unnoticed in the general commotion and came back later, spinning some tale about dining with friends,' said Cunningham.

Wilson stopped by his car. 'If only it had come to me earlier, but I'm always like that. *Staircase Wit*, Dorothy calls it, I always get the punchline of a joke hours later.'

'Probably in the middle of the night and start laughing in the dark. My ex used to do that and I took it personally,' Cunningham said sadly.

'We'll have to use our brains and start thinking like Fred Foster. What's the unlikeliest place he will go to ground in?'

Fred Foster was about to drive onto the car park in front of the Angel Mount Hotel when he noticed the inspector and his sidekick getting out of their car, walking towards the hotel. He drove on, past the cathedral, turned round and drove through and out of Bury St. Edmunds towards Cambridge, when it occurred to him he did have somewhere to go.

He turned round and drove back to Bury St. Edmunds. He parked his car in a side street and walked to *The Flats*.

A locksmith's van was in front of it with a uniformed policeman, so he retraced his steps, got his car and drove back to *'The Volunteer'*. In the heat of the moment, he'd clean forgotten the duplicate keys of the B&B he had made, he intended to use them once he knew the Warner's plan.

He ordered a pint and got on the mobile he had finally bought. 'My wife and I are planning to visit Bury St. Edmunds with our little girl,' he said after ringing the B&B's number. 'I'd like to make a reservation for a double room with a small bed for a child.'

He closed the 'phone, well satisfied; the B&B was closing down. When he asked for a recommendation elsewhere, Mr Warner told him to look it up himself if it wasn't too much trouble.

He drove into town and bought another set of clothes from a charity shop, a polo neck, trousers and jacket in a dinghy brown. He paid, and then asked if they had a hat.

The woman, some stupid bitch called Lena, (she told him) telephoned upstairs to enquire, but with no luck. He asked her if she had ever heard of stock control, whereupon she asked him if he wanted to volunteer in the shop.

He went to B&Q and bought a torch. Later, he treated himself to fish and chips, which he ate in the car, watching the B&B. He waited until the guests and the Warners drove away.

It was getting dark when he parked behind the deserted B&B. Next, the number plate. He smeared some dirt on it and let himself into the house where he went upstairs in the dark and fell over a chair and then onto the bed.

George had forgotten to put his dustbins out the night before. It was black bin day. When he wheeled it out before he left for work, he noticed it was overflowing.

George, who was keen on recycling, thought that he would have to have a word with Christine about sorting refuse into their proper bins, put the small bag with the watch and signet ring on top. Thank God, he thought, they are finally gone, all we've got to do now is burn Paul Willoughby's shoes and shirt, before he drove to work.

The dustman, or refuse operative, also noticed the bin was overflowing.

I'm not emptying that, he thought, I'm not doing my back in for anybody. When a package fell out, he thought there might be something nice in there for his partner. He wanted to make up for his loss of temper although it was her fault for annoying him. He thumped the van, which drove off to next door.

It wasn't such a good day for George after all.

Nonetheless, Mira, his secretary, thought it was hilarious when PC Connor appeared in his workshop. George was bending over a plan, explaining something to Mira, who was sitting to his right at her computer.

'What have you found out?' he said, after the introductions.

'There's nothing new concerning Fred Foster,' said Connor. 'I'm here on a different matter. It concerns fly-tipping in the woods on the Thelford Road, just before you leave Bury St. Edmunds. Last Saturday, about seven o'clock.'

'Yes?' said George, straightening up, his heart beating like a drum. 'How does this concern me? Or the police?'

Mira stifled a giggle, and then started to laugh.

'You think Mr. Hudson is a fly-tipper? That's the funniest thing I ever heard. He is tidiness personified. If you have some nut dropping rubbish, I'm afraid you have to look elsewhere. He actually keeps *his car* in the garage. Apart from which, the Hudsons hosted a dinner party on Saturday night.'

'The problem is not Mr Hudson as such, he isn't the fly tipper,' said Connor. *'He might have seen* who the fly-tipper was. He was seen walking a small dog and parking his car by the road. The man who reported it made a note of Mr Hudson's licence number.'

'A small dog?' George, said, completely mystified. I was burying a dead man, he thought, and I was dragging a spade. On the other hand, it had been raining and it was dark;so a nosy parker had been determined to see something and had probably made five when he put two and two together.

'I haven't got a small dog,' he said. 'I used to have a boxer dog, but that was before I was married.'

'And you were not in the vicinity?'

'Actually, now you come to mention it, I was. I went to see my father who lives in sheltered housing in Thelford. On my way back, I stopped and had a cigarette somewhere on the Thelford road. It might have been by the spot you describe, or it might not, but I didn't leave my car.'

Thank God I visited Dad, he thought. Double Thank God. How else could he have explained his presence?

'George visited his father after a falling-out, so naturally he was shook up, emotional, you know, and he wanted to collect himself,' said Mira importantly, 'because he was throwing a dinner party at his house and had to play the host.'

She had strong features that, illumined by the overhead florescent strip-light, became unattractive. 'My sister and I attended.'

Treble Thank God that Mira could vouch for him, but it was worrying. Before long, they would shift the rubbish, and then what? More visits from the police? Burials? Inquests? Natasha and Hester in tears?

'Isn't fly-tipping the Council's job? You'd think the police had more important things to do with all the goings-on on with Fred Foster,' said Mira primly, pursing her mouth.

'It ties in with a line of inquiry we are pursuing,' said Connor, he had no idea what that might be, but it always sounded good. 'We get all sorts of calls,' he added, 'we also have a report of a torch and a wheelbarrow gone missing and then returned on the allotments, would you believe.'

Mira thought it was hysterical, in contrast to George, although he pretended it was the funniest thing he had heard since.. but try as he might, the funny side of human nature escaped him completely.

CHAPTER 26

'DADDY,' SAID ROSIE ON Wednesday morning, looking at George over the cereal packets at the breakfast table.

'Yes?'

'Why is a bonfire called a bonfire?'

'What do you mean?'

'A fire is just *a fire* in the fireplace, but when it's in the garden it's called a bonfire. Why?'

'Good question, Rosie,' said George.

Rosie wasn't fooled.

'You don't know!' she said triumphantly. 'Do you know, Mummy?'

'What?' said Christine. She was busy working out how many people were coming to the party. Right, twenty-nine people equalled twenty-nine potatoes. 'Twenty-nine,' she said, 'better include us, that's thirty-two.'

'Good God,' said George.

'I've asked the neighbours as well, I think.'

'Why does no-one ever listen to me?' asked Rosie, so Christine promised to look it up later on.

'Emily is coming with Rosie straight from school,' she said to George. 'Her mother and I arranged it over the 'phone last night.'

Rosie hoped Emily would bring clothes to change into, it wouldn't be right to go to a party in a school uniform she said to her father, who had the day off, and was walking her to school.

'I'll come in the car for you and Emily tonight, and be sure to wait for me,' he said, bending down and kissing her. He watched her skipping up to the school and being counted in by the head mistress. Rosie put her heart and soul into everything she did. She had a zest for life, long may it last.

Several cars hooted at him as he walked down the road. Windows were lowered with shouts of 'see you tonight.'

When he got back, he changed his clothes and went outside. He was chopping up pallets for the fire and building them up into a pyramid shape, when Alf turned up.

'Where did you get those pallets from?'

'From the pallet shop,' said George, putting down his axe. 'And what are you clutching in your hot little hand?'

Two hands, actually. Alf was dragging what looked like half a tree across the lawn.

'It's from our greengage tree,' he explained,' and Margaret wants me to get rid of it. You are welcome to it. I've got the clothes, you know, for burning.' He wiped his face and looked up. The sky was dark; the heavy drizzle would soon give way to a proper downpour.

'We'll use paraffin,' said George, prepared like a good boy scout. They drenched the clothes with it, the clothes nestling in the middle of the banked-up wood.

'A fire needs air to burn,' said Alf wisely.

'A fire doesn't need water,' said George, 'and I think that's what we'll have. I'll build and you chop.'

It might have been better the other way round, thought George after mentioning he had a visit from the police about alleged fly-tippers on the road to Thelford.

'Some fool took my licence number and reported it to the police. Fortunately, I had been to see Dad and could explain why I was sitting in my car at that particular time in that god-forsaken spot.'

Alf dropped the axe, clutched the area in the middle of his chest and declared he would be glad when he had enough. He didn't say what of, but apparently that time hadn't yet arrived. Although

Christine did, tripping along daintily, leaving imprints on the wet grass.

'A bonfire takes its name from the Latin for 'bone', apparently it means 'purging of the soul when attached to fire',' Christine said, 'that is, after you die, obviously.'

Just what George had wanted to hear.

'Very interesting, I'm sure,' said Alf. 'Look, there's Ritchie.'

'Newsflash,' said Ritchie importantly.

George looked at Alf, who looked back at him and shrugged his shoulders.

'Go on, Ritchie.'

'Foster has been hiding in a B&B in Farn Road in Bury St. Edmunds, *'Homeward Bound.'* It's just up the road. They were going to arrest him THIS MORNING!'

'What do you mean *were*?'

'They missed him by minutes.'

Alf wondered if Christine would ever leave, but she did, eventually. He was dying to unload his knowledge.

'It was him in the Volunteer when we did that quiz,' said Alf. 'I knew I recognised the trainers, a sort of black what-you-call-it pattern. Chevron, that's it! So where is he now?'

CHAPTER 27

FRED FOSTER WAS in the deserted B&B's kitchen.

The cupboard was well-stocked with tins of sardines, tinned tomatoes, anchovies and peaches, and some eggs were shortly going bad in the fridge.

He debated switching on the electrics and doing a fry-up when he heard a car drawing up. He leaned over the sink, opened the window very slightly, in case he needed to make a quick exit. Then he ran upstairs and paused on the first landing, peering round the banisters.

Two women had been dropped by the back door. They came in, chatting, discussing switching on the electrics and the water. Cleaners. The Warners certainly didn't waste any time, he thought. He was put out. Somebody would have to pay for it, and they would.

'Get on with it,' he muttered up in his room, stowing his belongings in the wardrobe, putting on his anorak and trainers, getting his wallet, and opening the door.

He crept down the stairs, listening.

The cleaners were in the dining room facing the front, discussing TV. Bruce Bloody Forsyth, would you believe. Was that ugly sod still alive, he wondered.

'They're having the estate agents in tomorrow morning,' said one of them.

Now *that* was worth knowing.

'Not wasting any time, are they? But who will want a bloody great place like this?

'It's a lovely house; I wouldn't mind having a room to myself. I could watch all the soaps without *Himself* foaming at the mouth. Who is handling it? Is it that posh one?'

'I didn't know there was a posh one .When are they

changing the locks?'

'This afternoon, Mr Warner said, that's why we're here this morning. Let's go out the back and have a fag, Ivy.'

He gently closed the dining room door and raced to the back door and to his car. It started first time. He drove swiftly down the drive and joined the traffic.

'Was that a car, Ivy?'

'No, it can't be, nobody is here, so we can have a fag right here.'

'Better not, let's go outside. I can't smoke inside. I do believe I've been brain washed,' said Ivy. 'What if he's hiding on the top floor? They have bloody great wardrobes, so let's not do the top floor and do a runner.'

At two o'clock, Robert Watson closed his shop 'KEYS CUT WHILE U WAIT' in the Arcade. He popped into the barber's next door with his toolbox. 'Won't be long,' he said. If anybody was locked out, they would just have to wait a bit.

He debated fixing the board with his business particulars onto his white van. It was not worth it, he decided, he wouldn't be that long. In any case, he was going out tonight, and Rosemarie wasn't keen on being chauffeured around in van advertising his work.

The B&B was about ten minutes drive away. He parked in front of the house on the drive, opened the car door and walked to the front door with his toolbox. He started working on the locks, when he heard his mobile ringing faintly.

Blast, he had left it in the van

He leaned on the van roof when he answered it.

It was Rosemarie. She said that she was sorry for being so bad-tempered, was he still seeing her tonight?

'Of course, everybody has bad days,' he said.

It started to rain, and a man in an anorak with the hood pulled down was walking towards him.

'Sorry love, I'll have to go,' he said and closed the phone.

The man looked familiar.

'I'm Howard, from *Home About*, the estate agents,' the man said. He was maybe in his late forties, tidy-looking.

'Yes?'

'The Estate Agents. Mr Warner asked me to pick up the new house key from you. We're measuring the house up for sale tomorrow morning.'

Robert looked at him doubtfully. Just where had he met him?

'Sorry, mate, I can't. He gave me strict instructions to give the key to the manager.'

'I am the manager.'

'In that case you've had a sex change, mate,' said Rob. 'I'm ringing the police.'

Several things happened in quick succession. He was flung into the hedge, the man got into the van, drove past the house and turned round. Robert was up and blocking his path, arms outstretched, when the van accelerated.

He just about jumped clear. He still had his mobile, and this time he did phone the police. He still had his tools, thank god, but his van was gone. Rosemarie would be mad as hell.

'How the hell did Foster know the locks were being changed this afternoon?' asked Wilson, but first things first. He would interview Robert Watson, who told him the man coming up the drive had seemed familiar.

'He wanted the key to the house, he said he was

the estate agent's manager. Only the manager is a woman, so I didn't give it to him. He knocked me over and drove off with my van. What am I going to do without my van?'

Wilson said he would get Tomlinson onto it.

'Anyway,' Watson continued, 'afterwards, I realised it was the same man who had come into my shop a few days ago to have a spare key cut for his house. His so-called house, as it turns out. He wanted another key because his wife had lost hers, he said.'

After his interview, Watson was shown the CCTV footage of a man walking to the cash point on the market. He had been spotted by Connor, who had blown up the image of the man's face.

'That's him,' he said, pointing to the image of Fred Foster, alias Howard Cole, retrieved from the HSBC footage, also previously identified by Warner of *Homeward Bound.*'

'Bugger's wearing my hat,' Warner had said, put out about losing his hat would you believe, after all that had happened to him.

'Nought as queer as folk,' Wilson's dad used to quote; 'there's only me and thee, and I have my doubts about thee.'

After Watson had written a witness statement and was driven in a police car to finish changing the locks on the B&B, Wilson picked up the phone and talked to Mr Warner, who was in Great Yarmouth with his wife. Actually, he held the receiver away from his ear, marvelling at Warner's inventive use of a basic four-letter word.

He got the address of the cleaning women and sent Cunningham to bring them in for interviews and statements. As it turned out, they had been in the house. They had been talking about estate agents and locks being changed.

'So, Foster might have been in the house at the time,' Wilson concluded, which didn't exactly cheer them up when they left.

'Next, the urgent report about joy-riders from our colleagues from Thelford. Kids drive twenty miles and then set fire to a car. So how are they getting home? Any kids missing overnight? Perhaps you can go and see this lady tonight whose Lexus was stolen,' Wilson said to Cunningham, giving him the address.

'Unless you intend to celebrate Bonfire Night, although I don't know why anybody should celebrate Guy Fawkes's intention to blow up parliament. There's far too much blowing up these days.'

'We celebrate his failure to blow it up,' said Constable Smith, right on cue.

Right, history it was, when he retired, Wilson thought. But before that, he had to find Foster, who had been sighted in Bristol, according to the papers. What they didn't know they made up

The van.

Where would Foster hide it? You could hide a blade of grass in a meadow, so he had a word with Tomlinson who organised Traffic to search the streets.

Fred Foster cursed his luck. He was driving the white van badly with crashing gears, signalling right instead of left and reversing with difficulty into one of the remaining spaces in the nearest car park. He would have to walk back to his own car he had left in the car park of 'The Volunteer'.

His plan had been a non-starter from the word go. He had intended to get the key and have a spare one cut in "While U Wait," except the bloke from the shop was the very one who was changing the locks of the B&B and had recognised him.

He retrieved his car, drove to the B&B and

parked behind the house.

Trying to keep him out of *his* house, the bloody nerve, he thought, as he squeezed through the kitchen window onto the sink. When he peered out of the dining room window, a police car drew up in front of the house. Another car drew up, and a bloke with a bag of tools emerged.

The copper waited and chatted to the bloke who was finishing of changing the lock to the front door.

Foster hid in the pantry when the front door opened. He listened as the tools clattered and voices chattered, 'They want a strong safety chain fitted.' Would the copper walk round the back and see his car?

'Kitchen window's open, I'll close it,' a voice said. 'Are you finished?' The front door shut and the kitchen window had been closed, Foster saw when he emerged silently from the pantry, where he also noticed keys hanging up on a peg on the inside of the pantry door , keys to the garage and to the back door.

He was in a cold fury when he went upstairs to change his clothes. He was kept out of *his house*!

He had been crossed once too often.

Somebody would have to pay for it, he thought as he changed into his smart clothes, and he put his hat on as she had recognised him wearing it; that somebody was Emily Watson.

CHAPTER 28

IT WAS RAINING QUITE HARD when Fred Foster parked his car near the school. People were scurrying to get out the rain heads down, they wouldn't notice him, but Emily Watson did. She was standing by a teacher when he motioned to her. She waved and said something to her teacher who looked at him briefly and Emily ran towards him.

Ann Granger had been told by Emily he was her brother, Gregory. He had looked smart enough, but something about him worried her. The teacher looked after her and turned her attention elsewhere.

'Hurry up, Emily,' he said. 'You don't want to get wet.'

He opened the car door and almost threw her in the car, that wasn't very nice, and then he drove off very fast.

Rosie watched Emily walk off with the bad man, her mouth wide open. She couldn't believe it. Her daddy had told her the bad man was gone, and here he was. Well, I'm not going to talk to my daddy ever again, she thought, he tells lies, she thought, when he drew up and walked towards her.

'Hello, darling. Where's Emily, Miss Granger?' he asked, turning to the teacher.

'Mrs Granger.' she said. 'Emily was picked up by her brother a minute ago.'

She had watched Emily holding his hand, looking up at him and skipping along happily, she said.

'That is strange, she was supposed to come home with Rosie and me, but if you're quiet sure, we'll leave,' George said. 'Come along, Rosie. Did you have a nice day?'

'I'm not talking to you,' she said going to the

car and getting in, 'so there.'

'All right, but before you fold your arms in a strop, fasten your seat belt.'

Emily wasn't very happy. It was raining hard, the windscreen wipers were going swish, swish, swish.'Could you please stop,' she said, 'I can't do my seat belt up.'

'So?' he said. He sounded cross. 'You've been a very bad girl. You've been telling people about me. It was our secret.'

'I never did,' she said.

'Well, somebody did.'

'Well, it wasn't me, cross my heart and hope to die.'

'Did you tell them about the seaside and the caravan?'

'No, I didn't. I can't do my seat-belt up.'

He swore and said it didn't matter.

She thought about her new pink skirt and pink top with sparkly bits in her bag. She thought about fireworks red and yellow and green in the sky, and sparklers.

She thought about having a good time eating potatoes straight from the bonfire and playing with Rosie.

She had made a big, big mistake falling out with Rosie and pretending to the teacher Gregory was picking her up so she wouldn't have to go with her, but everybody made mistakes. Gregory said so. And how could she know *he* was a bad man when he turned up for her?

Perhaps if she asked him nicely, he would let her go.

'I think I have changed my mind, my friend Rosie is waiting for me,' she said politely. 'Can you please turn round? I made a mistake.'

She wasn't the only one.

He had turned onto the A14 automatically and was heading towards Cambridge, crawling with slow-moving evening traffic. It was some time before he found a slip road and turned back, towards Bury St. Edmunds and then onto the road to Clacton. He had planned to get to the caravan before Emily's absence was discovered, not driving along aimlessly in this fucking rain.

'Don't you want to go to the seaside?' the man said finally.

'I do. Have you got my passport?'

'Passport?

Every year Emily had four weeks holiday in a villa in Portugal with her father. That was the seaside.

'You need a passport to go on a plane,' she said, ' and you are going the wrong way now. You have to go where its says Stanstead. It's got a little plane on the sign.'

The bad man swore. 'Stop bleeding kicking me in the back,' he said.

Emily had put her legs out, trying to stop herself careering about on the backseat. She sat as still as she could on her seat.

She was feeling very small, clutching her backpack. She had known only goodness in her short life. Bad men were on television. When she was frightened of them Gregory said he would go and beat them up, but now it gradually dawned on her that she was in a car with a very bad man, a nasty man. He didn't care if her seat belt was done up or not, he didn't care about a passport for the seaside and he was on the wrong road, and *he swore at her*.

Oh, dear, she thought.

She waved at people in passing cars, but it was

getting dark, and the man told her to stop or she would be sorry. They didn't notice her because of the very bad weather. Oh dear. She had been a naughty girl. Willful. That's what came of it. Her mummy would be cross. She thought of her brother.

'My big brother Gregory will come and beat you up.'

'He'll never find me. Nobody will ever find you.'

She thought about it for a long time. Gregory always found her when they played hide-and seek, once she had fallen asleep behind the settee and he had found her. 'Hide, Emily, hide!' he urged her, but where could you hide in car?

After an hour's driving, the red light came on in Fred Foster's car. He needed petrol. 'Don't you dare move,' he said when the car stopped at a petrol station. She nodded.

He walked round the car and swore. He had stopped too far out and he couldn't reach the pump.

'Move back a bit, mate,' he said to the car that had drawn up behind him.

'What? Do you want me to shift the pumps for you?'

'Want to make anything of it?'

The bad man stopped arguing, the car reversed and stopped, he put petrol in, and then he came and opened her door. 'Don't you dare move,' he said again.

CHAPTER 30

WHEN THEY GOT HOME, Rosie gave her mother a kiss and her father a filthy look before she stomped up to her room and slammed the door.

'Where's Emily?' asked Christine. 'I thought you were picking her up.'

'There's been a change of plan. According to Miss Granger, sorry, *Mrs*. Granger, the Head, her brother Gregory, Emily said, picked her up. The girls must have fallen out, but it isn't my fault, although Rosie thinks it is.'

'She's skipped a few years and turned into a teenager by the sound of the slamming door,' said Christine. 'Let her stew for a bit, Rosie can't be quiet for long.'

When George went upstairs to change his clothes, he looked in on Rosie who sat on her bed, chin resting on her folded arms.

'Do you want to tell me what's wrong?'

She gave him a wounded look.

He shut the door quietly and went out to the garage, preparing some empty bottles for the rockets. It was tanking down outside. Was there anything worse than standing in the cold and rain watching a few fireworks go off? all those people with dirty shoes tramping into the house? he said to Christine when he came in.

She smiled. He always grumbled beforehand when they entertained and then he enjoyed himself, whereas she looked forward to it and was glad when everybody went home.

'We won't be eating until later, so we'll have sandwiches about five,' she said. 'I expect Madam will be joining us.'

It was getting dark already. He laid a fire in the

dining room, lit the fire in the living room, drew the curtains and got down to the crossword when Christine called him. 'Ready.'

'Rosie, tea,' she shouted up the stairs.

Rosie was put out. She hadn't said a word for about forever, and nobody cared. What's more, she had a bad feeling that she should have done.

'Good, ham,' she said, sitting at the table, picking up her sandwich. 'Emily wouldn't like it, Emily likes pizzas.'

Then she burst into tears.

'Just tell us what's bothering you. God's sakes,' said George. 'We'll try to make it better.'

'You tell lies,' she sobbed, pointing a shaking finger at him. 'You said the bad man had gone, but he hasn't. He did that thing with his hand and Emily went away with the bad man.'

His stomach clenched and time stood still.

'I didn't tell you a lie, Rosie,' he said. 'I thought he had gone. I don't know everything.'

He looked at Christine, who moved her lips in silent prayer.

'Rosie, listen carefully, did Emily go off with her brother like she told Mrs. Granger?'

'No, she didn't. It wasn't her brother like she said, it was the bad man.'

She took a shuddering breath

'We fell out because I played with Hester. Emily said Hester was stupid and I said she wasn't, and then she said she wouldn't come to my stupid party if Hester was my best friend, and she said Gregory was picking her up, but he couldn't, could he? because he didn't know. She was supposed to come home with me. I watched her go off with the bad man and I couldn't tell you because you said he was gone.'

'Dear God, please look after this child,' whispered her mother.

'Eat your sandwich, Rosie,' said her father gently. 'Mummy and me will have to do some telephoning.'

They left the room, but Rosie didn't feel hungry.

'Whatever happens, and God willing nothing will, Rosie must not be made to feel guilty for not telling us,' said George,' she's far too young to carry that sort of guilt.'

Guilt had already crept into their souls. Why didn't I make an effort and get to the bottom of Rosie's strop? he thought, like Christine.

'I'll 'phone the police,' he said. 'And then we decide who is next.'

'Emily's mother will have to be told, but what in God's name made her go with him? She was warned,' said Christine. '

The evening was dark, wet and cold. Rain beat against the window panes. Emily was in the clutches of a brutal child killer. The English language had untold words, but what were the words to tell a mother her little child had been abducted?

CHAPTER 31

AT A QUARTER TO FIVE, Inspector Wilson finished his paperwork and stretched his arms. He was ready to call it a day. He and Dorothy were dining at the *Old Fire Engine* in Ely. It wasn't a particular celebration, but every now and then they decided to push the boat out. Their food was very good, especially when compared with his own and Dorothy's home cooking.

Cunningham had telephoned the woman whose car had been stolen and found burnt out in Thelford, it was his ex-wife, as a matter of fact. 'She has arranged something for tonight, I'll interview her tomorrow evening, she works in the day,' he said.

'Why so glum? You're not married to her anymore for all her magnificent beauty.'

'It brings it all back,' said Cunningham. 'She could never be bothered to lock a car, you know, and when I told her it just needed a little click, was that too much to ask? she called me a control freak.'

Wilson thought about it.

'The car was stolen from a parking space opposite the railway station.'

'That's right, by people who frequent the Apple.'

It was a restaurant, not a lap top.

'And you suspect it wasn't locked.'

'She'll swear blind it was because of the insurance.'

'Let's assume it wasn't locked, and let's assume the Ford stolen from the forecourt of the railway station wasn't locked either because somebody was being picked up, what do we make of it?'

'Unlocked cars,' said Cunningham. 'Kids who haven't got the hang of opening cars, they are pretty foolproof these days but they can start them without a key, they know it's just a matter of creating a spark to get the engine going.'

'By rubbing two boy scouts together,' said Wilson rather unnecessarily and getting on his nerves, Cunningham thought before he got into his stride. 'They drove the car at great speed, couldn't handle it, landed in a ditch and abandoned it.'

'Little Johnny or Charlie and his mates getting used to driving. Could well be, the area round the station might well be worth looking into. Any joy yet on Watson's van nicked by Foster?'

'Not yet,' said Cunningham, about to leave the office, when an urgent call was put through to Wilson.

'Stay,' Wilson mouthed at him, motioning for Cunningham to listen on the other line.

'Mr. Hudson, I'll keep to the point to get it clear in my head, so can you just listen?' he said, after a short while.

'1) Emily's teacher told you she went off with her brother. She assumed the man she went off with was Emily's brother. Why was that?'

2) Your daughter saw Emily Watson go off with Fred Foster at a quarter-to four, and she has *just* told you. So Foster has an hour on us.'

He listened.

'No one is blaming you, we haven't got time for blame. I shall want a rapid response and I have to have the facts. Could you ask your daughter if she saw Emily actually getting in his car? And will you let me have Emily's parents telephone number?'

He wrote something, and then put the 'phone down, ashen-faced.

'You heard. Foster's abducted a little girl from the school, the sheer bloody nerve, maybe he is taunting us to show us his powers and he will let her go, but I don't think so,' he said to Tomlinson who had been summoned. 'I want Paula in here, pronto.'

He fumbled through his paperwork when the 'phone rang again.

'Right,' He listened. 'So your daughter didn't see Emily get into a car, she was just walking off with him. We'll contact Emily's parents to see if she's at home. I will do it. I will also contact the teacher who saw her go off with Foster. I have her name and telephone number on WPC Smith's report of the school right here. I'll get back to you.'

'Inspector Wilson here, Mrs. Watson,' he said when Emily's mother answered the 'phone. 'Tell me,' he said as gently as he was able to, 'are you on your own, or is there somebody with you?'

'My two sons are here and so is Natalie, the au-pair,' she said nervously. 'Why?'

'Is Emily with you?'

'Well, no, she's at the Hudson's for their party, as a matter of fact. We will go later. What is this all about?'

So Emily wasn't at home. He steeled himself and told her mother what had happened. Smith and Cunningham heard her scream over the telephone. 'I'll send you Constable Smith shortly, she is a mother herself, and she has met Emily, and I'll arrange for a family liaison officer for you as soon as possible.'

Next. HQ.

CHAPTER 32

WILSON WANTED wanted to keep his line kept open, so Cunningham 'phoned Storwich from his line. He informed Chief Superintendent Nicholson of events who promised to keep everyone at his station until he heard from Wilson.

'I hope to hear from him shortly,' Nicholson said. 'According to Wilson's report, this was one of the girls who was warned about Foster.' What could make a girl go with a man she had been warned about? he wondered.

'What sort of girl is Emily?' Wilson asked PC Smith.

'Delicate. Confident, pretty, clever, used to getting her own way, I suspect.'

But not yet six years old.

'Let's assume when Foster gets out of his car with her, Emily kicks up a stink.'

'Most people would assume she's having a tantrum, people want to get home, out of the rain, and to their Bonfire Night.'

'People would also assume she was in need of a smack, like in the good old days, if he was rough with her,' he said.

'He might get out in a lonely place, but of all the girls, Emily is the most likely to spot an opportunity to get away.'

'If there is one, we can but hope, but we have to be realistic. What was Fred's Foster's attraction for Emily?'

'The seaside. He promised her he would take Emily to the seaside, it's in the report,' Paula said.

'Good point, but which seaside? We're surrounded by bloody water,' said Wilson, when the 'phone rang.

'Gregory Watson here, Emily's brother. I'm in my car, I'll be at the station shortly,' said a voice when he answered it. 'Any news about my sister?'

'No, but apparently Foster promised to take her to the seaside. Which seaside would that be? Where was she particularly fond of?'

'Portugal,' said Wilson, putting the 'phone down. 'Bloody Portugal. She calls Portugal the seaside. Apparently they have a villa in Santa Eulalia, near Alberfura, and they spend a month there every summer.'

He repeated it after he had informed the Super of what had happened.

'A thought has occurred to me,' he added. 'Portugal might be Emily's idea of the seaside, but it certainly won't be Foster's. He might take her somewhere else. And we still haven't found Watson's white van.'

He listened.

'No, a different Watson, it's the key-cutter.'

'Right you are. We'll search garages, abandoned barns, allotments, and also keep looking for the van at our end. Cunningham and I will remain at the station.'

In Storwich, Nicholson swung into action. He got uniform together for a rapid response.

'Right. Foster has an hour's start, an hour and a quarter,' he said, looking at his watch. '*Seaside*. Could be Clacton, Hunstanton, Aldeburgh. Southwold. Great Yarmouth. I'll contact Essex as well as Norfolk Police and also Cambridgeshire as he might not be heading for the coast. Problem. He could drive a car, could be a pale blue Corrola, or a small white van.'

'Use your sirens,' he said as his men went off, and then he 'phoned the Assistant Chief Constable.

211

'Put an urgent alert on all the TV channels, as well as radio stations, and get Wilson to prepare a News Bulletin for the Six O' Clock News,' the ACC said. 'This isn't good. Why is Foster still at large? I thought he had broken his parole.'

The blaming-game had already started.

'Most likely because the Judiciary decided he was harmless and released him, and we have to deal with the fall-out,' said Nicholson. What they needed was support, not a broadside.

'I will call a press conference for tomorrow at HQ, at ten o'clock, after a nine o'clock news briefing. Inform Wilson,' said the ACC. 'I will be with you shortly.'

A press conference, where the finger-pointing would start in earnest.

'I have to keep my line free, there's a little girl in great danger,' said Nicholson, put down his receiver and dialed Wilson.

'The ACC is arranging a press conference, tomorrow, at ten o'clock. Here.'

'Hasn't he got a Bonfire Night to go to? asked Wilson, heavy-hearted. He wished he had never read that report on Foster.

Ann Robinson was interrupted in full flow of her 'rehearsed' impromptu, so-called witticisms, by *Breaking News*.

> *News has just come in Fred Foster, the missing paedophile released on licence has abducted a girl from her school this afternoon, at a quarter to four. Emily Watson is five-and-three-quarter-years old.*
>
> *Tall for her age, she has long, dark hair and blue eyes.*
>
> *She is wearing her school uniform, a red*

*jumper and fleece jacket, black skirt, tights
and shoes.*
*Foster is five foot eleven. Clothes worn not yet
known. Driving a white van or possibly a pale-
blue Corolla.*
*If you see them, please get in touch with
your nearest police station immediately.*

Fred Foster paid for his petrol and came out of the shop
and bumped into the bloke giving him agro, who had
wisely decided to shift his car to another pump. Foster
walked to his car and got in.

He looked in the back.

What the fuck.

He looked under the seats, and, stupidly,
opened the boot. There was no doubt about it; Emily
had vanished into thin air. Of course, there was no such
thing. He had forgotten to lock the car because of his
argument about the pump, so she had to be near-by. He
walked around all the pumps when the stroppy bloke
came out of the shop.

'I've lost my daughter,' he said. 'She's about
so high,' he gestured with his hand. 'She was in the
car.'

'Has she got dark hair?'

He nodded.

'She's in the shop, spending your money on
sweets, mate.'

Ann Granger finished some notes at the school and was
about to go home. She was reaching for her coat when
the 'phone rang. She debated if should answer it, but a
ringing 'phone can't be ignored as if it was a letter that
can remain unopened.

'Ridley Infants and Primary.' she said. 'Ann
Granger speaking.'

She listened.

'Dear God, what-ever next. Emily said her brother was fetching her, I knew he was a lot older than her, she pointed to him and went off with him.'

'Willingly?'

'Oh yes, very happily, she was running up to him and went off holding his hand, looking up at him.'

She listened.

'He was tall, and wore dark trousers, a grey jacket and hat, he may have worn white trainers. I didn't think anything of it apart from wondering about his age, but I pictured Foster with a beige raincoat as per his description. Just a minute. I'll come to the station, I'll just let my lot know they have to get on with the fireworks without me.'

Thank God her own girls were safe. She wasn't the only who thought so.

CHAPTER 33

GREGORY WATSON, Emily's brother, was in his twenties. A good-looking, square-jawed, long-legged country type, he wore blue jeans, a green sweatshirt and Wellingtons when he stormed into the station.

'And?' he barked.

'No news, I'm afraid,' said Wilson, after the introductions.

'I had just come into the house when you 'phoned, Inspector,' he said. 'I run stables with my brother Markus. Just what is going on with the police?'

'We're doing our best, but it looks like Emily went off with Foster willingly.'

'She's a five-year-old, for God's sake.'

'And there is a serious criminal out there with her. Let's try and find her first and blame the police later.' Wlison drew himself up. 'If you have no objections.'

Gregory Watson exhaled and steadied himself on the inspector's desk.

'I'm sorry. Can I do anything to help you?'

As a matter of fact, there was

'My DS is updating the News Bulletins. We have a recent picture of Fred Foster, as identified by two eye witnesses.'

This was courtesy of the fat woman's complaint of robbery which led to the surveillance on the HSBC tape. Cunningham had separated and printed off Foster's likeness which would be attached to the e-mail sent to HQ, and shortly to the TV stations, where it would be held and transmitted if nothing new broke.

'Have you got a recent photo of Emily, Mr. Watson?'

'Never thought of it, but I came out in such a rush. I do have a snapshot of her with her pony in my

215

wallet.'

The pony Emily was leaning against was brown, the same colour as Emily's hair. Emily was holding her riding hat in her hand, her head was bent at a slight angle, a huge grin on her face.

'She's not posing like she normally does, that's why I like it,' Gregory said, handing it over. 'Inspector, we are all going spare. My mother says she wishes she had never given birth to Emily, and I myself wish she had never been born rather suffering tortures by this man.'

His voice broke.

'Isn't imagination a curse?' he said when he recovered himself.

'Quite,' said Wilson.

'We are trying to contact my father. He is in Uganda with *Save The Children*, would you believe! He should be here.'

The Watsons' were separated but not divorced as Mrs. Watson was a Catholic. There were nineteen years between Emily and Gregory, seventeen years separated Emily and Markus. Mr. Watson, a doctor, had cleared off when Emily was two, and Gregory became the head of the household. Little Emily was the light of his life.

'Your father could be right here and it would make not make the slightest difference, 'said Wilson. 'Excuse me for a moment.'

He handed Emily's photo over to Cunningham and left the office. He went to the canteen equipped with an urn, which was fine if you liked stewed coffee. He had requisitioned an electric coffee maker and had been issued with a new kettle, so he made Instant and brought the mugs back into his office.

Coffee, he thought, when what he needed was a magic wand, when Sergeant Tomlinson reported his constable had located the white van Foster had made off in. He had simply asked a traffic warden if he had booked a white van.

'I reasoned Foster didn't care if the key-cutter got a parking fine,' he said. A white van had been booked. According to the license number it belonged to the key cutter, whose name he had forgotten.

'Well done,' said Wilson, and 'phoned HQ. Tomlinson was able to erase it as a possible vehicle for Foster, Wilson told the Super.

'Uniform have gone off,' he added, 'to check the B&B in Farn Road in case he has taken Emily there. Villains have been known to double back.'

Foster had no means of getting into the house, but Wilson was beginning to think of him as invincible.

He put down the 'phone and Ann Granger, the teacher, came in, confirming her telephone conversation.

'And what,' said Gregory Watson towering over her, 'were you thinking off letting her go off with him? I'll make sure you won't have a job when all this is over.'

'And I don't care if I don't, just as long as Emily comes back safely.'

The office was getting crowded but both Gregory Watson and Ann Granger were set for the duration, glaring at each other, when Wilson 's phone rang.

It was Connor.

Wilson shook his head and pointed to the door.

'Could you two go and argue somewhere else. Ask DS Cunningham to show you to the canteen, I'll let you know if anything breaks,' he said, watching the pair leave.

'We have checked the B&B. It's deserted and locked up. We are going to check sheds and garages in

217

the villages,' Connor said.

'Check the allotment sheds first. Break in if you have to.'

Wilson put the 'phone down. He rested his head in his hands when the 'phone rang again. He answered it, hoping for good news, which it was in a way. It was Warner from the B&B in Farn Road telephoning from Great Yarmouth.

'I've got a right shiner where he hit me, but the sight in my left eye is not threatened, so the doctors say.'

He wanted to know if he could shed any further light on Fred Foster, seeing he had spent some time in the same house and had the black eye to prove it.

'As a matter of fact, you can and I would be very grateful. We have a news conference tomorrow at HQ in Storwich. If you attended, the press could question you about your inside knowledge of Foster, but your photo might be in the paper.'

'Anything to get the bastard.'

Warner was going to attend. And that black eye wouldn't come amiss, Wilson thought, but it was going to be a long evening.

'I thought I would give one of the papers an exclusive afterwards,' added Warner. 'We're talking real money here, might as well make some money out of the evil old sod.'

He couldn't blame him, thought Wilson, but how could he think of making money right now? But of course, he wasn't any better by thinking how to make the best out of Warner's black eye.

He got one of Cunningham's cigarettes and went to the canteen for some more coffee, where he was greeted by an unusual sight; Gregory Watson and Ann Granger were sitting opposite each other, eyes closed, holding hands and concentrating, but on what exactly?

Gregory Watson broke off.

'We are trying to get into Emily's mind,' he said. 'At home. my mother, brother, Natalie, some neighbours and the police woman and the other officer are doing the same.'

He closed his eyes again.

'Emily, hide. Emily hide. Emily, hide.'

Ann Granger repeated the mantra, and Wilson left them to it. And pigs might, he thought, but on the other hand, people used to pray, so why not try it?

The first firework went off in the distance. Wilson had looked forward to a sparkling display against the magnificence of Ely cathedral after a good dinner with Dorothy. Bloody hell, Dorothy.

CHAPTER 33

DOROTHY WAS CROSS, not to put too fine a point, she was furious. Although she knew he didn't have a nine-to-five job and she was generally understanding about it, John had promised to leave work early.

'He promised faithfully to be on time. He knows it takes half-an-hour to get to Ely in this weather,' she said to the dog, who was hopefully lying in front of the unlit fire. He sighed, rolled his eyes and gave a great, jaw-breaking yawn as if to say, so, what's new?

She had showered and changed into her navy dress with the white collar and navy pumps he liked. Ralph would be left on his own, but unlike sensitive and sensible animals living in terror of loud noises, he wouldn't recognise a banger if it was let off under his very nose.

Might as well watch the news, she thought, depressing, as it usually was.

'Oh, my God,' she said, 'a child's been abducted,' putting her hands over her face. She now taught the little ones and knew all about their funny little ways. 'Oh, my God.'

She switched the news off and went to the phone, rang the station left a message for him.

'John, I've seen the news so I won't keep you, but let me know if anything happens if you can.'

The rain drummed against the window. She nearly jumped out her skin when several bangers went off in quick succession. She sat on the settee again, Ralph trotted over and put his handsome head on her lap, looking up at her with his soulful brown eyes.

She stroked his head. 'That poor child out in this weather with an evil man. No wonder I sometimes prefer dogs to people.'

Wilson went to the toilet. He sat in one of the cubicles, head in his hands. Detectives didn't cry, he told himself, but this detective had read a report on a child her mother had called a blessing, a child who wasn't recognisably human after Foster's brutality had finished with her. He shed tears of sheer frustration. If only he had been quicker, Fred Foster would now be behind bars where he belonged. If only!

He wiped his eyes and came out. Cunningham was washing his hands, his head bowed.

'I know,' said Wilson punching him lightly on the shoulder and going into his office, 'now let's get on with it. As they entered, the phone rang.

It was Storwich. Essex police had been contacted by a garage. The owner had recognised Fred Foster's mug shot and told them he had part-exchanged a pale-blue Corolla for a red Corolla.

'We are going nationwide with the index number,' said Nicholson.

It was going to be a long evening for George and Christine. Rosie was on Christine's lap, clutching her Snowy-White-Snowy-Leopard, her favourite toy. The fire spit in the grate. George thought he would have to put a match to the fire in the dining room soon. Far from wanting to be busy to get his mind off Emily, he felt as if he never wanted to move again.

'I'll give you a bath and you can choose what to wear,' said Christine.

'I am a big boy and I can wear what-ever I like,' he said, looking at Rosie's tear-stained face. It worked. 'She means me, Daddy,' she said, going off happily with her mother.

He sat there, idle, waiting for somebody to do something, when he heard a car draw up. God, not

221

guests already, he thought going to the front door.

'Hello, son,' said his father when he opened it.

'Am I pleased to see you,' George, who hadn't expected him, said. 'Come in.'

'I was having a cup of tea with my neighbour. She's in a wheelchair; nice lady, but a poor old thing and only my age. I'd been to the Post Office for her and watched a bit of telly and we saw that news flash.'

He'd recognised the school as Rosie's, so he had come over early with a DVD for her. He had come early, Christine must have asked him to the party.

Rosie, in new clothes, although George couldn't tell the difference between one pink outfit and another flew down the stairs.

'Granddad!' she yelled, ready to take a flying jump at him, so George quickly stood in front of him and caught her.

'Hello, Jim,' said Christine.

'My friend Emily Watson won't be here,' said Rosie, back on the floor. 'I saw her go off with the bad man but I only told Daddy later.' She looked up at him.

'*You* told him?' said her grandfather. 'Well, that was very clever of you. Not everybody would remember to do that.'

'Next time,' Rosie announced, 'I will tell him at once,' but instead of being pleased, the grown-ups just looked at each other with long faces.

'You're a good girl for telling,' said her granddad, finally. 'My neighbour lent me a DVD her granddaughter likes. *The Princess Dairies*. Apparently it's about a girl who discovers her daddy is a prince.'

He was an unlikely breath of fresh air, George thought, but then again, why was he so surprised?He had always been a hands-on dad, and now he was a hands-on granddad.

Of course, he was right. If Rosie had kept quiet

Emily's abduction would have been discovered much later. But please God, there wouldn't be a next time. If Foster was too slippery for the police, he, Alf and Ritchie might have to do something about him, and do it right this time. He sent himself a mental memorandum: Meeting at the pub.

'Her daddy is a real prince?' said Rosie and disappeared with him into the sitting room, while George finally lit the fire in the dining room and poured himself a large whisky.

'Don't forget that you're in charge of the fireworks,' Christine said warningly from the doorway, looking at his glass. 'Maybe you can make the salad while I change.' It all seemed so normal, yet somehow surreal. He went into the kitchen. Potatoes wrapped in silver foil, greenery and tomatoes on the chopping board, but he just couldn't deal with it.

In a week's time, they would light a candle in remembrance of their first son's death. He went upstairs, stood under a hot shower for five minutes, changed, discovered he had put his old clothes back on as he wondered what the hell had he done with Christine's Valiums. He sneaked into Rosie's room for the news where he found Christine, the TV was switched on.

'Forget the spuds, I'll order some pizzas,' he said, deciding not to mention tranquilisers, 'the kids will like it. Have we got any pink ice-cream?'

'Some strawberry, I suppose, but not enough, I'll ring Mum and ask her to bring some over.'

She dialled on her mobile and listened for a considerable time. Yes,' she said finally, 'and can you bring some pink ice cream?'

If you want to please children, you had to trust in the most obvious things.

The news came on after she switched off her

mobile, but it wasn't good. Foster and Emily hadn't been found.

'Ring the station,' Christine said, as the first two cars drew up.

It was Alf with his wife and two daughters, Victoria and Kylie, followed shortly by Lewis, Natasha and Hester, and then Ritchie, his wife and his two boys, who raced down to the snooker room.

After the initial greetings and introductions and a few minutes of silence, unburdening themselves of scarves, hats, coats, getting used to surroundings, more and more people arrived. Deriving comfort from each other's presence, they were all crammed together in the sitting room.

His mother-in-law had put herself in charge of the drinks and George heard the first audible conversation, the overlapping sentences, when Alf drew him, Ritchie and Lewis to one side. 'Keep Victoria away from the other girls,' he said urgently.

'Why?'

'She knows what bad men do to little girls, and she'll take great pleasure in informing the others.'

'Get you,' said Ritchie, 'does she play darts? There's a dart board in the snooker room.'

'She's a girl, thicko,' said Alf. 'She likes dressing up and music.'

'Do you like Opera, Victoria?' asked Lewis going to her.

Victoria didn't know what it was, but she stuck to him like glue, she was fascinated by this good looking, very smart man who didn't look at all like a daddy. And Natasha didn't look like a mummy either, more like a model.

'Good old Lewis,' said George. 'We'll have to do something about Foster. If he's not found, let's meet tomorrow.'

224

'Right,' said Ritchie, 'The Volunteer, eight o'clock.'

'Eight o'clock it is,' said Lewis, temporarily disengaged.

'And who the hell asked him?' said Alf after Victoria dragged Lewis away, 'and isn't it time for the fireworks?'

CHAPTER 34

IN SUDBURY, Emily had looked out of the car window as the bad man walked to the shop to pay for the petrol.

Pulling the door handle was no good, Emily Watson discovered, but when she pushed the door, it opened. It wasn't quite shut because the strap of her backpack had caught when the bad man had come and shouted at her. She got out and shut the car door as quietly as she could.

She had to be seen.

That's what you did when you got tired of playing hide-and seek, you had to be found. But Gregory hadn't found her yet.

Where could she go until he came to get her? Opposite the forecourt was the busy road, to the left was a place with grass and bushes. She would have to hide, but where? and then Gregory would find her, he always did. The man in the beret was a bad man, Emily knew it. He didn't care about seatbelts and he swore. He didn't even know the seaside was the sea, which was in Portugal, and you needed a passport and go on a plane.

Hide, she thought, looking around her.

Fred Foster went in the brightly lit shop, looking around. A small girl with long, dark hair had her back to him, choosing sweets. I'll give you sweets, he thought.

'There you are, you naughty girl,' he said, grabbing her by the shoulders.

The girl turned round. She had a flat face and wore glasses.

'Daddy!' she screamed.

'Sorry, my mistake, mate,' said Fred Foster

when a young, fit bloke approached, looking less than friendly. 'I thought she was my daughter. She must be in the car.'

If only!

But she had disappeared, so he beat a hasty retreat and roared off, not bothering with seatbelts. Emily wouldn't have liked it, but Emily was missing and therefore couldn't point it out to him. He had always known she was the wrong one, that shy kid would have been ideal. She was so much like Amelia when she had been that age. That would show.... he paused, her cow of a mother whose name he couldn't remember.

Sirens were blearing as he joined the traffic on the main road. They were already looking for him, how come? He took his foot off the accelerator, the last thing he needed was being stopped for speeding; although the police cars were going in the opposite direction. They were indeed looking for him, as he discovered when he switched the radio on.

He would have to stop in a lay-by and gather his thoughts, not to mention his shaking hands. After a while, he drove on to Bury St. Edmunds railway station. Parking the car, he noticed a couple of kids, hoodies as they called them, hanging around, head down, hands in pockets, looking at parked cars.

He also noticed a police car driving up the road, it was indicating a right turn. He rushed into the station as the police car cancelled the signal and passed by. Heaving a sigh of relief, he bought a ticket to York. What made him think of York was a mystery, perhaps it was the American couple touring English Cathedral Cities.

'Change at Cambridge and Peterborough,' he was told and handed his ticket.

That was a bit too quick. He would have to

make sure the ticket seller remembered him.

'Why?' he asked.

'You *do* you want to get to York?'

'I just bought a ticket, haven't I?' he said taking the ticket, waiting for the train from Stowmarket. There had to be a surveillance camera somewhere. As more people arrived, he went to the toilet where he turned his anorak inside out and removed his wig, his beret and his glasses.

He looked at himself in the mirror. His hair, not yet grey but a lighter brown than it used to be, had grown perhaps half an inch all over his head and into a widow's peak onto his forehead. His eyebrows, previously shaved off, had grown back.

He looked completely different, especially with brown spots all over his face; although they were present courtesy of the old mirror. There was nothing he could do about his trainers mentioned on the radio. What was so suspicious about trainers? he thought as he joined passengers alighting from the train and walked out of the station, close to a family with two children so it would appear they were together.

Outside, he went through his pockets for the car keys, only they weren't there, but neither was the car.

CHAPTER 35

SODDING KIDS had stolen his car, but he felt relieved; the decision had been made for him, he would stay here. He walked to the B&B. Another car was out of the question, still, two wheels also got you about; they were all the rage now what with saving the planet. Now that was one he hadn't seen coming, saving the fucking planet!

He waited until a police car parked in front of the B&B drove off. Right, they were looking for him. When the road and pavement were deserted, he tip-toed up the drive and round to the back of the house, fumbled for the back door key and let himself in, lighting the torch.

To his surprise, he found he was starving, but starving for hot food, not for tuna and anchovies. The Volunteer it had to be, but first he had to change into his black shoes.

His feet were killing him when he walked to the pub, which, to his surprise, was practically deserted.

'We don't get many customers until later, seeing what day it is,' said the barmaid.

'Of course,' he said. What bloody day was it?

He sat on the table nearest to the fire after he ordered some of their excellent gammon, egg and chips in his booming voice.

She paused momentarily. There was something familiar about him, was it the voice?

She was waiting for a drink order, he thought, but he decided against a beer, he could feel a migraine coming on. Decision-making did that to him.

'I'll have some coffee later,' he said.

'You're table is number five,' the barmaid said, coming over with the cutlery, condiments and a wooden spoon bearing the number five.

'To save confusion,' he couldn't help saying, seeing he was the only customer.

She laughed, then her face changed. She sat down opposite him on the edge of the chair, her upper body leaning towards him, her breasts -like large dinner plates-nearly under his nose.

Bugger off, he thought, and get my food.

'Isn't it terrible, that poor little kid, in the clutches of that awful man.'

'Absolutely,' he agreed. 'I know what I would do with him.'

Her eyes glittered.

'You know what will happen when they catch him, they'll put him in a maximum security prison where nobody can get at him.'

I wouldn't count on it, he thought, he had one ball missing to clinch the argument, fortunately his food arrived, saving him from further platitudes.

When he walked back to the B&B, he noticed a path running beside it. Where did it go to? he wondered, but it could wait for another day. He went round the back of what he now regarded as *his* house, and by the light of the torch, he wound his way upstairs.

The house was going on the market, so people would come in and measure up. He would have to make a move, and soon, but starting somewhere new made his headache worse. Deciding he hadn't left any traces of living downstairs, he took the second to last migraine pill and fell on the bed fully dressed, exhausted.

Before sleep overcame him, he thought how stupid he had been. If the police had stopped him for speeding, he could have denied taking the kid. 'What kid?' He could picture it. 'What are you hounding me for?' He could have sued them, how he would have loved that!

Sharp sounds of gunfire woke him up shortly afterwards. He sat up, the police were breaking in! He heard more gunfire, the house had to be surrounded. The police weren't as stupid as he had thought, they had probably found the kid and she would know him.

He groped his way to the landing. Disorientated after the migraine pill, his hands in the air, he went to the window where he discovered he was on the second floor and another rocket whistled up into the air and exploded into the air close by.

It was *that* bloody day, he thought. He fell asleep again when another rocket woke him up, followed by distant cheering from further down the road. I'll give them cheer, he thought.

That kid, a little thing like that, got the better of him, what else would they cheer about? He chased sleep for a long time, and while he did, he worked backwards to where his troubles had started, to the three blokes on the footpath, to the three blokes in the pub. He would make them pay, as well as the bloke from Keys Cut While U Wait, not forgetting Warner. Once that was out of the way, and then, only then, would he follow his plan and leave.

Fifteen-year-old James Harvey, Jimmy, and his mate Ronald were on the road to anywhere or possibly nowhere. Jimmy was driving for the first time. 'Not much of a car,' he grumbled, crawling along, 'and what's with all the coppers?'

Jimmy had a Jimmy Osborn face, round and really innocent, whereas Ronald was dark, thin-faced, moody and lanky. While girls liked Jimmy and laughed with him, they turned to Ronald who already had the seducer's smile girls found irresistible.

He wasn't smiling now.

'Where are we?' Jimmy asked, peering into the dark, finally finding the windscreen wipers.

'On the way to bloody Stow,' said Ronald.

'I've got an aunt in Stow,' said Jimmy.

Ronald thought of hitting him, but changed his mind.

'Turn right before the fuzz spots us. And for fuck's sake, get out of first gear. Gear stick up and then down to the right. We're supposed to burn up the road, not crawl like…' words failed him.'

'Right,' said Jimmy, starting to laugh. 'Burning up the road in first gear!'

He put his foot down in third and increased his speed. Bowling along, he found what he thought was fourth gear but was reverse, the car shuddered and bucked. It then slithered on the edge of the slippery road Jimmy was driving on, turned over and fell into a ditch. Hanging upside down didn't seem much of a thrill. They freed themselves, managed to open a door to get out and distance themselves from the car.

In films, it would have gone up in smoke, only it didn't.

'Why?' Jimmy asked.

'The petrol tank has to rupture and ignite, dickhead,' said Ronald.

Not a house or a car was in the sight.

'It's the end of the bleeding world,' said Ronald. 'Got any matches?'

'Safety matches,' said Jimmy going to the car, opening the back door of the car. The match went out in the gusty wind. They all flared up and then died. It seemed killingly funny, first burning up the road in first gear, and, as Ronald said, it was unfucking unbelievable how safe safety matches were.

'We can't always rely on a key left in a car, and

we can't smash a car window with a car alarm when people are about,' said Ronald, who could start an engine without a key but couldn't force a car door open, 'I can't ask my dad how it's done.'

'Seeing he is the Head,' said Jimmy, holding his stomach, laughing. 'I can't ask mine; he's absent. He might ask his friends, though. Where he is, they are bound to know.'

For joy riders they had done lot walking since taking up driving, but, as Jimmy pointed out. it wasn't as far as Thelford where Ronald had turned a car over. Ronald was in a mood, but Jimmy laughed all the way home.

'Isn't your mum going away soon?' Ronald asked. Instead of a party, they could take her car and drive to Eileen's and get some gear.

'But I do want to have a party,' said Jimmy, 'my flat will be empty.'

'Like your fucking head,' said Ronald.

Jimmy had to ring the bell when he got home.

'Forgot your key again?' said his mother when she opened the door. She sniffed. 'Where have you been? Can I smell burning?'

'Safety matches. Bonfire night, innit, at Ronald's,' said Jimmy.

Such a nice boy, such a good influence, that Ronald, and from such a good family, she thought.

CHAPTER 36

IN SUDBURY, Peter Robinson filled up with petrol. He had been to Clacton to clear out and shut the caravan for the winter. He and his wife had spent ten good summers in it; although, the place wasn't what it once was, flats full of immigrants and people on benefit. Nonetheless, they liked the Essex coast, its green, gentle slopes, the sandy beach, the blue sea and sky.

But there it was. After ten years on a site, paying rent, now three- thousand pounds a year, you were slung off unceremoniously when your caravan was ten years old. He felt betrayed, as betrayed as he had felt when the boss called him into his office and mentioned the unmentionable ten-letter word, Redundancy.

Only last year, he had been head-hunted by the very same man for a small engineering firm promising him rapid advancement.

'I left a good job for you,' he said.

'Sorry, Peter, there it is. Last in, first out,' said his boss. 'You'll soon get another job,' he added grandly, as if he was granting him an enormous favour.

He now clicked the car open and was about to get in it when his mobile rang. It was his wife wanting to know where he was.

'Not sure,' he said, 'probably Stowmarket or Sudbury, I'm not sure. I'm always getting the two mixed up. I'm half-way home, more than half-way. I'll soon hit the A14. Got to go, punters behind me are getting impatient.'

'Did you remember to bring the cutlery?'

Bloody hell, the cutlery. A few battered spoons, forks and knives could hardly be called cutlery.

'I did,' he said, knowing they had gone in the

bin, 'I must go now.'

He got in the car and set off, not knowing he had a small passenger curled up on the floor behind him, namely Emily Watson.

She had been beside Fred Foster's car when Peter Robinson came out of the shop.

Deciding where to hide, she saw the bad man was coming out of the shop. Opposite to the bad man's car, a man was about to get into his own car, when he stopped to talk on his mobile, looking the other way.

She crossed to the car, let herself in, shut the door and lay down, hardly daring to breath. The man was still talking on his mobile when she cautiously looked out of the window. The bad man was in his car, driving off.

The man got into the car. He switched the engine on and then the radio, turning the station from talking to music as he was driving. The rain beat on the car roof and she felt sleepy, except the floor was uncomfortable. When the car stopped, the radio was switched off and the man talked again on his mobile.

'I'm in a lay-by, I was going to phone you,' he said, 'but I forgot what about.' He laughed. 'I know, what am I like.'

The car floor felt stuffy, sweaty, hard, and the back seats of the car were piled high with blankets and pillows, so Emily -very carefully- lifted the top one off. She stopped.

'A pillow fell off the back seat,' said the man, 'I'll leave it, see you soon. Love you.'

As the car set off again, the windscreen wipers going, swish, swish, Emily Watson settled herself on the pillow and fell asleep.

Peter Robinson drove on carefully through the dark and

235

the pelting rain. He steered carefully, as if he was carrying a lost treasure and not a load of tat, oblivious to the fact he was, indeed, carrying a lost treasure.

Half-an-hour later, he pulled up in front of his house in Harston, Cambridgeshire. A chalet-type bungalow, with a huge living room and galleried landing, the house was the pride and joy of the childless couple. Situated near Addenbrook Hospital, it would raise a tidy sum when it was sold, as it would have to be now he was without a job, or, as they called it, a job seeker.

The porch light was switched on. Fiona, his wife, a pretty redhead, opened the door.

'Did you bring the cutlery?' she asked.

'Let me get in first,' he said, clicking the car door shut, turning round as a rocket went off in the distance.

He took off his coat and his shoes, hung up his car keys and sat on the settee in the living room while Fiona went into the kitchen and finished cooking.

Whatever it was, it smelled good.

They sat side by side, eating lamb chops, broccoli, mashed potatoes and gravy; Fiona was ace with gravy. He would have to come clean about the cutlery soon, he thought, switching on the television for the news.

'Oh, my God. That poor child.'

Meanwhile, Emily felt cold. She reached for a blanket, covered herself and wondered how much longer Greg would be, she badly needed the toilet, and then she slept on.

CHAPTER 37

FOR THE NEXT fifteen minutes or so Fiona talked, and Peter listened, although he was fully aware what ought to have been done with Foster.

'Shall we?' she said finally, taking the plates and getting up.

'Shall we what?'

'Shall we clear the car, of course.'

'Let's do it tomorrow, shall we?'

'All right,' she said, leaving the room.

He counted to twenty. Fiona was a 'better the day, better the deed,' person.

'I'll do it now,' she shouted from the hall.

He heard her open the front door, and then he heard a scream. He rushed out and found Fiona on the porch, clutching her heart. Apparently, there was an animal in the back of the car.

She'd decided to get the blankets and pillows and then she had felt something moving.

'I tell you, Pete, whatever it was, it was alive.'

She shuddered.

'I thought I'd leave the cutlery till later,' she said, being fond of telling it *CHAPTER and VERSE*.

'Bugger the cutlery,' he said.

'There's a pillow and a blanket on the floor, and something moved when I touched it. See for yourself.'

'Rubbish,' he said, opening the back door of the car where, to his surprise, he was looking at a small girl.

'Here, Fiona!'

The girl was sitting up and rubbing her eyes when the bright porch light hit her.

'Where's Greg?' she asked. 'He's supposed to find me.'

237

'He'll be her as soon as possible,' said Fiona, shrugging her shoulders at Pete, and helped Emily out of the car. 'What were you doing in there?'

Emily shouldered her backpack and shook her hair out of her eyes.

'I was playing hide and seek,' she said. She looked around her. 'Have you got a toilet?'

'Let her come in the house,' said Peter, 'and then we can get some sense out of her.'

It was a nice house, but it had a very small hall, Emily decided as the lady showed her the toilet where she did the longest wee ever. On and on it went, like her pony's which she called Pony. Imagination wasn't Emily Watson's strongest point, getting her own way was.

She wanted to get away from the bad man and she had, although she knew she shouldn't have gone with him in the first place, the police lady had said so at the school. She was being wilful, her Mummy called it.

An awful thought struck her.

'Will I get arrested?' she asked when she came out of the toilet.

'No, darling, tell me, have you run away?' the lady asked her.

'I was in the car and he was a bad man, he swore and wouldn't let me do my seatbelt up. He went the wrong way for the seaside. I didn't want to go with him, so I got out when he got some petrol. It's called hide and seek and when you want to be found, they have to see you, but I didn't want the bad man to see me. So I got into a car and hid from the bad man and he,' she pointed to Peter, 'drove away and stopped here.'

'The bad man isn't here, sweetheart,' said Fiona, hugging her, settling her onto the settee. 'Are you hungry?'

'I shall eat at Rosie's party, thank you, *I* have been invited,' said Emily. 'I've got some nice clothes in my bag. Where's my bag? I want to change.'

Peter handed it to her.

'What bad man?' whispered Fiona.

'Are you Emily Watson?' Peter asked her in a shaking voice.

'How did you know?' asked Emily, astonished. 'That's really, really clever of you,' while Peter rushed out and dialled 999.

'The emergency is over, I have found the missing girl,' he told the operator. 'Give me Bury St. Edmunds.'

He listened.

'All right, give me the number.'

The desk sergeant put him through to Inspector Wilson.

'Just one question, Mr Robinson, and I don't want to worry the little girl if it can be helped,' said Wilson after being informed of Emily Watson's whereabouts by Peter Robinson, 'did Foster release her, or did she manage to get away herself? And where was it? We want to trace Foster as soon as possible.'

'She got away, would you believe, a little thing like that,' said Peter Robinson. 'The bloke, Foster, I now realise, had an argument with another bloke at the pumps and went to pay for the petrol. I was parked by the opposite pump only a few steps away. I was about to get into my car when Fiona, that's my wife, rang me on my mobile, and Emily apparently got out of his car and sneaked into my car. Afterwards I drove off, completely unaware.'

'Form where exactly?'

'From the filling station in Sudbury.'

Wilson listened. Then he wrote down Peter

Robinson's telephone number, put down the receiver and inhaled deeply. He wished that Cunningham was there to share the moment, but he had been called out to a Domestic with Tomlinson. Instead, he raced to the canteen. He looked at Gregory Watson and Ann Granger for a minute, then he yelled and punched the air with both hands.

'Sorry to interrupt you, Mr Watson,' he said when they broke off, startled. 'There's a young lady who wants to speak to you on the telephone. She's safe and well, apparently she's been playing hide and seek, and she's waiting for you to find her.'

Back in the office, he gave Gregory Watson the Harston telephone number for Emily, and then he phoned the Watson's home, where he talked to WPC Smith.

'Emily's been found, she got away, what a kid! And guess what?'

'She's been playing hide and seek.'

'Amazing. How did you guess? Tell Mrs Watson will pick her up shortly,' said Wilson.

He phoned HQ and spoke to the Super, who sent a team to Sudbury and promised to prepare a statement for *Breaking News,* and then he phoned Dorothy. But he couldn't talk for long as it occurred to him to inform and recall his team.

Cunningham and Tomlinson came in from his Domestic. Cunningham processed the man and put him in the holding cell and then he went to Waitrose. He brought a whacking great box of doughnuts on expenses to celebrate Emily's safe return, when someone from a petrol station in Sudbury rang. A man fitting Fred Foster's description had been filling up with petrol about five-thirty. The shop had a surveillance camera.

The phone rang again. It was a Mr Brown from

the railway station, he had sold a railway ticket to a man answering Fred Foster's description, before he finished his shift at the desk.

'Where to?'

'To York.'

No sooner had he put the receiver down after informing HQ, Smith rushed in, beaming.

'What about this hide and seek business?' Wilson asked her.

'You mean meditating. I thought it was weird at first, but then anything was better than the worry and picturing the girl in the danger she was in. Mrs Watson goes in for meditation and she called in a few neighbours, apparently the more the better. We sat in a circle, holding hands, looking at a pot of cyclamen in the middle of the circle.'

Wilson looked incredulous.

'It's a plant with pink flowers and with heart-shaped green leaves,' WPC Smith explained.

'What was the plant's connection with Emily?' he asked, but she said she was coming to it.

'We were asked to concentrate on it. The flower had grown from a tiny seed, we had to picture the seed, then we shut our eyes, and imagined ourselves in a car, planting a seed in Emily's mind.'

'The hide and seek seed.'

'That's right. But the truly weird, peculiar thing is, for just a moment I left the bright living room and found myself in a dark place, moving along a road.'

'Even more peculiar, it seemed to have worked.'

Let us say it happened, thought Wilson, but did he believe these things? He could only say he was prepared to consider the evidence and accept it if he was satisfied, but first he had to talk it over with Dorothy.

He got his coat and let Cunningham to deal with the office as he left for the Robinsons and Emily in Harston. As he didn't like the voice on his Sat Nav system, he relied on his familiarity with the area.

It was the second turning after the nurseries that stocked a plentiful supply of the plants Dorothy was so fond of killing.

He was still too early, so he drew into the nursery's forecourt where he wished more than anything else for a cigarette. He went through his pockets, knowing it was a fruitless task and found a packet of Marlborough, courtesy of Cunningham, that unlikely miracle worker. Ten years of giving up, and it was still in his system.

Finally, he judged that he had given the Watsons enough privacy. He wanted to find out as much as he possibly could without actually debriefing Emily Watson, that would have to be done later, and possibly by a woman.

Watson's Land Rover was parked on the drive of Peter Robinson's house, so he left his car on the road and was about to ring the bell, when the porch light came on and Gregory Watson came out with Emily. Her legs were wrapped around his waist, her arms around his neck and her head was resting on his shoulders. She looked very small, baby-like.

'I knew Gregory would find me,' she said triumphantly.

He stopped her mother, who was behind them carrying Emily's backpack.

'I'm Inspector Wilson,' he said, whereupon she threw her arms around him, weeping.

'There, there,' he said. 'Get in touch with us tomorrow,' he added when she let go of his comforting male presence. He watched them drive off, and then he remembered.

Good God.

He was about to dial, beaming unnecessarily, but quite appropriately, as the bearer of good news for George Hudson, and then he closed his mobile. It wouldn't take him much out of his way and bearing good news would be a wonderful charge and pleasure.

CHAPTER 38

GEORGE HUDSON FOUND little or no pleasure in letting off fireworks, although the fire was a roaring success, Alf said, and Ritchie failed to see it.

'The fire is, it's roaring, thicko,' said Alf, 'never mind.'

It was a big bonfire, doused with paraffin and piled high with neighbours' rubbish, including an old mattress and an unpainted door. Although George had put his foot down when next door brought round a twisted bicycle frame without wheels.

Catherine wheels had whirled shooting out sparks, vulcans had shot sparks down the fence, rockets had r isen and exploded, their colours falling like rain, although their beauty by-passed Alf.

'How many more bleeding rockets? I'm frozen.'

Three more. They decided to leave them for next year. In any case, the fireworks in the near-by Abbey Gardens stole their thunder, every neck was craned in the opposite direction as the sky bloomed and exploded with bigger and better red, green and yellow sparks.

The children were well-wrapped up, and, with gloved hands, drew rings in the air with red and green matches,, always the best bit. Then, the doorbell rang.

Alf was indoors because he was cold and he answered the door.

A tall, thin, well-dressed man wearing a hat and beaming all over his face was revealed in the porch light.

'I'd like a word with Mr Hudson,' he said, 'I'm Inspector Wilson.'

'That's me,' said George coming behind Alf. 'This is my friend, Alf Butler. Would you like to come

244

in?'

'No thanks, I'm on my way home. I just want to tell you Emily has been found, safe and sound. In fact, she got away from Foster would you believe, she gave him the slip,' said Wilson. When the two mates embraced each other, thumping each other on the back, crying, Wilson beat a hasty retreat.

'Listen up, Emily has been found safe and sound. Mrs Granger will inform us as to how and where at school, tomorrow at ten o'clock. Emily is now safely at home with her family,' George announced when he had everybody's attention.

The doorbell rang again. It was the pizza delivery man in the black motor cycling gear he wore for riding a scooter. He wore a helmet and pulled up his visor when Christine opened the door. One-hundred-and fifteen pounds.

'Cash only,' said the delivery man to Christine. A sharp intake of breath.

She looked without much hope in George's wallet where, to her astonishment, she found nearly two-hundred pounds. It was unusual, she would mention it George, but later when he finished answering the phone. It was Emily's brother, Gregory. He said that Emily wanted to come to Rosie's party, but she wasn't allowed to go.

Although the Watson's couldn't bear to be parted from Emily, she thought of it as a punishment, which worked out well. She would think twice before she did anything silly, or was wilful, as Mummy called it. Furthermore, Rosie and the other children wouldn't see her treated as a heroine by all the grown-ups and so wouldn't think of doing something equally regrettable.

Hopefully.

Lewis put himself in charge of the pizzas while the children milled around; Emily was back.

The children did not seem surprised; they seemed to have expected it, nobody asked how she had got away. Perhaps they were just hungry, or perhaps they were young enough to believe in the redeeming feature of a fairy, who would wave her magic wand and would make the bad man disappear.

Alf's daughter Victoria, a most beautiful child in a Botticelli manner with a mass of red-gold hair and huge blue eyes in a delicate face, was well past that stage.

'I don't know,' she said to Lewis, 'two slices, please, I'm starved, but my sister Kylie is five, nearly six. She is the same age as Emily. Kylie can't even tell the time and she has only just learnt to tie her shoelaces.'

Victoria had tears in her eyes.

'Kylie would just cry and cry and cry.'

She looked up at him.

'I don't know how Hester would have coped either,' he said.

Lewis looked at Hester, deep in conversation with George's father who was sitting in an armchair. She was leaning on his knees, looking up into his face.

'They take it for granted, Emily getting away. I suppose it's to be expected at their age,' said Victoria wisely, 'I'm eight, but I was just the same when I was young.'

Natasha looked a bit like a statue, indeed everybody had that look of not allowing any feelings to show. They felt as if they had fallen from a great height and miraculously were still in one piece and testing their feet. But now she felt a bubble of laughter building up.

When George said they had three rockets left they all ran outside. The rain and the wind had both died down, and the fire was still burning pretty well.

George lit one rocket, the one that woke Fred Foster again. Their spirits soared by the combined spectacle of fire and fireworks celebrating Emily's safe return, and thirty-one people and assorted children raised a great cheer , the cheer that kept Fred Foster awake and planning his revenge.

'Odd, isn't it, how people never behave like we think they should,' said George to Christine, his arm around her, holding Rosie's hand and looking at a raggedy sky. 'We could hardly breathe when we heard Emily was safe.'

'It is certainly odd, we couldn't believe it, I suppose,' said Christine, 'and normal will take getting used to it,' but not as long as they thought. She asked him why he had nearly two-hundred pounds in his wallet.

'See you in The Volunteer,' said Lewis, taking a private leave from George, Alf and Ritchie.

'I'm a bit slow here, we are going to discuss our trouble,' said Alf after Lewis had left, 'what exactly has got our trouble got to do with him?'

'I like him. What exactly is our trouble?' asked Ritchie. 'Oh, Doctor Willoughby.'

Alf had plenty to say to him when they left, although George didn't say anything. The pizzas had been paid for by Dr Willoughby's money, and there was something in his coat pocket he wanted to investigate. Christine's Valiums. He lacked Ritchie's inner peace, so he washed two down with some leftover red wine. As he was a stranger to it as much as he was to an aspirin, it took hold of him immediately. He sank onto the settee and fell into a deep, drooling sleep. Now that wasn't normal, Christine thought.

'Granddad spent a lot of time with Hester, not with me.' Rosie complained, looking at her sleeping father. 'And I am his granddaughter.'

'Hester has lost her own granddad,' said her mother. 'At least Emily is back home. I expect that she'll be tucked up in her bed by her mother.'

Rosie opened her mouth again, arms in the air. She was about to utter something. Christine braced herself for the question she didn't know how to answer: what did a bad man do to a little girl?'

'I wonder what her new top was like. Spangely, I expect,' she said. 'Mummy, why do people say, "Next time you come don't leave it so long before you go?"'

Christine smiled, relieved, although Rosie had that wrong, but she wasn't so sure when she looked at the mess left behind in every room and George fast asleep on the settee. She resisted the temptation and stopped Rosie from poking her father into his ribs.

Instead of waking him up, she covered him with a blanket. He looked as if he needed his rest.

CHAPTER 39

PETER ROBINSON also felt that he needed something. The inspector had seen no reason why he
shouldn't contact one of the tabloids for an Exclusive
after he had heard about his recent redundancy. He
could maybe make fifteen or twenty k out of it.

'You found Emily, so you are tapping into
general relief and not into general misery, and also,
anybody who makes something out of Foster is to be
congratulated. We have a press conference in Storwich.
If you attend, you can also complete a criminal justice
statement,' Wilson had said as he left for the office,
'the press will find you eventually, so why don't you
find the press first?'

Wilson hoped he wouldn't regret it as he went
to inform the Hudsons, and then back to the office
where he entered the relevant data in his notebook.
Connor returned. He reported that he had searched the
wooded area towards Thelford for Emily, where he had
located a stained mattress.

'So?' the inspector closed his notebook.

'I dragged it away and turned it over. It was
stained and very smelly, but there was nothing under
it,' he said, 'and then the search was called off.'

The inspector thought about it. They would get
a lot of bad press, but they could make one man very
happy, namely, he opened his notebook again, 'a
certain Albert Rusty who is concerned with fly tippers.
I'll get it cleared up.'

By now everyone bar Travis from Traffic was
back in the office, tucking into the doughnuts. Very
nice, although Wilson thought Cunningham watched
too many American cop shows, when the phone rang. It
was the Super.

Wilson listened.

'Right, Sir,' he said. 'Yes, everybody is back.'

'E-mail me your summary leading up to the present for a press release and to familiarise the ACC with it before we get to the conference.'

'Right you are, sir.'

'And make sure everybody writes their reports before they leave, and bring them to the meeting tomorrow,' he said.

'I will,' said Wilson, putting the phone down.

'Everybody, you can bugger off home, all bar you.' He turned Cunningham. 'What about the Domestic in the holding cell?'

'It's a Luke Cole,' said Cunningham. 'He beat up his partner so badly that she is being hospitalised in Emergency Admissions. She is Polish, and she got on his nerves, he said, cooking beetroot, horseradish and sour crème with everything and not talking proper. It was time she learned our ways.'

'And beat the crap out of him for a change, I expect he'll be charged tomorrow,' said Wilson.

Another call came through. An abandoned car had been found in a ditch near Stow. No passengers were inside the red car.

'It's Foster's car, according to the licence number,' he said to Cunningham.

He listened.

'If you find a disorientated car driver wandering about, it could be Foster. Nab him regardless, although my money is on car thieves.'

He put the phone down.

'How can Foster buy a ticket for York and drive his car to Culham, all at the same time?' He sighed. 'The car will be cordoned off. Forensics will have to take fingerprints of the rear-view mirror first. That's our best early chance to determine who was driving it, everybody adjusts it and leaves their mitts on it.'

Cunningham left before the car was towed away and thoroughly examined. Wilson was finally leaving the office, having no answers but plenty of questions, when his mobile rang. Cunningham said he had found a small pair of pliers wrapped in a towel in Foster's Corolla.

Wilson looked up despairingly into the raggedy dark sky. He felt diminished. Just what made men, flesh and blood and brains like himself, into monsters?

Answer came there none, but a rocket overhead exploded into a shower of yellow stars. He got into his car and drove off.

Somewhere else, somewhere amongst Scot pines with straggly branches like useless umbrellas, an inquisitive fox pawed at a new piece of crumbly black earth.

CHAPTER 40

'YOU WOULDN'T EXPECT a child to go off with a bad man, a man it had been warned about, would you?' asked Wilson, back home.

'Children don't do the expected,' said Dorothy, waving a fork at Wilson, 'because children very rarely ask the questions we expect of them.'

'We ought to recruit them in that case, criminals absolutely hate the unexpected questions,' said Wilson, finishing a supper of eggs, bacon and baked beans, ignoring the dog whose routine had been broken and who sighed loudly from the door way.

Five-to-eight-year-olds, Dorothy explained, although like Emily, full of life and potential, were not old enough to make rational choices. Their brains were not yet equipped for reasoning, operating as they did on emotion.

'That's very much simplified, of course,' said Dorothy, 'and it's amateur psychology.'

'Based on your experience with children.'

'That's right. Purely amateur. What motivated Emily was that she didn't want to go with...'

'Rosie because Rosie had a new friend and she didn't like it. So, when Foster, having befriended her previously, turned up, she went off happily with him to get one over on her friend. She never asked herself why Foster turned up out of the blue and what he wanted her for,' said Wilson, 'because he told her he would take her to the seaside.'

'She would seem extraordinarily advanced to get away from him,' said Dorothy. 'She was also a much loved and protected child. Foster was bad because he didn't care about seat belts, from what you have told me, that was important to her, and she wanted to be with her brother. She has this deep, emotional attachment to him.'

'He played hide and seek with her and he always found her. What do you think of this mediating business?'

Dorothy was in two minds, she said, except it might have worked.

'Years ago, we would have called it the power of prayer,' said Wilson, none-the-wiser, getting up. Intending to write up his notes on the word processor, he opened his briefcase, looking in vain for his notebook, and as usual, with a shout of, 'Dorothy!' he panicked.

'Where's my notebook?' was a good game as far as Ralph was concerned, although, 'Where are my car keys?' was a better one, but he joined in enthusiastically, tail wagging, barking furiously. Panic over, game over, finding his notebook in his jacket pocket and having his face licked, Wilson started to transmute his brief jottings into gold. He hoped.

'Do you want me to put it on the computer for you?' asked Dorothy.

What a woman!

'I am a man in a million,' he said modestly.

'I know,' she said, going upstairs to the study, 'you're not married to the most marvellous woman in the world.'

It made sense in a way. They both understood the benefits of not being married, Wilson said, taking the dog for a walk. After he came back, the dog soaked through, drying the thick pelt with its marvellously earthy smell, Wilson found he was not yet ready for bed. With untold facts racing through his mind in no particular order, sleep would prove to be elusive. He thought of his own daughter, safe and grown up in New Zealand. Sort of.

'Yes?' she said when she answered the phone.

'Dad?'

'I just wanted to know how you were,' he said.

'I am rather busy just now,' she said, 'I do have a life.'

'He has absolutely no consideration,' Heather said, putting down the receiver, whilst Wilson wound his weary way upstairs. As always, Heather had chased every other thought from his brain, but the main thing was that she was safe.

Next morning he woke up refreshed, showered and smartly dressed as usual, he reached Storwich HQ at nine for the news conference at ten. It wasn't only the local East Anglian press who would be there; the Nationals had sent their big guns. Both Anglian TV and the BBC would have their cameras ready, and there would be questions from Crimewatch.

Mr Warner from the Farn Road B&B was waiting for him, sporting a horrible black, blue and yellow eye. Peter Robinson from Harston was also there.

'You're late,' said Nicholson when he entered his office after a few minutes chat, flanked by the Assistant Chief Constable. Apparently, the Chief Constable was in hospital having his appendix out.

A uniform did something for a man, Wilson thought, it enabled him to look down onto the lower ranks.

'Sorry, sir,' he said. 'I was looking after Mr Warner. From the B&B. Remember? And Peter Robinson, who found the girl. They will be attending our News Conference.'

'Why wasn't I informed of this?' asked Nicholson, handing him the Press *Release* that started with the Nationwide search for Foster.

'I informed you, as a far as I know, let me see,'

said Wilson, fumbling for his notebook. As if!

'Must have slipped my mind.' said Nicholson, 'but Warner will add to our err, assertion that Fred Foster is a dangerous and clever bloke. Having lived with him for err. '

'Five days, it's in my summary,' said Wilson.

'Yes,' said the ACC. 'Well done.'

'And Robinson will take on the hero's mantle, said Wilson. 'Two things,' Wilson, who wanted a coffee machine for his office, added. 'I'd like to request a bowl of fruit for our station. I believe other station canteens provide them daily.'

From their stunned expressions, he might just as well have asked for a crocodile skin handbag. It wasn't warranted, apparently. Wilson, who wanted a bowl of fruit a day as much as he wished for a crocodile handbag himself, accepted the refusal with good grace. 'Secondly, I would like to request a coffee maker for our canteen.'

His wish was granted.

'Last night, we've found Foster's car in a ditch about three miles outside Bury St. Edmunds,' said Wilson. 'When Cunningham retrieved the rear-view mirror from the car for fingerprints, he discovered a pair of small pliers, wrapped in a white towel.'

A shocked silence fell on the room.

'Fred Foster's tools, no doubt,' said Nicholson.

Then he got down to business in hand. It seemed likely Foster had left the area, despite the abandoned, or more possibly stolen, car, and was buying a rail ticket to York. Cambridge and Peterborough Police, as well as York, were looking at their CCTV cameras, it was important to keep vigilant.

Next, there was a spate of car thefts.

Wilson made a note of it.

Next. Sheds would have to be searched for the

missing man, Paul Willoughby. Finding the missing man was now a top priority for Bury St. Edmunds.

'Thoughts?'

'The Mobile Unit. Late afternoon to evening would be best to recreate the same conditions,' said Wilson. 'It'll be seven days since Dr Willoughby disappeared.'

'Thoughts?'

'When a person is missing, they're either dead, or they're hiding; but we can't assume he's dead until we find his body. Although his raincoat has been found with blood on it, indicating an assault.'

Nicholson nodded. 'DNA tests are not yet through due to our heavy case load. Officer reports?'

'Oh dear, I left them behind,' said Wilson, making a show of going through his briefcase.

Nicholson shook his head. Next, they went over the finer points of the tricky press interview, starting with the good, if not miraculous news, of Emily Watson's safe return, and the bad news, Fred Foster still being at large. This got worse when somebody rushed in and interrupted Nicholson with bad news, very bad news.

The *Press Release* had to be altered, and only two very serious officers took their seats behind the table next to Warner and Robinson. The ACC had to leave because he had to report to the recuperating Chief Constable, there was always someone higher-up, as well as lower down.

Time to go before the Press got their teeth into the latest calamity. 'And who could blame them,' Wilson said gloomily to Nicholson in the canteen, waiting for their caffeine shot.

'It wasn't us who released him,' said Nicholson. There was a hint of weakness in his voice, Wilson noted, but who wasn't affected by the horrific death of a young child who had all its life before it? Two children dead, and Foster was let loose on the public.

'Set free by the Judiciary,' Wilson said, rather unnecessarily, before they faced the press.

CHAPTER 41

NICHOLSON STARTED THE PROCEEDINGS with Emily Watson's miraculous escape from Foster..

The good news.

Now the bad news..

'Devon Police have this minute informed us that an unsolved child murder from 1977 has been linked to Fred Foster.'

A sharp intake of breath and rustling of paper.

'These are the bare details. The victim was five-year-old Denise Stocks.'

The audience sat up and took notice, faces turned up to Nicholson like flowers to the sun.

'I must emphasise that this cold case review was not originally sanctioned by Devon Police due to budget restrictions.'

He explored budget restrictions fully and at length.

'Dr Williams, a pathologist from Truro who was about to retire,' he said, 'tried to find the perpetrator of this crime because of its horrific nature. After reading pathologists' reports of similar crimes, he found a corresponding brutality in Fred Foster's victim.'

He paused.

'DNA testing on old fabric is by no means conclusive. Apparently, he had a piece of a hair-band worn by a five-year-old girl from which he was able to retrieve traces of sweat and blood containing Foster's DNA. We heard of the pathologist's investigations on the day Fred Foster went missing. I must stress that Dr Williams carried out these DNA tests, that is, until he realised Foster had been released on parole, at which point Devon gave him full assistance.'

He looked up from his notes.

'That was four weeks after Foster was released.'

He consulted his notes again.

'Fred Foster changed his appearance, and assumed a different name, under which he was a guest at Mr Warner's B&B,' he pointed to him, 'who will talk to you later.'

Wilson was next.

He kept this part brief. He also confirmed that the reason for Foster going underground was not known, but it was thought to be due to vigilantes. 'And let that be a warning! He is far more dangerous having gone to ground.'

Then he turned to the amazing escape of Emily Watson, which he followed by pointing to Warner who scored a bull's eye with his bad eye.

It wasn't lost on the journalists in front of them, and Wilson explained how they had missed Foster by a hair's breadth at the B&B.

'Would you say Fred Foster is at large because of police blunders?' Daily Mail.

'No, I would not,' said Wilson. 'He is at large because the powers-that-be judged him to be harmless and released him.'

'Why wasn't he kept under more strict supervision when he came out?' Daily Mirror.

'Perhaps you haven't heard Chief Superintendent Nicholson explaining the restraint of our budget to you. We were short-staffed, and Foster reported to the probation officer at our station.'

He didn't say how long for.

More questions of a similar nature followed, but next came the killer.

'Would you say if you had been more vigilant, or let's say more quick off the mark,' a journalist (The Times) started to ask, and Wilson's heart sank, 'Fred

Foster would no longer be at large, or did you regard him simply as a slippery fish?'

There is a God after all, thought Wilson.

'I thought I made it perfectly clear to you that Foster isn't just *a* slippery fish, as you call him, he is in fact a child killer, a most brutal double child killer as it turns out, and he still would be, judged by the Emily Watson affair.'

The journalist opened his mouth again.

'And I resent your implication,' said Wilson looking at him. 'However, leads are already coming in on Foster, on which I could not possibly comment.' Always a good stand by. 'And now, I will pass you over to Mr Warner. He ran the B&B Foster resided at, I do hope you are keeping up. Mr Warner has first-hand experience of sharing accommodation with Foster.' He turned to Warner. 'Mr Warner.'

Warner kept his interview brief. He eyed the assembled journalists speculatively with his good eye, possibly weighing up his best option for an exclusive; plus, he had lost the sight in the other.

He lost the sight overnight, thought Wilson when the meeting concluded.

'Peter Robinson will have the scoop for having found Emily Watson,' he said.

'Right, right. Don't forget the East Anglian meeting in Cambridge tomorrow morning,' said Nicholson. 'Someone from the Police Authority as well as the Chiefs will address us on the upcoming cuts.'

The Police Authority policed the Police, but who policed the Police Authority? Wilson was reminded of an old song. *Who takes care of the care taker's daughter when the care-taker's busy taking care?* There would be a new body for policing the Police Authority soon, Wilson was quite sure of it.

'I bet this cost-cutting exercise will include

new uniforms for our force,' he said.

'What?' said Nicholson changing tracks, not successfully. 'Why wasn't I told about Robinson attending this morning?'

He paused.

'And don't tell me again that I was,' he added in parting. 'I have a meeting, so I'll get in touch with you this afternoon. Make sure you are there.'

It would be a nice change not to have somebody breathing down his neck, Wilson thought, as he drove back to Bury St. Edmunds.

CHAPTER 42

HOW DID IT GO with the press, sir?'

'It was close,' Wilson said, back in his office. 'If one of them hadn't been too clever for his own good, I would have been forced to admit I had been slow to spot Foster. It still does my head in, as a matter of fact.'

'How do you think I feel? I never even connected Foster with Howard Cole,' said Cunningham. 'By the way, I interviewed my ex last night about her stolen car.'

He looked pleased with himself.

'And?'

'She left it unlocked when she went into the restaurant to cancel a booking. She got delayed, and when she came out it was nicked, and later found burned out in Thelford.'

'Juveniles. Joy riders, but isn't the restaurant opposite the railway station?'

Cunningham nodded.

'I thought so. So, before Foster bought a ticket to York, he might have left his car on the railway car park from where it was nicked. He might have, and I think this highly unlikely, walked out of the station and driven to Stow where he had an accident. Can you put something together for regional news, the usual thirty seconds. I'd like to know if anybody saw Foster there, or his car.'

Cunningham nodded.

'It's also timely. We have to concentrate on car thieves, the missing Dr Willoughby, and sheds. How did you get on with the Domestic?'

First thing, Cunningham had driven to Suffolk Hospital to interview Miss Wawrinska, the woman who was

262

attacked. She was out of bed and about to discharge herself. She had a split lip, a black eye, a bruised rib, and the full range of assorted bruises on her arms where she had tried to shield herself.

'She refuses to bring charges, she said, because, and now it get's interesting, it was her own fault. '

'So? Don't they all say that?'

'She says she shouldn't have mentioned something. Luke, that is Luke Cole in the holding cell, her Man, as she calls him, is a dustman or whatever they call them. Sometimes he scavenges from the bins, apparently. When he came home at lunchtime, they don't work afternoons, he had a silver signet ring and a watch. A Tag Heuer.'

He paused.

'From there it gets interesting.'

'Miss Wawrinska used to work for Dr Willoughby. She became upset because she thought it was Dr Willoughby's signet ring and his watch and he should return them to Willoughby's daughter, Natasha, who she sometimes works for.'

'Whereupon he set about her. So, Mrs Marshall, Willoughby's daughter, employs her. Wheels within wheels.'

Cunningham had put both items, the ring and the watch, in a plastic bag.

'I have spoken to Natasha Marshall, who was at the hospital. Incidentally, she and her daughter are laying flowers by the posters of her missing father this afternoon.' He pointed to the cellophaned bunch of flowers on his desk. 'She wants me to put it under her father's poster on the notice board.'

'I thought they were from your ex,' said Wilson.

Cunningham ignored him.

'Mrs. Marshall says she knows her father is dead, she feels that the connection between them has been severed and she wants to draw a line under it for her daughter's sake. A line in the sand, if you ask me; but she has identified both the ring and the watch.'

The ring bore an intertwined AA, Agnes was her mother's first name, Anthony her father's, although he used his second name, Paul. It had a Hallmark, and it bore the date, 1968.'

'I'm going to trace the serial number of the watch to make sure,' Cunningham said, before they went into the interview room to ask Luke Cole a few questions.

'We won't tell him that Miss Wawrinska won't press charges,' said Wilson, 'let him think being released is the dangling carrot. We'll make him sweat a bit. Any priors? Burglaries?'

'Clean sheet.'

Luke Cole was a pleasant-looking man in his early thirties. Slightly protruding upper teeth gave him a smiling Ken Dodd aspect. Wilson started the recorder and noted the time, date and who was present.

'I want a fag,' Cole said. 'I've been without and it's not good for me nerves.'

'Later, perhaps. We would like to talk to you about Miss Wawrinska, who is still in hospital with severe injuries.'

Cole thought she had some sort of illness, a bruising illness.

'I've only got to look at her and she's black and blue.'

'Can you tell us why she got an attack of this illness yesterday evening?'

Cole stated that he couldn't possibly say. Confronted with the familiar challenge of an uncooperative witness, Wilson might have coaxed out the truth, but looking at this bully, he didn't waste time on refinements.

'It isn't your job to say what is or is not possible, I would advise you to shape up,' he bellowed.

Cole explained he was a Refuse Operative. One of them bins was overfull and something fell out, he said.

'A small packet,' he said. Finders keepers, so he put it in his pocket and looked at it. 'Not when I got home, I forgot,' he explained, 'I looked at it later. It was a signet ring and a watch.'

'You know Avenue Lane?' asked Wilson. 'Have you ever been there?'

It was on his route, he said.

'So, Miss Wawrinska worked for Dr Willoughby, the missing man. You could have accompanied her, and when the coast was clear entered the premises and made off with these valuable items.'

Cole went a paler shade of green.

'You're trying to fit me up. I've never been inside the bungalow, so yes, I know it was a bungalow, I waited for her once or twice on the road.'

He had shown the ring and the watch to his partner, who started wailing in that annoying foreign way, he a added. So, he clocked her once, but she carried on something alarming, so he clocked her another one.

'It's only an old watch, so what?'

'This old watch, as you call it, is worth in the region of £10,000.'

'You're having me on,' said Cole, 'people don't pay that much for a watch. What? For telling the time?'

Wilson knew what a watch was used for.

'She screamed that it was the old man's, I had

to shut her up on account of the neighbours,' Cole finally added, and shouldn't he have a solicitor present?

'I don't think there is any need for that,' said Wilson. 'Can you remember where the bin the package fell out of was situated?'

'It was black bin day, Southern side of Bury St. Edmunds, maybe Farn Road or thereabouts. It was overflowing, the lid was pushed open halfway, that's why the packet fell out when I lifted it up,' said Cole. 'Don't ask me where exactly. We do that part of the town on a Wednesday, but one black bin looks like another.'

'What time was that?'

'Probably between eight and one,' he said helpfully, 'the next day we do the other side of Bury St. Edmunds.'

Wilson said Miss Wawrinska didn't want to bring charges; he could go after he had made a statement and had his fingerprints taken. 'To eliminate you from our enquiries when we examine Dr Willoughby's bungalow, so it's in your favour.' Privately, he hoped to find another fingerprint on the ring, whose, he wasn't sure of.

Cole left the station after that, got a taxi and went home. Aleska wasn't there, so he went to the hospital, all long corridors with arrows pointing God only knew where. Eventually he was told by a snotty nurse that Aleska had already discharged herself.

When he got home, he found the flat was still empty. Where the hell was she? Bloody foreign troublemaker, he should have stayed well clear of her, he thought, looking into her wardrobe, where he found her clothes had gone and her stuff had been cleared from the bathroom.

The doorbell rang. When he opened the door, it was the nosy cow who had reported him.

'Where is she?' he asked softly.

She backed off, but he caught her, the imprint of his thumb and fingers he left on her arms would take a while to fade.

He let her go, well pleased. She was in Wheystead, with Marshall's daughter.

'It's a right dog's breakfast, it looks like Willoughby was robbed, possibly attacked what with the blood on his coat. Plus, according to his son-in-law, he was also suicidal,' said Wilson, looking at one of the whiteboards.

When the phone rang, Cunningham answered it.

'It's Lena, from Oxfam,' he said. 'She says that she served a man answering Foster's description. He was buying a jacket and trousers, as far as she can recall. He was also rude and gave her the creeps. She'll come in and make a statement.'

Wilson put it on the whiteboard and then looked at the map of Bury St. Edmunds.

The Southern part included Avenue Lane and Farn Road. Warren of the B&B sprang to mind. George Hudson, who had also loitered in an unlikely spot at an unlikely hour in unlikely weather also lived in Farn Road. There was no connection and he tried to dismiss it from his mind, but George Hudson resolutely stayed there.

'We can't fingerprint the whole town,' said Cunningham when he told him, 'you can empty a lot of bins in four hours. I'll telephone Warner to see if he had emptied his bins before leaving the B&B.'

'Miss Wawrinska will have to make a statement and the items will have to be tested for fingerprints. Perhaps you can send them to the lab. Meanwhile, I'll leave the station in your capable hands.

It's time for my annual nervous breakdown.'

Cunningham wasn't surprised, but he lifted his eyebrows.

'If?'

'If? When he rings, tell Nicholson to stop breathing down my neck. Or tell him I'm giving blood.'

'You allegedly gave blood a few weeks ago.'

'Say anything you fancy, tell him I have been diagnosed with leprosy if you like,' said Wilson, getting up and gathering his belongings, 'just say that I'm not here. And I won't be here for long tomorrow morning, we have a meeting in Cambridge I have to attend. In the meantime, I leave it all in your capable hands.'

At four o'clock, with everything done, Cunningham wrote his report when the phone rang. It was the Super.

'Where is he?' he demanded when he was told Wilson was gone for the afternoon.

Cunningham coughed.

'He didn't like to mention it, but he's got a boil on his backside that needs a doctor's attention.'

Nicholson said he thought Wilson had been a bit tetchy.

'Lack of vitamins, but a bit of a nerve requesting fruit. What? I would have thought he could pay for it himself,' he added, much to Cunningham puzzlement.

'Fruit?'

'I was as surprised at his request as you are, but there it is. Vitamins.'

When Constable Smith returned from the lab, he said he had a phone call from the Super.

'I couldn't make any sense of it, Paula,' he said.

'You're the detective,' she said, 'so go and

detect.'

'Did your kid keep you awake?'

'My mother looks after her during the week, and a kid is a young goat,' she said coolly.

She had snapped at him all day. She didn't like him being in charge, he said to Sergeant Tomlinson in the canteen.

'I have told Paula before now there is no "I" in team,' he said sadly, stirring his tea, 'but she does give us 110%.'

Just as well Wilson wasn't there to hear it.

'And we did hit the ground running when the child went missing,' added Tomlinson for good measure.

As Cunningham clinched his teeth, Wilson drove home.

He pressed the doorbell testing the dog for alertness, which he passed with flying ears, slithering on the wooden hall floor towards the front door, barking madly. Then he went to the nursery for a big green plant for Dorothy, booked them in again into the Old Fire Engine in Ely, and then drove to Felixstowe, where he let the dog loose on the beach while his own mind dwelled on the child murder.

The pathologist had ignored procedure and carried on with testing the old samples. Strange, Wilson had always thought of himself as the last of a dying breed, going about in his old-fashioned way amongst shiny-faced whiz-kids who only had to look at a computer to find out what everybody had for breakfast last Tuesday.

He had nothing against people able to use technology; he just wished he knew more about it than telling the difference between software and hardware.

The wind in his hair, waves rolling in foaming, crashing rolls onto the shore, he finally left his mind to its own devices. At the moment, it resembled a jigsaw puzzle, emptied from its box into many pieces, with perhaps one or two corners resting in his trusty notebook.

That evening, driving with Dorothy to Eli, the illuminated Cathedral emerged like a large ocean-going vessel. *"The Ship of the Fens"* it was called, the distant views of its towers dominating the low-lying wetlands of the Fens.

'Oliver Cromwell shut it down for ten years and stabled his horses there,' said Dorothy.

Holy horse shit, thought Wilson, then he pondered on his general ignorance.

Finally, he laughed.

He told Dorothy Cunningham had said he had interviewed his ex about the stolen car last night. 'Interviewed. That's a funny word for it,' he added. 'She fancies him rotten like the rest of the female population, except she thinks policing is a nine-to-five job and she takes offence when it isn't.'

He paused.

'I also said something stupid to him a few days ago.'

Dorothy tried to look surprised.

'I said I didn't come over on a banana boat.'

'Well, you didn't, oh, I see.'

Cunningham was a very light-coloured black man.

'He took it calmly, perhaps I ought to apologise,' he said, 'but I never know what is permissible in this politically correct world. Can we still say "*Indian* Summer", or "Accident *Black* Spot?"'

In the restaurant, he looked at Dorothy fondly over the flickering candlelight. He took her small, elegant hand into his and proposed marriage to her.

'You don't really want to get married, do you?' she said. 'I'd marry you like a shot if I thought you really wanted to.'

'I don't want to spoil what we have got,' he said. 'What we have together.'

'What we have together,' she said. When she smiled and she left her hand in his. Wilson could feel in an interview coming on.

CHAPTER 43

THE NEXT MORNING, Wilson was sitting in his office with a cup of coffee. Wondering when the promised coffee-maker would turn up, he was having a quick look at the papers. The Mirror had landed the Peter Robinson scoop. MODEST HERO SAVES EMILY FROM BEAST, proclaimed the headline. Modest Peter Robinson, thirty-five, denied he was a hero. He was in the right place at the right time, he told our reporter. And so on.

The Mail had to make do with Warner from the B&B. BLINDED BY EVIL CHILD KILLER, ran the headline.

When the phone rang, it was Emily Watson's brother, ringing about Emily's debriefing. He said that for Emily's sake it should be done by Margaret, who turned out to be the liaison officer. Wilson suggested Constable Smith ought to accompany her, Gregory Watson agreed, and he suggested that the debriefing be done at their house, but not today, possibly tomorrow.

'Tomorrow it is then. How is Emily?' Wilson asked.

Apparently, she was coping well and her father was back. Although no press was camped outside their house, they intended to visit Portugal for a month.

'The papers only have a photo of Emily with long hair,' Gregory said, 'so my mother is doing something to alter it.'

He told WPC Smith about it, when his mobile rang. It was Nicholson, and he briefed him.

'Quite right, Emily's wishes have to come first.'

He paused.

'Where are you?'

'I'm on the A14,' said Wilson, and very

shortly, he was on the way to the meeting for Inspectors and above ranks from Cambridge, Essex and Suffolk. Parking would be a nightmare. He parked at the Grafton Centre, the shopping complex, and walked down Fitzroy Street and into town to the Guildhall, where he arrived late.

Squeezing into his seat, he noted the disapproving stare from Nicholson's swivelled head two rows in front of him.

The meeting, chaired by one of the Chief Constables started well, with no mention of benchmarking, always a puzzle to Wilson. Why not think of something else, like a touchstone?

Apparently, in these days of cutbacks, not to say rigorous pruning of budgets, the economical use of available resources was of the utmost importance.

Wilson looked out of the window.

'One way of looking after finances,' the voice droned on, 'is by ensuring that we get the most out of our teams, by which I mean,...'

After a finely judged point, he slipped out and went to King's College Chapel. He gazed in awe at the stained-glass windows with their marvellous blues, and at the reds in the painting of "*The Adoration Of The Magi*," by, Good Heavens, Rubens. The mighty sound of the organ swelled and filled the building, and he returned just in time for the coffee break.

'It has done me the world of good,' he said most sincerely to Nicholson, who wasn't as daft as he looked.

'There is a spare seat next to mine,' he said, when Wilson's mobile rang.

'Yes, thank you,' he turned to Nicholson and switched off the phone. 'Cunningham has heard from Cambridge. Vladimir Glubis, a friend of Foster who was banged up for downloading kiddy porn, absconded a few weeks before Foster's release. He disappeared, and he possibly managed to identify Foster's wife for Foster. Regarding the Foster leak, apparently an Alf Butler from Bury St. Edmunds is the brother of a secretary working there.'

A distant bell rang in his memory.

'I think you are barking up the wrong tree if you're thinking of vigilantes,' said Nicholson before Wilson could identify the peal, and lead the condemned man to his doom, next to him. 'Foster has left the area; we have definite sightings of him in Oxford.'

'And Bath, and Dover. He's had more sightings than Elvis.'

Nicholson ignored him.

'Have a word with the ACC after the meeting.'

'Part 2. Targets,' said the ACC, standing in for the Chief Constable for Suffolk.

'Appeals are to be issued to the residents in towns and suburbs to be watchful and increase security to prevent garden shed and garage burglaries. Metal grills should be fitted to shed windows, garage door locked, also oil tanks.... Freeing valuable police time for....

Common sense and gobbledygook, says it all, thought Wilson. Of course, householders looking after their belongings freed police time, but here I sit contemplating securing lawn mowers while a child killer is on the loose and a disturbed man is missing.

The force is accumulating a significant amount of expense claims for parking in Cambridge and for lunch, and apparently new uniforms were to be issued, whilst Nicholson sat rapt, his hat on his lap, until the next item.

The present officer numbers could no longer be sustained in the forthcoming cuts to the budget.

Wilson secretly dialled his own mobile phone

number.

'Got to go,' he mouthed, and so he did.

It could be seen as truanting, thought Wilson driving home, although, at his age, he preferred to call it preserving his sanity.

On Friday afternoon, the mobile unit was parked at the start of the lane where the lens was found. It was another dismal evening, rain fell heavily from a grey sky. DS Cunningham didn't have a lot to do, only a few people stopped to look at the posters of Paul Willoughby and Fred Foster.

At five o'clock, an irate man, a Mr Albert Rusty, came in and told him he was parked in the wrong place, didn't the police know anything? He was followed by the man whose wheelbarrow and torch had been borrowed and returned.

'And you are?'

'Claude.'

Claude what?'

'Why don't you find out?'

'Right, Claude, we are trying to trace the missing man, Dr Willoughby's, whereabouts last Friday.'

'A bit late, aren't you?' Claude said. 'A week too late, maybe?'

Cunningham told him that if the police officers could foretell the future, they would be redundant.

'With a nice fat pension, no doubt,' said Claude, exiting the van.

Maggie was, once again, on her way to do the evening shift at Somerfield when she spotted the van. 'I always thought you spoke through a window in one of these things,' she said inside, sitting down and facing Cunningham opposite her with notebook at the ready.

'Like an ice-cream van,' she added, but it's more like a caravan.'

Cunningham didn't write it down.

'Anyway, last week I was on my way to work. I work at Somerfield, the evening shift. My headscarf slipped off and I put it back on, that was after I crossed the road. That's when I spotted the mobile on the little wall.'

She rummaged in her bag and handed it over.

'I meant to hand it in, but you know what it's like, with kids and working it never ends, there's always something else to do.'

It was a bit like being in the police, Cunningham thought.

'Is there anything else you remember about last Friday evening?'

'Somebody was working on the allotments. It struck me as odd, being out and about in this awful weather.'

'Somebody? Just one person, or more?'

She thought about it.

'It might have been two, I didn't look closely; the weather was awful.'

She signed her statement and added that she best be off, she didn't want to be late.

Cunningham thanked her and, seeing nothing else transpired, stared to make his report. He was half-way through, when he remembered to call Wilson.

WPC Paula Smith, along with Connor, was dispatched at five o'clock to interview householders living on top of the lane.

'A a week is a long time if you ask me,' said Paula.

'We're not in politics, and I didn't ask you.' said Wilson. 'Ask them to cast their minds back, did something unusual occur last Friday? The cat got run over? An aunt died? Little Jimmy kept in detention?'

Wilson put the phone down, Cunningham told him they had Paul Willoughby's mobile, when Smith and Connor returned.

One of the householders, whose garden lead to the lane, had been disturbed.

'Not exactly disturbed,' said Connor. 'The side gate was open. Usually it was kept shut because of their dog, but last Friday, it was open and the dog ran away when they let him out. Normally, the sensor light out the back is triggered by the dog and when it didn't come on they realised the side gate was open. Their house faces more or less the middle of the lane.'

'Not more or less,' said Smith. 'Roughly.'

'Number 35,' said Connor.

'Right,' said Wilson. 'Time you weren't here. I suppose you have got a home to go to.'

He looked at his notes. One, or possibly two people leaving a gate open, jumping off the wall? Pretending to do some gardening? Borrowing a wheelbarrow? What had happened between jumping off the wall and gardening, he wondered, when the phone rang.

It was Dorothy.

'No, I haven't forgotten, Dorothy. The list is here somewhere.'

Weekend shopping at Waitrose. He got up, found his coat and wondered where the list was and what could possibly be on it if it had gone missing.

The aforementioned A. Butler, whose sister was a secretary in the open prison, had a busy schedule planned for Monday morning, although a hospital visit wasn't on his agenda.

He slid under the engine of an old Ford when

he realised he had forgotten to ring his supplier. He was about to slide out when he saw a pair of trainers on the ground quite close to his head. 'No, no, no, no, no,' he shouted. His heart began to hammer in his chest and then he felt sick and faint and he couldn't breathe.

'A heart attack? Alf? Are you sure, George?' said Christine that evening. 'Surely it's not possible.'

Alf was on the small and thin side, with an unremarkable face, distinguished by two deep worry lines running from nose to chin.

'He doesn't smoke, but he likes a fry up, and he worries a lot,' said George, 'But you never know. Margaret was quite annoyed when she saw me coming out of the ward.'

'But he asked for you. Margaret seems to be a disappointed woman, she always makes cracks about us, like we are in a different league.'

'That is just silly,' said Rosie, who had no idea what her parents were talking about, but she wanted to broadcast her own news. 'Daddy, you'll never guess who came to see me today.'

She looked at him expectantly.

'The Queen.'

'You are being silly again,' she said and opened her mouth. It was going to be Chapter and Verse. 'The doorbell rang, and when Mummy opened it, Emily Watson was standing there with her Mummy, only I didn't know it was Emily Watson. I wondered whoever could that be, and she said, "I am Emily Watson."'

She paused.

'She had her hair cut really short and coloured blond. Can I have my hair cut short? Mummy said that I couldn't. And guess what, Emily Watson is going to another school, it's called a Public School because it's a private school.'

'Now you are being silly,' said George.

'No, and before she goes to that school, she is going on holiday with her father. And that lady from the police, I forgot what her name is, is going to talk to her.'

Luckily the phone rang. He answered it in the hall.

'Ritchie.'

'I hear Alf's in hospital,' he said.

'Only overnight, he's had a mild heart attack. I've been to see him.' George pushed the hall door shut with his foot. 'He was under a car engine when he saw a pair of trainers next to the car.'

'Standing there.'

'That's right. He assumed it was Foster with a spanner in his hand, so he stayed where he was but it turned out to be his lad. When he pulled him out, Alf was hyperventilating and was rushed to hospital.'

'In an ambulance.'

'That's right.'

George paused. 'So Fred Foster got to Alf without being there,' he said.

He let that sink in.

'Lewis will be joining us at the pub. I think we ought to meet a bit earlier to decide what to tell him.'

'I get you,' said Ritchie, 'we tell him nothing about nothing.'

George heaved a sigh of relief.

'Who's Lewis?' asked Ritchie.

In Wheystead, Hester, Natasha, Aleska and Lewis finished their supper. 'Me and Mummy went and laid flowers by granddad's big photos because he's gone away and we won't see him any more. He was in a lot of bus stops.'

'Like Princess, much flowers,' said Aleska who

was out of hospital and was wincing as she leaned forwards. Aleska was very sore, but nothing had been broken and there was no fluid in her lungs.

'My Man, I go back to him. I am in way.'

'What way? Oh, you mean in our way.' For a minute, Lewis thought she might be in the family way. She was to stay there and take it easy, he said. He himself was perfectly capable of putting a few dishes in the dishwasher and a few clothes in the washing machine.

'In that order, I hope,' said Natasha.

'How about the bad man?' asked Hester.

'We're not washing his clothes, but don't you worry, I am here now, and so is Mummy and Aleska. You can teach her some English words,' said Lewis, but he added that was going out later in the evening.

'You are meeting George and his friends?' said Natasha. Men meet once or twice and they became mates, how do they do it?

Mates or not, Lewis was back in good time for a game of Scrabble, or so he was told.

'Is Hester still up? I'll take her up to bed.'

She was in her nightdress and was sleepy, so he carried her upstairs and put her to bed.

'Anything on the telly?' he asked hopefully when he came down.

'Nothing that I can see,' said Natasha. 'Scrabble will help Aleska with her English. How did you get on?'

'All right. They're nice blokes, George and Ritchie, that other one, you know the thin one with the amazing red-headed daughter?'

'You mean Victoria?'

'That's right. He's in hospital. Something to do with his ticker. Maybe we can ask the family over on Sunday. Do they deliver pizzas out here?'

'You're not on the moon; it's barely a mile out of town.'

Lewis was amazed, 'Anyway, a bloke in the black motor cycling gear they wear for riding a scooter passed me when I drew up. That made me think of it.'

'You are prepared to eat a pizza? A carpet tile as you call it, but why not? Anyway, Christine phoned me,' said Natasha. 'What an amazing escape for Emily! We can't stop talking about it and shuddering when we think how our children would have fared. But it looks like Foster has left the area, according to the police.'

Lewis shook his head.

'I wouldn't be too sure. I think the police are up shit-creek without a paddle, as Sherlock Holmes so often remarked to Dr Watson.'

After a game Aleska convinced was called Squabble, they went upstairs. Natasha looked out of the window where she saw the dark figure of a man leaning, once again, against the willow tree.

'It's only Frank, he's keeping an eye on the house since Dad went missing, He means well,' she whispered to Lewis.

He had to think for a moment who Frank was.

'Uncle Frank. I'll tell him to bugger off tomorrow,' he said. 'You never know, Aleska's Man might stalk her and meet him instead.' He got into bed and switched the bedside lamp off. Something was digging into him, a piece of a jigsaw, he discovered when he switched on the light once more.

'That's the missing corner piece for the Swiss scene,' said Natasha.

'How did that get very nearly up my..., never mind. I feel we are being watched, I can't rest until I see that old bugger off.' He jumped out of bed, put on his dressing gown and rushed downstairs.

'What on earth is this screaming?' Natasha

thought. Opening the bedroom window, she saw Lewis running after the disappearing figure of a man. He came back and went towards the willow tree. He was bending over the still figure of Aleska when Natasha rushed down.

The ambulance had been and gone, Hester was cuddled up to her father on the settee.

'Mummy has gone with Aleska to the hospital.'

'Was it the bad man?'

'No, moppet,' said Lewis, 'why would the bad man come here?'

She didn't look convinced. 'He doesn't know where we live, does he?' she said.

When Natasha came back by taxi in the early hours of the morning, Hester was fast asleep on the settee.

'Aleska is in the Intensive Care Unit, would you believe,' Natasha said. She shivered.'Lewis, what is happening to us?'

'I've been thinking,' said Lewis, drawing her to him. 'Why don't we move into my apartment in Cambridge? I'll talk to the school tomorrow. I believe something very nasty is on the loose.'

CHAPTER 44

FRED FOSTER PARKED HIS SCOOTER round the back of the B&B. He had been stupid again. Lurking by the bushes by *The Volunteer,* he had thought the red-headed bloke was the one he was looking for when he met up with the other two.

The power of three.

He waited and then he followed him through twisting country lanes and roads to an isolated house. He was standing under a willow tree for a long time letting the night gather around him when he noticed that the curtains were not drawn and that someone had left a space open on one of the downstairs windows.

Sash windows, not locked, he noticed, when he spotted a man, carrying a small girl, leaving the room.

After the lights went out downstairs and the bedroom lights came on, he padded to the house and inched the sash window up one foot. When all the house lights went out, he would enter the house through the window and let the occupiers know someone had paid them a visit.

He wouldn't touch the kid the man had carried, he didn't know the house layout, but he was bound to think of something filthy.

Except.

A woman came running out of the house. When he stared at her, she screamed at him and turned around to the house. One blow at her neck with his helmet and she fell conveniently at his feet. And then a bloke ran out of the house; he was tall, not short, and he was blond, not red-haired.

It was the wrong bloke, but there was no reason to panic, except later he had wheeled his scooter up the front to the B&B in plain sight, not through the council estate and through the back garden.

He sat in the kitchen, letting the torchlight flicker over his trump card. He chuckled. It was a good term for the business card of ...... He looked at the card he had pocketed from The Volunteer

Richard King, Painter and Decorator.
Plastering, Coving. Painting.
No Job Too Small, No Job Too Big.

When his torch gave out, he thought he would get a new battery. Then he sat up, the hairs of his neck bristling; a car was drawing up by the back door.

A car door slammed. A voice shouted, 'Hello,' and the kitchen door opened slowly.

Luke Cole spent the evening at the pub. He wasn't drinking heavily but he was losing heavily playing snooker.

As he stormed out and drove home to his empty flat, he was getting more and more worked up about the Polish bitch. He had opened his home to her, yes, he had opened his home. He had even brought her presents. She had set the police on him, that's how she repaid him.

He wouldn't get any sleep thinking about it, so why should she?

He drove off, watching his speed through the twisting lanes, he was over the limit. OK, it was getting late, but not that late, when he found the house.

Luke Cole parked a bit further by a farm and walked back to the house. Big. You bet whoever lived there had money; but all thoughts of comparative wealth were driven out of his mind by the spectacle played out in front him. He heard a well-known scream. Then silence. Next, a bloke in motorcycling gear was being chased by a bloke in a dressing gown who turned back to the house, while the other bloke put on his helmet, turned his scooter round and drove off.

Luke came out from the hedge he had melted against, ran to his car, reversed and caught up with the rider who drove up to the B&B that was supposedly deserted and up for sale.

'Hello!' he shouted stupidly but he really wanted to know what had happened back at the house, when the door opened and something heavy caught him a glancing blow. He fell down onto his back and looked up.

'You are Fred Foster,' he said.

Those were his last words.

CHAPTER 45

AFTER HEAVING THE BODY into the boot, he had to get rid of the dead man's car, Foster thought, and tonight. But who would have thought strangling an adult was such a hard work? Those legs kicking out? He felt worn out. One of the problems with squatting was that electricity and water were cut off, and he sometimes needed his caffeine from something other than Coke.

He got into the dead man's car, fumbled for the light, turned the headlights off and inched down the drive. When the road ahead was clear, he crossed over, switched the lights on, adjusted his rear-view mirror and drove onto the car park at the railway station. He went into the station's Gents, washed his hands and his face and then, at the bar, he bought a large coffee. It came in a plastic tub, complete with lid, but was far too hot. He carried it to the dead man's car, which was being closely inspected by two hooded youths.

'Sod off!' he shouted, attracting the attention of a copper patrolling the car park.

He waved his hands dismissively, got into the car and drove it to the estate and parked it. He then walked through the lane between the back gardens and let himself into the house. He sank into a chair he would call bed. Never had coffee tasted better, but of course, it kept him awake, allowing him to think back to the copper at the railway station.

'We weren't doing nothing,' Jimmy pointed out to the policeman.

'We were waiting for our father,' said Ronald, 'only he missed the train, he said, when I phoned him on his mobile.'

They didn't have to be told twice to clear off.

They had better wait until Jimmy's mum went away, leaving her car behind, said Ronald.

Jimmy had to ring the bell again when he got home.

'Got all your homework done with Ronald?' asked his mother when she opened the door.

'Revision, Mum, revision. I left it at Ronald's.'

An early morning, dark and depressing, found Foster clearing up his traces in the B&B. He stashed the scooter, helmet and dark jacket behind the shed and went back into the house.

Finally, he was satisfied. Dirty plates, cutlery, empty tins and coke bottles were in the three plastic bags he carried when he let himself out of the house.

He had a car again and it had a body in the boot.

He walked through the streets and around to the estate to get to the car, when a cold hand gripped his heart. What fucking colour was the dead man's Ford Focus? He had thought it was a dark blue, but it was a maroon actually. He inserted the key and the engine turned over.

He pulled his woolly hat further down on his curly dark wig and adjusted the large, horn-rimmed glasses he now wore. He looked into the rear-view mirror and drove off, straight into the slow-moving rush-hour morning traffic of Farn Road, where an interesting, heart-warming sight greeted him.

Barely twelve houses from the B&B, a man paused on the doorstep, kissing his wife, presumably. Then he got hold of his blond daughter's hand, and started to walk down the road.

It was him! The bloke who had smashed the bottle and thrown the money onto the path.

'Got you, and Richard King, I don't have to go

to that fucking sodding pub any more,' he said, before he got to grips with the A14.

Normal traffic would have been bad enough, but he got bogged down when three lanes had been narrowed to one due to an accident. Instead of in Cambridge, he ended up in a god-forsaken hole called Milton. In Milton's *"Paradise Lost,"* Pandemonium was where demons dwelled. Too right.

He turned off towards a river, which gave him an idea.

The day was grey, murky. It looked as if someone had switched off daylight; it was raining heavily now.

One or two people walking their dogs on a well-worn path kept their heads down. When he rounded a bend, the road as far as he could see was deserted, the river bank interposed with willows weeping into the water.

Further up, a tent was pitched; it was probably used by anglers although the season was over.

He remembered fishing, and he clearly remembered the last time he went.

'Go fishing, you two, and talk,' his mother said.

By the river, his father started using the rod, forwards and back, forwards and back like he was flogging a horse, a dead horse, as far as he was concerned. Pretty soon he had a bite, a flapping green fish. He sprang forward and cut out its eyes. There was a little blood, and his father gave him a thick ear.

His father said that he was wired wrong.

'You did that thing with the cat, didn't you? Your mother and I want you to live with your grandparents.'

Anger gripped him by the throat.

They never asked him, they *just told* him of the

new plans for his living arrangements.

They were eating fish paste sandwiches by the river's edge in silence. His father had nothing more to say on the matter, while he was thinking; living with his grandparents in their crummy little house with the stairs in the living room and the stinky little kitchen? He had to do something about it.

If the river was as wide as it was deep, the car would easily vanish.

He used some of the Wipes the bloke had in his car to wipe off his fingerprints. Wipes? Was he a doctor? Surely not, with all those empty beer cans littering the floor. He threw the cans into the river and cleaned everything he thought he had touched.

Finally satisfied, he got out of the car and opened the car boot and went through the dead man's jacket.

The dead man was a Luke Cole, according to his driving licence. He had a mobile and fifty pounds in his wallet as well as several credit cards, a Visa card amongst them, the pin number thoughtfully next to it, and a condom. He kept the money, the Visa card and the pin number, the rest went into the river.

He started the car and left it in gear, released the handbrake, and, one hand on the steering wheel, pushed it over the footpath and the coarse green grass at the water's edge. After an eternity, the car disappeared with a sucking sound.

He never noticed the aerial sticking out of the water, a beer can swinging gently in the breeze. He walked on and emptied his rubbish into a bin in some hole called Ditton, where he waited in a bus shelter next to a recreation ground, adjacent to a noisy old crow with more hair on her chin than on her head. He nodded while she explored the weather over the past fifty years.

'Old hags like you should be put down like old dogs,' he said pleasantly when the bus came in sight.

'What?' she said.

'You heard.'

When she tried to get away, he stuck his foot out against her ankle and she fell on her face, screaming.

The bus stopped.

'I'm trying to help her, but she won't let me,' he said to the driver through the open door before he boarded the bus and sat down. This pleasant diversion was interrupted when a smart woman in a beige raincoat planted herself next to the driver. 'Don't you dare drive off while I see to this lady,' she thundered.

When she was on the road the bus drove off, leaving the two woman in the rain.

'I've got a schedule to keep,' said the driver.

'Is there a mental home round here?' Foster asked an elderly male passenger, who shrugged his shoulders and leaned towards him. 'I have his number,' he whispered.

A village was missing its idiot, he thought.

Next on the list was a hotel. He wanted a television, a shower, room service and a wide bed.

When the bus stopped, he exited onto Drummer Street, crossed the road to John Lewis, where he bought all the essentials for a travelling man, with Cole's credit card.

He booked himself into The Crossed Arms nearby for two days as Luke Cole, 30 Ridley Road, Bury St. Edmunds. He paid for two days with Cole's credit card and went to ground, or that was his intention.

CHAPTER 46

'PERHAPS YOU COULD ask Warner from the B&B in Farn Road if we can inspect his house,' Wilson said the next morning to Cunningham.'

Cunningham had his number. Warner's, not Wilson's.

'To see if Foster is hiding there. What does Alf Butler do for a living?'

'Who?'

'Alf Butler, he is a mate of Hudson's.'

'He is a car mechanic, is he?' said Wilson, who would never learn, 'I think my car needs a service. Connor, perhaps you and Tomlinson can go and get Luke Cole. There's been some weird goings on, leaving Miss Wawrinska injured and in hospital.'

He turned to the DS. 'Perhaps you can go to the hospital and see if Miss Wawrinska is up to an interview yet.'

Aleska was out of intensive care and in the general ward, Natasha, he couldn't remember her last name for the moment, oh, Marshall, was by her side. While not sitting up, Aleska, who wore a neck brace, lay with her head propped up on pillows; the IV line was still attached to the side of her neck.

'I won't keep you long. How are you feeling?'

She muttered something long and complicated in Polish, which Cunningham translated correctly as 'like shit.'

Natasha took over.

Aleska didn't know who had attacked her. She didn't know if it was Luke Cole, it was a dark figure of a man, it was at night and it was dark under the overhanging branches of the willow tree. Aleska had turned round when Lewis opened the front door and something hit her from behind. Hard.

'She's got whiplash.'

She fell down, unconscious, but she must have had a kicking as well. Her ribs were no longer bruised, but broken.

'She's a smoker as well,' Natasha said. 'She coughs a lot.'

That just had to be painful, he thought.

'She wore her anorak over her nightdress. The hood was bunched up against her neck,' Natasha added. 'If she hadn't worn it, the doctor said, she would have broken her neck and she would be paralysed.'

'I want go home, Poland, she Lublin, ' said Aleska brokenly, when the ward sister shoed them both out.

'She's from Lublin,' Natasha interpreted.

'We'll need statements about last night, from both you and your husband, at some time,' said Cunningham, who walked with her to the car park.

Mrs Marshall pointed to a BMW, parked very near his old Saab. 'My husband is in the car,' she said, 'perhaps now would be a good time.'

They drove off, the Marshalls to the station, and Cunningham to Luke Cole's flat to assist Connor and Tomlinson. They broke the door down when they got no reply and got hold of a photo showing a dead-pan Luke Cole in a monkey suit at a wedding, while Wilson drove back from Alf's garage to the office.

He couldn't have his car serviced as not only Miss Wawrinska but also the said Alf Butler was in hospital, having suffered a heart attack. He was under the engine when it happened, the apprentice told him.

Apparently Alf was wanted on the phone by his supplier. He went to tell him and Butler shouted,'No', several times. 'I pulled him out after a bit and he was ill and couldn't breathe properly, shallow-like, so I phoned for the ambulance.'

He paused.

'They said they were on their way and I was to put a paper bag over Alf's head, only I couldn't find one so I phoned Hudson, his best mate, and asked him if I could put a plastic bag over Alf's head instead.'

'What did Hudson say?' Wilson asked, interested.

'He swore at me, and then the ambulance arrived.'

Hudson, the best mate.

'What shoes did you wear?' asked Wilson.

'Shoes? Trainers,' said the lad. Why was he asking stupid questions, he said later, when Alf was out of hospital, instead of making future appointments for his car. It didn't do Alf's blood pressure any good, especially when the lad said he thought the bloke was a copper.

Wilson was back in the office when the officers arrived with Cole's photo.

'We'll want that for the regional news,' he said to Paula. 'Can you fax it to HQ?'

'I will scan it electronically and....'

'Whatever you think best,' he said. 'And Connor, perhaps you can secure Cole's flat.

Now onto what Wilson called the beautiful people. The dark-haired woman with the exquisite face, wearing jeans and an oversized jumper, a scarf around her neck was a luminous beauty; the blond man with his height and his leanness was impressive. Both wore their good looks lightly, doubling the impact.

The beautiful people had made their statements

.   Spotting a man leaning against the willow tree, Mrs Marshall mistook him for a friendly uncle. Mr Marshall was uneasy, running out but not catching the man, coming back and bending over the unconscious

Miss Wawrinska.

'It happened so fast,' he said, 'and it was so unexpected.'

'What friendly uncle was keeping an eye on your house, Mrs Marshall?' asked Wilson.

'This is bit hard to explain. Frank Somersby was a colleague of my father's. I've known him since I was about ten, and he was keeping watch on my house.'

'You mean at night?'

She nodded.

'From the willow tree, that is, since my father disappeared. He thought I shouldn't be alone in that isolated house, but now that Lewis is with me I am not alone. Frank came onto the scene again before Lewis and I got together because he thought I needed looking after.'

'He'll have to be interviewed. Now, Mr Marshall, did anything else out of the usual happen on Saturday night?'

Lewis said it might be nothing, but one of the living room windows was open at the bottom, about a foot.

'They're sash windows, not locked,' he explained. 'Natasha opens the top one to get rid of the smell of curry.'

'But never the bottom window,' Wilson made a note of it. 'And?'

'I met up with George Hudson and Ritchie King at The Volunteer.'

He explained they were not old friends; he had met them through the Emily Watson business. 'I met them, we had a drink, and I drove home.'

'Nobody followed you?'

Not that he noticed, Mr Marshall said.

'Have you any idea what was used to inflict

Miss Wawrinska's injuries?'

Lewis said it hadn't crossed his mind.

'Could it have been a cricket bat?'

'I wouldn't know; I haven't thought about it, but it certainly wasn't mine,' said Lewis. 'I play at Fenners with my team and I keep my bat in the Cambridge apartment.'

'You're a Cambridge man?'

He got his degree in business studies from a technical college in Cambridge later acquiring University status. But being able to say her son had a degree from Cambridge kept his mother happy.

'I suppose you will want to examine our front garden, but I didn't see anything like a weapon, not that I was actually looking for one.'

'We will also take some fingerprints off the sash window, the glass. We have acquired quite a database of suspects and convicts,' said Wilson. 'We can run a sample against what we have, and we might get lucky.

'I do hope you do. We may well move into my father-in-law's bungalow when my parents arrive,' said Lewis. His parents had retired to Sardinia, he explained.

Where else, thought Wilson. But the family felt uneasy, understandable so.

As they left the station, Connor came in with a Mrs Beverly, a comfortable, unremarkable looking woman, wearing a coat and a head scarf, not unlike Her Majesty on her estate, a different estate perhaps. Connor explained that she lived in the same block of flats as Luke Cole.

'I felt sorry for Aleska, a lovely girl, always doing things for other people,' Mrs Beverley said, clutching her bag to her, when she was seated. 'He was mostly all right with her, but sometimes he became a monster, and she was a stranger in a strange land. I suppose it suited him that she had nobody to turn to.'

Wilson had never thought of that.

She didn't know if Cole was home or not last night, as Miss Wawrinska was absent she didn't keep a look-out for her.

When told she was in hospital after being attacked again, she went pale.

'I told him where she was,' she said. 'She pushed her sleeves back. Her wrists were black and blue. She had no other option, she said. 'After I reported him to you, he waited for me in the hall and punched me in the chest.'

She wouldn't show them her bruises, she added.

'Aleska can move in with me when she's out of the hospital,' she said, 'poor girl. What was she attacked with? I suppose you don't know yet.'

She had her wits about her, thought Wilson.

'I think Cole has done a runner, When I went to get my morning paper I noticed his car was parked over the road, and one of his mates drove off in it. He was probably picking him up somewhere.'

'Can you describe him?'

'Not really. It was drizzly, and he was bent over the steering wheel, but he wore a woolly hat and big glasses.'

Nice woman, he thought after she left, what they called salt of the earth, whatever that meant.

Cole's photo had been scanned and sent to Storwich, Constable Smith informed him.

Did she want a medal? he thought.

Frank Somersby, Willoughby's doctor, had been interviewed.

The previous evening he had attended a concert

by a string quartet held at the Fitzwilliam in Cambridge. Wilson thought the Fitzwilliam was a museum, which it was. But sometimes they held recitals there, that sort of thing, as Somersby, remarkably dark-haired for a man approaching fifty, explained. Somersby said he was looking out for Natasha Marshall, who he had known since childhood, because she was needing help when her father had developed a problem.

The phone rang after Somersby left.

'That was Storwich reporting on our Cambridge colleagues,' Wilson said after he replaced the receiver. 'The A14 monitors have traced Cole's car as far as Milton where it went off their screens. Cambridgeshire will take over from there.'

Five o'clock, the end of a busy day. Wilson was deep in thought, trying hard to remember what he had better not come home without.

'We have guests,' he said glumly. 'Dorothy's Head and his wife. Don't get me wrong, they are a nice couple, a bit up their own arses, I suppose, but they do love an intellectual discussion.' Unlike Wilson, who loved an intellectual discussion as much as the dog liked being shut in the kitchen due to the wife's allergy.

'What do you know about the John Donne you mentioned?'

'Metaphysical poet, seventeenth century,' said Cunningham. ' Metaphysical means his poems take in world sciences.'

He tried to think of an example.

'*No man is an island/ entirely unto himself.* He was Dean of St. Paul and he died of syphilis.'

'Interesting, I might sprinkle that in the conversation,' said Wilson, for whom there was now only one composer, Mozart, and only one poet, A.E.

Houseman.

> *'Loveliest of trees, the cherry now,*
> *Is hung with bloom along the bough,*
> *And stands about the woodland ride*
> *Wearing white for Easter tide.'*

He was transformed into a boy in short trousers, visiting Kent in the spring. He was lifted up by his father into a sea of blossoms, the scent making him dizzy, when the phone rang and brought him out of his reverie, placing him onto the ground and right into the manure.

He replaced the receiver and told Cunningham, who was engrossed in the spectacle of his inspector reciting poetry, that he would be needed for another hour, at the very least.

At five o'clock, the clearance team from the Council reached the woods and got to grips with the mattress reportedly dumped by fly tippers, when one of the men noticed a bony hand sticking out of the earth next to it.

He screamed and ran off.

'I swear to it, mate,' he gasped, 'that hand wagged a finger at me. And there is a body attached to it. We better ring the station.'

CHAPTER 47

'RIGHT, SAID WILSON. 'The environmental lot have discovered a hand waving out of the ground belonging to a body in the very spot reported to us used by fly-tippers.'

'Right,' said Cunningham, 'monkey suits?'

'We'd better,' said Wilson. He added that he recalled a time when cross contamination was barely thought of. 'Not that I am knocking it, it's a valuable tool.'

'I won't be home very early, something has come up, I think you had better start without me, just in case,' he reported back to Dorothy.

'I'm sorry,' she said. 'Did you remember to get the grapes, the Stilton and the crackers?'

'Of course I did,' he said, and he did, locating Dorothy's list after summoning the Scene of Crime Team and dispatching Connor to search the Marshall's front garden for the weapon used on Miss Wawrinska.

He stopped in Somerfield before he drove onto the Brandon Road, turning off towards Thelford, just before the sign Welcome to Norfolk, Nelson's County. Albert Rusty had come in useful after all.

The clearing van was parked on the edge of the trees. A man in overalls, who introduced himself as Ron, and -once Wilson and Cunningham were suited and booted up- pointed out the spot through scot pines where the mattress had been located.

'So as soon as I saw the hand sticking up from the ground, I said to my mate that something was not right here and we saw what looked like a body attached to the hand.'

'Well spotted,' said Wilson, interrupting him in full flow, but he was sympathetic. It wasn't every day you found a dead hand, possibly attached to a dead body.

'I didn't touch anything on the body,' said Ron, 'as I believe this is a crime scene. I suppose you are waiting to cordon it off, or wait for the Soccer, SOCO team or what-ever you call it.'

'Scene Of Crime Officers. Well, off you go, have a strong cup of tea,' said Wilson, booted and suited up, 'you have been very helpful. We'll need a statement from both of you you later.'

The hand was well-gnawed, they discovered after Ron departed.

'A fox probably,' said Wilson. 'There is a connection. The mattress was moved in the search for Emily Watson, a fox smelled out the body and unearthed his hand,' but he was talking to himself.

The DS, a sensitive and imaginative soul now picturing the post mortem, was inhaling smoke through his kneecaps at the edge of the trees after the team had arrived, cordoned off the area, and unearthed the body, now in a body bag and in an ambulance.

'Can you say roughly,' Wilson said.

The pathologist, Sandra Pearson, a pretty blonde woman, was sitting in her open car, making notes.

''Interesting,' she said.' I don't do roughly, and don't get in the way of the photographer..All I can say is Rigor Mortis has worn off, and there is some infestation.' She looked up. 'One week possibly, the weather has been mild of late. I'll have to do some more tests, but it's interesting.'

He asked her a few more questions before he joined the DS.

'Do you think you could inform the Marshalls of our find? It isn't only that sometimes I hate my job, I think you were there at the start and I think it is best done personally.'

Cunningham agreed reluctantly. Informing relatives of a loved one's often brutal death always lingered in the mind.

'Can you also tell them that the body can be viewed for identification? Sandra said tomorrow morning at ten. You can tell them that I shall be meeting them in the hospital car park.'

He paused.

'Sandra thinks the man was killed somewhere else. Apparently, there was dirt, fertilised soil, found on his trousers.'

'Whereas he was buried in sandy soil full of dead pine needles,' the DS said, getting in the car and driving away to Wheystead, leaving the team to carry out a fingertip search of the surrounding area, while Wilson drove home.

A car was in front of the house, Angela and Godfrey, he supposed. The dog looked up miserably from his basket when he let himself into the kitchen.

'How did it go today?' asked Godfrey, when he went into the living room.

Not a question to ask of someone who had just looked on death.

'Bloody awful,' he said. 'Thank you for asking.'

Angela, a pretty, soft-looking blonde woman with a hard centre, poked her husband in the ribs.

'Don't even think of questioning him about Foster,' she said.

'I suppose not,' said Godfrey, 'anyway, it will be in the papers.'

Godfrey added he thought it would be nice not to find Bury St. Edmunds mentioned in the news and in the papers.

'Unnecessary would be better,' said Wilson.

He thought it would be an awful evening but it

wasn't.

He just had to make a few polite noises, and, to his surprise, he found he was starving. He lifted his cutlery and attacked the food with relish. Rashers of bacon, thin, crispy red rashers that splintered when the knife touched them, roast chicken, moist and fragrant, potatoes both roasted and mashed fluffy.

He ate with appetite while giving a good impersonation of a man with interest in the conversation flowing around him, now reaching vegetarianism.

'Oh, Lord, Ang, you're not eating much, ' said Godfrey, 'you're not on the beans-and-greens kick again, I hope.'

'I will no longer eat anything I could look into the eye,' said Angela, leaving the meat on her plate. 'What say you, John?'

That had to be him.

'I have never looked a chicken in the eye, nor am I likely to.'

When she gave him a sharp look, he wondered if he ought to sign a witness statement to that effect, but inspiration struck right out of the blue.

'As George Bernard Shaw said, We are the living graveyard of animals. I believe John Donne, the poet and Dean of St. Paul, was also a vegetarian. As he wrote in one of his poems, "*No Man Is An Island*."

He was loading the dishwasher as he congratulated Dorothy on her cooking after they had left. 'A bit of pain, those two, if you ask me,' he said., '

'I nearly pinched Angela's chicken right off her plate,' said Dorothy,'Angela ought to have told me she had given up eating meat.'

She started to laugh.

'But honestly, John Donne, the famous

vegetarian, and then you told them they were free to go,' she started laughing again. 'I enjoyed the evening after they left, and perhaps you will sleep better tonight.'

Not very likely, he thought, I would have to show Natasha Marshall her father's dead body. Still, he had the best night's sleep for a long time, he said next morning to the dog looking at him hopefully over his dish. Dorothy had left, which could only mean he would be late at the station.

CHAPTER 49

GEORGE HUDSON WAS READY to go out and fetch his father when the phone rang.

'That was Lewis Marshall,' he said, replacing the receiver. 'Where's Rosie?'

'Rosie? She's in her room. I hope you're not starting that again. What has brought this on?'

'I don't want her to overhear us. They have found Natasha Marshall's father's body, today, and somebody attacked Lewis Marshall's Polish help last night, she's in hospital, seriously injured.'

Christine was glad Rosie wasn't listening, perhaps it was best if George's father didn't know about it either, she said, before George drove to fetch him for dinner with a heavy heart.

What was happening?

Last night, Ritchie had left his wallet on the bar when he got the drinks in. When he went to get it back, it was gone, except later a customer had found it on the floor and handed it to the barmaid. What it had to do with Aleska getting attacked in Lewis's front garden he had no idea, but connected it was.

George replayed the scene in his head. Coming out of the pub into a dark night, Ritchie was pleased he had his wallet back, Lewis was getting into his car, when George noticed the popping sound of a scooter starting up. The scooter was breaking the routine, which is why it lodged in his memory.

All thoughts of that night vanished when he saw the police presence at the wood's edge before he reached Thelford; the body had been discovered.

One thing was certain, he didn't want to see *that* on TV. He parked his car and walked to the flat. His father, after letting him in, eased into the chair in front of the television.

'Just watching the headlines, son, and then we're off,' his father said. 'I like that dark-haired news reader,' he added, 'she could rattle my cage any time she wanted. Have you noticed how all the birds on the telly flash their knockers these days? Can she cook?'

'How should I know?' said George.

'I don't mean her, I mean Dawn by name, dawn by nature, your mother-in-law with that awful cackle she calls a laugh we're having dinner with, in case you've forgotten.'

He was beginning to get on George's nerves. Everybody would tonight.

His father said his neighbour had made a pie. 'You could kill somebody with her pastry,' he said, 'but she's a right laugh.'

He was definitely getting on George's nerves, but then a headline on the TV caught his eyes: a Luke Cole, wanted for a serious assault on a Polish woman. It was Lewis's Aleska, but who exactly was Luke Cole? he wondered.

His father turned the TV off and got his coat.

'The Poles had a raw deal, during the war,' his father started. The Poles had helped win the war (there was ever only one war, World War II for him) and then they were thrown aside like so much rubbish.'

He paused.

'Polish soldiers were banned from attending the Victory Parade, but they had guts, by God! Still have.'

'A leopard doesn't change his socks,' said George, 'according to Rosie. And if she tells you that, don't laugh at her, or she'll sulk for hours.'

CHAPTER 50

FRED FOSTER HAD no complaints about his hotel room. Everything worked, the bathroom had a shower and a bath as well as soap, shampoo and a hair-dryer, the mini bar was well-stocked, the room had tea and coffee facilities and a TV with 98 channels.

But first things first, a bath, when had he last seen one of those? He filled the bath close to the brim and as hot as he could bear it. The tub was deep and the hot water kept him still. His body remembered all sorts of old pains and injuries, while his mind remembered his mother clashing saucepans downstairs while the water was cooling.

When he got up, he slipped, trying to right himself.

Wonderful, he thought, I could break a leg in a bathtub, when he slipped again on the water that had splashed over the rim of the bath onto the floor.

'You OK,' his mother used to shout, 'or are you going to be in there all night? There's other people in the house wanting to use the bathroom. He remembered his slowly rising anger, and the next day he released it. His mother ran a bath in the evening when the phone rang. When she switched the taps off and went downstairs, he switched them on again. He went downstairs and did his homework on the table, his father reading the paper in the armchair, his mother in the hall on the phone for a long time. When he looked up, there was water coming through the ceiling.

He stopped daydreaming and dressed, made some coffee and got to grips with the amount of TV channels when Luke Cole's ugly mug was flashed on the new bulletin. That was quick, he thought, but he felt like a new man after his bath and hot coffee. He packed up, cleared the mini bar, pocketed the silk flowers because they got on his nerves, and secured the wig and the glasses. While he waited for the sirens, he flicked through the phone book and found a small hotel not far away. Grenville House, near Addenbrook hospital, it said. Handy for visiting relatives, he supposed.

He closed the book when, sure enough, they were stupid enough to sound their sirens and warn him of their imminent arrival. He looked nothing like Luke Cole but he waited in the first floor corridor, where the lift stopped.

Shortly after, a man with his hands fastened behind his back was lead out by two coppers and dragged down the stairs. They hadn't come for him after all.

Reception was hardly busy, people came and went past it, it had probably something to do with electronic keys eliminating the need to hand in a door key. Finally, a new client arrived and although he had paid, he slipped through the door and into the street, where he caught a bus to the hospital and walked to Grenville House.

He signed in under the name from the card he had pocketed from the B&B in Farn Road. Michael Oliver, 21 Gloucester Road, Stroud, Wiltshire.

'Wife's at the hospital,' he said sadly to one of the queers in their ridiculous cardigans who ran the place, wearing name tags, Geoffrey and Jeffrey. 'I may have to come and go.'

'Room fifteen,' said Geoffrey, handing him his key. 'It gets the sun in the morning.'

'And the moon at night,' said Jeffrey. 'Irvine Berlin.'

He went to his room, pausing on the half landing.

'Old lag,' one of them said.

'Takes one to know one, but even old lags have wives.'

'Some of them. His wig was on crooked.'

They wouldn't laugh if he was in charge, flaunting it they were, they wouldn't do anything after he had put them down slowly and painfully like the scum they were. He was so infuriated that he knew he had to get out.

Brandishing the silk flowers he handed in his key and walked to the hospital. It had everything including pay-phones, hot water and soap in the Gents. Even second-hand books were sold and you could eat there, and how! Why hadn't he thought of that before? he thought, ordering a bowl of soup with wholemeal bread, a piece of quiche and a piece of walnut cake with pink icing. Must be thirty years since his Nan had made one of those.

She had adored him. He had quite liked her, but she died because he wet his bed and all the washing was strung on the landing. She groped her way through the wet sheets, missed the top two step and fell down the stairs. She died, fortunately, not a wrinkly old crone, but a handsome woman, after he had pushed her down the stairs. He went back home to live with his parents where he, thankfully, no longer had to piss his bed and lay in wet sheets, and where he learnt to keep his other side absent. Or at least tried to.

He glanced around him at a few families, a few Asians, Pakis, they used to call them. A tall, supremely handsome youth with dark curly hair, wearing an army surplus coat left over from the Crimea probably, was nibbling a plain girl's ear. Nobody paid anybody the slightest attention. A small burp escaped him after he finished.

He went to the phone and dialled Vladimir

Glubis's mobile. Glubis had four infected front teeth removed by a dentist in Lithuania before he did a runner. He didn't know anything about sound-proofed rooms, as he had told to the immigration officers. Except for looking for the winning side, politics passed him by. Children did not, but torture and the fear of it was a credible cover story for someone who had to get out in a hurry. Credibility was the immigrants' password.

'Listen, my friend, I know you have been very busy,' said Vladimir, 'I have your new passport here. You owe me one thousand Euros. Come soon, I am getting a trifle impatient.'

Vladimir never swore; he had to remember that. He was a mate. They recognised each other as if they had met and liked each other in a former life. They shared the same interests, both were educated and intended to vanish abroad just as soon as Foster was ready.

'One week,' said Vladimir, 'I haf missed you, but if I do not hear after that, at the most, the passport will go elsewhere and I vil visit Thailand on my own.'

'Thailand. Wouldn't I need a visa?

'Everything is possible, my friend. Attention. Photo on passport. You have a shaved head, thin eyebrows, no beard, small glasses with black rim. Note my address and memorise.'

'But I don't know London.'

'Take tube train to Embankment station, walk to Chelsea bridge, always crowded, telephone me, take out card from mobile and destroy, and wait for me,' said Vlad. 'And listen. Do not make your life complicated.'

Which was all very well, but how could he help it?

When he walked back to the guest-house, a

woman was removing luggage from a car, a Honda Accord, leaving the car door open and the keys in the ignition.

He drove off in the Honda Accord, parked it one street away, got his belongings back from his room, sympathised with the woman about her stolen car, and paid with Luke Cole's credit card for the bed and breakfast he hadn't had.

Then, in sheer desperation to get away, he drove to Huntingdon and eventually back to Cambridge and onto Bury St. Edmunds along the B roads -all through the night. After a god-awful journey, he parked the Honda in a side street near the hospital and walked back to the B&B in a grey dawn. A blackbird was trying to pull a worm out of the earth, or one-and half blackbirds.

He had to get shot of this migraine and join Vlad, leaving unfinished business behind him, he thought, letting himself into the kitchen, where he stopped, stunned. The kitchen door leading to the hall was half open and the armchair he had used as a bed had been moved. A fierce anger grabbed him by the throat; somebody had been in *his house* while he was away. Somebody would have to pay for it

Now look out, Richard Butler, Painter and Decorator, No Job Too Small, No Job Too Big.

CHAPTER 51

WILSON WAS BACK at the office after taking Natasha and Lewis Marshall to the Suffolk hospital to identify her father's body. He had been told by Cunningham that Lewis Marshall would do it, so he was surprised when Natasha was by Lewis's side.

He had waited for them in the car park and guided them through long, bleak corridors and into the room marked PRIVATE. He looked at Natasha, and when she nodded, he gave the sign. The sheet was pulled away by the mortuary attendant, revealing the corpse's head. As she saw her father's shrunken face with eyes bulging beneath the eyelids, Natasha said yes, and then she leaned towards the ground, bent double, gasping, as if she had been hit in the stomach.

He led them out of the room and let her recover.

Sandra, Dr Pearson, who was doing the autopsy in a day or two, asked for their permission to use Dr. Willoughby's doctor's notes.

'For eliminating purposes. It's normal practice so we know what we are dealing with,' she said.

Natasha nodded before he took them out into the fresh air where she grabbed the car keys off Lewis and ran off to the car.

'She likes to face things alone. He looked so dead, not if he was sleeping,' Lewis said, leaning against the wall, letting his tears run down his face, quite unashamed. 'Paul has got his wish, the family has come together. My parents are due, and so is Natasha's brother. But lying in a steel cabinet in a steel drawer with a label on his big toe, what a price to pay!'

'He doesn't know it,' said Wilson gently.

'For once, when I opened my mouth, the right thing came out of it. I told him not to be so stupid, it

311

was a privilege to know him, I changed his mind about suicide,' said Lewis. He wiped his face, blew his nose, and walked towards the car. He opened his arms wide and Natasha ran to him.

They had each other, Wilson thought.

His daughter had once asked him how much he liked Dorothy.

As much as I like breathing, he had thought.

It was the same for these two.

There's nothing on the CCTV from Asda, Sainsbury, and Tesco,' said Cunningham back in th eoffice, 'Connor is about to start on Somerfield.'

'Carry on.'

Wilson made notes on the whiteboard and in his notebook, the DS wrote out his report when they were interrupted by Connor, who had located a man who could be Dr Willoughby on the CCTV surveillance from Somerfield.

Wilson was out of his chair faster than a chosen contender on a game show.

They all crowded around the computer.

Dr Willoughby seemed to be in involved in some sort of an argument with a big woman with bleached hair. A man, in his thirties, appeared to put his oar in, Willoughby bought cigarettes, put them in his bag and left the Supermarket. Date: 31 October. Time: 5.35 pm. Both the blonde woman and the interfering man left shortly afterwards.

Connor rewound the tape back to the time when Willoughby entered the supermarket. They saw him stop at the frozen food section and later in the alcohol aisle, where he bought a bottle of sherry, a blue bottle, Harvey's Bristol Cream, probably. He bought cigarettes and went out of the door into the unknown.

'Interesting,' said Cunningham. 'He might have

taken the shortcut where the lens was found.'

'Very interesting,' said Wilson.

'Look,' said Connors, pointing at the screen.

Willoughby left the supermarket just as another, similar figure in a raincoat entered, walked down the aisles where he stopped at the frozen food, the bread counter, and the medicine sections. He paid and left the store barely five minutes later.

Two men in beige raincoats.

'Fred Foster, I'll be damned. Now this is really interesting,' said Wilson. 'We know the lens found in the shortcut was Foster's, the blood on Willoughby's coat was also Foster's.'

'What if,' said Connor.

'Yes?' said Wilson, always open to suggestions.

'What if Foster met up with Willoughby, attacked and robbed him.'

'We know the dead man is Willoughby, but we can't assume Fred Foster assaulted him, slung him over his shoulder, carried him away and buried him.'

'No,' said Cunningham, 'but there is the missing wheelbarrow, besides, he might have been using his car and was waiting for Willoughby in the lane, attacked him and somehow got his own blood on the coat.'

'Dr Pearson wants his medical notes, but whatever Willoughby suffered from, or not, he didn't walk out of the supermarket and down the road, turn into the lane, get a wheelbarrow from a shed, wheel himself to the woods and bury himself.'

'Forensic are on the phone,' said Connor. 'They will identify fingerprints left by the intruder on Marshall's window as soon as possible.

CHAPTER 52

'DON'T WORRY ABOUT ANYTHING,' said George to Alf who was sitting on his hospital bed. He was all packed up ready to go home, and he was brandishing a piece of paper.

George was at the hospital to pick up him up. Fully dressed, Alf looked more like himself, not like the scrawny bloke in striped pyjamas.

'I might as well be dead, mate, and it was only a mild heart attack not the whole Cardiac thing. This is a diet sheet. Nothing fried, lots of vegetables and salad.' He put the paper down. 'Don't they know anything in this bloody hospital? Don't they know salad is a vegetable?'

He took a deep breath.

'And another thing, they give you cocoa at night, and in the morning, the nurse says, "Have you opened your bowels this morning?"'

'All right, Jim?' he said to a man loaded up with machinery, inching his way out of the ward.

'I had some trouble last night, mate,' he said in a confidential voice, 'but please don't tell anyone. I'm on a catheter and I had an erection last night.'

After he had shuffled off, George and Alf laughed so long and so hard that the nurse came in.

'I don't approve of swearing,' she said.

'I never bloody swear, never. Do I, George?' said Alf, indignant.

George started to laugh again, and she threw them both out.

'We're having Hester today,' Christine said when they got home. 'Lewis and Natasha went to the hospital. The body found last night was her father as the police thought, she said, when she telephoned. And her father's ring and watch were found in the possession of Luke Cole, Aleska's lover.'

RING AND WATCH? LUKE COLE HAD THEM?

George and Alf nearly did a John McEnroe. They waited until they were in the car when George drove Alf home and George stopped in a lay-by.

'*They cannot be serious,*' they screamed.

'How come Cole had them?' asked George? 'I put them in my dustbin myself.'

'Sometimes,' Alf said dreamily, 'I have a whole other mad world going on in my head.'

Ritchie would have said he got him, doing that gesture with his hand over his face when he spoke.

'I'll have nightmares about white trainers,' said Alf as he got out of the car when they reached home.

'Nightmares don't kill you, heart attacks do,' said George. 'Why don't you get out of here, have bit of a holiday? I mean, the sun must shine somewhere.'

'It doesn't shine up my arse with all that cocoa at the hospital,' said Alf.

What would I do without Alf, George thought after he finished laughing, but he didn't say so, there were limits.

The sun didn't shine on the angler dismantling his tent. A cold rain came at him sideways as he rolled it up and started to walk to his car to put it on the roof rack of his car. He vaguely recalled a story about a dead grandmother on a car roof when he noticed a beer can on the water, swaying gently in the in the wind. On closer inspection, the beer can was lodged on a car aerial, which in turn was attached to a car.

'A car, yes, in the river,' he said to the officer answering the phone at Parkside Police station in

Cambridge. He listened. 'I'll wait, but you better not be long or I'll catch it from my wife.'

CHAPTER 53

'DEVELOPMENTS,' said Wilson. 'A man believed to be Foster has been arrested in Oxford,' when the phone rang again.

'I don't believe it,' said Wilson, putting down the phone. 'Listen up. Cambridge have recovered the car belonging to Luke Cole from a river, the Cam, in Ditton. Guess what they found in the boot?'

'Not Foster, he can't be in two places at once.'

'I wouldn't put it past him. Luke Cole's body was in the boot of his car. They want his fingerprints for Forensic. His face was badly damaged by some sort of heavy blow. Forensic will examine the car for other fingerprints, but whose? And they are looking closely at CCTV surveillance from highway traffic. As we know, they lost sight of the car when it turned off at Milton in Cambridge.'

He paused.

'Somebody will have to identify the body.'

He went to the second whiteboard and looked at what they already knew.

Luke Cole, 32, divorced. Childless.
Ex-wife lives in Devon.
Parents, both retired teachers,
Live in Thelford.
COLE: Moved to Bury St. Edmunds two years ago.
No previous.
Flat abandoned. Car driven off
the Ridley estate by a stranger,
Woolly hat, thick glasses.
Seen by Mrs Beverley, neighbour.

No weapon in the car.

He informed his opposite number in Norfolk of the latest events and the need for Cole's parents to identify their son, and put down the phone.

'The flat is now a crime scene and forensics will get to work. Norfolk will deal with Cole's, parents who will probably identify the body, as it has to be a relative if possible. Cole's face was smashed in. Any suggestions as to who smashed something against Miss Wawrinska's neck and Luke Cole's face and drove the car away with the dead body in the boot and - hopefully-left his mitts on the car?'

'Perhaps it was not Cole who attacked Miss Wawrinska,' said the DS. 'Somebody else attacked Miss Wawrinska, perhaps Cole observed the attack and paid for it.'

'And all under a willow tree at night in a peaceful village. Whatever happened to nightingales?'

He went to the whiteboard and added, Why? What? How? Then he noticed Lewis Marshall's office number on the other whiteboard.

'Stone me,' said Lewis answering the 'phone, 'Luke Cole is dead? In his own car boot? I better get home and deal with Natasha and Aleska. But as far as last Saturday night goes, since you asked, I didn't notice anything when I got back, except.'

He paused.

'It sounds silly, and it's probably nothing, but a bloke dressed in black, driving a scooter delivering pizzas, passed me. Noisy little thing, I had a Honda once, 50 cc.'

'What makes this stand out in your mind?'

'I didn't think they delivered as far out as Wheystead.'

'Right, Paula, perhaps you can get to grips with pizza parlours, deliveries concerning Saturday night,' said Wilson after he put down the 'phone.

He went to the canteen and got a mug of coffee out of the urn which had produced coffee continuously since the Boar War, probably. He took it to his office and shut the door, he wanted to think. He looked at his notebook and wandered out of his office once again, staring at the whiteboards, when Paula reported on pizza deliveries.

His 'phone rang.

'What?' he bellowed.

It was Nicholson.

'Where is my coffee machine?'

'I have put in the requisition form,' said the Super. 'Developments regarding Luke Cole?'

'It might be nothing, but we have drawn a blank with pizza deliveries in that area and that time of night, but it might have been somebody on a scooter on his way home.'

Sandra Pearson was next. The autopsy had to be rescheduled.

The phone was red-hot. A Miss Williamson wanted to speak to him next.

'Who?'

'She lost her purse in a car park and identified Foster's mug. She insists on talking to you.'

'Put her through.'

He would have to tell her that the theft of her purse had led to Foster's CCTV image.

She was thrilled out of her mind and was probably straight onto one of the tabloids. He could expect a gory headline, and he wasn't wrong when he briefly glanced at the headlines the next day: *'Attacked And Robbed By Evil Killer.'*

He didn't intend to read any more, no doubt the police would come in for a bashing. However, when the paper was shoved under his nose, she actually gave the

Suffolk Police the thumbs up.

His officers completed their reports and all the statements were in. He went home early with his trusty notebook and let his trusty non-wife put it together with a proper narrative while he took the dog out. The dog stopped and sniffed at various interesting places on the grass verge, coming to no firm conclusion. His master didn't have much luck either, not until the early morning hours. Staircase wit, Dorothy called it.

'Scooters! Helmets! Pizza deliveries!' he shouted.

Fortunately he was in the spare bedroom with only the dog, sighing and rolling his eyes at him, for company. Aleska Wawrinska, neck smashed, Luke Cole, face smashed in, no weapon found. Could it be the handiwork of the mysterious scooter driver wielding his helmet?

He expounded his theory the next day to Cunningham.

'Could be a helmet, it certainly was a smooth instrument, it didn't leave any splinters,' he said, 'but how did Luke Cole end up in the boot of his own car? Did the attacker sling him over his shoulder and ride off, or what? And by the way, I have passed my inspector's exam.'

'I knew you would,' said Wilson, 'I will buy you a coffee maker. Drinks after work?'

'Amanda is taking me out, but thanks, perhaps another time.'

The phone rang.

'Cambridge,' he mouthed, 'Just a minute, I'll have a word with Cunningham. I'll ring you back.'

Luke Cole, who wasn't Luke Cole because he was dead, had booked in as Michael Oliver, 21 Gloucester Road, Stroud, Wiltshire, at a guest-house in Cambridge but paid with Cole's credit card. The name

Michael Oliver rang a distant bell.

He went through his notebook.

'The B&B at Farn Road,' he said. 'Mrs Warner said a Michael Oliver, 21 Gloucester Road, Stroud, Wiltshire, had booked in.'

'And Foster had been the other guest.'

'I'll 'phone Cambridge and let them know. They have his fingerprints. They can deal with the nutter in Oxford posing as Foster.'

He telephoned Cambridge and then the Super.

'The autopsy is due today, in half an hour,' said Cunningham, 'and I am not actually an inspector until a position becomes vacant.'

Wilson, who was supposed to attend a meeting in Storwich, thought about it.

'Perhaps you can go in my place and report back to me. Tell Nicholson I can't be in two places at once, and perhaps you can take all the reports and statements with you.'

'I am willing to attend with you, sir,' said Paula, 'two officers have to attend an autopsy.'

Wilson, who already knew this, declined and took Connor to the Suffolk hospital.

'You are aware that all human life is but a handful of dust,' he said when they entered the mortuary, 'well, eventually.' He had to remind himself every time he attended an autopsy. The human body was a thing of beauty, well, relatively speaking, when all the bits and pieces that made it function were nicely enclosed by beige skin. Or any colour skin, he said to himself, even his thoughts seemed to be politically incorrect.

Connor told him not to worry, his father was a butcher, he was used to blood and bones. 'I used to bag them up and we got three pounds for them. Nowadays he has to pay someone to take them away.'

The throw-away society, how sad, Wilson thought briefly, but the sound of water running continuously from the dissecting table's channels made him feel glad his prostate was still intact.

Sandra, Dr Pearson, was a beautiful, golden girl, who was made to do - he didn't really know what, but she wasn't made to beckon him impatiently with what looked like a sharp instrument.

'I'll just explain a few things as we proceed.'

She glanced at Dr Willoughby's notes. Wilson couldn't help thinking that Lewis had said that it had been a privilege knowing him, and now he was a cadaver -he despised the word as it rendered a corpse inhuman- being cut up. Connor, the butcher boy, was leaning against the wall by the sink, looking as green as Sandra's gown while she explained as she went along.

'Very interesting indeed,' Wilson said when Sandra lifted out the heart and held it tenderly, like a trophy. A red, important looking organ, not heart-shaped, more lump-shaped.

'It can tell you how a person lived, or how they died, but sometimes the heart has nothing to do with a death, something causes it to stop pumping.'

'Very interesting, don't you thinks so, Connor?' He turned round.

'Certainly,' said Connor faintly, 'are we done yet?'

'You go outside and get some fresh air,' he said.

Sandra was coming to the head and was reaching for the saw.

'When will you know for certain?'

'A day or so at the most.'

'You've done very well for a first time, they had to scrape somebody I know off the floor,' said Wilson back in the car. Everybody- animals- was made of the same stuff, but a cow's carcass hanging in a butcher shop was just meat, whereas a corpse on a table reminded them of their own mortality, the mortality facing them and which they did their best to ignore.

Cunningham was back after lunch and reported to Wilson.

'Not the niceties, and the not-niceties,' said Wilson. 'perhaps you can just stick to the facts, if you don't mind.'

'Right you are,' said Cunningham. Cambridge Police were alerted by a man who reported a bus driver, as well as a lady who had been assaulted by a man in Ditton, where Luke Cole's car was found in the river. His description: dark curly hair, tall, woolly hat, anorak.

A man fitting this description used Cole's credit card to book in at The Crossed Arms, it was also used in a guest-house, where he checked in as Michael Oliver, 21 Gloucester Road, Stroud. From there, he stole a 2001 Honda Accord; the car was traced to Huntingdon, where it went off the screen.'

'A right trail blazer,' said Ron Nash, the DI from Cambridge who was on the telephone. 'We simply followed Foster's purchases with Cole's credit card. We are still looking for the car he nicked from the guest-house, the Honda Accord. Incidentally, Cunningham is a good man; I only wish we had a vacancy for him.'

Cunningham was pleased but not surprised to hear he was a good man, he already knew that. Traffic was out looking for the Honda, and so was Norfolk and Essex, which was good news. How did a stolen car connect to a scooter rider and fit into the scheme of things? Wilson thought, when forensic reported back to him; the fingerprints found on the sash window on the

323

Marshall's house in Wheystead were indeed those of Fred Foster.

CHAPTER 54

RICHARD KING, No Job Too Small. No job Too big, wasn't worried about scooters, he was more worried about a particular shade of paint. His customer had changed her mind again. Two o'clock, and he was off once more to B&Q to find a member of staff familiar with the store. Or even a member of the staff.

He walked to his car and was about to get in, when somebody sitting on a scooter parked on the grass verge waved him over.

'Can you direct me to Norman Road?' said the rider, his helmet in his right hand.

Ritchie thought about it.

'Never heard of it, mate,' he said. He was running his right hand over his face to push the hair out of his sweaty face when the helmet came at him, hard. He was on the ground and looked at his hand, stupefied, it was full of blood. When he realised it came from his face, the scooter had vanished.

'Yes, yes,' said Wilson, he was on the telephone. 'Can you take a deep breath and tell me what happened.'

'My decorator was attacked, and in broad daylight, we're not safe in our beds,' the woman screamed. As if it would be better to be attacked at night, when, presumably, she would be in bed.

'Can you give me your name and address and we'll be right there.'

'The scooter rider has struck again, Cunningham, perhaps you can come with me.'

Mrs Roxby, who had reported the incident, lived on a new development of red-brick mock-Tudor houses with white portico and front gardens the size of a handkerchief. She was a small, pretty, blonde woman dressed in black trousers and top.

'What am I going to do now?' she said, ushering Wilson and Cunningham into the living room which had wooden floors, shrouded furniture and bare walls, one of which was a horrible shade or purple.

'It's an accent wall,' she said, 'but I wasn't sure I liked it, so Mr King went out to get some shade called Summer Lavender.'

She had run after him to remind him to get *Pale Sunrise* for the rest of the walls when she saw Mr King talking to a man sitting on a scooter.

'He took a swipe at his face with his helmet ' she said, 'it was totally uncalled for, Mr King couldn't be a nicer man.' She paused. 'He broke his nose, there was a lot of blood, so I called the ambulance and then the police.'

She couldn't describe the rider, he drove off down the road, a cul-de-sac, and when he came back, he wore his helmet.

She looked at her purple accent wall and then at Cunningham.

'What do you think?'

'Very nice,' he said, 'especially with a gilt-framed mirror.'

Gilt-framed mirror? Does he think he is that poncy git with the long name and longer hair? Wilson thought.

Cunningham took Mrs Roxby back to the station to make a statement and then dropped him off at the hospital to talk to Mr King, if he was fit enough for it.

Of course, Cunningham's ex-wife ran a decorating business. Perhaps they were getting back together.

He took out his notebook. Just as he had thought, the attacked Ritchie King was a mate of George Hudson, and, for some good reason, Fred

Foster was the scooter driver. He was convinced of it, and Fred Foster was no friend of either.

Dorothy had a meeting, so Wilson indulged in what was in these days of labelling the bleeding obvious called guilty pleasures; he bought a Melton Mowbray pork pie and a Crunchie bar.

The dog, whose routine was interrupted, could hardly be bothered to get out of his box. He padded after him with drooping ears and sad eyes, while Wilson expounded his theory.

'Something has clicked in my brain, and it's all due to Connor. I'm very impressed by him, not so impressed by somebody else. Do you know what he said to me concerning Fred Foster?'

The dog had no idea.

'He said, "What is Foster's End Game?" So. Why didn't he just clear off after he was released? Or when Emily Watson had her amazing escape? What is he after?'

'What is more, Alf Butler and Ritchie King are friends of George Hudson.'

The dog put his head on one side. So what?

'Could they be vigilantes and upset Foster in some way? Somebody got attacked in Lewis Marshall's garden. I suppose you could say, so what? Alf Butler is a mate of George's, Ritchie King is a friend, Lewis is a friend. They are just friends. If a cat has kittens in the larder it doesn't make them into cheese, does it.'

The dog got ready to lick his balls. One leg behind his ear, he watched the fork spearing a piece of pie. He started to worry about his ten percent, forgot what he was doing and lowered his leg to the ground.

'My view is simple; if offenders were kept in prison and not released they would not re-offend, and, contrary to popular opinion, some people deserve no second chances. I have a gut feeling that these mysterious or non-existent vigilantes could lead us directly to *Fred Foster, the scooter rider,* who, I believe, is still in the area. His End Game, you see. Once he's done with them, he disappears '

The dog yawned one of his great, jaw-breaking yawns.

'And that makes me believe that George Hudson is in great danger, he is the only one of the circle left unscathed. But, and this is important, Hudson will have to come to me. Mohammed and the mountain, if that is still politically correct, you see.'

The dog didn't see it, but he was hugely relieved when Dorothy's car wheels finally crunched on the gravel.

CHAPTER 55

GEORGE HUDSON picked up Alf for a visit to Ritchie. Alf's children were in their bedrooms to give their father some peace, Margaret, Alf's wife, said.

The tidy living room seemed lifeless.

'It would be nice to see something of the girls,' Alf said. 'They could watch EastEnders down here with me.'

'EastEnders? I should think not, not with your heart condition.'

'She treats me worse than a baby,' Alf said when they finally drove to Ritchie, 'Kylie is allowed to watch it, and she's five.'

Ritchie was at home with a sore face, two broken fingers on his right hand and a bottle of painkillers. Luckily, there was no damage to his eyes, so his wife, whatever her name was, said, or possibly said. Their two blond boys were racing around the house, chasing each other, squealing and throwing themselves at their father, whose broken nose was encased in what looked like a small cage.

'I'll give them Darth Vader, I'm supposed to have complete rest, and peace and quiet,' said Ritchie.

'They've had their one allowed hour on the computer, we must stick to it, otherwise they take over,' said his wife, a small, dark-haired woman who, for some reason, wore a pair of cut-off jeans over black leggings. She had hips like a young boy and looked extremely sexy, and she was as unlikely match for Ritchie, as the glorious Victoria was as a daughter of Alf.

'Can't you take them out, Iris?' Ritchie asked.

Ah, Iris.

'Where to, at this hour? They are just happy you are back, and boys will be boys,' she said.

'I'm sure Christine will be happy to see Iris and the boys,' George said hopefully, 'why don't you take Ritchie's car and surprise her?'

Finally, the two boys, only two? with promises of the snooker room were driven off by their mother to a certainly surprised Christine.

'Talk about famine and plenty, you two, with your kids,' said George.

'What?'

'As my old Dad would say.'

'How is he?'

'He is thinking of getting married again,' said George.

'Not the one who is knocking seventy and uses the stair lift.'

'It's between her and the warden, one makes him laugh, and the other lives in a house and is fifteen years younger.'

'Can he still?'

'Apparently so,' said George.

November had settled in dull, foggy days, uneventful days as a rule, with people looking forward to Christmas. But the three facing each other on the settee and two armchairs had other things on their mind.

'You won't be able to work for a while, but you are insured, aren't you?' asked George.

'Against accidents,' said Ritchie sadly, 'I suppose that includes Foster, only I can't put his name on the form, can I?'

He had worked it all out, he said.

Alf and George stared at him, stupefied.

Somebody, Ritchie said, had returned his wallet to the barmaid at *The Volunteer,* but his business card was missing.

'How did you know it was missing?'

330

Ritchie kept birthday dates on his business card.

'You know what they're like when you forget a birthday,' he said.

'Right. Do you remember standing outside the pub talking to Lewis in the drizzle, hearing a scooter?'

'So?'

'You see, Lewis's Polish help was attacked later that evening and Lewis also mentioned a scooter. We made it easy for Foster, don't you see? He just had to come to *The Volunteer* and look us over.' He paused. 'I suppose you are sure it was Foster who attacked you?'

'Dead sure, but I recognised the mad eyes too late,' said Ritchie. 'I ran my hand over my sweaty face when he struck out with his helmet. If I hadn't put the tin of paint down I could have lifted it up and protected my face'

He paused.

'But it might have dented the tin and B&Q might not have changed it.'

'I wish I could joke if I was in his condition,' said George after they left.

'Except he wasn't joking,' said Alf.

Gallows humour, a safety valve. George had never understood it, but now he realised it was a guilty man's last defence. They laughed all the way home and George wished he could have told Christine. But they had made a pact, their wives had to be ignorant of the whole saga as long as possible, which might not be too long; George, with Alf and Ritchie's consent, had decided to get in touch with the police.

George knew for certain that he would be next on Foster's list, and after that, it might well be their children who were in danger.

He had promised to keep Alf and Ritchie out of it, it would be bad enough..just one of them doing time. What an awful thought doing time was; nevertheless, he would contact the police soon.

Soon was also a word much used by Jimmy and , and his mate Ronald.

'When's your mum clearing off?' Ronald asked.

'Soon,' Jimmy said, when, to his horror, his mother said one morning she might take the car and drive to Buckingham instead of taking the train.

'Train fares are so expensive, you have no idea.'

Jimmy nearly choked on his cornflakes.

'So is petrol, Mum,' he said, 'so is petrol. Is,' he paused, whatever was her friend's name? 'Is Norman going with you?'

'Norman was a friend I put up for two nights when Elaine threw him out, did you really think I would have a boyfriend with your dad gone?'

'But we never go and see him.'

'Because he doesn't want to see us where he is,' his mum shouted. 'He is getting out in two weeks, and it won't be easy for him,' she said, lowering her voice.

'I get you Mum,' said Jimmy. 'But if you go on the train, you will have a nice rest and could look out of the window, or read.' He couldn't think of anything else, but his mother did.

'Yes, I could enjoy some of the countryside,' she said looking at his round, his cherubic face. 'You are a nice boy, always thinking of your mother, I don't deserve you, I'm sure.'

'You do, Mum, you do,' said Jimmy, 'where's my sandwiches?'

CHAPTER 56

TIME TO DITCH THE SCOOTER, thought Fred
Foster. He could walk from the B&B to George
Hudson's house, the last on his list to be punished.
Vlad had to told him not to complicate his life, so he
abandoned revenge on KEYS CUT WHILE U WAIT.

Warner, however, he could deal with. The
B&B had a basement reached by concrete steps. There
was nothing much in it except wooden packing cases.
He pushed them together. Tomorrow morning he would
put a match to them. He would leave the cellar door
open, a fire needed air to burn, and once it spread
upwards and into the house, it would be a welcome
diversion.

Next was George, whatever else his name was.
He might be the last of the three, but he also deserved
the best. He had a little blond daughter he seemed very
fond of.

Foster rode the scooter to the Suffolk Hospital
where he parked it and had some sort of a pie in their
restaurant. He retrieved the Honda Accord from the
side street and drove to the B&B, where he packed up
and then parked the car in the car park of *The Volunteer*
before he settled down in the armchair for the night, his
last night there.

'Take tube train to Embankment station, walk
to Chelsea bridge, always crowded, telephone Vlad,
take out card from the mobile, destroy it and wait for
him,' he murmured before he went to sleep.

Next morning he waited until the rush hour and school
runs had finished. He gathered all the leaflets collecting
dust in the hall, donned his leather jacket and walked
down the road and back to the B&B again where he set
fire to the packing cases. A fire, eventually reaching

333

upstairs ,would summons the fire engines, and fire engines would cause a marvellous diversion.

Afterwards he went down the road, went up the drive of number twenty-two and looked at the top leaflet.

He pressed the door bell.

A blonde, slim woman opened the door, a phone in her hand.

'Good morning Madam,' he said, 'can I have a few minutes of your time? Have you heard of Everest double glazing?'

'Yes, I have' she said, 'but we are listed,' and shut the door.

Listed. A Victorian or Edwardian building, he thought as he went to the back door which opened straight into the kitchen. He went in and listened.

'I don't know, Mother,' he heard the woman say. She was in one the living rooms chatting on the 'phone. No problem.

'I might finish that painting of Rosie,' said Christine to her mother. 'She wants that toy her granddad bought for her painted in.'

'But the light won't be good enough,' said her mother, who had no idea what light had got to do with painting except she had heard it mentioned often enough.

'I have to do something to take my mind of George, I'm so worried about him. He is as bad as ever about Rosie.'

'Oh, dear, I don't like you worrying,' her mother said

'I can't help it. He can't sleep, he tosses and turns, and then he gets up early and pounds the roads.'

'What? With his fists?'

'No, Mother, he jogs.'

'It's what men do, well, some men do in the

morning. Sometimes I wish I had picked a man like that and not one who thinks he's in with a chance.' She paused. 'I know, too much information.'

She paused.

'Why don't we go shopping, darling. I've seen a wonderful little black cocktail dress, sleeveless, quite short, it would suit you to the ground '

'Or to the knees. What would I do with a cocktail dress? We don't go anywhere.'

'You could wear it for the firm's dinner dance,' said her mother.

George employed four people, including Mira.

'Or the work's outing,' Christine said.

Laughing.

The woman was laughing. She wouldn't laugh tomorrow morning, he thought, before winding his way to the second floor.

'George,' Christine said on the 'phone, 'Mum and I are going to do some shopping in town. See you later. Love you.'

High heels clicked on the parquet floor, a door shut. He peered out of the window as she inched out of the garage, stopped at the end of the drive and double-checked the traffic. What did she want, a written guarantee?

The top story of the house, stretching across the entire width of the house, wasn't used as living space. One part of it was a studio, smelling of turps and paint. It had a few boring Still Life paintings -fruit and bottles- stacked against the wall. But there was also one good painting of a little blonde girl sitting on a chair, a toy on her lap.

The other section of the attic was used for storing old carpets, blankets, pillows and a skate board.

She won't want to look at that painting once he had done with the little girl, he thought as he explored the rest of the house which was big, expensive and lived in by well-to-do people.

On the first floor, a pink bedroom with a shop-full of soft toys was the first bedroom next to the stairs. He selected a white toy animal from the bed, something to tease her with.

'Quiet, or he will get it,' a finger against his lips.

Further down the landing was the master bedroom. Excellent, they wouldn't hear him creeping into her bedroom.

It was another house with a basement. The fire in the B&B should smoulder nicely by now he thought as he went into the kitchen and made himself a cup of Instant and a sandwich; he needed something to sustain him until the small hours. Bloody woman hadn't heard of cut-loaves, he thought as he cut a couple of slices from a round loaf.

His hand started throbbing from the pressure of the knife and he felt a headache coming on. He took two painkillers and his last migraine pill, cleared up every trace and put everything back the way it was.

He wound his way to the top floor where he curled up in a large wardrobe with a pillow and a blanket. He wrestled with his headache and cursed George Hudson. He was here because of him and not safely in London with Vlad.

George would be sorry.

CHAPTER 57

'THE ACC IS IN YOUR OFFICE,' Cunningham informed Wilson when he arrived at the station at nine. 'He has a meeting to attend and he is not happy, I must warn you.'

'Make him some of our god-awful coffee, would you, Connor?'

The Assistant Chief Constable was sitting behind Wilson's desk. With his pink cheeks, blond crew cut and his pressed uniform, he looked as fresh and shiny as the new dawn Wilson had missed through sleeping late.

'Sorry to keep you waiting, Sir,' said Wilson, standing there, 'only I didn't know.'

'You didn't know what?'

'I was keeping you waiting.'

The ACC looked at him. When Wilson made no move to sit down he got the message, he came from behind the desk and sat on the visitors chair, now facing Wilson.

The ACC wanted a progress report.

Wilson asked if that meant the investigation of Foster, or of Willoughby's death, or a brief account of all that he knew in connection to both.

The ACC waved the coffeee and Connor away with a tight gesture. He obviously prayed for self-control, or else he had tasted their coffee before.

'The man arrested in Oxford was not Foster,' he said. 'He has been released. One good thing, the press have decamped for Oxford, and also for Cambridge with the Luke Cole murder.'

Now he asked for a brief statement on both cases, starting with Foster.

'Enquiries are proceeding Sir.'

'Is that all?'

'Not quite. Forensic have discovered Foster's fingerprints on a sash window, on the glass, on Mr Marshall's house, where Luke Cole's girlfriend was attacked. But I have sent in full and detailed reports of every aspect of the investigations. Do you want me to summarise? I have listed all the statements.'

'Good. I'll read the reports. I would like to suggest, however, that you keep budgets in mind.'

'Sergeant Tomlinson was able to use Uniform on shift work as best he could, apart from Connor and Smith under my command.'

'It appears you have sanctioned a lot of overtime.'

'Yes, Sir,' said Wilson. 'Next time we find a dead body, I suggest we leave him to rot in the ground until we can find a convenient time slot.'

When the ACC left, Wilson thought he would not make an exception in his case.

'Who does he think he is, the Home Secretary?'

'Something has annoyed him,' said Cunningham. 'He was put out when he arrived. I believe he doesn't see eye to eye with the Super.'

Nicholson assumed almost saintly qualities in Wilson's eyes.

'Someone has been in our house,' said Christine, wringing her hands, when George came home at lunchtime.

His heart fell right down to his boots.

'What makes you think so?'

'The kettle was warm when I got in,' she said, 'and I haven't used it since I went out after eleven. Plus,' she stopped, 'I hope you don't think I'm being stupid, but there was some water in the sink, and when I went upstairs to check all the rooms for intruders there was dirt on the first floor landing, I vacuumed it when you took Rosie to school.'

She steadied herself on the sink.

'Rosie's Snowy-White-SnowyLeopard is missing, and I know I put it on her bed this morning after I made it.'

'And did you check every room? All the floors?' he asked as he raced off to check the rooms himself.

'Whoever it was has gone,' he said when he came down.

'Do you think it was Foster? You have been worried about him, and Rosie was a friend of Emily Watson,' she asked, surprisingly steady.

'I thinks so. And it's my belief he is coming back for Rosie. I think you will have to fetch her from school and go with her and stay with your mother for the time being.'

Christine gasped.

She had better get some things for herself and for Rosie, he urged her, while he paced the hallway. Finally, she came down with her bag and he took her to his mother-in-law.

'I think if I was in trouble again, I would go to her,' he had said to Lewis at one time, and now trouble had found him, he was prepared to trust her.

'My mum can cope with anything,' said Christine, 'and she's got Eddy. I think if we tell them the truth, they'll cope with it.'

And so they did after George left them and went to the police.

'I think these will be long hours, darling,' said her mother, 'we must think hard how to entertain Rosie without her noticing anything is wrong. What do you think, Eddy?'

'We'll buy her a new toy when she comes out of school and let her choose a DVD,' he said. 'She can also bake some biscuits and make a real mess with it.'

It was a start for them as well, keep busy, don't think, they'll catch him soon, soon.

Wilson finished talking to Sandra Pearson and put the phone down. The autopsy report would be with him tomorrow, she's said, although what she had told him confirmed what he had suspected, when Cunningham reported that Hudson had arrived at the station.

'Hudson is here? At last, bring him in, and tell Connor we do not want to be disturbed,'

George Hudson was the sort of man who couldn't be ignored merely by being in the room. Tall, square-faced, square-shouldered, blue-eyed, well dressed, feet firmly planted on the ground, he made the office seem smaller.

'Please sit down,' said Wilson after the introductions.

Hudson glanced at Cunningham.

'It might be easier,...'

'I'm not here to make it easy for you, and DS Cunningham is my right hand. So, let's have it.'

They both made notes, and Wilson asked questions, as George explained why he was certain somebody had been in his house.

'A barely-warm kettle?'

'It's an upright stainless steel kettle, it retains the heat for a long while.'

'Right. What about water in the sink?'

'My wife is neurotic about her stainless steel sink, she keeps polishing it.'

Wilson used to be a compulsive sink polisher himself, he said. And why not? he thought. Sherlock Holmes had his violin, he had his sink until they had a Belfast, as Dorothy called it.

'Please continue."

'Dirt on the landing?'

'She had hoovered it when I took Rosie to school.'

'And what about the missing toy?'

'She put it on the bed after she made it.'

'Right.' Wilson put down his pen. 'And who do you think was in your room?'

'Fred Foster,' Wilson repeated.

'And what makes you think so?'

And so the whole sorry saga was laid bare, and it was just as Wilson had thought.

'Thank you, I'll recap. Foster, an ex-inmate, was a creature of habit. He walked to Somerfield at the same time on the same day. He went to the school at break time, in the morning and in the afternoon. He would enter the lane on Friday evening when you jumped off the wall and gave him a beating, only it was Dr Willoughby who collapsed, just as the real Fred Foster came down the lane. Dr Willoughby's coat fell on the floor. When you smashed the sherry bottle to beat Foster off, he tried to get away, slipped, cut his hand and wiped it on the coat. You got a wheelbarrow from a shed, put the corpse into the back of the car and buried him in the woods.'

He paused.

'You watched Foster every day and in the evening all by yourself, and then you went home to your family. When did you actually find time to run your business?' said Wilson. 'And it has nothing to do with Ritchie King and Alf Butler, who have both recently been injured?'

Hudson glanced sideways before he spoke, a sure sign of a liar.

'Absolutely nothing, I swear. It was just me.'

'Let's assume you're right and Foster was in your house. I suppose he got in through the back door you left by when you took Rosie to school.'

'That's right, we never lock it during the day when we are there.'

'Have you a burglar alarm, and if you have, is it connected to Bury St. Edmunds or to Newmarket?'

George said no alarm, it was just an empty box on the front wall.

'I searched the whole house but there was nobody in any of the rooms, but .Christine and Rosie will stay with her mother and her husband,' he said, 'they know what our suspicions are and they are able to deal with it.'

'You are right; Foster is coming back to your house at some point. When you go back home, first thing: lights,' said Wilson, 'don't switch the lights on in the front room.'

The lights were on an electric timer when it got dark, Hudson said. The living room and dining rooms were actually facing the road on either side of the hall, but the light was switched on in only one room.

'Good, carry on as normal. Who lives directly opposite to you?'

Farn Road was a wide, tree-lined avenue with semi-detached houses, except for a large block of flats. The occupants were mostly elderly, possibly widowed people, but able to live independent lives. 'It has three stories,' George added. 'The top flats have balconies, and there is a car park at the back.'

And now Hudson was at home along with PC Connor, who was in the kitchen watching the path to the back door. Hudson was in one of the front rooms, watching the drive.

Both were under strict instructions not to move from the spot and keep their eyes peeled. Wilson's number was keyed into their mobiles and on speed.

Both men were armed with a Thermos of coffee, George had a plant pot and Connor had the kitchen sink if it was needed.

And every two hours they had to change places.

CHAPTER 58

'ARE WE TAKING ARMED RESPONSE,' asked the Chief Superintendent when Wilson phoned him.

'I don't think so. There is a long back garden Foster might use as a route to the house, he might hide in the shed until he can slip in through the back door, but he has no weapons except his brain,' said Wilson.

'Banged up for twenty years with only a routine for company,' he added, ' and he is running rings around us. Tomlinson will use Traffic to monitor the streets, Uniforms will be out as well. But as we don't actually know if he is on foot or drives a car or a scooter we can't cordon off the area. One thing is certain, though, he will have to approach the house either from the back or the front.'

'I'll be there as soon as I can and bring two officers for the back garden. I'll speak to Tomlinson and oversee the operation from there.'

'Thank you,,' said Wilson. 'I will join Cunningham at the flat and watch out for Foster, that's all we can do.'

He drew onto the car park at the block of flats to join Cunningham, when his mobile rang.

'It's number eighteen,' reported Cunningham, 'and it is a Mrs Maxwell, in her sixties, she lives alone. She's a former school teacher, retired due to bone trouble, but there is a lift, and she likes to watch the life of the street below.'

Some life, thought Wilson, climbing the stairs, greeting a neighbour, an elderly, neatly dressed man, who stopped with an enquiring look on his face.

'I'm here to see my cousin, Mrs Maxwell,' he said.

'Oh, good, she hardly ever gets any visitors, apart from what we call the *Sisters*, of course.'

The Sisters? Is she religious?'

'Oh, no. It's a sewing circle, apparently.'

Mrs Maxwell was a stout woman who used a walking stick. She had bright, blue eyes and curly white hair, like a woolly lamb.

'Exciting, isn't it, a surveillance team in my flat. As I told your colleague just now, I saw a man in dark clothes looking at a leaflet and ringing the doorbell of the house. Mrs Hudson answered the door. They are a nice family. Sometimes I see them sitting together in one of their rooms and I imagine their perfect life.'

She paused.

'I hope you do not think I am snooping or that I am envious; it's just that sort of life escaped me when I was married. It's rare, I suppose.'

There was life to be observed from Miss Maxwell's flat. Young mothers pushing pushchairs, pregnant woman and old people on sticks came and went from the nearby supermarket.

The wide street was lined with exactly spaced plane trees hanging onto their autumnal leaves.

'They're heavily pollarded. Plane trees collect pollution in their bark, it falls off when it's full, hence their camouflage appearance,' said Mrs Maxwell.

'A tray with tea things is ready in the kitchen. And now it is time for my siesta,' she announced after she had watched Countdown and the various antique shows in an armchair, where she fell asleep.

A light drizzle fell. Car passed in both directions down below, school was out, and it started to get dark.

Fred Foster fell asleep in his wardrobe just as the children came out of school.

'Oh, goody,' said Rosie being counted out,

Hester in tow,' there's my mum and my grandma and my Uncle Eddy.'

'Uncle Eddy?' said Ann Granger, 'Where? Oh, right, Mrs Hudson, just making sure.'

'Can Hester come to play, Mum?' she asked, tugging at her skirt.

'No, she can't, we are busy today.' said Christine, 'Come along and don't make a fuss, we are going into town.'

'She spoke quite severely,' reported Natasha to Lewis later. 'She made Hester cry.'

What's up now? thought Lewis, as if he needed anything else to contend with. Aleska Wawrinska decided to stay where the love of her life would be buried, his parents had arrived and so had Natasha's brother and his family. He had suggested eloping to Natasha, but interestingly, she had said, 'not yet,' but she did not opt for, 'not likely.'

Soon had become now, Jimmy was really getting the hang of using the gears and steering, Ronald said after three evenings out. Too right, he wasn't going to ruin his mum's car. Tomorrow evening was the soon for Ronald, who said he would collect the car and get some birds, pick up Jimmy. He was going to take them out and treat them.

'Where?'

'In the car, man. The girls in the car and then back to my house. I'll get some weed. Got any money?'

'Only what's in the jar,' said Jimmy, 'but it's money she owes to the debt collector. I can't touch that, my mum would kill me.'

Ronald asked him did he want some fun or not? Jimmy said he would think about it.

'Think about it?' said Ronald. 'What's to think about?'

346

He was right; there was nothing to think about. Ronald was as good as his word. Before he drove away that evening in Jimmy's Mum's car, he said he was off to fetch Ruth and Eileen. 'Hot Babes, Jimmy, hot Babes, one for you, and one for me.'

'They don't sound hot to me,' said Jimmy who had no idea who they were, 'I mean Ruth and Eileen! Are they like a hundred?'

Ronald tapped the end of his nose meaningfully, what was that supposed to mean?

'Be ready with the money, I'll get the weed,' he said, 'or you won't be able to complete your sex education, know what I mean?'

It was all very well for Ronald, Jimmy thought, his father was a headmaster and he earned more than the prime minister and his Mum, all right, she was a step-mum and they hated each other, was something big on the council, whereas Jimmy's mum worked in a shop during the day and in a pub at weekends.

He missed her, especially at night. He had never slept by himself in his life and he kept listening out for unknown noises.

He heated up some spaghetti his mother had left for him and finished his homework; he always did any school-related work on the quiet, he didn't want to be known as a snotty swot.

It was Shakespeare, Othello. Ronald had given him a book where it was all done for him, the jealousy and that, double jealousy, in fact, with that Iago calling Othello *a circumcised dog*. It had to mean something, he thought. When the doorbell rang, he hoped it was his mum, but why she should ring the bell he had no idea.

It was Ronald, so he went downstairs. Two blonde girls were in his mum's car, one in the front seat, the other in the back.

'Money, mate,' said Ronald stretching out his

hand as if he had every right to his mum's money.

'I've got twenty quid from my paper round you can have.'

'I've got the weed and something else, and Hargreaves wants paying,' said Ronald.

'You can't drive the car like that, what have you done to it?' Jimmy said, looking at the car, horrified. 'There's a big crack in the windscreen.'

'It was a stone,' said Ronald. 'The car got stoned.'

'It isn't funny, I changed my mind. I want the car keys, I don't want you to use the car, I forbid it, my mum needs it for work.'

Ronald grabbed Jimmy's twenty pounds and stormed off, Jimmy vainly trying to catch up with him, Ronald laughing and waving the notes and the keys at him through the open car window.

Jimmy went back and let himself into the flat, where he went into the sitting room, switched on the DVD player and watched Norman's porno films, thus finishing his sex education.

In Buckinghamshire, Mrs Rendell picked up the phone. It was Irene, her friend from the downstairs flat who had promised to keep an eye on Jimmy in case he threw any wild parties.

'I tell you, I saw him with my own eyes, that nasty boy he hangs around with, he had your car keys and he grabbed Jimmy's money, and then he drove off.'

CHAPTER 59

RONALD WAS NOT keeping an eye on his speed, he was too bloody annoyed with Jimmy as he drove up Farn Road and to the road junction controlled by traffic lights. Ruth sat with her legs bent on the backseat and leant forward, passing Eileen a roll-up. Eileen had undone her seatbelt as well and was kneeling on her seat, her blonde mane across Ronald's lap as she gave his crotch some serious attention.

'Give over,' he said, 'and sit up properly.'

She straightened up, almost standing, when he noticed the traffic light was about to change. He accelerated furiously to beat the lights when, all of a sudden, they loomed up in front of him, close into his vision. He covered his face with his hands.

'What the fuck,' he said as something flattened him against his seat. His air bag had inflated. He wasn't hurt, and then it was all cars and hooting and coppers and ambulances and Ruth laying half-way across the front seat and Eileen halfway on the bonnet.

At six o'clock, Wilson looked at his watch.

'I've just remembered something that might well be relevant,' said Miss Maxwell, who was busy stitching something on her embroidery frame. 'A good sleep often does clear the brain.'

'Let's have it,' said Wilson.

'As I said, Inspector,' said Mrs Maxwell, 'something has come to mind about this morning. When Mrs Hudson shut the front door, the caller walked round to the back of the house.' She paused. 'I never saw him coming back.'

'He's in the house,' shouted Wilson into Hudson's mobile. 'Let's go,' he said to Cunningham when there was an almighty crash and a cacophony of

349

blaring car horns. His phone rang. Some kids had wrapped a car round the traffic lights, he said, when the phone rang again.

'I don't believe it,' he said,' we'll be right over.'

Time passed slowly, '*on leaden feet*,' as they called it in books, and George Hudson could well understand the sentiment. He was about to change rooms with Connor when they heard the noise of a door opening over their heads. Connor put a finger to his lips and went back into the kitchen, while George's heart, frozen for a moment, started beating rapidly and he went back to the living room

The noise of the blaring sirens woke Fred Foster. Good God, the B&B was going up in smoke. He better get out or he would burn to death.

BUT HOW AND WHY HAD HE ENDED BACK IN THE B&B?

He stumbled silently without his shoes out of the wardrobe and out into a silent house and ran down the stairs.

He paused on the top step of the long and steep stairs leading into the hall when he saw two men staring up at him, one was wielding a poker, the other a knife.

WRONG HOUSE.

He changed his mind and turned round, when a phone rang. He lost his footing wearing socks, tripped over and fell forward, bouncing on every tread. As he accelerated, he lifted his head and came to rest when his head hit the hard corner of a small bookcase, splitting his forehead into two.

'Take tube train to Embankment Station,' he said when the two men turned him over and bent over him, deeply shocked. It was a corpse they were looking at.

'What did he say?' said Wilson after he and Cunningham had rushed across the road, looking at the corpse with distaste

'Take tube train to Embankment Station? I don't suppose he said who he was meeting.'

As these were Foster's last words, nobody would ever know. Or so Wilson thought.

'I didn't know anybody could die so quickly,' Connor said.

'Better make sure he is dead,' said Wilson, bending down with an 'Ah' of disgust and feeling for a pulse, but there was none.

'I have to ask you, but you had better be prepared, could you have stopped him?'

The two men looked at each other.'

'We could have under normal circumstances,' said Hudson, 'except...

'These were not normal circumstances,' said Connor.

'Foster was actually in the house, and now he has gone off in an ambulance, but he is dead. He fell down the stairs and whacked his brain into two, the two front lobes,' reported Wilson to Nicholson. 'Connor and Mr Hudson witnessed it.'

'Could they have stopped him?'

'Too shocked. You had better let your men know. And perhaps you could send the photographer, there is a certain amount of blood on the hall floor and he has possibly left some other evidence in the house.'

Conner bagged the kettle for forensics, while Wilson accompanied George Hudson on his search of the house. Nothing seemed disturbed until they reached the top floor, where they found an open wardrobe. On investigation, the interior revealed a pillow and a blanket, a half-eaten cheese sandwich, a used mug and a packet of painkillers.

'I think we can safely say we have cured his headache,' said Wilson.

Then he spotted the white toy animal George Hudson held up.

'Rosie's toy.'

'If your wife wasn't such a good housewife and if you had dismissed her fears as silly, we would have an entirely different set of circumstances to look at.'

George felt faint.

'Well done. Foster got the better of me, but not of you,' said Wilson.

He paused.

'The house is yours again after the photographer leaves, it isn't a crime scene, and we will leave you to spread the good news around. However, I'm afraid you and I will have to talk again. Perhaps you can call in a the station tomorrow morning at ten 'o'clock when I have Dr Pearson's autopsy report.'

Wilson dispatched Connor to talk to Mrs Maxwell at her flat, to put her out of her misery, as he called it, while Cunningham drove them to the station.

'Foster's gone at last, but we don't know yet where he was operating from,' said Nicholson who had made himself at home behind Wilson's desk. 'I've arranged the press interview for tomorrow morning at Storwich. I see that you will be in possession of Pearson's autopsy report tomorrow, and that you expect to make an arrest for Willoughby's murder. It's all coming together nicely, but I expect one of you to attend the briefing.'

'Right you are, Sir,' said Wilson.

'You had better interview the boy who was

driving the car into the traffic lights. He is unharmed, but his two passengers, two young girls, are in hospital in a serious condition. Their parents have been informed.

'Tonight?'

'If we do it now, the youth can spend a night in a cell; might do him good. The traffic diversion at the junction is in operation, and one side of Farn Road is blocked to traffic,' Nicholson added. 'Sergeant Tomlinson is a good man, I think you should really make an effort to get to know all the officers in the station.' He cleared his throat. 'Better.'

'Better than what? Better than nothing?'

'Than you do now.'

'I will,' said Wilson, puzzled, they had worked together really well, even if Tomlinson expressed himself in clichés and talked about the best laid plans of mice and men and ticking all the boxes. And yes, he had quite forgotten that he had disliked him

.   'Yes, yes,' said Nicholson, and waved him away.

'I don't know how you put up with the Super,' said Cunningham, who was driving Wilson to the Suffolk hospital. 'Like the Peace of God, he passes all understanding.'

'The Super? I wouldn't want his job for a pension. Sitting in an office all day, brown-nosing to his Superiors, co-ordinating evidence and passing it on to the right quarters. He is all right, but sometimes he just doesn't think about what comes out of his mouth when he opens it. Besides, I turned it down at the Met.'

Cunningham looked surprised.

'There are rumours on the grapevine that you will be offered a promotion,' he said, positively confounding Wilson -before he laughed. 'It would explain the ACC's tantrum,' he said, 'but you don't get an offer once you have turned it down.'

Or so he thought.

Ronald was in A&E, being patched up and giving some blood for analysis. All he had was a sore neck, not even a whiplash. No bruises on the face either, as he had covered it with his hands before the air-bag smacked into him. He was relaxed after the stuff Hargreaves had given him. Not given, he thought, somebody would have to come up with the money for it.

'Can I see my friends? Ruth and Eileen?' he asked the nurse who led him to a bed in A&E to be on the safe side.

'I'll see if it's possible.'

When she came back, she said that Ruth was in theatre undergoing surgery.

She didn't mention Eileen, so he didn't either.

The nurse gave him some painkillers and he lay down reluctantly, reliving the moment over and over when he saw that pole in front of him. He knew that there was nothing, absolutely nothing, he could do about it. Then the shock of the air-bag deploying, Eileen flying through the windscreen, had he seen that? Suddenly, he heard voices from behind the cubicle curtains.

'My son is a good lad,' said his father.

'I expect he is.'

Not my fault, he thought, nobody could have stopped the car, except there was the little matter of him driving it too fast, he was under-age and on drugs.

He must have been seen stealing the car from Jimmy; that neighbour was looking at him when he was waving the car keys. Then, there was Ruth being wheeled off to theatre. There was the little matter of Eileen... He stopped.

And now he was in the police station sitting

next to his Dad and facing two coppers, Wilson and Cunningham, who were recording the interview.

'A minor has to have a parent or a solicitor present,' said DI Wilson, looking at his notes. Ronald was two days short of his sixteenth birthday.

His dad said that they didn't want a lawyer.

'That is right. We do not need one,' said Ronald.

'Why not?' asked the other copper, Cunningham.

'I was given a lift when the accident occurred,' he said, 'Eileen was driving.'

'Whose car was it?'

He shrugged his shoulders.

'She didn't say.'

The other policeman, Cunningham, looked at his notes.

'Is this really necessary?' asked his dad. 'He was involved in a car accident, that's all. Being a passenger is not a crime.'

'If Eileen was driving,' said Wilson, 'she was driving it on the left-hand side of the car, the side without a steering wheel.'

Somebody came in. Wilson stopped the tape at eight-forty-five, and went out. When he came back, he whispered something to the other copper and turned the recording on again, saying that he had entered the room at eight-forty-seven.

'Right. I have just been told that Eileen Bishop died a few minutes ago.'

'Oh, my God,' said Ronald's dad. 'How terrible. She's one of my pupils. Bright girl.'

Ronald thought and thought, and finally he knew whose fault it was. Jimmy's.

'Jimmy Rendell said I could have his mother's car because she is away. He asked me to go fetch some weed and I was going to pick him up when I had it.'

'And you got the cannabis and what else?'

'Nothing else?'

'Coke,' said Ronald. 'But Jimmy asked me to get it, that's why I did it. I got it from one of Jimmy's mates, Paul Hargreaves.'

'And this Jimmy lives where?'

'Jimmy Rendell lives on the North Estate.'

His father said Jimmy was one of his pupils as well.

'I have to do as Jimmy says,' said Ronald. 'You see, his father is in prison and his mother works in a pub.'

'So?'

'He's dangerous. Scum.'

'But the North Estate is in the opposite direction you were driving, you were driving away from it in fact, and you were already in possession of the drugs. You are under-age, you drove a stolen car dangerously and used drugs. Consequently a fifteen-year-old girl is lying in the hospital mortuary.'

'Have you been joyriding before?' asked Cunningham.

Co-operate, thought Ronald, co-operate, and he came clean.

Somebody came in and whispered something to the DI.

'Ruth Kendall has undergone surgery, she is in the Intensive Care Unit,' he said. 'We will have to hold your son in a youth facility until he appears before the Magistrate.'

'Go easy on him,' said Ronald's father after his son was led away.

'We will go easy on him if you tell the dead girl's parents your son is responsible for her death,' said Cunningham.

'I thought not,' Wilson said into the silence.

'He had a great future ahead of him,' said Ronald's father after he mentally faced the next days morning assembly. 'He has a couple of cautions,' he added. 'He drove my neighbour's car into a brick wall, plus, you'll find out, anyway, he forged some of my wife's cheques and she reported him. She is his stepmother.' He straightened his back. 'Ronald used to play Internet Poker, his money problem was not caused by drugs. My wife and I are busy people, you understand, we can't be with him all the time.'

Ronald had some sort of a future, thought Cunningham, but he wouldn't call it great. However, knowing the case an experienced lawyer could make out of police interviewing a boy who might possibly be in shock, he arranged for the doctor to look Ronald over when the boy complained of a neck ache.

Ronald was sent back to the hospital for an x-ray, to be on the safe side. Wilson sent Connor to sit with him.

The following Wednesday. the Magistrate decided to send him to trial.

Jimmy woke up when his mother shook him.

'Mum? Where did you spring from?'

'Ron drove me back after Irene phoned.' she said. 'What have you been up to?'

Two coppers were in the living room. He rubbed his eyes, the light was so bright, but they were still there. They asked him about the car.

'Ronald took the car,' he said. 'He wanted me give him Mum's money for the debt collector for some weed. Ronald is well off, but we ain't; my mum works hard for it, so I wouldn't give it to him. he wouldn't take no for an answer, so he grabbed my paper round money and he just took the car as I said and drove off and the windscreen has a big crack in it.'

One of the policemen made a note of what he said.

'You see, in school, if Ronald is a mate, you are big. We all do as he wants us to, but not for long, he's a bully.'

'I asked Irene to keep an eye on him,' his mum said, 'when she phoned me and said the boy grabbed the money off Jimmy and went off in my car, Edward drove me back.'

More notes by the police.

'Where is my car? Mum asked, and that was when it all came out ? Ronald arrested, Eileen dead and Ruth seriously injured, the car wrecked.

'I know you are shocked, Jimmy,' said the tall policeman, 'but I have to ask you, are you and Ronald in the habit of joyriding?'

'Would I?' Jimmy said, looking at him with the limpid eyes of innocence.

'We rather think you would. Do you remember what you did on the fifth of November?'

They had driven a car away from the station and turned it over somewhere near Stow.

He was told he would have to make a formal statement and was sent back to bed, so the coppers could talk to his mother.

His father and his mother lost their jobs when the pickle factory burnt down, reported Wilson afterwards. Their house was repossessed, and someone who called him a benefit scrounger once too often ended up in hospital.

'Four years, no previous. I suppose it's the law, but is it justice?' He paused. 'We can sort out the debt collector without pointing the finger at Mrs Rendell, and Mr Rendell will be out in a fortnight.'

'Plus, we can add obtaining money with menaces to Ronald's sheet, but not speeding, he's too young to hold a licence,' said Cunningham.

'Jimmy is a good lad at heart,' said Wilson back in the car, 'a very good lad under the circumstances. And he loves his mother.'

He wished he could say the same for Mrs Hargreaves, sobbing broken-heartedly the last time he had seen her over her son Paul, out on bail. He was definitely dealing and heading for a lengthy sentence.

'So, back to the old chestnut, nature versus nurture.'

Wilson backed nature every time. Every possible care and love had been lavished on his own daughter with the fragrant name, Heather.

'She's not a bad kid, you understand, she works hard and looks after herself. Unfortunately she takes after my Aunt Agatha, a big woman wielding tweed-clad hips, always on the lookout for a sore spot she can inflame.'

He started the car.

'Why Heather couldn't take after Agatha's sister, my mother who was a lovely, gentle, woman I shall never know, or her own mother, for that matter.'

Jane, his late wife, had been a loved daughter, later becoming a loved wife; she had never seen the need to fight for anything.' She never saw herself in competition with my job.'

'And Heather did.'

Oh, yes, every time. Jane was eventually diagnosed with stomach cancer; you see, an aggressive cancer, Grade three. It was eating her up. There was nothing that could be done, she was dead within three months. When she died, Heather said it was my fault, she still does, she says that if Jane didn't fight it, it was because I had made her soft.'

'And the worst of it was that Heather was a nurse, she still is.'

And now he was at home with Dorothy and Ralph, getting a rapturous welcome. Dorothy opened a bottle of champagne she had kept in readiness for this momentous occasion.

'You finally got Foster,' she said, 'so let's concentrate on a safer world and worry about today's youth another day.'

They sat down at the table with the discerning epicure Wilson's favourite meal, egg and chips. Champagne and chips.

'Nicholson is a good bloke at heart, he looks after his men,' said Wilson, 'but Cunningham had better look out for it if he isn't transferred, or he may go nuts, well, he is bound to find a vacancy for him very soon.'

'What are you talking about?'

'A rumour is going round that I am in line for promotion,' said Wilson. 'Do you fancy me in a blue uniform?'

CHAPTER 60

NOTHING PASSED FOR NORMAL for George Hudson. Foster's demise elated him, but he knew what was marching towards him tomorrow. Or rather, he knew who he had to go and see tomorrow at ten o'clock.

Rosie and Christine stayed with her mother while he went back to the house in the late evening. He went up to his office, sorted out his papers and made notes for Christine. Rates, house insurance, car insurance, MOT, dustbin collection. It was surprisingly little, he thought. Sleep was out of the question, so he settled down in the armchair he had spent the best part of the afternoon in, certain only of two things; one, he would keep Alf and Ritchie out of it, and two, he could expect a lengthy prison sentence.

'The autopsy report has arrived, and it is as Sandra thought,' said Wilson to Cunningham the next morning. 'You might as well attend the press conference and get into the groove. Perhaps you can make my excuses to the Super; say that I have an arrest to make. And don't forget, you have Fred Foster's post mortem examination this afternoon.'

Cunningham departed with no intention to be back for it, while Connor and Wilson went off to arrest Frank Somersby for the murder of Paul Willoughby. Connor parked the car in the Angel Mount surgery car park and they entered the reception area.

'Can you call Frank Somersby?' said Wilson.

'He's not here,' the receptionist said, 'he's on leave. Dr Graham might see you later.'

'Do you know where Dr Somersby spends his leave?'

'Who wants to know? Oh, I am sorry, you're

the inspector, you've been here before,' she said accusingly.

'Quite right,' said Wilson, using his authoritative voice, 'and I need to know where he is this moment.'

She sniffed

'He wouldn't tell the likes of me where he goes,' she said, 'he barely passes the time of day with us,' but she went to the computer and printed out Somersby's particulars.

Somersby lived in a whitewashed, detached house in Harbinger. Set in a garden, unremarkable in this weather, it was pleasant, but modest. They walked up the front path to the door and Wilson pressed the doorbell. Nothing stirred. He stepped back and looked up at the upstairs windows when Connor called him, pointing to a long, dark shape hanging in the hall, dimly glimpsed through the frosted-glass door.

'Bloody hell,' said Wilson, racing round to the back of the house, where Connor broke the glass of the back door. They looked at each other, but there was nothing for it. And so they went into the hall where the shape turned out to be Frank Somersby gently swinging from a hook in the ceiling by the banisters, an envelope at his feet.

'I think he's been there for some days,' Wilson reported to Pearson through his handkerchief. 'The central heating is on full blast.'

He 'phoned Storwich and spoke to the Super, who was not yet at the press conference.

'I'll send the crime team over,' Nicholson said, 'leave it with me. How long has he been dead do you think?'

'I think since the day we discovered Dr Willoughby's body, we have not cut him down. We also found what looks like a letter, it's not addressed to anybody,' said Wilson. 'Can I have Cunningham back? There really is a case for more officers on the crime team.'

The Super sighed and replaced the receiver.

Wilson and Connor went upstairs. Carefully avoiding looking at the dark-red face, the swollen blue tongue sticking out, they inspected the noose, which appeared to be made out of some strong, thick, blue twine, before going into the bedroom.

'Bloody hell,' said Wilson, going downstairs with Connor.

Leaving him at the house with the body, he drove back to the station and dispatched Smith to guard the house with Connor until the team arrived from Storwich. He had barely five minutes to digest Somersby's suicide before George Hudson arrived. He was there on the dot of ten o'clock, dark hollows under his eyes telling a story of another sleepless nights.

Wilson began.

'I might as well put you out of your misery,' he said. 'When we went to arrest Frank Somersby for the murder of Dr Willoughby this morning we found him swinging from the banisters.'

'WHO IS FRANK SOMERSBY?' asked Hudson, completely bemused, his arms in the air, his hands fluttering like birds.

'He was Paul Willoughby's own doctor, and from his note it seems he has harboured an obsession with his daughter Natasha for years, since she was ten years old. His bedroom was plastered with Natasha Marshall's photographs and posters from her modelling days.'

He paused.

'I haven't had time to digest all the information yet, as there is more from Dr Pearson, the pathologist's results, and the contents of the note.'

A knock on the door.

'Coffee, thank you, Paula. You can go.'

'He was kind of a favourite uncle' Wilson added, 'or that was how he saw himself when she was a child. When she grew into her teens, he disapproved of her modelling career as he felt that she was wasting her beauty.' He glanced at the note again. 'He disapproved of her marriage to Lewis Marshall, a puffed-up peddler of rubbish.'

Lewis Marshall ran a nation-wide chain of converted warehouses where he sold cheap or bankrupt goods at a higher price, he explained.

'After Natasha Marshall and Lewis began to live separately, he saw his chance, except Natasha became very attached to her father.'

He paused.

'If her father was removed, he thought, she would turn to him instead. He turned into a mind game, he persuaded Willoughby he was losing his reason. As Dr Pearson said, doctors know what can go wrong with the human body and are often the worst hypochondriacs.

He looked at his notes.

`Willoughby was probably glad to have Somersby to lean on, especially after his wife had died a long, agonising death. When Somersby first prescribed strong tranquilisers, inducing drowsiness and irritability when substituted with placebos, he persuaded Willoughby that he suffered the onset of Alzheimer's disease. Advising him to leave Post-it notes for everyday tasks, enforced Willoughby's belief he was losing his mind. Somersby prescribed what Willoughby thought was a new drug, Aricept, except it was actually a strong dosage of Dioxin. One of the side effects of Dioxin is confusion, and thirst.'

He paused.

'He didn't have Alzheimer's. According to Dr Pearson, Alzheimer's disease can only be correctly identified through a post-mortem, that is, through the snares and flats it causes in the brain.'

Where was his coffee-maker when he needed it?

'To continue. Dr Pearson found high levels of toxicity in his body not absorbed by the kidneys, he didn't die of renal failure although there was some renal damage.'

'But how do you know it was Dioxin and not Aricept?' asked Hudson.

'Because,' Wilson said, wagging a finger at him, getting finally to why he had laid the case open before Hudson, 'you didn't remove Willoughby's trousers before you buried him. A bottle of water and the medicine bottle were in his trouser pocket and have been analysed by the lab.'

'But,' Hudson started.

'He had but the slightest of bumps on his head, cranium ridges and his forehead were intact, that was what caused Dr Pearson's suspicion when I asked her how he died. Dr Willoughby's collapse had nothing to do with vigilante activity and with wheelbarrows from a shed and burying a corpse in the woods.'

He paused.

'You, or one of your friends, gave Dr Willoughby a mild tap on the head, as Dr Pearson put it, but his system simply broke down; he was poisoned. Who exactly was it who wielded the sherry bottle?'

'It was .. it was me,' said George.

'Let's say I believe your Spartacus moment. Now think on.'

George Hudson did his best, but he couldn't.

'If you had jumped off the wall five minutes later you would have found a dead body, summoned an ambulance and encountered an entirely different set of circumstances.'

Hudson was sitting in his chair with his head in his hands, and Wilson thought he had sweated long enough.

'What I am telling you now is entirely due to Mrs Maxwell, your neighbour from the flat opposite to you who has been much impressed with the good life you and your family lead, and your friends, I believe. Furthermore, I am impressed with your loyalty to your friends.'

He pointed a finger at Hudson.

'My official version will be that Foster chanced on the dead man in the lane, robbed him, thought he had been observed by somebody walking by, put him in the boot of his car and buried him in the woods. He deposited the ring and watch in a dustbin about to be emptied. No discernible fingerprints were found on these items, but they were in Luke Cole's possession as he was a dustman. So we will forget all that nonsense we have talked about, like three men jumping off a wall.'

George Hudson stared at him.

'Perhaps it will be best if you stick to my official version with everybody, including a certain Alf Butler and Richard King. Before you leave, you will have to make a statement about Foster's death in your house, and you will also have to attend a coroner's inquest to give evidence.'

George Hudson tottered out of the station hardly believing his luck.

A glorious vista opened out wide before him; they were not responsible for Paul Willoughby's death, he would become an ordinary man again, an ordinary man coming home to his family after a day's work, a man without a burdened conscience. What more could any man want? he thought. He parked his car in the garage, and before he opened the front door, he did something very unlike George Hudson. He turned round, looked at the top flat opposite and blew Miss Maxwell a kiss.

'We're in the clear, Alf. I have talked to the police. No, just listen. Willoughby was poisoned by his doctor who wanted Willoughby's daughter, Natasha, for himself. Foster robbed the dead man who collapsed in the lane, put him in his car and buried him under the trees.'

'And I'm Hans Christian Andersen,' said Alf.

'I'll explain it all later. Meet me at *The Volunteer*.'

He telephoned Ritchie and told him the same story.

'What?' said Ritchie, 'you mean we are not even accessorised?'

'No, Ritchie, just forget all about it, and remember, not a word to anybody else.'

Ritchie said that he got him, sort of, although he was a bit confused.

George put the phone down, picked it up again, and then he spoke to Christine's mother, who put the phone down, puzzled.

'That was George. He wants you to come home at once. I thought he was crying, but he said he had a cold coming on.' Apparently a shock could bring on a cold, said her mother. A villain bumping down the stairs and dropping dead at his feet with his nose buried in his neck was a certainly a shock.

Christine said it wasn't like that, Foster had split the frontal lobes of his brain when he hit the book case.

'And what have I always told you?' demanded her mother? 'Haven't I always said it was a silly place for a book case?'

She recommended a hot toddy for George, but Christine, who had read the letter he had left for her last night, didn't listen and ran for her car; George was back, how on earth had he managed it?

CHAPTER 61

Fred Foster's autopsy was next, and Lewis Marshall needed to be informed of developments, said Wilson to Cunningham who was back, having explained the situation with regard to sending off Hudson with merely a flea in his ear.

'I just couldn't send three hard-working family men to prison and deprive three families of husbands and fathers. And a hefty prison term it would most certainly have been, charged with robbing and illegally burying a dead body and perverting the course of justice.'

'All that indeed, sir,' said Cunningham. 'But I seem to have developed a sudden spot of amnesia. I can't recall a word of what you have just told me.'

Wilson sighed with relief.

'Perhaps you can deal with Lewis Marshall.'

He paused.

'Ironic, Somersby started his mental reign of terror. And it was an act of mental cruelty to make an elderly man, a man living on his own, convince he was losing his reason. All to get rid of him and get Natasha Marshall to lean on him instead. And yet, her father's death reunited the estranged pair. Read the autopsy report and the suicide note, read the last line out.'

'*A dying sun leaves a long shadow,*' read Cunningham.

'Precisely, he didn't repent, he wanted to punish Natasha through his death.'

'Or,' said Cunningham, 'Somersby was vainglorious.'

Wilson wondered if that wasn't a flower.

'Because?' he asked.

'He thought only Natasha was worthy of him. Only him.'

Wilson said he thought it was time Cunningham turned his mind from the – he was about to say the metaphysical except he didn't know what it meant- the philosophical to the real world of policing.

'Right you are, Sir,' said Cunningham, 'but how did you know it was Somersby?'

'This case had more twists and turns than a maze, but every maze has a centre,' said Wilson, back on firm ground..

'Two things alerted me. 1) Seventy-one percent of murder victims are killed by somebody they know well. So, who knew Dr Willoughby? His daughter, Lewis Marshall and Dr Somersby.'

'And 2.) A man doesn't know what he knows until he knows what he doesn't know, my old inspector used to say,' he added. 'Some philosopher said it first. I knew Somersby watched Natasha Marshall's house, but although I didn't know why, it seemed important. Why didn't he just phone her, or why didn't he go and see her, he didn't have to stand in the cold and watch the house unless... '

He paused.

'Unless he had something her father had and wanted to get to him first if he turned up at his daughter's house, a mostly routine visit on a Saturday,' said Cunningham.

'Precisely, he was looking for the Aricept, which we now know wasn't Aricept but Dioxin, a heart medicine which doesn't do a healthy heart a lot of good and can cause confusion, the so-called Aricept which was missing from Willoughby's cabinet.'

Wilson drove off to Foster's autopsy, quite sure there would be nothing more to surprise him, but he was wrong.

Foster had suffered a bad cut to his hand, Sandra said, but that wasn't the surprise, he fallen on the broken glass in the lane.

'According to his notes, Foster suffered from migraines,' said Sandra, saw in hand, opening the skull, 'but he also had a brain tumour. See?'

Wilson declined the offer.

'He got off lightly in that case,' he said, but he did wonder if Foster had known about it. Did "Take tube train to Embankment station," mean anything?

Foster was a predator/hunter/psychopath and probably intended to do his hunting as part of a pair. He would never know, or so Wilson thought, all he knew was that he would have to see Nicholson the next day. He discussed this with Dorothy, who totally agreed with him.

'Do you think I ought to?'

'Yes,' she said, 'I think you should.'

What more was there to say?

'So, to recap,' said Wilson to Nicholson the next day.

'Foster chanced on the dead man, poisoned by Frank Somersby, and robbed him. He took the coat off, slipped and cut his hand badly on a broken bottle left in the lane, it will be in the autopsy report, and that is how Foster's blood was found on Willoughby's coat.'

Nicholson nodded.

'He took it to Oxfam to muddy the waters, we have a helper's two statements. The first one was taken when the coat was discovered, and the second was when Foster came in to buy some clothes and was rude to her. Thus, he knew about the shop.'

He paused.

Foster thought he had been observed by somebody on her way to Somerfield, we have a worker's statement, so he rolled the body onto the allotment, borrowed a wheelbarrow, put him in the boot of his car and buried him in the woods. That is why he went to ground as Howard Cole in Warner's B&B on the same night.'

'Right.'

'He disposed of the ring and the watch in a dustbin down the road from the B&B, where it was found and pocketed by Luke Cole who was emptying the dustbin. He was observed by Foster, who *wrongly* thought his fingerprints would be on the items. Cole fell out with Miss Wawrinska and followed her when she moved in with the Marshalls. In turn, he was followed by Foster, who killed him but failed to find the items, and drove with the body to Cambridge.'

'Well, that's nicely cleared up, everybody will be well impressed,' said Nicholson who was in receipt of all relevant reports and statements. If he was impressed with the prompt paperwork he didn't say so. Wilson resented that, given that had been sitting up with it for half the night.

'Anyway,' Nicholson added, 'I never believed in all that vigilante nonsense theory of yours if you don't mind me saying so. I readily believe in the obvious if it is obvious.'

And you can see no ships if you put your telescope to your blind eye, thought Wilson.

'And you were right too,' said Wilson, who was sweating. Lying and falsifying facts went as much against his nature as remembering the lies; he felt sick.

'And now,' said Nicholson, 'I am the bearer of good news, or rather the whisperer. I am pleased to tell you that you will be offered promotion to Chief Inspector. A vacancy has arisen in Cambridge, so you will be able to commute.'

He leaned back in his chair.

'You would have to appear in front of the Promotions Board, but it will be a mere formality with your results.'

Chief Inspector. Wilson savoured the word for a moment.

'I am grateful to have the offer, flattered really, but I'm afraid can't accept it.'

Nicholson leaned forward.

'I would like to hand in my resignation.'

'Resignation? Are you angling after a sabbatical? It's not wise in this financial climate.'

Wilson shook his head.

'You want to resign? But why?'

'I was turning into a policeman twenty-four hours a day,' Wilson said, 'with nothing else on my mind.'

That was true. He recalled waking up in the spare room, the dog by his bed and rolling his eyes when he shouted, 'motor cycle helmets, pizza deliveries.' He had looked at a willow tree and spouted off something about nightingales. It was almost certifiable.

'And dealing with Foster has been very unpleasant.'

'Dealing with a psychopath is, fortunately, rare, but policemen have to deal with these cases. I can see you are not yourself, you have gone red in the face. Health reasons, blood pressure and that, you will have to see the police surgeon,' said Nicholson. 'However, promotion carries a substantial increase not only in salary but also pension, don't forget.'

Wilson had half of the money left from the sale of his house in London, Dorothy earned good money, and so did he.

'We have savings,' he said, 'and our needs are few.'

But what will you do with yourself? You don't play golf, and a man can get tired of his own four walls.'

Wilson frowned.

'Long term, we want to do something for disadvantaged children,' he said.

'Like what?'

'Advantage them. Dorothy is a teacher so she knows something about it.'

Nicholson looked puzzled.

'Short term?' he asked

'I will grow a ponytail and join the Open University. Dorothy and I also want to travel in France during the school holidays; their guest houses accommodate dogs.' He paused. 'Dorothy suggested studying psychology, I would have a head start, but trying to find out what makes people function has lost its appeal, so I intend to study history.'

Nicholson said that he wouldn't have to grow a pony tail for that and hoped he would see the inquests through.

'The Magistrates in Suffolk will deal with Foster and Frank Somersby. Luke Cole's will have to be dealt with by Cambridge where he was found. The respective coroners will summon relatives, and you may have to give evidence. And,' he looked at the papers, but couldn't find what he was looking for, 'the teenage joy rider has gone before the Magistrates and will stand trial. It has been judged a Capital Crime.'

That was how he would lay it before the Chief Constable.

'Just one more thing. As it says in my report, the scooter and helmet with Foster's fingerprints were abandoned in the hospital car park. Foster has been hiding in the B&B at Farn Road. He started a fire in the basement, but that had burnt itself out. The stolen Honda Accord was found in the car park of *The Volunteer*, reported by the pub's landlord.'

Nicholson nodded, and then onto the nitty-gritty. There would be a vacancy for an inspector. Unfortunately, Tomlinson was stuck on that particular rung of the promotional ladder because -he paused- 'he is happy where he is. Worrying, th.s general lack of ambition.'

Cunningham sprang to mind, although internal promotions could be tricky.

'Cunningham will cope easily. Connor has passed the exam and could become DS, they would make a good pair,' Wilson said.'Connor, definitely not Smith.'

'Oh? You surprise me. Anything to do with family reasons?'

'No,' said Wilson, 'although...' He paused. They had a baby, left with her mother most of the time. Paula had said they fetched the baby on a Sunday and looked after it all day. What did she want, Wilson had thought, a round of applause?

'Paula is dedicated, but she is not a team player, not yet,' he settled on, which was the truth. 'Oh, she's very intelligent, no doubt, but she thinks it makes her superior to anybody else. If you want to get anywhere in detective work, you have to be prepared to listen. She is young, she has had an exhausting year, now is not the right time for her. But there might well be trouble ahead,' and he wasn't wrong. It would turn out to be sexual discrimination.

'I'll have a word with Cunningham first, if you don't mind,' he said before he left Storwich.

'Don't raise his hopes,' said Nicholson, 'he will face fierce competition as the Chief Constable explained at the meeting.'

'Staffing levels are subject to cuts,' said Wilson. 'I was present.'

Some of the time, he thought.

And now Wilson was in Cunningham's hands.

CHAPTER 62

'I'm resigning,' he said to Cunningham. He would be drawing a pension, he thought, a pension into which he had invested a lot of money. No conscience about that. 'I have discussed it at length with Dorothy. Even a well-fitting uniform will not tempt her.'

He wasn't fit for the job of a police officer because his status had changed, he said.

'How can I put it? I am not a spectator any more, if you like, or a bystander. By suppressing and falsifying clear evidence I have not enforced the law, I have taken the law into my own hands; my status has changed.'

He paused and looked at Cunningham.

'Five minutes later, as I told Hudson, and circumstances would have changed. It was what my old guv used to call *a quarter turn of the screw*.

'Ah,' said Cunningham, 'Henry James, *The Turn Of The Screw*, it's a famous ghost story.'

No ghosts in this case, or so Wilson thought.

'Perhaps you had better make whatever you want of what I have told you.'

'What did you say? I do believe the spot of amnesia has returned,' said Cunningham, 'but whatever it was you were talking about, I'm sure you were right.'

Miss Maxwell was in bed with Dan Brown, when her scoffing at the *Da Vinci Code* was interrupted by the sound of rockets whistling up into the air and exploding nearby, reminding her that she ought to be somewhere else.

'Smashing,' she'd said, 'absolutely smashing,' when the Hudson's asked her to their New Year's party. However, it had   completely slipped her mind and now she would have to apologise.

She needn't have worried; the year 2008 was toasted in with the usual Hudson confusion.

Christine had arranged a huge party and forgot whom she had invited. But there was one difference; George Hudson was entirely happy to go along with her plans, which included inviting some strangers.

Natasha's brother and his two sullen teenage boys were standing about, the burden of boredom weighing heavily on their slumping shoulders, Lewis' parents were comparing symptoms of old age with George's father and his fiancée, the Warden.

George, Ritchie and Alf went into the garden. Alf kept asking how many more bleeding rockets there were, but that was only because he couldn't stand fireworks.

After everybody had left and Rosie was in bed, George and Christine stood amongst the debris and raised a glass to normality.

We'll take a cup of kindness yet
For the sake of Auld Lang Syne

Neither knew or cared who or what Auld Lang Syne was, much to Rosie's disgust, but everybody had a need of a cup of kindness now and then, especially George and Christine. They had walked away from the edge of the precipice just as surely as Emily Watson had on Bonfire Nigh;, but they had glimpsed its unfathomable depth.

Dr Willoughby's inquest involved Dr Pearson, the pathologist. The verdict was he was murdered by Frank Somersby, whose inquest was a verdict of suicide. Luke Cole's inquest was held in Cambridge and didn't involve him to give evidence, Wilson said thankfully. He sent Cunningham, the officer who had arrested Cole, instead.

Paul Willoughby was buried in Stow, the small village where he was born, in a private burial. The burial was short; eulogies were reserved for a memorial service. The coffin was covered in yellow flowers, his favourite colour, and the choir sang, 'All things bright and beautiful,' his favourite hymn.

The little girl, Hester, wore a yellow hat and a yellow scarf over her coat. She carried a sheaf of yellow gladioli and was walking carefully behind the coffin. She squatted on the artificial turf covering the mound of soil around the trench and lowered the flowers onto the coffin before the commencement of the burial rite.

'Phew!' she said to Lewis, who -squatting behind her- had kept his arms arm around her. A job well done, that was how she would remember her granddad's funeral.

Wilson hadn't wanted to attend but he was glad he had; it was uplifting to see the spirit of youth living on in the face of an undeserved death.

'We now commit his body to the ground: Earth to Earth, Ashes to Ashes, in the sure and certain hope of the resurrection to eternal life,' intoned the parson.

It was only a sure and certain hope, thought the analytical policeman, when George Hudson came towards him and introduced his wife, Christine, who most certainly was and looked exceedingly grateful.

Foster's inquest was held in Storwich, and both Wilson and Cunningham gave evidence, as did George Hudson and Lewis Marshall.

The coroner's conclusion was that Hudson and Marshall's' daughters were part of a group that included Emily Watson, the girl Foster had tried to abduct.

'Foster, knowing that the girl, Hester Marshall,

was taken upstairs by her father, waited until later when he would cause her some injury. His plan was foiled when the Polish help, Miss Wawrinska, rushed out, thinking the man watching the house was her lover, Luke Cole.'

'In George Hudson's case, Foster actually entered the house and waited for nightfall. His plan was foiled when traces he left behind were detected, and he fell down the stairs later and died of head injuries.'

Verdict: Misadventure.

'And you can say that again,' said Lewis in front of the court house. 'And now for the gentlemen of the press.'

'What do you mean?' asked George Hudson.

'I suggest taking the bull by the horn. They will hound us unless we collar one of them for an Exclusive. *Selbst is der Mann*, as Kant said.'

'Who?'

'A German philosopher, old son. I once wrote an essay on him and promptly gave up. Roughly translated, it means a man stands on his own two feet, or that there is no society according to Ma Thatcher, basically, it means whatever you can pontificate on. We'll get some money from one of the papers between us and put it away in a university fund for our daughters.'

This would be some time in the future, he added. Hester had told him she had a dream. 'When I asked her what the dream was about, she gave me a pitying look and said, "Stone me, Lewis, I was asleep."'

Wilson was present at Foster's cremation, although it had been difficult to find an undertaker willing to take on the task.

The cremation was held in secret, although Miss Wawrinska was there with Mrs Beverley from the flats. Miss Wawrinska had also attended Luke Cole's cremation. She said she wanted to see Fred Foster go up in smoke. At least that is what he thought she said; or, perhaps, it was his own thought, unworthy of a policeman.

Fred Foster's wife and her daughter attended, accompanied by an old couple, a sharp-faced woman in black and a pleasant-looking man, a Mr and Mrs Foster. Fred Foster's wife had introduced them.

The coffin was in front of the curtains and not one word or sound broke the eerie silence. An attendant gave a nod and the coffin slipped silently away.

Mr. Foster approached Wilson afterwards.

'He was our son,' said Foster, 'but you see, Alfred was wired wrong.'

'Sometimes good people have bad children,' said Wilson.

'You try and live with it,' said the old man.

They watched the couple slowly walk away.

'Bad children?' said Cunningham. 'He was a monster, but I suppose you couldn t tell that to his father.'

Perhaps he knew it already, although he wasn't aware that another unsolved child murder under investigation, that of five-year-old Stephen Wright, was possibly connected to Foster'

Young Mrs Foster, Heidi Foster, the scar sharp and visible in the cold air on her white face, said they were here to make sure Foster had gone, and also that the ten thousand pounds Foster had left would go to the Polish girl whose lover had been murdered.

'It is the ten thousand pounds he wanted and that I gave to him when he came out. I thought he would get out of the country with the friend he made.'

'Ah,' said Wilson. 'Vladimir Glubis.'

He took his leave from the two women and

walked back to his car. '*Take tube train to Embankment station,*' had a foreign ring to it; Foster had intended to meet Glubis, but Glubis, who presumably watched TV and read the papers, would be long gone by now.

Wilson went back to the station and cleared his desk. Nicholson wanted to arrange a proper send-off, but he wisely cleared it first with Wilson.

'I had a feeling you might be truanting again if it was arranged,' he said, disappointed, when Wilson declined.

'Me? Truanting?'

Wilson didn't want a send-off, but he had agreed to treat his officers to a drink at *The Volunteer* the next night. Tomlinson came into the office shortly after and asked him and Dorothy to dinner at his house on Saturday night.

'He was surprised when I accepted,' he reported to Dorothy that evening. 'He thought I would say I would be washing the dog down.'

'So what did you say?'

'I said we were all heading to the pub tomorrow night, would he like to come.'

'

'I was wrong, but I always thought that you knew more about my father-in-law's death than you let on,' said Lewis to George Hudson later in The Volunteer.

'Whatever gave you that idea?' asked George.

When Ritchie opened his mouth and said that was an easy one, he and Alf nearly crossed themselves,

'George likes to worry, he even worries about the state of the planet, carbon footprints,' Ritchie said knowingly. He was about to add, 'But not just lately,' except George asked him to get another round in.

When he came back and George and put their drinks on the table, Lewis announced this was his Swan Song. They were buying a house in Cambridge, the bungalow and the house in Wheystead had been put on the market.

He had his wallet out and was fishing for something. When he found it, he passed it onto Alf.

'I can't quite make it out,' said Alf who liked Lewis a whole lot better since he was leaving, looking at a square of paper, black, with criss-crossing, spidery lines. 'But I do believe this is a heel and up there is a fist.'

'Spot on, Alf. We had a scan on Friday,' said Lewis. 'We don't know what it is yet, but Natasha thinks it's a boy.'

He looked at George. 'Perhaps,' he started, but George assured him he was perfectly content with his own family. 'I have never been happier,' he said, when laughter caused him to look to a corner where two tables had been pushed together.

'Looks like a leaving-do,' said George, 'and I do believe it's DI Wilson's.'

A slim, dark-haired woman in a green coat was sitting next to him.

'Prim, but very sexy,' said Lewis, 'the man has got taste.'

Wilson might have had taste, but now he was making a leaving speech.

'In conclusion, ladies and gentlemen of the jury, I will miss you all,' he said, 'well, some more than others,' whereupon Paula Smith left the room. 'If I may quote some poetry, some A.E. Houseman:

> And now the fancy passes by
> And nothing will remain
> And miles around they'll say then, I
> Am quite myself again.'

Applause.

'Thank you. I have been asked what I will do with myself in retirement. Well, for a start, I can listen to my Mozart operas again.'

'OOOOOOH!'

'I will ask for a respectful silence. Dorothy and I intend to tour France, in particular the Dordogne area with Ralph during the school holidays.'

'Better let Dorothy handle the Sat Nav,' said Cunningham, who was there with his ex-wife, a bony-faced, thin blonde woman, who was gorgeous.

Wilson laughed.

'I believe you are right. I will also study for a degree with the Open University where I will find out the meaning of words like *metaphysical*,' he continued.

'You won't have to grow a ponytail for it,' said Nicholson, who got a surprise laugh, much to his satisfaction after his own witty speech had been ignored, but speak he would.

'You will be a hard act to follow, John, and I will just say that a leader has to be followed, not imitated, otherwise we would all walk around with only one arm or an arrow in our eye.'

Baffled silence.

'Nelson, and 1066 and all that,' he finished lamely, 'I was never good at making a joke.'

After a baffled pause followed by a generous round of applause, he bent down and put a big package on the table.

Wilson looked at it from all angles. He said that was one bloody big carriage clock and when he started to unwrap it, it turned out to be A COFFEE-MAKER!

Espresso machine, Nicholson said, there were little cups to go with it, but it was lost in the great cheer going up, almost shaking the rafters.

CHAPTER 63

Before Wilson's days became his own, he had to attend young Ronald's trial..

The charge was Involuntary Manslaughter. Two young girls, bright, beautiful girls at the brink of womanhood, had life snatched away. Eileen Bishop was dead, and Ruth Kendall, who had been in what was called a "vegetative state", that is, her brain wasn't functioning and some of her organs had stared to die.

Her life support was switched off.

Ronald's father employed a top defence lawyer, a smooth-talker, who could persuade judge and jury as well as a snowflake that black was white.

However, he didn't have much to work with, procedures had been followed, the car did not have faulty brakes. Paul Hargreaves (sentenced for seven years for dealing when on bail for similar offences) had not forced drugs on him to sell but had been visited by him, so young Jimmy was his best plan.

He paused, finally coming to the nitty-gritty.

'James Rendell.' He paused again. 'You don't mind if I call you Jimmy, do you?'

'No, everybody else does,' said Jimmy, all shiny-faced innocence, 'it's my name.'

'You have said previously that you ran after the car as fast as you possibly could.'

'I did.'

'Do you love your mother?'

'Funny question,' said Jimmy looking at his rapt audience in the court room. 'Course I do.'

'Now, wouldn't you have run faster if your mother had been threatened?'

'No, I wouldn't, I ran as fast after Ronald as I could, and my mum wasn't there.'

Jimmy might have lacked imagination, but so

did Ronald who wanted to give evidence against all advise and who ignored the grieving families in the gallery.

'They didn't do their seatbelts up,' he ended up saying sulkily, 'and they were anybody's. Ask anybody in the school.'

Wilson met DI Cunningham, who had been talking to Jimmy Rendell outside the court house. Young Jimmy wanted to become a policeman, Cunningham reported.

(Ronald, with previous cautions and the severity off the offence, received a sentence of four years in a unit for juveniles as the verdict would reveal. Another two days and he would have been sixteen and would not have been tried as a juvenile.)

'Jimmy asked me if you had to pass exams if you wanted to become a policeman,' said Cunningham. 'He said he wasn't any good at exams.'

'Exams, exams. There's more to policing than passing exams. The lad has a good core at his heart. There's hope for the police yet,' said Wilson. 'By the way, Ronald's father has been transferred to Devon. He told me that he wanted to discover his inner landscape.'

'So what did you say?' asked Cunningham, interested.

'I hoped he would find a lot of trees to hide behind, he still thinks his son was led astray.'

So Wilson's days were now his own, although he was not yet quite himself. He had wanted one less predator stalking children behind bars, but he had given up on Vladimir Glubis on the Super's recommendation.

'Interpol? Are you mad? What for?'

'He absconded from Open Prison.'

'Haven't you heard of budget cuts? And aren't you supposed to be retired?'

What neither of them knew from the headline of a bomb exploding in Bangkok was that Glubis was one of the unidentified casualties among the back packers crowding a nightclub on Christmas day.

Foster might have gone up in smoke, but he was haunting Wilson at night, a dream ghost silently padding just out of reach, a dream ghost he could not off-load.

Wilson opened a letter from his daughter, a pleasant letter, announcing she was coming home with her partner, Agnetha, to have their union blessed.

'Blessed by who? Does the Church of England do that sort of thing?'

'I don't think so, I suppose she means by us,' said Dorothy, who had known Heather in London. 'But she does sound happy at long last.'

'As you say, she is happy. Funny name for a bloke though,' he said to Dorothy, except Agnetha was a girl's name, so Dorothy said.

'It's Swedish,' she added. 'Maybe that was wrong with her all along, do you remember the girl in the boarding house she got close to? Nicky?'

'I do indeed, but Nicky had her beady eye on me,' he said modestly. 'Interesting, don't you think?' he said to the dog, who yawned his jaw-breaking yawn.

He gave up thinking about his daughter and opened the second envelope. Two tickets to Glyndebourne to a performance of Mozart's "*The Marriage of Figaro*," and a voucher for a hamper from Harrods. Plus an unsigned note.

FROM A GRATEFUL FRIEND.

'Hudson was in the pub when I talked about Mozart,' he said to Dorothy. If it was a bribe, he would have to hand it over.

He paused and looked at Dorothy's threatening

face.

'But as I can no longer be bribed, we will be able to swank it on Glyndebourne's lawns with the best of them.'

Then he unwrapped the big package from the OU, which turned out to be books. Or rather texts called Units, and a paper with eight essay questions he would have to answer on top of them. He also found a schedule with dates and venues of tutorials he had to attend.

Who-ever had heard of *The Corn Law*s, or of *Constable's Leaping Horse*? This could be interesting, he had no idea what they were talking about, he thought. He got up to see what Dorothy was up to and left the dog to demolish the brown packing paper with his usual gusto.

Dorothy was on the computer, mapping out routes for travelling in France. She pointed to the Dordogne on the screen when the dog rushed to the front door, barking furiously.

'Ken Brogue,' said the man on the door step when Wilson answered the door, rather unnecessarily, as Wilson recognised him as a muckraker from one the lower tabloids.

'Yes?'

'I am a reporter.'

'So?'

'I intend to write a book about Fred Foster. And I have to know what made Foster tick, not just what he did, but why he did it, what made him tick.'

The first of the many who thought they were dealing with a clock, thought Wilson, but he was more than welcome to take on Foster and take him off his shoulders.

'So what exactly has it got to do with me?'

'Aren't you John Wilson, the lead detective on

the case?'

'He has relocated,' said Wilson, 'just a minute.'

'Where has Wilson relocated to?' he shouted up the stairs.

He came back, holding the golden retriever, who was about to lick the caller to death, by the collar.

'Wilson has relocated to France, to the Dordogne,' he said. Perhaps you had better get a move on, I believe it is a very big area.'

The End

NOTES:

I have used the search engine Google for A.E. Houseman, Dioxin and Alzheimer's disease.